...ler's precision
and a playwright's deployment of dramatic irony."
Edmund White, *Times Literary Supplement*

"Armistead Maupin has this uncanny way of providing a
different sort of mirror on life, which he then rotates to a
particular angle, so that we can see the backs of our own
heads—that wayward cowlick, the bald spot we've been trying
to cover up, what's really on our minds."
Amy Tan

"Maupin has a genius for observation. His characters have
the timing of vaudeville comics, flawed by human frailty
and fueled by blind hope."
Denver Post

"Armistead Maupin is a first-rate, world-class novelist, creating
characters so vivid, complicated, tender, and true as to seem
utterly timeless. . . . I'm willing to bet that fifty years from now
Maupin's work will be read for its detailed descriptions of late-
twentieth-century America, its rollicking humor and kind heart,
its Chekovian compassion, its Wildean wit, its
intricate . . . sometimes unbelievable but always utterly
irresistible plotlines."
Stephen McCauley

"Like those of Dickens and Wilkie Collins, Armistead Maupin's
novels have all appeared originally as serials. It is the strength
of this approach, with its fantastic adventures and astonishingly
contrived coincidences, that makes these novels charming and
compelling. Everything is explained and everything tied up
and nothing is lost by reading them individually. There is no
need even to read them chronologically."
Literary Review

BY ARMISTEAD MAUPIN

Novels

Tales of the City
More Tales of the City
Further Tales of the City
Babycakes
Significant Others
Sure of You
Michael Tolliver Lives

Maybe the Moon
The Night Listener

Collections

28 Barbary Lane
Back to Barbary Lane

TALES

OF THE

CITY

Armistead Maupin

HARPER ● PERENNIAL

NEW YORK ● LONDON ● TORONTO ● SYDNEY

HARPER ● PERENNIAL

First Perennial Library edition published 1978. Reissued 1989.
First Harper Perennial edition published 1994. Reissued 2007.

Designed by C. Linda Dingler

LIBRARY OF CONGRESS CARD CATALOG NUMBER 77-11781
ISBN 0-06-096404-9

ISBN: 978-0-06-135830-2 (pbk.)
ISBN-10: 0-06-135830-4 (pbk.)

18 LSC 30 29 28 27 26 25 24

*For my mother and father
and my family at The Duck House*

It's an odd thing, but anyone who disappears is said to be seen in San Francisco.

OSCAR WILDE

Tales of the City

Taking the Plunge

MARY ANN SINGLETON WAS TWENTY-FIVE YEARS old when she saw San Francisco for the first time.

She came to the city alone for an eight-day vacation. On the fifth night, she drank three Irish coffees at the Buena Vista, realized that her Mood Ring was blue, and decided to phone her mother in Cleveland.

"Hi, Mom. It's me."

"Oh, darling. Your daddy and I were just talking about you. There was this crazy man on *McMillan and Wife* who was strangling all these secretaries, and I just couldn't help thinking . . ."

"Mom . . ."

"I know. Just crazy ol' Mom, worrying herself sick over nothing. But you never can tell about those things. Look at that poor Patty Hearst, locked up in that closet with all those awful . . ."

"Mom . . . long distance."

"Oh . . . yes. You must be having a grand time."

"God . . . you wouldn't believe it! The people here are so friendly I feel like I've . . ."

1

"Have you been to the Top of the Mark like I told you?"

"Not yet."

"Well, don't you dare miss that! You know, your daddy took me there when he got back from the South Pacific. I remember he slipped the bandleader five dollars, so we could dance to 'Moonlight Serenade,' and I spilled Tom Collins all over his beautiful white Navy . . ."

"Mom, I want you to do me a favor."

"Of course, darling. Just listen to me. Oh . . . before I forget it, I ran into Mr. Lassiter yesterday at the Ridgemont Mall, and he said the office is just falling apart with you gone. They don't get many good secretaries at Lassiter Fertilizers."

"Mom, that's sort of why I called."

"Yes, darling?"

"I want you to call Mr. Lassiter and tell him I won't be in on Monday morning."

"Oh . . . Mary Ann, I'm not sure you should ask for an extension on your vacation."

"It's not an extension, Mom."

"Well, then why . . .?"

"I'm not coming home, Mom."

Silence. Then, dimly in the distance, a television voice began to tell Mary Ann's father about the temporary relief of hemorrhoids. Finally, her mother spoke: "Don't be silly, darling."

"Mom . . . I'm not being silly. I *like* it here. It feels like home already."

"Mary Ann, if there's a boy . . ."

"There's no boy. . . . I've thought about this for a long time."

"Don't be ridiculous! You've been there five days!"

"Mom, I know how you feel, but . . . well, it's got nothing to do with you and Daddy. I just want to start making my own life . . . have my own apartment and all."

"Oh, *that*. Well, darling . . . of *course* you can. As a matter of fact, your daddy and I thought those new apartments out at Ridgemont might be just perfect for you. They take lots of young people, and they've got a swimming pool and a sauna, and I could make some of those darling curtains like I made for Sonny and Vicki when they got married. You

2

could have all the privacy you . . ."

"You aren't listening, Mom. I'm trying to tell you I'm a grown woman."

"Well, act like it, then! You can't just . . . run away from your family and friends to go live with a bunch of hippies and mass murderers!"

"You've been watching too much TV."

"O.K. . . . then what about The Horoscope?"

"What?"

"The Horoscope. That crazy man. The killer."

"Mom . . . The Zodiac."

"Same difference. And what about . . . earthquakes? I saw that movie, Mary Ann, and I nearly died when Ava Gardner . . ."

"Will you just call Mr. Lassiter for me?"

Her mother began to cry. "You won't come back. I just know it."

"Mom . . . please . . . I will. I promise."

"But you won't be . . . the same!"

"No. I hope not."

When it was over, Mary Ann left the bar and walked through Aquatic Park to the bay. She stood there for several minutes in a chill wind, staring at the beacon on Alcatraz. She made a vow not to think about her mother for a while.

Back at the Fisherman's Wharf Holiday Inn, she looked up Connie Bradshaw's phone number.

Connie was a stewardess for United. Mary Ann hadn't seen her since high school: 1968.

"Fantabulous!" squealed Connie. "How long you here for?"

"For good."

"Super! Found an apartment yet?"

"No . . . I . . . well, I was wondering if I might be able to crash at your place, until I can . . ."

"Sure. No sweat."

"Connie . . . you're single?"

The stewardess laughed. "A bear shit in the woods?"

3

Connie's Place

MARY ANN DRAGGED HER AMERICAN TOURISTER into Connie's apartment, groaned softly and sank into a mock zebra-skin captain's chair.

"Well . . . hello, Sodom and Gomorrah." Connie laughed. "Your mom freaked, huh?"

"God!"

"Poor baby! I know the feeling. When I told *my* mom I was moving to San Francisco, she had an absolute hissy-fit! It was a zillion times worse than the summer I tried to join Up With People!"

"God . . . I almost forgot."

Connie's eyes glazed nostalgically. "Yeah . . . Hey, you work up a thirst, hon?"

"Sure."

"Sit tight. I'll be right back."

Thirty seconds later, Connie emerged from the kitchen with two airlines glasses and a bottle of Banana Cow. She poured a drink for Mary Ann.

Mary Ann sipped warily. "Well . . . look at all this. You're practically a native, aren't you? This is . . . quite something."

4

"Quite something" was the best she could manage. Connie's apartment was a potpourri of plastic Tiffany lamps and ankle-deep shag carpeting, needlepoint Snoopy pictures and "Hang in There, Baby" kitten posters, monkey pod salad sets and macramé plant hangers and—please, no, thought Mary Ann—a Pet Rock.

"I've been lucky," Connie beamed. "Being a stew and all . . . well, you can pick up a lot of art objects in your travels."

"Mmm." Mary Ann wondered if Connie regarded her black velvet bullfighter painting as an art object.

The stewardess kept smiling. "Cow O.K.?"

"What? Oh . . . yes. Hits the spot."

"I love the stuff." She downed some more of it to demonstrate her point, then looked up as if she had just discovered Mary Ann's presence in the room. "Hey, hon! Long time no see!"

"Yeah. Too long. Eight years."

"Eight years . . . Eight years! You're lookin' good, though. You're lookin' real . . . Hey, you wanna see something absolutely yucky?"

Without waiting for an answer, she leaped to her feet and went to a bookshelf made of six orange plastic Foremost milk crates. Mary Ann could make out copies of *Jonathan Livingston Seagull*, *How to Be Your Own Best Friend*, *The Sensuous Woman*, *More Joy of Sex* and *Listen to the Warm*.

Connie reached for a large book bound in burgundy vinyl and held it up to Mary Ann.

"Ta-*ta!*"

"Oh, God! *The Buccaneer?*"

Connie nodded triumphantly and pulled up a chair. She opened the yearbook. "You'll absolutely *die* over your hair!"

Mary Ann found her senior picture. Her hair was very blond and meticulously ironed. She was wearing the obligatory sweater and pearl necklace. Despite the camouflage of an airbrush, she could still remember the exact location of the zit she had sprouted on the day of the photograph.

The inscription read:

Mary Ann shook her head. "Rest in peace," she said and winced.

Connie, mercifully, didn't offer her own biography for examination. Mary Ann remembered it all too well: head majorette, class treasurer for three years, president of the Y-Teens. Connie's waters had run fast and shallow. She had been popular.

Mary Ann struggled back into the present. "So what do you do . . . like for fun?"

Connie rolled her eyes. "You name it."

"I'd rather not."

"Well . . . for instance." Connie bent over her hatch-cover coffee table and dug out a copy of *Oui* magazine. "You read that?" asked Mary Ann.

"No. Some guy left it."

"Oh."

"Check out page seventy."

Mary Ann turned to an article entitled "Coed Baths—Welcome to the World's Cleanest Orgy." It was illustrated by a photograph of intermingling legs, breasts and buttocks.

"Charming."

"It's down on Valencia Street. You pays your money and you takes your chances."

"You've been there?"

"No. But I wouldn't rule it out."

"I'm afraid you'll have to count me out, if you're planning on . . ."

Connie laughed throatily. "Relax, hon. I wasn't suggesting we . . . You're a new girl. Give it time. This city loosens people up."

"I'll never be that loose . . . or desperate."

Connie shrugged, looking vaguely hurt. She took another sip of her Banana Cow.

"Connie, I didn't . . ."

"It's O.K., hon. I knew what you meant. Hey, I'm hungry as hell. How 'bout a little Hamburger Helper?"

After dinner, Mary Ann napped for an hour.

She dreamed she was in a huge tile room full of steam. She was naked. Her mother and father were there, watching *Let's Make a Deal* through the steam. Connie walked in with Mr. Lassiter, who was furious at Mary Ann and began to shout at her. Mary Ann's mother and father were shouting at Monty Hall's first contestant.

"Take the box," they screamed. "Take the box. . . ."

Mary Ann woke up. She stumbled into the bathroom and splashed water on her face.

When she opened the cabinet over the sink, she discovered an assortment of after-shave lotions: Brut, Old Spice, Jade East.

Connie, apparently, was still popular.

A Frisco Disco

THE DISCOTHEQUE WAS CALLED DANCE YOUR ASS OFF. Mary Ann thought that was gross, but didn't tell Connie so. Connie was too busy getting off on being Marisa Berenson.

"The trick is to look bored with it all."

"That shouldn't be hard."

"If you wanna get laid, Mary Ann, you'd better . . ."

"I never said that."

"Nobody ever *says* it, for Christ's sake! Look, if you can't deal with your own sexuality, hon, you're gonna get screwed but good in this town."

"I like that. You should make it into a country-western song."

Connie sighed in exasperation. "C'mon. And *try* not to look like Tricia Nixon reviewing the troops." She led the way into the building and staked out a battered sofa against the wall.

The room was supposed to look funky: brick-red walls, revolving beer signs, kitschy memorabilia. Henna-rinsed women and rugby-shirted men clustered decoratively along the bar, as if posing for a Seagram's ad.

8

While Connie was buying their drinks, Mary Ann settled uncomfortably on the sofa and commanded herself to stop comparing things with Cleveland.

Several yards away, a girl in cowboy boots, sweat pants and a red squirrel Eisenhower jacket stared haughtily at Mary Ann's polyester pantsuit. Mary Ann turned away from her, only to confront another woman, looking blasé in a macramé halter, black fingernails and a crew cut.

"There's a dude at the bar who looks *exactly* like Robert Redford." Connie was back with the drinks. A tequila sunrise for herself, a white wine for Mary Ann.

"Warts?" asked Mary Ann, taking the wine.

"What?"

"That guy. Does he have warts? Robert Redford has warts."

"That's sick. Look . . . I feel like a little heavy bumping. Wanna hit the disco?"

"I think I'll just . . . soak it in for a while. You go ahead."

"You sure now?"

"Yeah. Thanks. I'll be O.K."

"Suit yourself, hon."

Seconds after Connie had disappeared into the disco, a long-haired man in a Greek peasant shirt sat down next to Mary Ann on the sofa. "Mind if I join you?"

"Sure . . . I mean, no."

"You're not into boogying, huh?"

"Well, not right now."

"You're into head trips, then?"

"I don't know exactly what . . ."

"What sign are you?"

She wanted to say, "Do Not Disturb." She said, "What sign do you think I am?"

"Ah . . . you're into games. O.K. . . . I'd say you're a Taurus."

He rattled her. "All right . . . how did you do it?"

"Easy. Taureans are stubborn as hell. They *never* want to tell you what sign they are." He leaned over close enough for Mary Ann to smell his musk oil, and looked directly into her eyes. "But underneath that tough Taurus hide beats the heart of a hopeless romantic."

9

Mary Ann moved away slightly.

"Well?" said the man.

"Well, what?"

"You're a romantic, right? You like earth colors and foggy nights and Lina Wertmuller movies and lemon candles burning when you make love." He reached for her hand. She flinched. "It's all right," he said calmly. "I'm not making a pass yet. I just wanna look at your heart line."

He ran his forefinger gently across Mary Ann's palm. "Look at your point of insertion," he said. "Right there between Jupiter and Saturn."

"What does that mean?" Mary Ann looked down at his finger. It was resting between her middle finger and forefinger. "It means that you're a very sensual person," said the man. He began to slide the finger in and out. "That's true, isn't it? You're a very sensual person?"

"Well, I . . ."

"Do you know you look exactly like Jennifer O'Neill?"

Mary Ann stood up suddenly. "No, but if you hum a few bars . . ."

"Hey, hey, lady. It's cool, it's cool. I'll give you space. . . ."

"Good. I'll take the other room. Happy hunting." She headed for the disco in search of Connie. She found her in the eye of the storm, bumping with a black man in Lurex knickers and glitter wedgies.

"What's up?" asked the stewardess, boogying to the sidelines.

"I'm beat. Could I have the keys to the apartment?"

"You O.K., hon?"

"Fine. Just tired."

"Hot date?"

"No, just . . . could I have the keys, Connie?"

"Here's an extra set. Sweet dreams."

Boarding the 41 Union bus, Mary Ann realized suddenly why Connie kept an extra set of keys in her purse.

*   *   *

Mary Ann watched *Mary Hartman, Mary Hartman,* then turned off the television and fell asleep.

It was after 2 A.M. when Connie got home.

She wasn't alone.

Mary Ann rolled over on the sofa and buried her head under the covers, pretending to be asleep. Connie and her guest tiptoed noisily into the bedroom.

The man's voice was fuzzy with whiskey, but Mary Ann knew immediately who he was.

He was asking for lemon candles.

Her New Home

MARY ANN CREPT OUT OF THE APARTMENT JUST before dawn. The prospect of sharing Trix for three at breakfast was more than she could take.

She wandered the streets of the Marina in search of For Rent signs, then ate a mammoth breakfast at the International House of Pancakes.

At nine o'clock she was the first customer of the day at a rental agency on Lombard Street.

She wanted a View, a Deck and a Fireplace for under $175.

"Jees," said the rental lady. "Awful picky for a girl without a job." She offered Mary Ann "a nice Lower Pacific Heights studio with AEK, wall-to-wall carpeting and a partial view of Fillmore Auditorium." Mary Ann said no.

She ended up with three possibles.

The first one had an uptight landlady who asked if Mary Ann "took marijuana."

The second was a pink stucco fortress on Upper Market with gold glitter in the ceiling plaster.

The last was on Russian Hill. Mary Ann arrived there at four-thirty.

The house was on Barbary Lane, a narrow, wooded walkway off Leavenworth between Union and Filbert. It was a well-weathered, three-story structure made of brown shingles. It made Mary Ann think of an old bear with bits of foliage caught in its fur. She liked it instantly.

The landlady was a fiftyish woman in a plum-colored kimono.

"I'm Mrs. Madrigal," she said cheerfully. "As in medieval."

Mary Ann smiled. "You can't feel as ancient as I do. I've been apartment-hunting all day."

"Well, take your time. There's a partial view, if you count that little patch of bay peeping through the trees. Utilities included, of course. Small house. Nice people. You get here this week?"

"That obvious, huh?"

The landlady nodded. "The look's a dead giveaway. You just can't wait to bite into that lotus."

"What? I'm sorry. . . ."

"Tennyson. You know: 'Eating the lotus day by day, To watch the crisping ripples on the beach, And tender curving lines of creamy spray; To lend our hearts and spirits wholly To the influence of' . . . something, something. . . . You get the point."

"Does the . . . furniture go with it?"

"Don't change the subject while I'm quoting Tennyson."

Mary Ann was shaken until she noticed that the landlady was smiling. "You'll get used to my babbling," said Mrs. Madrigal. "All the others have." She walked to the window, where the wind made her kimono flutter like brilliant plumage. "The furniture is included. What do you say, dear?"

Mary Ann said yes.

"Good. You're one of us, then. Welcome to 28 Barbary Lane."

"Thank you."

"Yes, you should." Mrs. Madrigal smiled. There was something a little careworn about her face, but she was really quite

13

lovely, Mary Ann decided. "Do you have any objection to pets?" asked the new tenant.

"Dear . . . I have no objection to anything."

Elated, Mary Ann walked to the corner of Hyde and Union and phoned Connie from the Searchlight Market. "Hi. Guess what?"

"You got kidnaped?"

"Oh . . . Connie, I'm sorry. I've been looking for a place. . . ."

"I was freaked."

"I'm really sorry. I . . . Connie, I've found this darling place on Russian Hill on the third floor of the funkiest old building . . . and I can move in tomorrow."

"Oh . . . that was quick."

"It's so *neat!* I can't wait for you to see it."

"Sounds nice. Look, Mary Ann . . . like, if there's any problem with money or anything, you can stay with me until . . ."

"I've got some saved. Thanks, though. You've been wonderful."

"No sweat. Hey . . . what's on for tonight, hon?"

"Let's see. Oh, yeah. Robert Redford is picking me up at seven, and we're going to Ernie's for dinner."

"Ditch him. He's got warts."

"For what?"

"The hottest spot in town. Social Safeway."

"Social *what?*"

"Safeway, dink. As in supermarket."

"That's what I thought you said. You sure know how to show a girl a good time."

"For your information, dink, Social Safeway just happens to be . . . well, it's just the . . . big thing, that's all."

"For those who get off on groceries."

"For those who get off on *men,* hon. It's a local tradition. Every Wednesday night. And you don't even have to look like you're on the make."

"I don't believe it."

"There's only one way to prove it to you."

Mary Ann giggled. "What am I supposed to do? Lurk behind the artichokes until some unsuspecting stockbroker comes along?"

"Meet me here at eight, dink. You'll see."

Love with the Proper Shopper

A DOZEN CARDBOARD DISKS DANGLED FROM THE ceiling of the Marina Safeway, coaxing the customers with a double-edged message: "Since we're neighbors, let's be friends."

And friends were being made.

As Mary Ann watched, a blond man in a Stanford sweatshirt sauntered up to a brunette in a denim halter. "Uh . . . excuse me, but could you tell me whether it's better to use Saffola oil or Wesson oil?"

The girl giggled. "For what?"

"I don't believe this," said Mary Ann, taking a shopping cart. "Every Wednesday night?"

Connie nodded. "It ain't half bad on weekends, either." She grabbed a cart and charged off down a busy aisle. "See ya. It works better if you're alone."

Mary Ann strode to the produce counter. She intended to *shop*, Connie's pagan mating ritual notwithstanding.

Then someone tugged on her arm.

He was a puffy-faced man of about thirty-five. He was wearing a leisure suit with a white vinyl belt and matching shoes.

"Are those the things you use in Chinese cooking?" he asked, pointing to the snow peas.

"Yes," she said, as uninvitingly as possible.

"Far out. I've been looking for some all week. I've really been getting into Chinese cooking lately. Bought a wok and everything."

"Yeah. Well, those are the ones. Good luck." She wheeled sharply and headed for the check-out counter. Her assailant followed.

"Hey . . . like, maybe you could tell me a little about Chinese cooking?"

"I doubt it very seriously."

"C'mon. Most chicks in this town are really into Chinese cooking."

"I'm not most chicks."

"O.K. I can dig it. Different strokes for different folks, right? What *are* you into, anyway?"

"Solitude."

"OK. Skip it, just skip it." He hesitated a moment, then delivered his exit line. "Get off the rag, bitch!"

He left her standing in the frozen food department, white knuckles clamped around the rim of the freezer, her breath rising like a tiny distress signal. "Jesus," she said in a frosty whisper, as a single tear plopped onto a box of Sara Lee brownies.

"Charming," said a man standing next to her.

Mary Ann stiffened. "What?"

"Your friend there . . . with the sparkling repartee. He's a real prince."

"You heard all that?"

"Only the parting endearment. Was the rest any better?"

"Nope. Unless you get off on discussing snow peas with Charlie Manson."

The man laughed, showing beautiful white teeth. He was about thirty, Mary Ann guessed, with curly brown hair, blue eyes and a soft flannel shirt. "Sometimes I don't believe this place," he said.

"Really." Had he seen her crying?

"The hell of it is that the whole goddamn town talks about

relating and communicating and all that Age of Aquarius shit, and most of us are *still* trying to look like something we aren't . . . Sorry. I sound like Dear Abby, don't I?"

"No. Not at all. I . . . agree with you."

He extended his hand. "My name is Robert." Not Bob or Robbie, but Robert. Strong and direct. She gripped his hand. "I'm Mary Ann Singleton." She wanted him to remember it.

"Well . . . at the risk of sounding like Charlie Manson . . . how about a little culinary advice for a hapless male?"

"Sure. Not snow peas?"

He laughed. "Not snow peas. Asparagus."

Mary Ann had never found the subject so exciting. She was watching Robert's eyes respond to her hollandaise recipe when a young man with a mustache approached with his cart.

"Can't leave you alone for a minute." He was talking to Robert.

Robert chuckled. "Michael . . . this is Mary Ann . . ."

"Singleton," said Mary Ann.

"This is my roommate, Michael. She's been helping me with hollandaise, Michael."

"Good," said Michael, smiling at Mary Ann. "He's *awful* at hollandaise."

Robert shrugged. "Michael's the master chef in the house. That entitles him to make life miserable for me." He grinned at his roommate.

Mary Ann's palms were sweating.

"I'm not much of a cook, either," she said. Why in the world was she siding with Robert? Robert didn't need her help. Robert didn't know she was there.

"She's been a lot of help," said Robert. "That's more than I can say for some people."

"Temper," Michael grinned.

"Well," said Mary Ann feebly. "I guess I'd better . . . finish up."

"Thanks for your help," said Robert. "Really."

"Nice to meet you," said Michael.

"Same here," said Mary Ann, pushing her cart in the direction of the paper-supplies aisle. When Connie rounded the corner several seconds later, she found her friend standing glumly by herself, squeezing a roll of Charmin.

"Hot damn!" said the stewardess. "This place is Pickup City tonight!"

Mary Ann threw the toilet paper into her cart. "I've got a headache, Connie. I think I'll walk home. O.K.?"

"Well . . . hang on a sec. I'll come with you."

"Connie, I . . . I'd like to be alone, O.K.?"

"Sure. O.K."

As usual, she looked hurt.

Connie's Bummer Night

ONNIE CAME HOME FROM THE MARINA SAFEWAY AN hour after Mary Ann did.

Noisily, she dropped her groceries on the kitchen counter. "Well," she said, walking into the living room, "I'm ready for Union Street. I suppose you're ready for bed?"

Mary Ann nodded. "Job-hunting and moving tomorrow. I need my strength."

"Abstinence causes pimples."

"I'll remember that," said Mary Ann, as Connie stalked out the door.

Mary Ann ate dinner in front of the television. She had steak, salad and Tater Tots, the fare that Connie swore by for keeping men happy. She checked out Connie's record collection (The Carpenters, Percy Faith, 101 Strings), then looked at the pictures in *More Joy of Sex*. She fell asleep on the sofa shortly before midnight.

When she awoke, the room was filled with light. A garbage

truck rumbled along Greenwich Street. A key chain was clinking against the front door.

Connie lumbered in. "I cannot *believe* the assholes in this town!"

Mary Ann sat up and rubbed her eyes. "Bad night, huh?"

"Bad night, bad morning, bad week, bad year. Weirdos! Goddammit, I can pick 'em. If there's a weirdo around for a hundred goddamn miles, good ol' Connie Bradshaw will be there to make a date with him. Fuck!"

"How 'bout some coffee?"

"What's the matter with me, Mary Ann? Will you tell me that? I have two tits, a nice ass. I wash. I'm a *good* listener. . . ."

"C'mon. We both need coffee."

The kitchen was too perversely cheerful for an early-morning soul-baring. Mary Ann winced at the Doris Day yellow walls and the little windowed boxes full of dried beans.

Connie devoured a bowl of Trix. "I think I'll become a nun," she said.

"They'll love your outfit at Dance Your Ass Off."

"Not funny."

"O.K. What happened?"

"You don't wanna know."

"Yes I do. You went to Union Street, right?"

"Perry's. Then Slater Hawkins. But the *real* bummer was at Thomas Lord's."

Mary Ann poured her a cup of coffee. "What happened?"

"Fuck if I know. I was having a perfectly innocent drink at the bar when I noticed this guy sitting over by the fire. I recognized him right away, because him and me did a little number last month on his houseboat in Sausalito."

"A little number?"

"Fucked."

"Thank you."

"So . . . I walked over to where this guy was sitting. Jerry something. A German name. Buckskin pants and a turquoise squash blossom necklace and a pair of those John Denver-type glasses. *Gorgeous,* in a . . . you know . . . Marin kind of way. And I said, 'Hi, Jerry, who's keeping the houseboat warm?' and the asshole just stared at me like I was some whore on Market Street or something. I mean, like he didn't even *recognize* me. I was *mortified.*"

"I guess so."

"So, finally, I said, 'Connie Bradshaw from the Friendly Skies of United.' Only, I said it in . . . like a real bitchy tone of voice so he'd get the point."

"But he didn't?"

"Fuck, no! He just sat there looking stuck-up and spaced out. He finally asked me to sit down, and he introduced me to this friend of his named Danny. Then the asshole just got up and walked out, leaving me with this Danny person, who had just finished his goddamn est training and was spouting all this shit about making a space, et cetera."

"What on earth did you do?"

"What *could* I do? I went home with Danny. I sure as hell wasn't gonna let *him* get up and leave me there munching pretzels all by myself. There's such a thing as pride!"

"Of course."

"Anyway, Danny had this really neat redwood apartment in Mill Valley, with lots of stained glass and all, but he was an absolute *nut* about ecology. As soon as we smoked a joint, he started babbling about saving the whales in Mendocino and screwing up the ozone layer with feminine hygiene spray."

"*What?*"

"You know. Aerosol cans. The fucking ozone layer. Anyway, I was really bent out of shape at that point, and I said I thought it was a woman's unalienable . . . inalienable . . . which is it?"

"Inalienable."

"Inalienable right to use a feminine hygiene spray if she wanted to, ozone layer or no ozone layer!"

"And . . . ?"

"And he said that just because I have some *bizarre* notion that my . . . you know . . . smells bad is no reason for me to expose the rest of the world to ultraviolet rays and skin cancer. Or something like that."

"Well . . . delightful evening."

"I mean, get *him.* Not only does he subject me to all this ecology crap, but . . . nothing happened."

"Nothing happened?"

"Nada. Zilch. He drives me all the way across the bridge just to talk. He says he wants to *relate* to me as a person. Ha!"

"So . . . what did you say?"

"I told him to drive me home. And you know what he said?"

Mary Ann shook her head.

"He said, 'I'm sorry you sprayed for nothing.' "

Later that day, Mary Ann moved out of Connie's apartment into 28 Barbary Lane. The move involved only a suitcase. Connie was visibly depressed.

"You'll still come see me, won't you?"

"Sure. And you'll have to come visit me."

"Cross your heart?"

"Hope to die."

Neither one of them believed it.

The Employment Line

ON HER FIRST MORNING AT BARBARY LANE, MARY Ann scanned the Yellow Pages for the key to her future.

According to a large, daisy-bedecked ad, the Metropolitan Employment Agency was "an individualized job placement service that really cares about your future."

She liked the sound of it. Solid yet compassionate.

Gulping an Instant Breakfast, she put on her low-key navy-blue suit and caught the 41 Union to Montgomery Street. Her horoscope today promised "matchless opportunities for a Taurus who takes the bull by the horns."

The agency was on the fifth floor of a yellow-brick building that smelled of cigars and industrial ammonia. Someone with an eye for contemporary Californiana had decorated the walls of the waiting room with Art Nouveau posters and a drift-wood-and-copper sculpture of a seagull in flight.

Mary Ann sat down. There was no one in sight, so she picked up a copy of *Office Management* magazine. She was reading an article about desktop avocado gardening when a woman appeared from a cubicle in the back.

"Have you filled out a form yet?"

"No. I didn't know . . ."

"On the desk. I can't talk to you until you've filled out a form."

Mary Ann filled out a form. She agonized over the questions. Do you own a car? Will you accept employment outside San Francisco? Do you speak any foreign languages?

She took the form to the woman's cubicle. "All done," she said, as cheerfully and efficiently as possible.

The woman grunted. She took the form from Mary Ann and readjusted her chain-guarded glasses on a small, piglike nose. Her hair was done in a salt-and-pepper DA.

As she examined the form, her fingers manipulated an executive desk toy. Four steel balls suspended on strings from a walnut scaffolding.

"No degree," said the woman at last.

"Like . . . college?"

The woman snapped. "Yes. Like college."

"I had two years at a junior college in Ohio, if that . . ."

"Major?"

"Yes."

"Well?"

"What?"

"What did you *major* in?"

"Oh. Art history."

The woman smirked. "We've certainly got enough of *those* for a while."

"Does a degree really matter that much? I mean . . . for secretarial work?"

"Are you kidding? I've got Ph.D. candidates doing clerical work." She used the first person as if these struggling scholars were her personal serfs. She wrote something on an index card and handed it to Mary Ann. "This is a small office-supply company on Market Street. The sales manager needs a Girl Friday. Ask for Mr. Creech."

He turned out to be a red-faced man of about fifty. He was wearing a burgundy polyester jacket with an oversized hound's-tooth pattern. His trousers and tie were the same color.

"You ever done sales work before?" He smiled and leaned back in a squeaky swivel chair.

"Not . . . well, not exactly. For the past four years I've worked as a secretary for Lassiter Fertilizers in Cleveland. I wasn't exactly *in* sales, but I had a lot of . . . you know . . . contact and all."

"Sounds good. Steady work. Always a good sign."

"I was also an admin assistant for the past year and a half, and I was attached to several of . . ."

"Fine, fine . . . Now, I suppose you know what a Girl Friday is?"

"Sort of gofer . . . right?" She laughed nervously.

"Pay's good. Six fifty a month. And we're pretty relaxed around here . . . this being San Francisco." His eyes were fixed on Mary Ann's face. He began to chew the knuckle of his forefinger.

"I like . . . an informal office," said Mary Ann.

"You like Vegas?"

"Sir?"

"Earl."

"What?"

"Name's Earl. Informal, remember?" He smiled and wiped his forehead. He was sweating profusely. "I asked if you like Vegas. We go to Vegas a lot. Vegas, Sacramento, L.A., Hawaii. Lotsa fringe benefits."

"Sounds . . . really nice."

He winked at her. "If you're not . . . you know . . . uptight."

"Oh."

"Oh, what?"

"I'm uptight, Mr. Creech."

He plucked a paper clip off the desk and tore it apart slowly without looking up. "Next," he said quietly.

"Sir?"

"Get out."

*　*　*

She went home to her new apartment and cried, falling asleep as the afternoon sun spilled in the window. She woke up at five and scoured the kitchen sink for therapy. She ate some blueberry yogurt and made a list of things she would need for her apartment.

She wrote a letter to her parents. Optimistic, but vague.

There was a noise outside her door. She listened for a moment, then opened it. Plum-colored silk fluttered at the top of the stairway and descended out of sight.

There was a note on Mary Ann's door:

> Something from my garden to welcome you
> to your new home.
>
> ANNA MADRIGAL
>
> P.S. I'll shoot you if you write
> your mother about this.

Taped to the note was a neatly rolled joint.

Enter Mona

THE WOMAN DOWN BY THE GARBAGE CANS HAD FRIZZY red hair and was wearing a country-chic cotton sharecropper's dress.

She dropped her Hefty bag with a disdainful wrinkle of her nose and smiled at Mary Ann. "Garbage, you know, is *very* revealing. It beats the shit out of tarot cards!"

"What would you say about . . . let's see . . . four yogurt cartons, a Cost Plus bag, some avocado peels and assorted cellophane wrappings?"

The woman pressed her fingers to her forehead like a psychic. "Ah, yes . . . the subject takes care of herself . . . nutritionally, that is. She is probably on a diet and is . . . furnishing a new apartment!"

"Uncanny!" Mary Ann smiled. "She also . . . likes growing things. She didn't throw out the avocado pit, so she's probably rooting it in her kitchen."

"Bravo!" Mary Ann extended her hand. "I'm Mary Ann Singleton."

"I know."

"From my garbage?"

"From our landlady. The Mother of Us All." She shook Mary Ann's hand firmly. "I'm Mona Ramsey . . . right below you."

"Hi. You should have seen what Mother taped on my door last night."

"A joint?"

"She told you?"

"Nope. It's standard operating procedure. We all get one."

"She grows it in the garden?"

"Right over there behind the azaleas. She's even got names for the plants . . . like Dante and Beatrice and . . . Hey, want some ginseng?"

"What?"

"Ginseng. I'm brewing some upstairs. C'mon."

Mona's second-floor apartment was adorned with Indian wall hangings, assorted street signs, and Art Deco light globes. Her dining table was an industrial cable spool. Her armchair, a converted Victorian toilet.

"I used to have curtains," she smiled, handing Mary Ann a mug of tea, "but after a while paisley bedspreads seemed so . . . Sixties Vassar." She shrugged. "Besides . . . like . . . who am I hiding my body from?"

Mary Ann peered out the window. "What about that building over . . ."

"No . . . I mean . . . you know . . . *nobody's* really hiding anything from the Cosmos. Beneath the rays of the White Healing Light, we are all . . . like . . . capital *N* Naked. Who gives a shit about the little *n?*"

"This tea is really . . ."

"Why do you want to be a secretary?"

"How did you know . . . ?"

"Big Mother. Mrs. Madrigal."

Mary Ann couldn't hide her irritation. "She gets the news out quick enough, doesn't she?"

"She likes you."

"She told you that?"

Mona nodded. "Don't you like her?"

"Well . . . yes . . . I mean, I haven't really known her long enough to . . ."

"She thinks you think she's weird."

"Oh, great. Instant rapport."

"*Do* you think she's weird?"

"Mona, I . . . yeah, I guess I do," she smiled. "Maybe it's my fault. We don't have people like that in Cleveland."

"Too bad for Cleveland."

"Maybe so."

"She wants you in the family, Mary Ann. Give it a chance, O.K.?"

Mona's condescension irked Mary Ann. "There's no problem here."

"No. Not now."

Mary Ann sipped the weird-tasting tea in silence.

The best news of the day came minutes later. Mona was a copywriter for Halcyon Communications, a well-respected Jackson Square ad agency.

Edgar Halcyon, chairman of the board, needed a woman to replace the personal secretary who had "gotten pregnant on him."

Mona arranged an interview for Mary Ann.

"You're not planning to run back to Cleveland, are you?"

"Sir?"

"You're staying put?"

"Yes, sir. I love San Francisco."

"They all say that."

"In my case, it happens to be the truth."

Halcyon's huge white eyebrows leaped. "Are you that sassy with your parents, young lady?"

Mary Ann deadpanned. "Why do you think I can't go back to Cleveland?"

It was risky, but it worked. Halcyon threw back his head and roared. "O.K.," he said, regaining his composure. "That was it."

"Sir?"

"That's the last time you'll see me laugh like that. Go get some rest. Tomorrow you'll be working for the biggest son-of-a-bitch in town."

Mrs. Madrigal was weeding the garden when Mary Ann returned to Barbary Lane.

"You got it, didn't you?"

Mary Ann nodded. "Mona call you?"

"Nope. I just knew you would. You always get what you want."

Mary Ann smiled and shrugged. "Thanks, I think."

"You're a lot like me, dear . . . whether you know it or not."

Mary Ann headed for the front door, then stopped and turned around. "Mrs. Madrigal?"

"Yes?"

"I . . . Thank you for the joint."

"You're welcome, dear. I think you'll like Beatrice."

"It was nice of you to . . ."

The landlady dismissed her with a wave of her hand. "Go say your prayers or something. You're a working girl now."

The Ad Game

HALCYON COMMUNICATIONS HAD BEEN A FOOD-PRO-cessing warehouse in an earlier incarnation. Now its mellow brick walls blazed with supergraphics and rental art. Matrons shopping for Louis Quinze bargains in Jackson Square often mis-took its secretaries for top fashion models.

Mary Ann liked that.

What she didn't particularly like was her job.

"Is the flag out, Mary Ann?"

That was Halcyon's first question of the morning. Every morning.

"Yes, sir." She felt less like Lauren Hutton every second. Who would make Lauren Hutton raise the American flag before nine o'clock in the morning?

"Are we out of coffee?"

"I set it up for you in the conference room."

"Why in God's name would . . . Oh, Christ . . . Adorable's here?"

Mary Ann nodded. "Nine o'clock conference."

"Goddammit. Tell Beauchamp to hustle his butt up here on the double."

"I've already checked, sir. He's not in yet."

"Christ!"

"I could check with Mildred, if you want. Sometimes he has coffee down in Production."

"Do it."

Mary Ann did it, feeling vaguely like a fifth-grader who had snitched on a classmate. She *liked* Beauchamp Day, actually, despite his irresponsibility. She may have even liked him *for* his irresponsibility.

Beauchamp was Edgar Halcyon's son-in-law, the husband of post-post-debutante DeDe Halcyon. A graduate of Groton and Stanford, the handsome young Bostonian had been a natural for The Bachelors when he moved to San Francisco as a Bank of America trainee in 1971.

According to the social columns, he had met his wife-to-be at the 1973 Spinsters Ball. Within months, he was savoring the delights of pool parties in Atherton, brunches on Belvedere and ski treks to Tahoe.

The Halcyon-Day courtship had been whirlwind. DeDe and Beauchamp were married in June 1973 on the sunlit slopes of Halcyon Hill, the bride's family estate in Hillsborough. At her own insistence, the bride was barefoot. She wore a peasant dress by Adolfo of Saks Fifth Avenue. Her maid of honor and Bennington roommate, Muffy van Wyck, recited selections from Kahlil Gibran, while a string quartet played the theme from *Elvira Madigan*.

After the wedding, the bride's mother, Frannie Halcyon, told reporters: "We're so proud of our DeDe. She's always been *such* an individualist."

Beauchamp and DeDe moved into a fashionable Art Deco penthouse on Telegraph Hill. They entertained lavishly and were frequently seen at philanthropic extravaganzas . . . by almost everyone, it seemed, but Mary Ann Singleton.

Mary Ann had chatted with DeDe once at an interagency softball game (Halcyon vs. Hoefer Dieterich & Brown). Mrs. Day didn't strike the secretary as snobby, but Mary Ann concluded that a Dina Merrill hairdo looks *ridiculous* on a twenty-six-year-old.

Beauchamp, on the other hand, had looked magnificent

that afternoon, transforming the pitcher's mound into a mini-Olympus.

Blue eyes, black hair, brown arms glistening under a faded green Lacoste . . .

She was right. He was drinking coffee in Production.

"His Majesty requests your presence in the royal chambers." She didn't hesitate to use that kind of irreverence with Beauchamp. She was sure he was a kindred spirit.

"Tell him the Bastard Prince is on his way."

Within seconds, Beauchamp was standing next to her desk, flashing his self-assured post-preppie grin. "Don't tell me. I screwed up the Adorable account, right?"

"Not yet. There's a conference at nine. He was nervous, that's all."

"He's always nervous. I didn't forget."

"I know you didn't."

"You think I'm O.K., don't you?"

"As an account executive?"

"As anything?"

"Not fair. Want a Dynamint?"

Beauchamp shook his head and slumped into a Barcelona chair. "He's a real fart, isn't he?"

"Beauchamp . . ."

"How about lunch tomorrow?"

"I think he's booked."

"Not him. You. Will he let you out of your cage for an hour?"

"Oh . . . sure. Dutch?"

"Italian."

Mary Ann giggled, then jumped as Halcyon buzzed her. "I'm ready for him," said her boss.

Beauchamp rose, winking at Mary Ann. "Well, it ain't bloody mutual."

Edgar Blows Up

EDGAR GLARED AT HIS SON-IN-LAW, WONDERING HOW anyone so well-groomed, articulate and generally *presentable* could be such a royal pain in the ass.

"I think you know what this is about."

Beauchamp leaned forward and brushed a speck of dust off his Guccis. "Yeah, the pantyhose pitch. I think we might as well forget about the Bicentennial angle."

"I'm talking about DeDe and you know it!"

"I do, huh?"

Edgar's eyes narrowed. His fist tightened around the neck of a mahogany decoy Frannie had bought him at Abercrombie's. "Where were you last night, Beauchamp?"

Silence.

"I don't get a big bang out of this, you know. It doesn't thrill me to remember that my own daughter called me up last night, crying her eyes out . . ."

"Frankly, I don't see what business this . . ."

"Goddammit! Frannie spent two hours on the phone with DeDe, trying to calm her down. What the hell time did you get in last night, anyway?"

35

"Why don't you ask DeDe? I'm sure she wrote it in the log!"

Edgar spun his chair around and faced the wall. He studied a hunt print and tried to calm himself. He spoke quietly, deliberately, knowing that tone implied the greatest menace.

"One more time, Beauchamp. Where were you?"

The answer was addressed to the back of his head. "I had a committee meeting at the club."

"Which club?"

"University. Not *quite* as grand as PU, but Nob Hill nonethe . . ."

"You were there till midnight?"

"We had a few drinks afterwards."

"We? You and some chippie from Ruffles?"

"That's Ripples. And I didn't pick up any . . . what's that quaint word? I was at the club. Ask Peter Cipriani. He was there."

"I'm not running a detective agency."

"You could have fooled me. Is that all?"

Edgar massaged his forehead with his fingertips. He didn't turn around. "We have a conference."

"Right," said Beauchamp, leaving.

Promptly at noon, Mary Ann headed for the Royal Exchange with Mona.

"Shit," groaned the copywriter over a Pimm's Cup. "I am *so* spaced today."

Not surprising, thought Mary Ann. Mona was *paid* to be spaced. She was the resident freak at Halcyon Communications. Clients who weren't immediately impressed with her creativity changed their minds when they saw her office: an assortment of hookah pipes, an oak icebox which served as a bar, an antique wheelchair, a collage of *Playgirl* beefcake photos, and a neon martini glass from a Tenderloin bar.

"What's the matter?" asked Mary Ann.

"I did mescaline last night."

"Oh?"

"We went to Mission Street and tripped through all those

godawful tacky furniture stores with the tassled lampshades and round beds and . . . you know . . . those phony waterfall things in the glass tubes. It was so *plastic,* but . . . you know . . . like *cosmic* plasticity . . . and in a weird way it was sort of, like, spiritual, you know."

Mary Ann did *not* know. She avoided the issue by ordering a turkey sandwich and a bean salad. Mona ordered another Pimm's Cup.

"Guess what?" said Mary Ann.

"Yeah?"

"I'm going to dinner at Mrs. Madrigal's tonight."

"Congratulations. She likes you."

"You already told me that."

"Well . . . then she trusts you."

"Why do I have to be trusted?"

"Nothing . . . I just meant . . ."

"How should I handle it, Mona?"

"Handle what?"

"Her. I don't know . . . I feel like she *expects* something of me."

"Bourgeois paranoia."

"I know . . . but you're really close to her, and I thought you might be able to tell me . . . you know . . . her quirks."

"She's decent. That's her quirk. She also makes a fabulous rack of lamb."

Mona left work at four o'clock, deliberately skirting Mary Ann's alcove near the elevator. When she got home, she found Mrs. Madrigal in the garden.

The landlady was wearing plaid slacks, a paint-smeared smock and a straw hat. Her face was ruddy from exertion. "Well . . . home so early from the fields, dear?"

"Yeah."

"Just so many things you can say about pantyhose, eh?"

Mona smiled. "I wanted to tell you something. It's no big deal, really."

"Fine."

"Mary Ann's been asking me about you."

"Have you told her anything?"

"I figure that's *your* business."

"You think she's too green, don't you?"

Mona nodded. "Right now, yeah."

"We're having dinner tonight."

"She told me. That's why . . . well, I didn't want you to be embarrassed, that's all."

"Thank you, dear."

"I should mind my own business, shouldn't I?"

"No. I appreciate your concern. Would you like to come tonight?"

"No, I . . . no, thank you."

"You're very special to me, dear."

"Thank you, Mrs. Madrigal."

Anguish in Bohemia

AFTER WORK, EDGAR SWILLED A DOUBLE SCOTCH AT the Bohemian Club.

The rules of a well-ordered life were never enough when other people refused to obey them. Beauchamp was only one of many.

The Cartoon Room was crowded. Edgar sat alone in the Domino Room, preferring silence. The dread had begun to grow again.

He rose and went to the telephone. His hands grew slippery around the receiver.

The maid answered.

"Halcyon Hill."

"Emma . . . is Mrs. Halcyon available?"

"Just a moment, Mr. Halcyon."

Frannie's mouth was full. "Uhhmm . . . darling . . . *marvelous* cheese puffs I doggy-bagged from Cyril's party! And Emma's whipped up a divine *blanquette de veau!* When are you coming home?"

"I have to pass tonight, Frannie."

"Edgar! Not those damn pantyhose again?"

"No. I'm at the club. There's a . . . committee meeting."

Silence.

"Frannie?"

"What?" She was icy.

"I have to do these things. You know that."

"We do what we *want*, Edgar."

Blood rushed to his face. "All right, then, goddammit! I *want* to go to this meeting! That make you happy?"

Frannie hung up.

He stood there, holding the phone, then put it down and mopped his face with a handkerchief. He took several deep breaths. He reached for the directory and looked up Ruby Miller's phone number.

He dialed.

"Evening. Ruby here." She sounded more grandmotherly than ever.

"Edgar Halcyon, Mrs. Miller."

"Oh . . . how nice to hear your voice. Gracious, it's been a long time."

"Yes . . . you know . . . business."

"Yes. Busy, busy."

His brow was drenched again. "Can I see you tonight, Mrs. Miller? I know it isn't much notice."

"Oh . . . well, just a minute, Mr. Halcyon. Let me check my book." She left the phone. Edgar could hear her rummaging around. "All right," she said at last. "Eight o'clock, O.K.?"

"Thank you so much."

"Not at all, Mr. Halcyon."

He felt much better now. Ruby Miller meant hope to him, however vague. He decided to have a drink at the bar in the Cartoon Room.

"Edgar, you old bastard, why aren't you home pruning the rosebushes?"

It was Roger Manigault, senior vice president of Pacific Excelsior. The Manigault tennis courts bordered on the Halcyon apple orchard in Hillsborough.

Edgar smiled. "Past *your* bedtime too, Booter." The nickname was a hangover from Stanford days, when Manigault had been beatified on the gridiron. Nothing since then had pleased him.

He was currently angered by the demise of the Stanford Indian.

"Everybody's so goddamn *sensitive* nowadays! Indians aren't Indians anymore . . . oh, no! They're Native Americans. I spent ten years learning to say 'Negroes' right, and now they've turned into Blacks. Goddammit, I don't know *what* to call the maid anymore!"

Edgar took a slug of his drink and nodded. He had heard it all before.

"Now, you take the word 'gay,' Edgar. That used to be a perfectly normal word that meant something wholesome and *fun,* goddammit! Jesus God! Look at it now!" He polished off his scotch and slammed the glass down. "A decent young couple is almost embarrassed to mention they've been to the Gaieties!"

"Good point," said Edgar.

"Damn right! Say . . . speaking of that, Roger and Suzie say they bumped into Beauchamp and DeDe at the Gaieties. Beauchamp's a damn good dancer, Suzie says . . . hustling or whatever they call it."

Hustling is probably the word, Edgar thought. He had wondered about Beauchamp and Suzie on several occasions. "Excuse me, Booter. I promised Frannie I'd be home early tonight."

For the lies she required, Ruby Miller might as well have been Edgar's mistress.

Up the hill at the University Club, Beauchamp sought solace from Peter Cipriani, heir to a fabled San Mateo flower fortune.

"I'm getting paranoid, I guess."

"The Old Man again?"

"Yeah. He put the screws to me about DeDe."

"He's suspicious?"

"Always."

"What does DeDe think?"

41

"You're assuming she knows how to."

"She's a tad thick, but she *does* pay for your Wilkes Bashford addiction . . . and she's got a nice box."

Beauchamp frowned.

"At the *opera,* Beauchamp."

"Very funny."

"I thought so."

"I didn't come here to talk about my wife, Peter."

"Hmm . . . that's funny. Everybody else did."

Silence.

"Sorry. Cheap shot. Wanna hear about the Bachelors Ball?"

"Do I look like I do?"

"Well, we missed you, anyway. Actually, we missed your Navy dress whites. They were always just the right touch. Very Gilbert and Sullivan."

"Thank you."

"The Prune Prince wore his great-uncle's opera tails this year."

"John Stonecypher?"

"The one. Are you ready for this? He spilled a bottle of amyl in the breast pocket."

"C'mon!"

"While he was dancing with Madge!"

"What did she do?"

"Oh . . . she just kept waltzing around like a Cotillion deb, presumably pretending that all her dance partners smell like dirty sweat socks. . . . You're going to her do tonight, aren't you?"

"Shit!"

"Forgot, huh?"

"DeDe will shit a brick!" He downed his drink. "I'm off."

"More than likely," said Peter.

The Wrath of DeDe

DEDE WAS SITTING AT HER LOUIS QUINZE *ESCRITOIRE* making notations in her Louis Vuitton checkbook.

"You forgot about Madge's party, didn't you?"

"I hauled ass to get here."

"It starts in half an hour."

"Then we'll be late. Pull in your claws. Your old man's been bitching at me all day."

"Did you make the Adorable presentation?"

"No. He did."

"Why?"

"Why don't *you* tell *me?*"

"I don't know what you're talking about."

"He was pissed, DeDe. Royally."

Silence.

"You know why, of course."

DeDe looked down at her checkbook.

Beauchamp persisted. "He was pissed because his darling daughter called him up last night and told him I was a son-of-a-bitch."

"I didn't do anything of . . ."

"Bullshit!"

"I was worried, Beauchamp. It was after midnight. I tried the club and Sam's and Jack's. I . . . panicked. I thought Daddy might know where you were."

"Of course. Little Beauchamp doesn't make a fucking *move* without checking with the Great White Father!"

"Don't talk about Daddy like that."

"Oh . . . fuck him! I don't need his permission to breathe. I don't need him for a goddamn thing!"

"Oh? Daddy would be interested to hear that."

Silence.

"Why don't we call him up and tell him?"

"DeDe . . ."

"Me or you?"

"DeDe . . . I'm sorry. I'm tired. It's been a bitch of a day."

"I'll bet." She moved to the hall mirror and made last-minute adjustments to her makeup. "How's Little Miss Whatshername?"

"Who?"

"Daddy's secretary. Your little . . . after-work amusement."

"You've gotta be kidding!"

"No. I don't think so."

"Mary Ann Singleton?"

"Is *that* her name? How quaint."

"Christ! I hardly know her."

"Apparently that hasn't stopped you before."

"She's your father's secretary!"

"And she's not exactly an eyesore."

"I can't help that, can I?"

DeDe pursed her lips to blot her lipstick. She looked at her husband. "Look . . . I've had it with this. You dropped off the face of the earth last night."

"I told you. I was at the club."

"Well, *quelle coincidence!* You were at the club when you stood me up for the reception at the de Young last Wednesday *and* last Friday when we missed the Telfairs' party at *Beach Blanket Babylon.*"

"We've seen it five times."

"That isn't the point."

Beauchamp laughed bitterly. "You are too much. You really are. . . . Where in God's name did you dig *this* one up?"

"I've got eyes, Beauchamp."

"Where? When?"

"Last week. I was shopping with Binky at La Remise du Soleil."

"How very chic of you."

"You were crossing the street with her."

"Mary Ann?"

"Yes."

"That *is* incriminating."

"It was lunchtime, and you were looking *very* chummy."

"You missed the good part. You should have been there earlier when I ravaged her in the redwood grove behind the Transamerica Pyramid."

"You're not gonna smartass your way out of this one, Beauchamp."

"I'm not even trying." He snatched the keys to the Porsche from the hall table. "I stopped with you a long time ago."

"Tell me," said DeDe, following him out the door.

The Landlady's Dinner

MARY ANN STOPPED BY MONA'S ON HER WAY TO Mrs. Madrigal's for dinner.

"Wanna mellow out?" asked Mona.

"It depends."

"Coke?"

"I'm on a diet. Have you got a Tab or Fresca?"

"I don't *believe* you." Mona placed a hand mirror on her cable spool table. "Even *you* must have seen *Porgy and Bess?*"

"So?" Mary Ann's voice cracked. Mona was spading white powder from a vial with a tiny silver spoon. The handle of the spoon was engraved with an ecology emblem.

"Sportin' Life," said Mona. "Happy dust. This stuff is an American institution." She made a line of powder across the surface of the mirror. "All the silent film stars snorted. Why do you think they looked like this?" She moved her head and arms spastically, like Charlie Chaplin.

"And now," she continued, "all we need is a common, ordinary, all-purpose food stamp." She flourished a ten-dollar food stamp like a magician, presenting both sides for Mary Ann's examination.

"Do you get food stamps?" asked Mary Ann. She makes four times what I do, thought the secretary.

Mona didn't answer, absorbed in the operation. She rolled the food stamp into a little tube and stuck it in her left nostril. "Stunning, eh? Verry sexy!"

She went after the powder like an anteater on the rampage. Mary Ann was horrified. "Mona, is that . . . ?"

"It's your turn."

"No, thank you."

"Aw . . . go ahead. It's good for social occasions."

"I'm nervous enough as it is."

"It doesn't make you *nervous,* dearheart. It . . ."

Mary Ann stood up. "I have to go, Mona. I'm late."

"God!"

"What?"

"You make me feel like such . . . an addict."

Mrs. Madrigal looked almost elegant in black satin pajamas and a matching cloche.

"Ah, Mary Ann. I'm grinding the gazpacho. Help yourself to the hors d'oeuvres. I'll be right back in two shakes of a lamb's tail."

The "hors d'oeuvres" were arranged symmetrically on two plates. One held several dozen stuffed mushrooms. The other, half a dozen joints.

Mary Ann chose a mushroom and gave the apartment a once-over.

Two rather gross marble statues flanked the fireplace: a boy with a thorn in his foot and a woman holding a jug. Silk fringes dangled everywhere, from lampshades, coverlets, curtains and valances, even from the archway that led to the hall. The only photograph was a picture of the 1915 Panama-Pacific Exposition.

"Well, what do you think of my little bordello?" Mrs. Madrigal was posing dramatically under the archway.

"It's . . . very nice."

"Don't be ridiculous! It's depraved!"

47

Mary Ann laughed. "You planned it that way?"

"Of course. Help yourself to a joint, dear, and *don't* bother to pass it around. I *loathe* that soggy communal business! I mean . . . if you're going to be degenerate, you might as well be a lady about it, don't you think?"

There were two other guests. One was a fiftyish, red-bearded North Beach poet named Joaquin Schwartz. ("A dear man," Mrs. Madrigal confided to Mary Ann, "but I *wish* he'd learn to use capital letters.") The other was a woman named Laurel who worked at the Haight-Ashbury Free Clinic. She didn't shave under her arms.

Joaquin and Laurel spent dinner discussing their favorite years. Joaquin believed in 1957. Laurel felt 1967 was where it was at . . . or where it *had* been at.

"We could have kept it going," she said. "I mean, it had a life of its own, didn't it? We shared *everything* . . . the acid, the music, the sex, the Avalon, the Family Dog, the Human Be-In. There were fourteen freaks in that flat on Oak Street, fourteen freaks and six sleeping bags. It was fucking beautiful, because it was . . . was, like, history. *We* were history. We were the fucking cover of *Time* magazine, man!"

Mrs. Madrigal was polite. "What do you think happened, dear?"

"They killed it. Not the Pigs. The Media."

"Killed what?"

"Nineteen sixty-seven."

"I see."

"Nixon, Watergate, Patty Fucking Hearst, the Bicentennial. The Media got bored with 1967, so they zapped it. It could have survived for a while. Some of it escaped to Mendocino . . . but the Media found out about it and killed it all over again. Jesus . . . I mean, what's left? There's not a single fucking place where it's still 1967!"

Mrs. Madrigal winked at Mary Ann. "You're being awfully quiet."

"I'm not sure I . . ."

"What's *your* favorite year?"

48

"I don't think I have one."

"Mine's 1987," said Mrs. Madrigal. "I'll be sixty-five or so . . . I can collect social security and stash away enough cash to buy a small Greek island." She twirled a lock of hair around her forefinger and smiled faintly. "Actually, I'd settle for a small Greek."

After dinner, on the way to the bathroom, Mary Ann lingered in the landlady's bedroom. There was a photograph on the dresser in a silver frame.

A young man, a soldier, standing beside a 1940s car. He was quite handsome, if a little awkward in his uniform.

"So you see, the old dame does have a past."

Mrs. Madrigal was standing in the doorway.

"Oh . . . I'm prying, aren't I?"

Mrs. Madrigal smiled. "I hope it means we're friends."

"I . . ." Mary Ann turned back to the photograph, embarrassed. "He's very good-looking. Is that Mr. Madrigal?"

The landlady shook her head. "There's never been a Mr. Madrigal."

"I see."

"No you don't. How could you? Madrigal is . . . an assumed name, as they say in the gangster movies. I cleaned up my act about a dozen years back, and the old name was the first to go."

"What was it?"

"Don't be naughty. If I'd wanted you to know it, I wouldn't have changed it."

"But . . . ?"

"Why the Mrs.?"

"Yes."

"Widows and divorcees don't get . . . what's Mona's word? . . . hassled. We don't get hassled as much as single girls. You must have figured that out by now."

"Who's hassled? I haven't had so much as an obscene phone call since I moved to San Francisco. I could use a little hassling, frankly."

"The town is full of charming young men."

49

"To each other."

Mrs. Madrigal chuckled. "There's a lot of that going around."

"You make it sound like the flu. I think it's terribly depressing."

"Nonsense. Take it as a challenge. When a woman triumphs in this town, she *really* triumphs. You'll do all right, dear. Give it time."

"You think?"

"I *know.*" The landlady winked and put her arm across Mary Ann's shoulder. "C'mon, let's go join those *tedious* people."

Rendezvous with Ruby

RUBY MILLER'S HOUSE WAS ON ORTEGA STREET IN THE Sunset district, a green stucco bungalow with a manicured lawn and a bowl of plastic roses in the picture window. A Rambler parked in the driveway bore a bumper sticker that said: HONK IF YOU LOVE JESUS.

Edgar parked the Mercedes across the street. He was locking the doors when he saw Mrs. Miller waving from the window.

He returned the wave. Christ! He felt like a shoe salesman coming home to the wife.

Mrs. Miller turned on the porch light, took off her apron and fussed with a strand of gray hair. "You're a sight for sore eyes, you are! I'm a mess. . . . I didn't plan . . ."

"I'm sorry. I hope it's not too much trouble."

"Don't be silly. I'm tickled to death." She gave his hand a pat and led him into the house. "Ernie . . . look who's here!"

Her husband was seated in front of the television set in a Danish Modern chair. His arms were the shape and color of provolone cheese.

"Hiya, Mr. Halcyon." He didn't get up. He was engrossed in the box before him.

"How's everything, Ernie?"

"Bob Barker just reunited a Marine with his loved one."

"I'm sorry . . . ?"

"Truth or Consequences. They brought this Marine back from Okinawa and reunited him with his fiancée. She was dressed up like a frog. They made him kiss her . . . blindfolded."

Mrs. Miller took Edgar's arm. "Isn't that sweet? You don't watch much TV, I guess."

"No. I'm afraid not."

"Well, enough chitchat. Let's get to work. Something to eat first? Hi-C, maybe? Fritos?"

"I'm fine, thank you." At the last minute, out of nervousness, he had gorged himself on chicken livers at the club. "I'm ready whenever you are."

"Then let's you and me go out to the garage. Ernie, don't you play the TV too loud, hear?" Her husband grunted his reply.

Mrs. Miller led Edgar through the kitchen. "That Ernie and his TV! I guess it relaxes him . . . and it's much more Christian than the movies these days, what with . . . you know . . . all that nasty stuff."

"Mmm," he said vaguely, trying to sound polite but disinterested. Mrs. Miller could slip into a monologue with all the precision of a New York cabby or an Italian barber. Edgar didn't want to spend this session hearing about Smut in the Cinema.

In the semidarkness of the garage, she went about her business. She cleared muddy garden tools off the ping-pong table and removed a couple of candle stubs from an old MJB can. Humming softly to herself, she donned the familiar purple velveteen robe.

"Have you noticed any changes?"

"In the garage?"

Mrs. Miller chuckled. "In *you.* This is your fifth visit. You should be feeling . . . changes."

"I'm not sure. I may . . ."

"Don't force it. It will come."

"I wish I shared your confidence."

"*Faith,* Mr. Halcyon."

"Yes."

"Faith is different than confidence."

She was beginning to irritate him. "Mrs. Miller . . . my wife is expecting me home shortly. Could we . . . ?"

"Of course." She was all business now. She brushed some imaginary lint off the front of her robe and kneaded her fingers for a moment. "Assume the posture, please."

Edgar loosened his tie and climbed onto the ping-pong table. He lay down on his back. Mrs. Miller lit a candle and placed it on the table near Edgar's head.

"Mr. Halcyon?"

"Yes?"

"Forgive me, but . . . well, I was wondering if . . . You mentioned Mrs. Halcyon. I was wondering if you told her."

"No."

"I know you don't like to talk about it . . . but sometimes it helps if a loved one joins in and . . ."

"My family is Catholic, Mrs. Miller."

She was visibly jarred. "Oh . . . I'm sorry."

"That's all right." He waved it away.

"I didn't mean I was sorry you're Catholic. I meant . . ."

"I know, Mrs. Miller."

"Jesus loves Catholics too."

"Yes."

She pressed her fingertips against Edgar's temples and made small circular strokes. "Jesus will help heal you, Mr. Halcyon, but you must believe in Him. You must become a little child again and seek refuge in His bosom."

A motorcycle roared down Ortega Street, spluttering blasphemously, as Ruby Miller began the incantation that Edgar Halcyon now knew by heart:

"Heal him, Jesus! Heal thy servant Edgar. Heal his failing kidneys and make him whole again. Heal him, Jesus! Heal thy servant. . . ."

The Boy Next Door

MARY ANN LEFT MRS. MADRIGAL'S JUST AFTER TEN o'clock. Back at her own apartment, she put her feet up, sipped a Tab and checked her mail.

There was a short, gloomy note from her mother, a Contemporary Card from Connie implying desertion, and a box containing her Scenic San Francisco checks from Hibernia Bank.

The personalized message on her checks was "Have a Nice Day."

Despite her pathetic income, the choice of a bank had somehow seemed crucial to the establishment of her identity in the city.

In the beginning, she had wavered between the Chartered Bank of London and Wells Fargo. The former had a wonderfully classy name and a fireplace in the lobby, but only one branch in the entire city. The latter had a nice Western ring to it and lots of branches.

But she had never considered Dale Robertson all *that* cute.

In the end, she had gone with Hibernia.

Their jingle promised they would remember your name.

Someone rapped on her door.

It was Brian Hawkins, who lived across the hall. He was a waiter at Perry's and they had chatted briefly only once or twice before. His hours were extremely irregular.

"Hi," he said. "Mrs. Madrigal just called."

"Yeah?"

"What is it? Furniture?"

"I'm sorry, Brian. I don't . . ."

"She said you needed help with something."

"I can't imagine what . . ." The light dawned. Mary Ann laughed, shaking her head, taking stock once more of Brian's chestnut curls and green eyes. Mrs. Madrigal was pushy, but her taste wasn't bad.

Brian looked vaguely irked. "You wanna let me in on it."

"I think Mrs. Madrigal is matchmaking."

"You *don't* need furniture moved?"

"It's kind of embarrassing. I . . . well, I just finished telling her there weren't enough straight men in San Francisco."

He brightened. "Yeah. Ain't it great?"

"Oh, Brian . . . I'm sorry. I thought you . . ."

"Relax, will ya? I'm straight as they come. I just don't like *competition.*"

He invited her over for a nightcap. His tiny kitchen was decorated with empty Chianti bottles and Sierra Club posters. The carcass of a neglected piggyback plant hung grimly from a pot on the window sill.

"I love your stove," said Mary Ann.

"Funky, huh? Anywhere else it's called squalor. Here we pass it off as Old World charm."

"Did it come with the apartment?"

"Are you kidding? The stereo and the incline board are mine. The rest belongs to Dragon Lady."

"Mrs. Madrigal?"

He nodded, looking her over. "She's trying to fix us up,

huh?" His smile was approaching a leer.

Mary Ann chose not to deal with it. "She's a little strange, but I think she means well."

"Sure."

"Has she always had this place?"

He shook his head. "I think she used to run a bookstore in North Beach."

"Is she from here?"

"Nobody's *from* here." He refilled her glass with Almadén Pinot Noir. "You're from Cleveland, aren't you?"

"Yeah. How did you know?"

"Mona told me." The green eyes were burning into her. She looked down at her glass. "Well, no secrets at *all.*"

"Don't count on it."

"What?"

"We've *all* got secrets in this town. You just have to dig a little deeper for them."

He's being mysterious, she thought, because he thinks it's sexy. She decided it was time to leave.

"Well," she said, rising. "Work tomorrow. Thanks for the wine . . . and the tour."

"Anytime."

She was sure he meant exactly that.

The Matriarch

WHEN EDGAR GOT HOME AT ELEVEN-FIFTEEN, IT was clear that Frannie had been drinking.

"Well, how was the club, darling? You make like a little hooty owl?"

She was perched on the sofa on the sun porch. Her legs were curled up under her Thai silk muumuu. Her wig was askew. She smelled of rum and Trader Vic's Mai Tai Mix.

"Hello, Frannie."

"Awful long committee meeting."

"We were planning for the Grove Play." He tried to sound nonchalant about it, though Frannie was too far gone to appreciate the effort.

"Lotta work, huh?"

"We had a few drinks afterward. You know how those things go."

Frannie nodded, stifling a hiccup. She certainly knew how those things went.

He changed the subject. "How about you? You have a fun day?" His tone was that of a kindly father to a small child.

What had happened to the debutante who once looked like Veronica Lake?

"I had lunch with Helen and Gladys at that *darling* place on Polk Street . . . The Pavilion. Then I bought a ceramic duck. *Precious.* Maybe it's a goose. I think it's supposed to be for soup, but I thought it would look darling in the den with some ivy or something."

"Good."

"Annnd . . . I went to my Opera Guild meeting this afternoon and made the most marvelous discovery. What do you think it is?"

"I don't know." Christ, how he hated this game!

"C'mon. One eensy-weensy guess."

"Frannie, I've had a long day. . . ."

"Don't you wuv me?"

"For Christ's sake!"

"Oh, all *right!* If you're going to be a grouch about it . . . Guess who's in town?"

"Who?"

Frannie sustained the suspense as long as possible, shifting her torso on the sofa and adjusting her wig. She needs attention, thought Edgar. You haven't been giving it to her.

"The Huxtables," Frannie said at last.

"The who?"

"Really, Edgar. Nigel Huxtable. The conductor. His wife is Nora Cunningham."

"It's coming back to me."

"You slept through their *Aïda.*"

"Yes. Marvelous evening."

"They're here to do a benefit for Kurt Adler. Practically *nobody* knows they're staying at the Mark . . . and we're going to give a party for them!"

"We are?"

"Aren't you excited?"

"We threw a party last month, Frannie."

"This is a *coup,* Edgar! The Farnsworths will just *die.* Viola's been gloating for two months over that absurd little barbecue she gave for Baryshnikov."

"I don't even remember it."

"Yes you do. She hired those seedy Russian waiters from

some place on Clement Street, and they served Russian dressing and Russian tea, and the organist played 'Lara's Theme' when Baryshnikov made his entrance. It was too ghastly for words!"

"You just did fairly well."

"Edgar . . . the Huxtables make Baryshnikov look like . . . Barney Google. I *know* I can get them, darling."

"Frannie, I just don't think . . ."

"Please . . . I didn't complain when you wouldn't let me have Truman Capote or Giancarlo Giannini."

Edgar turned away. He couldn't face that Emmett Kelly expression. "All right. Try and keep the cost down, will you?"

Emma warmed up some leftover quiche for him. He ate it in his study, while he scanned the new book he had ordered: *Death as a Fact of Life.*

"Whatcha reading, darling?" Frannie was propped against the doorway.

He closed the book. "Consumer research. Boring."

"You coming to bed?"

"In a minute, Frannie."

She was out cold and snoring when he got there.

Stranger in the Park

EDGAR SPOKE TO MARY ANN ON THE INTERCOM. "I NEED the Adorable script as soon as possible. I think Beauchamp has a copy."

"He's out right now, Mr. Halcyon."

"Check with Mona, then."

"I don't think she . . ."

"Ask her, goddammit! Somebody's got one!"

As soon as Mary Ann was gone, Edgar dialed Jack Kincaid's number.

"Dr. Kincaid's office."

"Is he in?"

"May I tell him who's calling?"

"No, you may not!"

"One moment, please, Mr. Halcyon."

Kincaid's tone was much too jovial. "Hello, Edgar. How's the pantyhose game?"

"When can you see me?"

"What about?"

"The tests. I want new ones."

"Edgar, that won't make a damn bit of . . ."

"I'll pay for them, goddammit!"

"Edgar . . ."

"You were wrong about Addison Branch. You told me so yourself."

"That was different. His symptoms weren't so pronounced."

"Symptoms can change. It's been three months."

"Edgar . . . look . . . I'm telling you as a friend. Stop fighting this thing. You're beating your head against a wall. You're not being fair to yourself or the people who love you."

"What the hell has fairness got to do with it?"

"Face it, Edgar. You've got to. Tell your family. Buy yourself a yacht and take Frannie on a cruise around the world. Hell . . . rent a castle in Spain or run off with a whore or keep right on raising hell in Jackson Square . . . but face it! For God's sake . . . no, for *yours* . . . make these next six months count."

When Mary Ann returned, he was waiting at her desk. "I'm going out. If anyone wants me, I'm at lunch with a client."

"Doro's?"

"Never mind where. Just say I'm out."

He strode out of the building, furious that a contract he had never signed was being carried out anyway.

Tell Frannie? Christ! What kind of mileage could she get out of *that* one in the social columns?

Frances Halcyon, Hillsborough hostess par excellence, scored another triumph Friday night with an intimate little dinner for operatic greats Nora Cunningham and Nigel Huxtable.
Frannie, who just saw *A Chorus Line* in New York ("Adored it!"), delighted some very well-bred palates with beef roulades and potato puffs. Hubby Edgar (he's the advertising giant) surprised the assembled guests with the announcement of his impending death. . . .

He headed away from Jackson Square, up Columbus into the frantic heart of North Beach. Carol Doda's electric nipples winked at him cruelly, flaunting a revolution in which he had never even been an insurgent.

In front of The Garden of Eden, a walleyed derelict bellowed: "It's all over. It's time to make peace with the Lord. It's time to get right with Jesus!"

He needed a place to clear his head.

And time to do it. Precious time.

He sat down on a bench in Washington Square. Next to him was a woman who was roughly his age. She was wearing wool slacks and a paisley smock. She was reading the Bhagavad Gita.

She smiled.

"Is that the answer?" asked Edgar, nodding at the book.

"What's the question?" asked the woman.

Edgar grinned. "Gertrude Stein."

"I don't think she said it, do you? No one's *that* clever on a deathbed."

There it was again.

He felt a surge of recklessness. "What would *you* say?"

"About what?"

"The end. Your last words. If you could choose."

The woman studied his face for a moment. Then she said: "How about . . . 'Oh, shit!' "

His laughter was cathartic, an animal yelp that brought tears to his eyes. The woman watched him benignly, detached yet somehow gentle.

It was almost as if she knew.

"Would you like a sandwich?" she asked when he stopped laughing. "It's made from *focaccia* bread."

Edgar said yes, delighting in her charity. It was nice to have someone taking care of *him* for once. "I'm Edgar Halcyon," he said.

"That's nice," she said. "I'm Anna Madrigal."

Relating at Lunch

BACK AT THE AGENCY, MARY ANN WAS GLOSSING HER lips when Beauchamp approached on little cat feet.

"Has the Blue Meanie gone to lunch yet?"

"Oh . . . Beauchamp . . ." She dropped the lip gloss into the wicker pocketbook she had decoupaged with frogs and mushrooms. "He's . . . he left over an hour ago. I think he was upset about something."

"News."

"This was different."

"Maybe they asked him to be a wood nymph in the Grove Play."

"What?"

"Nothing. We've got a lunch date, remember?"

"Oh . . . that's right."

She had thought of nothing else all morning.

At MacArthur Park, they both ordered salads. Mary Ann nibbled hers half-heartedly, put off slightly by the restaurant's caged birds and Urban Organic aloofness. Beauchamp sensed her discomfort.

"You're freaked, aren't you?"

"I . . . how do you mean?"

"You know. This. Us."

"Why do you say that?"

"Uh uh. You have to answer first."

She killed time by hunting for a chunk of avocado. "It's . . . new, I guess."

"Lunch with a married man?"

She nodded, avoiding his French Racing Blue eyes. "Could I have some ice water, Beauchamp?"

He signaled for a waiter without shifting his gaze from her. "You shouldn't be nervous, you know. You're the one who's free. There's a lot to be said for that."

"Free?"

"Single."

"Oh . . . yeah."

"Single people can call the shots."

The waiter appeared. "The lady would like some ice water," said Beauchamp. He smiled at Mary Ann. "You don't mind being called a lady, do you?" She shook her head. The waiter smirked and left.

"You know what?" said Mary Ann.

"What?" The eyes were locked on her now.

"I used to pronounce your name 'Bo-shomp' instead of 'Beechum.' "

"Everybody does that."

"I felt so dumb. Mildred finally corrected me. It's English, isn't it?"

He nodded. "My parents were shamelessly affected."

"I think it's nice. You should have told me when I said it wrong."

He shrugged. "It doesn't matter."

"I even said Greenwich Street wrong when I first got here."

"I called Kearny 'Keerny.' "

"Did you?"

"And Ghirardelli 'Jeerardelli,' and . . . blasphemy of blasphemies . . . I called the cable cars trolleys!"

Mary Ann giggled. "I *still* do that."

64

"So big deal! Fuck 'em, if they can't take a joke!"

She laughed, hoping it would cover her embarrassment.

"We're all babes in the woods," said Beauchamp. "At one point or another. Use it to your advantage. Innocence is very erotic." He picked a crouton out of his salad and popped it in his mouth. "It is to me, at least."

The waiter was back with her water. She thanked him and sipped at it, considering a new course for the conversation. Beauchamp beat her to it.

"Have you ever met my wife?"

"Uh . . . once. At the softball game."

"Oh, yeah. What did you think?"

"She's very nice."

His smile was wan. "Yes . . . very nice."

"I read about you two a lot."

"Yes. Don't you?"

She was squirming. "Beauchamp . . . I think Mr. Halcyon's gonna be back in . . ."

"You want a scoop you won't find in the social columns?"

"I don't want to talk about your wife."

"I don't blame you."

She dabbed at her mouth with a napkin. "This has been really . . ."

"We haven't slept together since the Fol de Rol."

She decided not to ask what the Fol de Rol was. "I think we should go, Beauchamp."

"DeDe and I aren't even *friends,* Mary Ann. We don't talk like you and I do. We don't *relate.* . . ."

"Beauchamp . . ."

"I'm trying to tell you something, goddammit! Will you stop being so fucking . . . Middle American for about ten seconds?" He dropped his head and rubbed his forehead with his fingertips. "I'm sorry . . . God . . . please, help me, will you?"

She reached across the table and squeezed his hand. He was crying.

"What can I do, Beauchamp?"

"I don't know. Don't leave . . . please. Talk to me."

"Beauchamp, this is the wrong place for . . ."

"I know. We need time."

"We could meet for a drink after work."

"What about this weekend?"

"I don't think that would . . ."

"I know a place in Mendocino."

A Piece of Anna's Past

THE SUN IN THE PARK WAS WARMER NOW, AND THE BIRDS were singing much more joyously.

Or so it seemed to Edgar.

"Madrigal. That's lovely. Aren't there some Madrigals in Philadelphia?"

Anna shrugged. "This one came from Winnemucca."

"Oh . . . I don't know Nevada too well."

"You must've been to Winnemucca at least once. Probably when you were eighteen."

He laughed. "Twenty. We were late bloomers in my family."

"Which one did you go to?"

"My God! You're talking about the Paleolithic period. I couldn't remember a thing like that!"

"It was your first time, wasn't it?"

"Yes."

"Well, then you can remember it. Everybody remembers the first time." She blinked her eyes coaxingly, like a teacher trying to extract the multiplication tables from a shy pupil. "When was it—1935 or thereabouts?"

"I guess . . . it was 1937. My junior year at Stanford."

"How did you get there?"

"Christ . . . a dilapidated Olds. We drove all night until we reached this disappointing-looking cinder-block house out in the middle of the desert." He chuckled to himself. "I guess we wanted it to look like the Arabian Nights or, at least, one of those gaslight-and-red-velvet places."

"San Franciscans are spoiled rotten!"

He laughed. "Well, I felt we deserved more. The house was ridiculously tame. They even had a photo of Franklin and Eleanor in the parlor."

"One has to keep up appearances, doesn't one? Do you remember the name now?"

Edgar's eyebrows arched. "By God . . . the Blue Moon Lodge! I haven't thought of that in years!"

"And the girl's name?"

"She was hardly a girl. More like forty-five."

"That's a girl. Believe me."

"No offense."

"What was her name?"

"Oh, Christ . . . No, that one's impossible."

"Margaret?"

"Yes! How did you . . . ?"

"She read me all the *Winnie-the-Pooh* books."

"What?"

"Are you sure you want to hear this?"

"Look, if I've . . ."

"My mother ran the Blue Moon Lodge. That was my home. I grew up there."

"You're not making that up, are you?"

"No."

"Christ!"

"Don't you *dare* apologize. If you apologize, so help me, I'll take my sandwich and run home."

"Why did you let me go on like that?"

"I wanted you to remember who you were then. You don't seem too happy with who you are now."

Edgar stared at her. "I don't, huh?"

"Nope."

He took a bite of his sandwich. His own present made him much more uneasy than this woman's questionable past. He shifted the focus. "Did you ever . . . you know . . . ?"

She smiled. "What do you think?"

"No fair."

"O.K. I ran away from home when I was sixteen, several years before you patronized the Blue Moon. I never worked for my mother."

"I see."

"I'm currently running a house of my own."

"Here?"

"At 28 Barbary Lane, San Francisco, 94109."

"On Russian Hill?"

She gave up the game. "I'm a garden-variety landlady, Mr. Halcyon."

"Ah."

"Are you disappointed?"

"Not a bit."

"Good. Then tomorrow . . . *your* turn to buy lunch."

Mona's New Roomie

THE UNCOSMIC JANGLE OF THE TELEPHONE BROUGHT AN abrupt end to Mona's mantra.

"Yeah?"

"Hi. It's Michael."

"Mouse! Jesus! I figured you got kidnaped by the CIA!"

"Long time, huh?"

"Three months."

"Yeah. That's about my average."

"Oh . . . you got the shaft?"

"Well, we parted amiably enough. He was terribly civilized about it, and I sat in Lafayette Park and cried all morning. Yeah . . . I got the shaft."

"I'm sorry, Mouse. I thought this one was gonna work out. I kinda liked . . . Robert, was it?"

"Yeah. I kinda liked him too." He laughed. "He used to be a Marine recruiter. Did I ever tell you that? He gave me this little key ring with a medallion that said, 'The Marines Are Looking for a Few Good Men.' "

"Sweet."

"We used to jog every morning in Golden Gate Park

". . . right down to the ocean. Robert had a red Marine tank top, and all the old mossbacks would stop us and say how nice it was to know there were still some decent, upstanding young men left in the world. Boy, we'd laugh about that . . . usually in bed."

"So what happened?"

"Who knows? He panicked, I guess. We were buying furniture together and stuff. Well . . . not exactly *together.* He'd buy a sofa and I'd buy a couple of matching chairs. One has to plan on divorce at all times . . . still, it was a landmark of sorts. I'd never gotten to the furniture-buying stage before."

"Well, that's *something.*"

"Yeah . . . and I never had anyone read me German poetry in bed before. In German."

"Hot stuff!"

"He played the harmonica, Mona. Sometimes when we were walking down the street. I was so fucking proud to be with him!"

"Talk much?"

"What?"

"Could he talk? Or was he too busy playing the harmonica?"

"He was a nice guy, Mona."

"Which is why he dumped on you."

"He didn't dump on me."

"You just said he did."

"It just wasn't . . . meant to be, that's all."

"Bullshit. You're a hopeless romantic."

"Thanks for the words of comfort."

"All I know is I haven't laid eyes on you in three months. There are other people in the world besides Mr. Right . . . and we love you too."

"I know. Mona, I'm sorry."

"Mouse . . . ?"

"I really am. I didn't mean to . . ."

"Michael Mouse, if you start crying on me, I'll never boogie with you again!"

"I'm not crying. I'm being pensive."

"You've got ten seconds to snap out of it. Jesus, Mouse, the woods are full of jogging Marine recruiters. Christ! You and

71

your Rustic Innocent trip! I'll bet that asshole had a closetful of lumberjack shirts, didn't he?"

"Lay off."

"He's down at Toad Hall right now, stomping around in his blue nylon flight jacket, with a thumb hooked in his Levi's and a bottle of Acme beer in his fist."

"You're a real hardass."

"Just your type. Look . . . if I learn a little German poetry, will you come stay here till you find a place? There's plenty of room in this barn. Mrs. Madrigal won't mind."

"I don't know."

"You're out on your can, right? You've got money?"

"A couple of thousand. Savings account."

"Well, I'm sick of playing Edna St. Vincent Millay. It's perfect. You can live here till you find another studio . . . or another harmonica player. Whichever comes first."

"It'll *never* work."

"Why the hell not?"

"You're into TM and I'm into est. It'll never work."

That night, he moved all his earthly goods into Mona's apartment:

The literary works of Mary Renault and the late Adelle Davis. Assorted work boots, overalls and denims from Kaplan's Army Surplus on Market Street. An Art Deco lamp in the form of a nymph perched on one foot. Random sea shells. A T-shirt that said DANCE 10, LOOKS 3. A hemostat roach clip. An exercise wheel. An autographed photo of La Belle.

"The furniture's at Robert's," he explained.

"Fuck him," said Mona. "You've got a new roomie now."

Michael hugged her. "You've saved my life again."

"Don't mention it, Babycakes. Let's just get the ground rules worked out, O.K.?"

"I squeeze the toothpaste from the bottom."

"You know what I'm talking about, Mouse."

"Yeah. Well . . . we've each got a bedroom."

"And the living room is off limits for tricks."

"Of course."

"And if I bring any switch hitters home with me, it's hands off, right?"

"Do I look like that kind of cad?"

"What about that Basque gardener last summer?"

"Yeah." Michael smiled. "He was all right, wasn't he?"

Mona stuck her tongue out at him.

Their First Date

ANNA SUGGESTED THEY LUNCH AT THE WASHINGTON Square Bar & Grill. "It's a hoot," she laughed over the phone. "Everybody's trying to be so godawful literary. For the price of a hamburger, you can look like you've just completed a slim volume of verse."

Edgar was wary. "I think I'd prefer something less boisterous."

"More private, you mean?"

"Well . . . yes."

"For God's sake! This isn't a shack-up! If one of your cronies spots us, you can say I'm a client or something."

"My clients don't look as good as you do."

"You naughty man!"

They ended up sitting two tables away from Richard Brautigan. Or someone who was trying to *look* like Richard Brautigan.

"That's Mimi Fariña over by the bar."

Edgar drew a blank.

"Joan Baez's sister, you philistine. Where have you been all your life? The Peninsula?"

He grinned sleepily. "You're mighty uppity for a slum lord."

"Slum lady."

"Sorry. I'm not very good on celebrities."

Anna smiled at him unaccusingly. "Doesn't your wife entertain them all the time?"

"You read the papers?"

"Sometimes."

"My wife *collects* things, Anna. She collects porcelain ducks, old wicker furniture, nineteenth-century French Provincial birdcages that look like the château at Blois. . . . She also collects people. Last year she collected Rudolf Nureyev, Luciano Pavarotti, several Auchinclosses and a bona-fide, first-edition Spanish prince named Umberto de Something-or-Other."

"You can't hardly get them no more."

"She also collects bottles. Rum bottles."

"Oh."

"Shall we stop talking about her?"

"If you like. What *would* you like, by the way?"

"I'd like a good-looking . . . how old are you?"

"Fifty-six."

"I'd like a good-looking fifty-six-year-old woman to walk on the beach with me and tell me a few jokes."

"How soon?"

"Right away."

"Crank up the Mercedes."

The beach at Point Bonita was almost empty. At the north end, a group of teen-agers was flying a huge Mylar kite with a shimmering tail.

"Goddammit," said Edgar. "Remember how much fun that used to be?"

Anna trudged along beside him through the coarse black sand. *"Used* to? I fly kites all the time. It's *delicious* when you're stoned."

"Marijuana?"

Anna arched an eyebrow wickedly. She dug into her tapestry shoulder bag and produced a neatly rolled joint. "Please observe the cigarette paper. I thought it might appeal to your stern businessman's heart."

The paper was a counterfeit one-dollar bill.

"Anna . . . I don't mean to be a spoilsport . . ."

She dropped the joint back in the bag. "Of course you don't. Well! Let's have a nice little stroll, shall we?"

He was hurt by her artificial cheeriness. He felt older than ever. He wanted to reach out to her, to establish some link between them that would last.

"Anna?"

"Yes?"

"I think you're incredible for a fifty-six-year-old woman."

"Bullshit."

"I do."

"This is *exactly* what a fifty-six-year-old woman is *supposed* to be like."

He laughed weakly. "I wish you approved of me."

"Edgar . . ." She took his arm for the first time. "I approve of *you.* I just want *you* to climb out of that tough old hide of yours. I want you to see how wonderful you . . ."

She let go of his arm and ran down the beach toward the teen-agers. In less than a minute she was back, trailing the great silver kite behind her.

She presented the string to Edgar. "It's yours for ten minutes," she panted. "Make it count."

"You're insane." He laughed.

"Maybe."

"How did you talk them into it?"

"Don't ask."

At the end of the beach, the teen-agers were huddled in a circle, watching Anna's bribe go up in smoke.

Off to Mendocino

BEAUCHAMP'S SILVER PORSCHE CAREENED DOWN A Marin hillside like a pinball destined for a score.

Mary Ann fidgeted with her Mood Ring. "Beauchamp?"

"Yeah?"

"What did you tell your wife?"

He smiled like an errant Cub Scout. "She thinks I'm sending a kid to camp."

"What?"

"I told her the Guardsmen were having a weekend for underprivileged kids on Mount Tam. It doesn't matter. She wasn't listening. She and her mother were planning a party for Nora Cunningham."

"The opera singer?"

"Yes."

"Your family knows a lot of famous people, don't they?"

"I suppose."

"You didn't tell Mr. Halcyon, did you?"

"About what?"

"About us . . . going off."

"Christ! Are you crazy?"

She turned and looked at him. "I don't know. Am I?"

The place was located on a wooded bluff overlooking the Mendocino coast. There were half a dozen cabins in varying states of disrepair. It was called the Fools Rush Inn.

The lady innkeeper kept winking at Mary Ann.

When she had gone, Mary Ann said, "There's only one bed."

"Yeah. I'll get her to bring in a rollaway."

"She'll think we're really weird."

"She will, won't she?"

"Beauchamp, you said we wouldn't . . ."

"I know. And I meant it. Don't worry. I'll tell her you're my sister or something."

He built a fire in the fireplace while Mary Ann unpacked her bag. Out of habit, she had packed the tattered copy of *Nicholas and Alexandra* she had been reading for the past three summers.

"Scotch?" he asked.

"I don't think so."

"It helps me to unwind."

"Go ahead, then."

"I really appreciate this, Mary Ann. I needed the space."

"I know. I hope it helps."

He sat on the hearth and sipped his scotch. She sat next to him. "You don't have many friends, do you?"

He shook his head. "They're all DeDe's friends. I don't trust any of them."

"I want you to be able to trust me."

"So do I."

"You *can,* Beauchamp."

"I hope so."

She put her hand on his knee. "You *can.*"

*   *   *

They drove into the village at nightfall and ate dinner at the Mendocino Hotel.

"It used to be wonderful," said Beauchamp, surveying the dining room. "Funky and cheap and the floors slanted . . . the real thing."

Mary Ann looked around. "It looks fine to me."

"It's too precious. It knows what it is now. The charm is gone."

"They have sprinklers on the ceiling, though."

He smiled. "Perfect. That was the perfect thing for you to say."

"What did I say?"

"You're the same way, Mary Ann. Like this building. You should never know what you are . . . or your magic will disappear."

"You think I'm naïve, don't you?"

"A little."

"Unsophisticated?"

"Oh, yes!"

"Beauchamp . . . I don't think that's . . ."

"I worship it, Mary Ann. I worship your innocence."

When they returned to the cabin, there were still a few embers glowing in the fire. Beauchamp knelt down and threw a pine log onto the grate.

He stayed there, immobile, golden as a Maxfield Parrish faun. "They haven't brought the rollaway. I'll check at the office."

Mary Ann sat down next to him on the floor. Gently, she stroked the dark hair on his forearm.

"Forget about the rollaway, Beauchamp."

Brian Climbs the Walls

BRIAN RANG MARY ANN'S BUZZER THREE TIMES, MUT-
tered "Fuck" to no one but himself, and skulked
back across the hall to his own apartment.

It figured.

A girl like that didn't spend Saturday night sack-
ing out with Colonel Sanders and Bob Newhart. A girl like
that was out gettin' down . . . boogying and boozing and
nibbling on the Brut-flavored ear of a junior Bechtel exec
with a 240 Z, a trimaran in Tiburon, and a condominium at
Sea Ranch.

He stripped off his blue denim Perry's shirt and did two
dozen feverish push-ups on the bedroom floor. What point
was there getting a mental hard-on over Mary Ann Singleton?

She was probably a dumb cunt, anyway. She probably read
Reader's Digest Condensed Books and swapped chain letters and
dotted her *i*'s with little circles.

She was probably *dynamite* in the sack.

* * *

He climbed into the shower and sublimated his sex drive in a Donna Summer song.

So what would it be tonight? Henry Africa's. It was far enough away from Perry's and Union Street to provide at least *token* escape. Some of the girls there had been known to master witticisms beyond "Really!" and "Far out!" Two, at least.

He couldn't get into it.

He was dying of fern poisoning, OD'ing on Tiffany lamplight. He was sick of the whole plastic-fantastic scene. But where else . . . ?

Christ! The Come Clean Center.

He had picked up some *hot* women there last month. Hot women flocked to the Come Clean Center like lemmings headed for the Sea of Matrimony. But you didn't have to marry 'em to nail 'em!

Perfect! He toweled off hurriedly and climbed into corduroy Levi's and a gray-and-maroon rugby shirt. Why the hell hadn't he thought of it before?

He slapped his belly in front of the closet mirror. It made a solid sound, like a baseball hitting a mitt. Not too shabby for thirty-two!

He headed for the door, then stopped, remembering.

He grabbed a pillowcase off the bed, returned to the closet and stuffed the pillowcase with dirty boxer shorts, shirts and sheets.

He almost sprinted down Barbary Lane.

The Come Clean Center squatted unceremoniously at the intersection of Lombard and Fillmore, across the street from the Marina Health Spa. It was blue and Sixties Functional, bland enough to have sprouted up in Boise or Augusta or Kansas City. A sign by the doorway said: NO WASHING AFTER 8 P.M. PLEASE.

Brian smiled at the notice, appreciating the management's chagrin. Some people stayed until the bitter end. He checked the time: 7:27. He had to work fast.

Inside, along a wall of tumbling Speed Queens, a dozen young women pretended to be engrossed in their laundry. Their eyes darted briefly toward Brian, then back to their machines. Brian's heart felt like a Maytag agitator.

He took stock of the men he could see. Not much competition, really. A couple of leisure suits, a bad toupee, a wimp with a rhinestone in his ear.

Tucking in his shirt and sucking in his belly, he moved with pantherlike grace toward the detergent dispenser. Every detail mattered now, every ripple of a tendon, every flicker of an eyelid. . . .

"Psst, Hawkins!"

Brian spun around to see Chip Hardesty grinning his worst game show grin. Chip was a bachelor who lived in Larkspur and practiced dentistry in a converted warehouse on Northpoint. His office was full of stained-glass panels and silken Renaissance banners. People frequently mistook it for a fern bar.

Brian sighed peevishly. "O.K. . . . So this turf's already staked out."

"I'm leaving. Don't get your bowels in an uproar."

That was pure Chip Hardesty. *Don't get your bowels in an uproar.* He may *look* like a TV sportscaster, thought Brian, but his wit is straight out of the Chi Psi Lodge, circa 1963.

"No luck?" asked Brian, goading him.

"I wasn't looking."

"You weren't, huh?"

Chip held up his laundry basket. "See?"

"I guess they don't have laundromats in Larkspur."

"Look, man, I've got a date tonight. Otherwise I'd be scarfing up on a sure thing."

"In here?"

"As we speak, ol' buddy."

"Where?"

"Hey, man, do your own legwork."

"Fuck you very much."

Chip chuckled and cast his eyes to the corner of the room.

"She's all yours, ol' buddy. The one in orange." He slapped Brian on the shoulder and headed for the door. "Don't say I never did you any favors."

"Right," muttered Brian, as he regrouped for the attack.

Post-mortem

BEAUCHAMP?"

"Yeah?"

"Is that side O.K. for you?"

"Yeah. It's fine."

"Are you sure? I don't mind changing."

"I'm sure."

Mary Ann sat up in bed and chewed her forefinger for a moment. "You know what I think would be neat?"

Silence.

"I saw a sign out on the highway for one of those rent-a-canoe places. We could pack a picnic lunch and rent a canoe and spend a nice lazy Sunday morning paddling up . . . What's the name of that river, anyway?"

"Big."

"The Big River?"

"Yes."

"Well, *that* could be improved on, but I'm an expert paddler, and I could recite all the poetry I wrote during my senior year in . . ."

"I have to get back early."

"I thought you said . . ."

"Mary Ann, could we get some sleep, huh?" He rolled away from her, inching closer to the edge of the bed. Mary Ann remained upright and kept silent for half a minute.

Finally:

"Beauchamp?"

"What?"

"Are you . . . ?"

"What?"

"It doesn't matter. My mind was wandering."

"What, goddammit!"

"Are you . . . upset about tonight?"

"What the hell do you think?"

"It doesn't matter, Beauchamp. I mean, it may matter to you, but it doesn't matter to me at all. You were probably just tense. It was a fluke."

"Terrific. Thank you very much, Dr. Joyce Brothers."

"I'm only trying to . . ."

"Skip it, will you?"

"You could've had too much to drink, you know."

"I had three fucking scotches!"

"Well, that's enough to . . ."

"Skip it, goddammit!"

"Look, Beauchamp, I personally resent the implication that . . . this . . . was the purpose of this trip. I came up here because I *like* you. You asked me to help you."

"Fat lot of good it did!"

"You're just concentrating too hard. I think your troubles with DeDe probably . . ."

"Christ! You have to bring *her* up?"

"I just thought that . . ."

"I don't wanna talk about DeDe!"

"Well, what if *I* wanna talk about her, huh? I'm the one who stands to get burnt in this deal, Beauchamp. I'm the one who's sticking my neck out. You can run home to your penthouse and your wife and your goddamn society parties. I'm stuck with . . . computer dating . . . and singles dances at the goddamn Jack Tar Hotel!"

She leaped out of bed and headed for the bathroom.

"What are you doing?" asked Beauchamp.

"Brushing my teeth! Do you mind?"

"Mary Ann, look . . . I . . ."

"I can't hear you. The water's running."

He shouted. *"I'm sorry, Mary Ann!"*

"Mrrpletlrp."

He joined her in the bathroom, standing behind her, stroking her stomach appeasingly. "I said I'm sorry."

"Would you mind getting out of the bathroom?"

"I love you."

Silence.

"Did you hear me?"

"Beauchamp, you're making me spill the Scope!"

"I love you, goddammit!"

"Not *here*, for God's sake!"

"Yes, here!"

"Beauchamp, for God's sake! Beauchamp!"

She propped her chin on her elbow and studied his sleeping Keane-kid face. He was snoring so softly that it sounded like a purr. His right arm, tanned and dark-furred, was flung across her waist.

He was talking in his sleep.

At first it was gibberish. Then she thought she heard a name. She couldn't make it out, though. It wasn't DeDe . . . and it wasn't Mary Ann.

She leaned closer. The sounds grew more obscure. He rolled over on his stomach, withdrawing his arm from her waist. He began to snore again.

She slipped out of bed and tiptoed to the window. The moon was slashing a silvery wake across the ocean. "That's a Moon River," her brother Sonny had told her when she was ten. She had believed him. She had also believed that someday she would be Audrey Hepburn and someone would come along to be George Peppard.

For the next two hours, she sat by the fire and read *Nicholas and Alexandra*.

Coming Clean in the Marina

BRIAN'S PREY WAS SITTING IN A PLASTIC CHAIR IN THE Come Clean Center's shag-carpeted waiting area. She was wearing orange slacks that could have protected a road crew at night.

Her Mao Tse-tung T-shirt was stretched so tightly across her chest that the Chairman was grinning broadly.

And she was reading a *People* magazine.

Brian hesitated for a moment in front of the dispenser, feigning indecision. Then he turned around.

"Uh . . . excuse me? Could you tell me the difference between Downy and Cheer?"

She looked up from an article on Cher and peered at him through cobalt-blue contacts. Chewing the cud of her Carefree Sugarless, she sniffed out the new bull who had pawed his way into her pasture.

"Downy's a fabric softener," she smiled. "It makes your clothes all soft and sweet-smelling. Here . . . wanna try some of mine?"

Brian smiled back. "Sure you got enough?"

"Sure."

She dug a bottle of Downy out of her red plastic laundry basket. "See? It says here . . ."

Brian moved next to her. "Where?"

"Here . . . on the label under . . ."

"Oh, yeah." Her cheek was *inches* away. He could smell her Charlie. "I see . . . April fresh."

She giggled, reading from the label. "And it helps eliminate static cling."

"I *hate* to cling statically, don't you?"

She turned and looked at him quizzically, then continued to read. "Whites white and colors bright."

"Of course."

"Softens deep and luxurious."

"Mmm. Deep . . . and luxurious."

She jerked away from him suddenly, then faced him, grinning coyly. "You are *fresh*, you know that?"

"April fresh, I hope?"

"You're too much!"

"That's what they tell me."

"Well, you can just . . ."

"You must not be from around here, huh?"

"Why?"

"I don't know. You just have a kind of . . . no, forget it."

"What?"

"It'll sound like a line."

"Will you just let me be the judge of that?"

"Well, there's something kind of . . . cosmopolitan about you."

After blinking at him for a moment, she looked down at her T-shirt, then back at him.

"Why did you do that?" he asked.

"I couldn't remember if I was wearing my *Paris Match* T-shirt."

He chuckled smoothly. "It's not your clothes. There's just . . . something . . . an air. Oh, forget it."

"Are you from around here?"

"Sure. Third drier from the right."

"C'mon!"

"I know it doesn't *look* like much, but it's really pretty inside. Crystal chandeliers, flocked wallpaper, Armstrong linoleum . . . Where do you live?"

"The Marina."

"Near here, huh?"

"Yeah."

"How quick could we walk it?"

"I don't think . . . five minutes."

"You don't think what?"

"Nothing."

"Good. Shall we?"

"Look, I don't even know your name."

"Of course. How stupid. Brian Hawkins."

She took his hand and shook it rather formally. "I'm Connie Bradshaw. From the Friendly Skies of United."

... And Many Happy Returns

THE FLOOR AROUND CONNIE'S BED WAS LITTERED WITH the bodies of its daytime occupants: a five-foot plush Snoopy dog, a chartreuse beanbag frog, a terry-cloth python with eyes that rolled (Forgive her, Sigmund, thought Brian) and a maroon pillow that said: SCHOOL SPIRIT DAY, CENTRAL HIGH, 1967.

Brian was propped against the headboard. "Do you mind if I smoke?"

"Go ahead."

He chuckled. "That's very New Wave, isn't it?"

"What?"

"You know . . . the couple sacked out afterwards with . . . It doesn't matter."

"All right."

"Would you like me to leave?"

"Did I say that, Byron?"

"Brian."

"You can go if you want."

"Are you pissed or something?"

Silence.

"Ah, methinks the lady is pissed."

"Oh . . . you're *such* an intellectual, aren't you?"

"My *brain* offends you?"

Silence.

"Look, Bonnie . . ."

"Connie."

"So we're even. Look . . . I'll be guilty if you want. I'm the quintessential liberal. Ring a bell, I'll salivate, flog myself, feel guilty for *weeks.* Just tell me what I *did,* will you?"

She rolled over and hunched into a fetal position. "If you don't know, there's no point in discussing it."

"Bonnie! Connie!"

"Do you treat all your bed partners that way?"

"*What* way?"

"Wham, bam, thank you, ma'am!"

"Well, that's getting to the point."

"You asked me."

"So I did."

"I don't think it's *abnormal* to require a little tenderness."

" 'She may be weary, women do get weary . . .' "

"Blow it out your . . . !"

" 'Wearin' the same shabby dress . . .' "

"You're really an asshole, you know that? You are truly a . . . *pathetic* human being! You've got about as much warmth as . . . I don't know what!"

"Nice simile."

"Go fuck yourself!"

She was up now, sitting at her French Provincial vanity, brushing her hair with a vengeance.

"I'm sorry," he said. "O.K.?"

"What's to apologize for? We don't even know each other."

"We shared a fabric softener. Doesn't that mean anything to you?"

"Yeah. The end of a horrible day."

"Jesus. What *else* happened to you today?"

"Nothing. Not a goddamn thing."

"So?"

"So it's my birthday, dink!"

He held her until she had stopped crying, then dried her eyes with a corner of her Wamsutta floral.

"I'm hungry," he said. "How 'bout you?"

She didn't answer. She sat on the edge of the bed like a broken Barbie Doll. Brian left for the kitchen.

He was back several minutes later, holding a tin pie plate with mock solemnity. "Don't those North Beach bakeries do a nice job?" he said.

From the top of a triple-decker peanut butter and jelly sandwich four kitchen matches were blazing festively.

"Make a wish," he said, "and no wisecracks!"

Mrs. Day at Home

DEDE WAS TICKED. IT WAS ALREADY MIDAFTERNOON Sunday and Beauchamp wasn't home from his Guardsmen weekend on Mount Tam.

She slammed around the penthouse in search of something to occupy her mind. She had already read *Town and Country,* watered the ficas, walked the corgi, and chatted with Michael Vincent about the twig furniture for the living room.

There was nothing left but bills.

She sat down at her *escritoire* and began to disembowel windowed envelopes. The latest tally from Wilkes Bashford was $1,748. Daddy would be *livid.* She had already got three advances on her allowance that month.

Screw it. Beauchamp could sweat out the bills for once. She was sick to death of it.

Angrily, she rose and went to the window, confronting a panorama of almost ludicrous exoticism: the sylvan slope of Telegraph Hill, the crude grandeur of a Norwegian freighter, the bold blue sweep of the bay . . .

And then . . . a sudden slash of electric green as a flock—no, *the* flock—of wild parrots headed north to the eucalyptus trees above Julius Castle.

The birds were a legend on the hill. Once upon a time they had belonged to human beings. Then, somehow, they had fled their separate cages to band together in this raucous platoon of freedom fighters. According to most accounts, they divided their time daily between Telegraph Hill and Potrero Hill. Their screeching en route was regarded by many locals as a hymn to the liberated soul.

But not by DeDe.

In her opinion, the parrots were annoyingly arrogant. You could buy the most beautiful one in town, she observed, but that wouldn't make it love you. You could feed it, care for it and exclaim over its loveliness, but there was nothing to guarantee that it would stay home with you.

There had to be a lesson there somewhere.

She locked herself in the bathroom and poured half a cup of Vitabath into the tub. She soaked for an hour, trying to calm her nerves. It helped to think of old times, carefree days in Hillsborough when she and Binky and Muffy would snitch the keys to Daddy's Mercedes and tool down to the Fillmore to tease the black studs lurking on the street corners.

Good times. Pre-Cotillion. Pre-Spinsters. Pre-Beauchamp.

But what was there now?

Muffy had married a Castilian prince.

Binky was still living it up as the Jewish American Princess.

DeDe was stuck with a Shabby Genteel Bostonian who thought he was a parrot.

Lying there in the warm, fragrant water, she realized suddenly that most of her ideas about love and marriage and sex had solidified when she was fourteen years old.

Mother Immaculata, her social studies teacher, had explained the whole thing:

"Boys will try to kiss you, DeDe. You must expect that, and you must be prepared for it."

"But *how?*"

"It's as close as your heart, DeDe. The scapular you wear around your neck."

"I don't see how . . ."

"When a boy tries to kiss you, you must pull out your scapular and say, 'Here, kiss this, if you must kiss something.' "

DeDe's scapular bore a picture of Jesus or St. Anthony or somebody. Nobody ever tried to kiss it.

Mother Immaculata knew her stuff, all right.

DeDe climbed out of the tub and stood in front of the mirror for a long time, smearing her face with Oil of Olay. The flesh under her chin was soft and spongy. Nothing drastic. It could still pass for baby fat.

The rest of her body had a certain . . . voluptuous quality, she felt, though it would certainly be nice to have an outside opinion again. If Beauchamp didn't want her, there were still people who did. There was no goddamn reason in the world why she had to act like Miss Peninsula Virgin of 1969.

She found her address book and looked up Splinter Riley's number.

Splinter of the massive shoulders and molten eyes. Splinter, who had begged her one balmy night on Belvedere (1970? 1971?) to follow him to the Mallards' boathouse, where he brutalized her Oscar de la Renta and took his manly pleasure with gratifying thoroughness.

God! She had forgotten none of it. The mingled odors of sweat and Chanel for Men. The scrape of the damp planks against her fanny. The distant strains of Walt Tolleson's combo playing "Close to You" up on the hillside.

Her hand trembled as she dialed.

Please, she prayed, don't let Oona be at home.

The Chinese Connection

MERCIFULLY, IT WAS SPLINTER WHO ANSWERED THE phone.

"Hello."

"Hi, Splint."

"Who's this, please?"

"Here's a hint: 'Sittin' on the dock of the bay, wastin' tiiiiime . . .' "

"DeDe?"

"I thought that might remind you." Her tone was tantalizing, but ladylike, she felt.

"Good to hear from you. What have you and Beauchamp been up to?"

"Not much. Beauchamp's off with the Guardsmen."

"Shit! Did I miss a meeting?"

"What?"

"Beauchamp and I are on the same committee. They'll skin my ass if I . . ."

"It may not have been Guardsmen, Splint . . . come to think of it." Well, that answered *that.*

"I hope to hell not. What can I do for you?"

"I can remember when it used to be the other way around."

Silence.

"Beauchamp's away till this evening, Splint."

"DeDe . . ."

"No strings attached."

"I don't think . . ."

"Is Oona there? Is that it?"

"No. DeDe, look . . . I'm flattered to death, honest to God . . ."

"No emotional commitments. I've changed a lot, Splint."

"So have I."

"What could have changed that much?"

"I'm in love with Oona."

She hung up on him.

Almost immediately, she picked up the phone and dialed Jiffy's Market. She ordered half a gallon of milk, a box of Familia and some bananas. There was something very comforting about cereal. It made her think of childhood at Halcyon Hill.

The delivery boy arrived in fifteen minutes.

DeDe knew him. It was Lionel Wong, a muscular eighteen-year-old suffering from a Bruce Lee fixation.

"Shall I put it in the kitchen, Mrs. Day?"

"Thanks, Lionel. I'll get my purse out of the bedroom."

"No sweat, Mrs. Day. We can put it on your tab."

"No . . . I want to give you something for your trouble." She went into the bedroom, returning with a dollar bill.

"Thanks a lot."

DeDe smiled. "Have you seen the exhibit at the de Young?"

"What?"

"The People's Republic exhibit. It's *stunning*, Lionel. You should be very proud of your people."

"Yes, ma'am."

"Truly stunning. The culture is amazing."

"Yeah."

"Would you like something to drink, Lionel? I don't have any Cokes in the house. How about a bitter lemon?"

"I've got a couple more stops, Mrs. Day."

"Just for a little while?"

"Thanks a lot, but . . ."

"Lionel . . . please . . ."

Half an hour later, Beauchamp arrived home. He met Lionel at the elevator.

"Working Sundays, Lionel? That's a bummer."

"No sweat."

"Anything for the Days?"

"Yeah . . . Mrs. Day needed a few things."

"How's the Kung Fu coming?"

"Fine."

"Keep it up. You're getting some nice definition."

"Thanks. See you later."

"Take it easy. Don't do anything I wouldn't do."

Upstairs, DeDe was basking in her second Vitabath of the day.

Confession in the Nude

THE PARKING LOT AT DEVIL'S SLIDE WAS JAMMED WITH vehicles: flowered hippie vans, city clunkers, organic pickups with shingled gypsy houses, and a dusty pack of Harley-Davidsons.

Mona had to park her '64 Volvo almost a quarter of a mile from the beach. "Shit," she groaned. "It must be wall-to-wall flesh down there."

"I hope so," leered Michael.

"That's sexism, even if you *are* talking about men."

"So I'm sexist."

They trekked along the dirt road with dozens of other wayfarers headed for the beach. "This reminds me of the Donner party," said Mona.

Michael grinned. "Yeah. Drop by the wayside and you get eaten."

When they reached the highway, Mona gave the ticket-taker a dollar for both of them.

"This is on me," she said. "You're in mourning."

Michael skipped down to the stairway on the cliff. "Just watch me recover, Babycakes!"

Two minutes later, they were standing on a broad stretch of white sand. Michael flung a pebble into the air. "Where shall we go? The gay end or the straight end?"

"Let me guess."

Michael grinned. "It's less windy down at the gay end."

"I'm not real crazy about climbing over those rocks."

"I shall carry you, my lovely."

"You're one helluva gentleman!"

They headed, arm in arm, for the sandy cove nestled amid the rocks at the north end of the beach. On the way they passed five or six frolicking bathers, all naked and brown as organic date bars.

"Look at them!" sighed Mona. "I feel like a goddamn fish belly."

Michael shook his head. "That's no good. They haven't got a tan line."

"A what?"

"A tan line. The contrast between brown and white when you take off your trunks."

"Who needs it? I haven't taken off my trunks before an audience in ages. I'd rather be brown all over."

"Suit yourself. I want a tan line."

"You're a prude, that's what."

"Five minutes ago, I was a sexist."

She snatched a piece of seaweed off the sand and draped it over his ear. "You're a sexist, faggot prude, Michael Mouse."

There were thirty or forty naked men on the tiny patch of beach. Mona and Michael spread a towel. It displayed the words *Chez Moi ou Chez Toi?* and a life-size picture of a naked man.

Mona looked around her, then down at the towel. "How redundant. Aren't you afraid people will make comparisons?"

Michael laughed, stripping off his sweatshirt, tank top and

Levi's. He stretched out in his green-and-yellow satin boxing trunks.

Mona removed her own Levi's and tank top. "How do you like my impression of the Great White Whale?"

"Bullshit. You look fabulous. You look like . . . September Morn."

"A fat lot of good it'll do me here."

"Don't be so sure. There's a nasty epidemic of heterosexuality afoot. I know lots of gay guys who're sneaking off to the Sutro Baths to get it on with women."

"How bizarre."

"Well . . . everything gets old after a while. I personally get a little sick of wrecking my liver at The Lion for the privilege of tricking with some guy whose lover is in L.A. for the weekend."

"So you're going straight?"

"I didn't say *that.*"

Mona rolled over on her stomach and handed Michael a bottle of Bain de Soleil. "Do my back, will you?"

Michael obliged, applying the lotion in strong circular strokes. "You do have a nice bod, you know."

"Thanks, Babycakes."

"Don't mention it."

"Mouse?"

"Yeah?"

"Do you think I'm a fag hag?"

"What?"

"I do. I'm sure of it."

"You've been eating funny mushrooms again."

"I don't mind being a fag hag, actually. There are worse things to be."

"You are *not* a fag hag, Mona."

"Look at the symptoms. I hang around with you, don't I? We go boogying at Buzzby's and The Endup. I'm practically a *fixture* at The Palms." She laughed. "Shit! I've drunk so many Blue Moons I feel like I'm turning into Dorothy Lamour."

"Mona . . ."

"Hell, Mouse! I hardly know any straight men anymore."

"You live in San Francisco."

"It isn't that. I don't even *like* most straight men. Brian Hawkins repulses me. Straight men are boorish and boring and . . ."

"Maybe you've just been exposed to the wrong ones."

"Then where the hell are the *right* ones?"

"Hell, I don't know. There must be . . ."

"Don't you *dare* suggest one of those mellowed-out Marin types. Underneath all that hair and patchouli beats the heart of a true pig. I've been *that* route."

"What can I say?"

"Nothing. Not a damned thing."

"I love you a lot, Mona."

"I know, I know."

"For what it's worth . . . sometimes I wish that were enough."

Two hours later, they left hand in hand, parting a Red Sea of naked male bodies.

They ate dinner at Pier 54, boogied briefly at Buzzby's, and arrived back at Barbary Lane at ten-thirty.

Mary Ann passed them on the stairs.

"How was your weekend?" asked Mona.

"Fine."

"You go away?"

"Up north. With a friend from school."

"Have you met Michael Tolliver, my new roommate?"

"No, I . . ."

"Yes." Michael smiled. "I believe we have."

"I'm sorry, I don't . . ."

"The Marina Safeway."

"Oh . . . yes. How are you?"

"Hangin' in there."

Back at the apartment, Mona asked, "You met Mary Ann at a supermarket?"

Michael smiled ruefully. "She tried to pick up Robert."

"You see?" said Mona. "You see?"

Miss Singleton Dines Alone

AFTER UNPACKING HER SUITCASE, MARY ANN PADded restlessly through her apartment in the pink quilted bathrobe her mother had sent her from the Ridgemont Mall.

She *hated* Sunday nights.

When she was a little girl, Sunday nights had meant only one thing: unfinished homework.

That's how she felt now. Anxious, guilty, frightened of recriminations that were certain to follow. Beauchamp Day was homework she should have finished. She would pay for it. Sooner or later.

She decided to pamper herself.

She quick-thawed a pork chop under the faucet, wondering if it was sacrilegious to Shake 'n Bake meat from Marcel & Henri.

Lighting a spice candle on the parsons table in the living room, she dug out her Design Research cloth napkins, her wood-handled stainless flatware, her imitation Dansk china, and her ceramic creamer shaped like a cow.

Solitude was no excuse for sloppiness.

She scrounged in the kitchen for a vegetable. There was

nothing but a Baggie full of limp lettuce and a half-eaten package of Stouffer's Spinach Soufflé. She decided on cottage cheese with chives.

She supped by candlelight, bent over a *Ms.* article entitled "The Quest for Multiple Orgasm." Music was provided by KCBS-FM, the mellow station:

> *Out of work, I'm out of my head.*
> *Out of self-respect,*
> *I'm out of bread,*
> *Underloved and underfed,*
> *I wanna go home . . .*
> *It never rains in California,*
> *But, girl, don't they warn ya,*
> *It pours, man, it pours.*

After dinner, she decided to try the "monster mask" formula from her herbal cosmetics book. She cooked a saucepan of the glop—using oatmeal, dried prunes and an overripe fig— and smeared it relentlessly over her face.

For twenty minutes, she lay perfectly still in a sudsy tub.

She could feel the mask drying, chipping off in gross, leprous flakes and sinking into the water above her chest. This would kill another ten minutes. Then what?

She could write her parents.

She could fill out her application to the Sierra Club.

She could walk down to Cost Plus and buy another coffee mug.

She could call Beauchamp.

Lurching out of the bathtub like a reject from a Japanese horror film, she examined her face in the mirror.

She looked like a giant Shake 'n Bake pork chop.

And for what?

For Dance Your Ass Off? For Mr. Halcyon? For Michael Whatshisname downstairs? For a married man who mutters strange names in his sleep?

She would *not* call him. The love he offered was deceitful, destructive and dead-end.

He would have to call *her.*

She fell asleep just before midnight, with *Nicholas and Alexandra* in her lap.

Over on Telegraph Hill, DeDe was eyeing Beauchamp malevolently as he adjusted the ship's clock in the library.

"I talked to Splinter today."

He didn't look up. "Mmm."

"Apparently he had forgotten about your little Guardsmen function on Mount Tam."

"Oh, well . . . Did he call here?"

"No."

"I don't get it."

"I . . . I called Oona. He answered the phone."

"You *detest* Oona."

"We're doing a League project together. The Model Ghetto Program in Hunters Point. Beauchamp, why do you suppose Splinter forgot such an important meeting? He says you two are on the same committee."

"Beats me."

She grunted audibly. Beauchamp turned and whistled to the corgi, half asleep on the couch. The dog yelped excitedly when his master opened a desk drawer and produced his leash.

"I'm taking Caesar for his constitutional."

DeDe frowned. "I've walked him twice already."

"O.K. So I need the air myself."

"What's the matter? Not enough air on Mount Tam?"

He left without answering, stopping by the bedroom on his way downstairs. He closed the door quietly and dug in his underwear drawer for an object he had brought with him from Mendocino.

Then, slipping it into the breast pocket of his sports coat, he descended into the dark of the garage, where he planted it in the glove compartment of the Porsche.

A nice touch, he told himself as Caesar led him up the Filbert Steps to Coit Tower.

A very nice touch.

Mona vs. the Pig

ON THE WORST OF ALL POSSIBLE MONDAY MORN-ings, Mona stopped by Mary Ann's desk en route to a conference with Mr. Siegel, the president of Adorable Pantyhose.

"What's the matter with *you*, Babycakes?"

"Nothing . . . everything!"

"Yeah. The moon's in ca-ca. Speaking of which, I have a dog-and-pony show for Fartface Siegel this morning. Have you seen Beauchamp?"

"Nope."

"If you see him, he's got ten minutes to get down there. Hey . . . are you O.K., Mary Ann?"

"I'm fine."

"I have a Valium, if you want one."

"No. Thanks. I'm fine."

"I probably should have taken it myself."

Mona stood next to Beauchamp, her hand clamped rigidly to the storyboard.

"Our approach should be carefree," she explained. "We're not backtracking . . . we're simply *improving*. The old nylon crotch wasn't unsafe. The new one is simply . . . better."

The client's expression didn't change.

"The youth image is important, of course. The cotton crotch is young, vibrant, hip. The cotton crotch is for with-it women on the go."

Buddha would have to forgive her.

She revealed the first card on the storyboard. It showed a young woman with a Dorothy Hamill haircut hanging off the side of a cable car. The copy read: "Under my clothes, I like to feel Adorable."

Mona gestured with a pointer. "Notice we don't mention the crotch in the headline."

"Mmm," said the client.

"The *idea* is there, of course. Hygienic. Safe. Functional. But we don't come right out and say it. The effect is subtle, low-key, subliminal."

"It's not clear enough," said the client.

"The crotch comes in later . . . down here in the fourth paragraph. We don't want to hit people over the head with the crotch."

Hit people over the head with the crotch? *This* was the woman who was going to be another Lillian Hellman?

The client grunted. "We're not selling subtlety, honey."

"Oh? What *are* we selling . . . honey?"

Beauchamp squeezed Mona's arm. "Mona . . . Perhaps we could move the crotch up to the first paragraph, Mr. Siegel?"

"The young lady doesn't seem to be pleased with that."

"*Woman,* Mr. Siegel. Young *woman.* Please don't call me a lady. I wouldn't *dream* of calling you a gentleman."

Beauchamp was scarlet. "Mona, goddammit . . . Mr. Siegel, I think I can handle these revisions myself. Mona, I'll talk to you later."

"Don't you patronize me, you prick! I'm not married to *my* job."

"You're *way* out of line, Mona."

"Thank God for that! Who the hell wants to be in line with that fat, sexist, capitalist sack of . . ."

"Mona!"

"You want crotch, Mr. Siegel. Is that it? Well, I'll give you crotch. Crotch, crotch, crotch, crotch, crotch, crotch . . ."

She stormed to the door, stopped, and wheeled around to confront Beauchamp. "Your karma is *really* fucked!"

That evening, she broke the news to Michael.

"What are you gonna do, Mona?"

She shrugged. "I don't know. Collect unemployment. Join a women's collective. Shop at the dented-can store. Give up coke. I'll manage."

"Maybe Halcyon would reconsider if you . . ."

"Forget it. That was my finest hour. I wouldn't take it back for nothin'!"

"Maybe I could get my old job back at the P.S."

"We'll hack it, Mouse. I can free-lance. Mrs. Madrigal will understand."

Michael sat down on the floor, slipped off Mona's Earth Shoes and began massaging her feet. "She's crazy about you, isn't she?"

"Who? Mrs. Madrigal?"

"Yeah."

"Yeah."

"Yeah . . . I guess so."

"It shows. Have you told her about getting fired yet?"

"No . . . I'll have to, I guess."

Where Is Love?

DESPITE HER DEFIANCE, MONA WAS CLEARLY DE-
pressed over losing her job. Michael tried his
usual ploy for cheering her up: He read her the
classified from the "Trader Dick" section of *The
Advocate.*

"God! Listen to this one! 'Clean-cut, straight-looking court
reporter, 32, sick to death of bars, baths and bitchiness, seeks
a permanent relationship with a *real man* who's into white-
water rafting, classical music and gardening. No fats, fems or
dopers, please. I'm *sincere.* Ron.' "

Mona laughed. "Are you *sincere?*"

"Who the hell isn't?"

"You'd leave me in a second, wouldn't you?"

Michael thought for a moment. "Only if he had a cottage
on Potrero Hill with a butcher-block kitchen, a functioning
fireplace and . . . a golden retriever in the small but tastefully
designed garden."

"Don't hold your breath."

"You know . . . when I moved here three years ago, I had
never seen so many faggots in my whole goddamned life! I
didn't know there were that many faggots in the *world!* Jesus!

I thought all I had to do was go to a party and pick somebody out. Everybody wants a lover, right?"

"Wrong."

"O.K. . . . So *almost* everybody. Anyway, I thought I'd be snapped up in six months. At the very most!"

"You were. Hundreds of times."

"Not funny."

"What about Robert?"

"Affairettes don't count."

"What if I grew a mustache?"

Michael grinned and tossed a paisley pillow at her. "C'mon. Let's go to a movie or something."

"I don't know . . ."

"There's a Fellini double bill at the Surf."

"Downer."

"Nah. Lotsa big tits and pretty boys and dwarfs. Very up."

"You go ahead. Take the car, if you want."

"What are *you* gonna do?"

Mona shrugged. "Curl up with Anaïs Nin, take a Quaalude. I don't know."

"Is my MDA still in your stash box?"

"Yeah. Christ, you don't need that for a movie!"

"I might not *see* a movie, Mother!"

"Ah."

"I hate movies when I'm alone."

"Michael, I just don't feel like . . ."

"I hear you."

"Where are you going?"

"Here and there."

"Trashing, huh?"

"Maybe."

"Be careful, will you?"

"What?"

"Don't do anything risky."

"You read the papers too much."

"Just be careful . . . and cheer up. Someday your prince will come."

Michael blew a kiss to her from the door. "Same to you, fella."

* * *

She rattled around the apartment for half an hour, talking to her rosy fishhooks cactus and fiddling with her I Ching coins.

She decided against a Quaalude. Quaaludes made her feel sleazy. What was the point in feeling sleazy if you had no one to sleaze with?

Could you conjugate that? To sleaze. I sleaze. You sleaze. We all have sleazen.

Words constantly annoyed her like that, reminding her of the gulf between Art and Making a Living. "Mona's good with words," her mother used to say matter-of-factly, "if she can just learn to Make a Living at it."

Her mother Made a Living in real estate.

Mona hadn't spoken to her in eight months, not since mother had joined the Reagan campaign in Minneapolis and daughter had written home breezily about her Sexual Awareness Retreat at the Cosmic Light Fellowship.

It didn't matter.

More and more it seemed that Mona's *real* mother was a woman so in tune with creation that even her marijuana plants had names.

So Mona trudged downstairs to tell Mrs. Madrigal the news.

If the Shoe Fits

MICHAEL DECIDED AGAINST THE MDA. THERE WERE rumors afoot that someone on MDA had dropped dead at The Barracks the week before. It probably wasn't true, but what point was there in pressing your luck?

Actually, there were *lots* of murky legends like that among gay people in San Francisco. God only knew where they originated!

There was the Doodler, a sinister black man who sat at the bar and sketched your face . . . before taking you home to murder you.

Not to mention the Man in the White Van, a faceless fiend whose unwitting passengers never found their way home again.

And the Dempster Dumpster Killer, whose S & M fantasies knew no limit.

It was almost enough to make you stick with Mary Tyler Moore.

* * *

Once again, he ended up in the Castro. True, he badmouthed the gay ghetto at *least* twice a day, but there was a lot to be said for sheer numbers when you were looking for company.

Toad Hall and The Midnight Sun were wall-to-wall flannel, as usual. He passed them up for The Twin Peaks, where his crew-neck sweater and corduroy trousers would seem less alien to the environment.

Cruising, he had long ago decided, was a lot like hitchhiking.

It was best to dress like the people you wanted to pick you up.

"Crowded, huh?" The man at the bar was wearing Levi's, a rugby shirt and red-white-and-blue Tigers. He had a pleasant, square-jawed face that reminded Michael of people he had once known in the Campus Crusade for Christ.

"What is it?" asked Michael. "A full moon or something?"

"Got me. I don't keep up with that crap."

Point One in his favor. Despite Mona's proselytizing, Michael was not big on astrology freaks. He grinned. "Don't tell anybody, but the moon's in Uranus."

The man stared dumbly, then got it. "The moon's in your anus. That's a riot!"

Go ahead, Michael told himself. Ply him with cheap jokes. Have no shame.

The man obviously liked him. "What are you drinking?"

"Calistoga water."

"I figured that."

"Why?"

"I don't know. You're . . . healthy-looking."

"Thanks."

The man extended his hand. "I'm Chuck."

"Michael."

"Hi, Mike."

"Michael."

"Oh . . . You know what, man? I gotta tell you the truth. I scoped you out when you walked in here . . . and I said, 'That's the one, Chuck.' I swear to God!"

What *was* it with this butch number? "Keep it up," Michael grinned. "I can use the strokes."

"You know what it was, man?"

"No."

The man smiled self-assuredly, then pointed to Michael's shoes. "Them."

"My shoes?"

He nodded. "Weejuns."

"Yeah?"

"And white socks."

"I see."

"They new?"

"The Weejuns?"

"Yeah."

"No. I just had them half-soled."

The man shook his head reverentially, still staring at the loafers. "Half-soled. Far fucking out!"

"Excuse me, are you . . . ?"

"How many pairs you got?"

"Just these."

"I have six pairs. Black, brown, scotch grain . . ."

"You like 'em, huh?"

"You seen my ad in *The Advocate*?"

"No."

"It says . . ." He held his hand up to make it graphic for Michael. " 'Bass Weejuns.' Big capital letters, like."

"Catchy wording."

"I get a lotta calls. Collegiate types. Lotta guys get sick of the glitter fairies in this town."

"I can imagine."

The man moved closer, lowering his voice. "You ever . . . done it in 'em."

"Not to my recollection. Look . . . if you've got six pairs, how come you're not wearing any tonight?"

The man was aghast at his *faux pas.* "I always wear my Tigers with my rugby shirt!"

"Right."

He held his foot up for examination. "They're just like Billy Sive's. In *The Front Runner.* "

Sherry and Sympathy

MRS. MADRIGAL SEEMED ODDLY SUBDUED WHEN she opened the door.

"Mona, dear . . ."

"Hi. I thought you might like company."

"Certainly."

"That's a lie, actually. I thought *I* might like company."

"Well, it works both ways, doesn't it? Come in."

The landlady poured a glass of sherry for her tenant. "Is Michael out?"

Mona nodded. "Taking the vapors, I think."

"I see."

"God knows when he'll be back."

"He's a sweet boy, Mona. I approve of him wholeheartedly."

Mona sniffed. "You make it sound like we're *married* or something."

"There are all kinds of marriages, dear."

"I don't think you understand the trip with me and Michael."

"Mona . . . lots of things are more binding than sex. They last longer too. When I was . . . little, my mother once told me that if a married couple puts a penny in a pot for every time they make love in the first year, and takes a penny out every time after that, they'll never get all the pennies out of the pot. . . . Damn! I haven't thought of that in years."

"That's a trip."

Mrs. Madrigal smiled. "It's also a comfort to those of us who never put in too many pennies in the first place."

Mona sipped her sherry, embarrassed.

"Have you and Michael talked, dear?"

"About you?"

The landlady nodded.

"I . . . no. I think that's up to you."

"You're very close. He must have asked you questions."

"No. Nothing."

"I don't mind, you know . . . with him."

"I understand . . . but I think it's up to you."

"Thank you, dear."

"I lost my job," Mona said at last.

"*What?*"

"The old son-of-a-bitch fired me."

"Who?"

"Edgar Halcyon. His son-in-law put the badmouth on me, and the old man tossed me out on my can."

"Mona . . . why on earth would he . . . ?"

Mona snorted. "You don't know Edgar Halcyon. He's the biggest asshole on the Barbary Coast."

"Mona!"

"Well, he *is*. It was a relief, actually. I *loathed* that job . . . all that crap about demographics and consumer profiles and . . ."

"Did you . . . do something, Mona?"

"I was honest with a client. The Ultimate No-No."

"What did you say?"

"It doesn't matter."

"Mona! It matters to me!"

"Jesus! What's with you?"

"I . . . I'm sorry. I didn't mean . . . Are you all right, Mona? Financially, I mean?"

"Yeah, sure. I can pay the rent."

"I didn't mean that."

"I know. I'm sorry. I didn't mean to snap. I'm fine, Mrs. Madrigal. Really."

She wasn't fine. She left ten minutes later, returned to her apartment and took the Quaalude. It put her to sleep.

Michael was back at one-thirty. He woke her on the couch. "You O.K., Babycakes? Don't you wanna go to bed?"

"No. This is O.K."

"This is Chuck, Mona."

"Hi, Chuck."

"Hi, Mona."

"Sleep tight, Babycakes."

"You too."

The two men went into Michael's bedroom and closed the door.

The Rap about Rape

DEDE FOUND HER MOTHER ON THE TERRACE AT HAL-
cyon Hill, aghast over the 1976 San Francisco
Social Register.

"I don't believe it! I *don't* believe it!"

"Mother, will you put that down for a . . ."

"They *are* listed. They are actually *listed*."

"Who?"

"Those dreadful people who bought the old Feeney place
on Broadway. Viola told me they were listed, but I simply
couldn't . . ."

"He speaks seven languages, Mother."

"I don't care if he *tap-dances*. They used to live in the *Castro*,
DeDe . . . and now they're living with his boyfriend . . . or is
it *hers*?"

"Binky says it's both of theirs."

"No! Do you think? Of course, they never take *him* anywhere . . . and he's even got a side entrance, so his address
is different. . . ."

"Mother, I need to talk to you."

"Viola says they even have different *zip codes!*"

"Mother!"

"What, darling?"

"I think Beauchamp has a mistress."

Silence.

"I'm sure of it, in fact."

"Darling, are you . . . ? You poor baby! How did you . . . ? Are you . . . ? Hand me that pitcher, will you, darling?"

DeDe dug into her Obiko shoulder bag and produced the offending scarf. Frannie studied it at arm's length, sipping her Mai Tai all the time.

"You found it in his car?"

DeDe nodded. "He walked to work on Monday. Binky and I drove the Porsche to Mr. Lee's at noon, and I found it then. I tried to act like nothing was . . ." Her voice cracked. She began to cry. "Mother . . . I'm sure this time."

"You're sure it's hers?"

"I've seen her wearing it."

"He could have given her a ride home, DeDe. Anyway . . . don't you think your father would have noticed, if she was . . . carrying on with . . ."

"Mother! I know!"

Frannie began to sniffle. "The party was going to be *so* lovely."

DeDe went to lunch at Prue Giroux's townhouse on Nob Hill.

Under the circumstances, she might have canceled, but this wasn't just *any* lunch.

This was The Forum, a rarefied gathering of concerned matrons who met monthly to discuss topics of Major Social Significance.

In previous months, the topics had been alcoholism, lesbianism and the plight of female grape-pickers. Today the ladies would discuss rape.

Prue's cook had whipped up a *divine* crab quiche.

DeDe was nervous. This was her first lunch at The Forum, and she wasn't sure of protocol. For guidance, she sat next to Binky Gruen.

"Keep your eye on Prue," whispered Binky. "When she rings that little silver bell, it means she's heard enough and you're supposed to stop talking."

"What am I supposed to *say*?"

Binky patted her hand. "Prue will tell you."

DING-A-LING!

The ladies dropped their forks and leaned forward, a dozen thoughtful faces hovering intently over the asparagus.

"Good afternoon," Prue beamed, surveying her guests. "I'm delighted you could be here today to share your personal insights into a subject of grave importance." Her face fell suddenly, like a jarred soufflé. "Our very special guest today is Velma Runningwater, a Native American who successfully defended herself against an attempted gang rape by sixteen members of the Hell's Angels in Petaluma."

Binky whistled under her breath. "This is better than the day she brought the bull dyke in!"

"Pass the rolls," whispered DeDe.

"But before we hear Ms. Runningwater's truly remarkable tale, I would like to try a very special experiment with those of us assembled here at The Forum. . . ."

"Here it comes," said Binky, nudging DeDe under the tablecloth. "She's always got a kicker."

"Today," said Prue, pausing dramatically, "we are going to rap about rape. . . ."

Binky pinched DeDe. "Can you believe this?"

DeDe gnawed nervously on her roll. Dark circles had begun to form under the arms of her Geoffrey Beane shirtwaist. She *hated* public speaking. Even at Sacred Heart, it had terrified her.

"This is going to be difficult," continued Prue, "but I want each of you to share an experience that you have probably tried to block from your memory . . . a time when your

. . . person . . . was violated against your will. This is a time for openness, an opportunity for sharing with your sisters."

"Shugie Sussman is not my sister," whispered Binky. "She puked in my Alfa after the Cotillion."

"Shhh," hissed DeDe. She was counting the seconds until the moment of truth. What could she say? She had never been raped, for Christ's sake! She had never even been *mugged.*

"Perhaps it would help," purred Prue, sensing the reticence of her guests, "if I began by sharing my own tale with you."

Binky giggled.

DeDe kicked her.

"This is the first time," continued Prue, "that I have told this story to a living soul. Not counting Reg, of course. It happened, not in the Tenderloin or the Fillmore or the Mission, as you might think, but in . . . Atherton!"

The ladies gasped in unison.

"And," said the hostess, aborting a pregnant pause, "it was someone you all know *very well.* . . ."

Prue lowered her head. "It serves no purpose to dwell on the morbid details. . . . Now perhaps someone else would like to share with us. What about you, DeDe?"

Shit. It never failed.

DeDe rose haltingly, folding and refolding her napkin. "I . . . I'm . . . not sure."

Binky tittered.

Prue rang the silver bell gently. "Please . . . DeDe is going to share with us. We're your sisters, DeDe. You can be up front with us."

"It was . . . awful," DeDe said at last.

"Of course it was," Prue said sympathetically. "Can you tell us where it happened, DeDe?"

DeDe swallowed. "At home," she said feebly.

Prue clutched the front of her sari. "Not . . . an intruder?"

"No," said DeDe. "A grocery boy."

*   *   *

When she got home, she picked up the phone and dialed Jiffy's, ordering a box of doughnuts and a can of Drano.
Lionel was up in ten minutes.

Romance in the Rink

MONA CELEBRATED HER FIRST DAY OF FREEDOM with a leisurely morning cappuccino at Malvina's. When she returned to Barbary Lane, Michael was in the shower.

"Christ! Didn't you get enough steam at the tubs last night?"

Michael stuck his head around the curtain. "Oh . . . sorry. Open a window, O.K.? No, here . . . I'll do it." He climbed out of the stall, dripping wet, and cranked open the window.

"Uh . . . Michael, dearheart?"

"Huh?"

"Why are you doing that?"

"Doing what?"

"Wearing your Levi's in the shower."

"Oh . . ." He laughed, hopping back into the stall. "I'm wire-brushing my basket. See?" He picked up a wire brush from the floor of the stall. "Just the thing for achieving that well-worn shading in just the right places." Scraping the brush gingerly across the crotch of his jeans, he screwed his face into an expression of mock pain. "Arrrggh!"

Mona was bland. "Do-it-yourself S & M?"

Michael flicked water at her. "They'll be *devastating* when they're dry."

"Where'd you pick that one up? *Hints from Heloise?*"

"This is *no* frivolous matter, woman. These babies have to be perfection by tonight."

"Date with Chuck?"

"Who? . . . Oh, no. I'm going to the Grand Arena."

"New bar?"

"Nope. A skating rink."

"*You're* going ice-skating?"

"Roller-skating. Tuesday is Gay Night."

Mona rolled her eyes. "Now I *know* I'm gonna kill myself."

"It's a scream. You'd love it."

"I never even *heard* of it."

Michael climbed out of the shower, shucked the wet jeans and toweled off. "Some fag hag *you* are."

"I didn't hear that," said Mona, heading into the hallway.

He didn't make it to the Grand Arena until eight o'clock, so he was prepared for the worst.

It happened, of course.

They had already run out of men's skates.

Small wonder. The giant South San Francisco rink was jammed with flannel-shirted men, circling the floor in predatory delight.

Michael caught his breath.

He shed his navy-blue cotton parka, submitted to the indignity of women's skates (white, with nelly-looking tassels) and clopped his way awkwardly to the edge of the rink.

He grinned when he recognized the recorded organ music: "I Enjoy Being a Girl."

There were half a dozen girls on the rink. Four of them were under twelve. The others were beehived Loretta Lynn lookalikes in sherbet-colored skating costumes. They were welded to sherbet-colored partners of the opposite sex, who propelled them across the floor like Brisbane's answer to Baryshnikov.

The other hundred men were less graceful.

Arms flailing and teeth flashing, they rolled around the rink in a swelling tide of denim. Some were alone; others snaked along merrily in lines of four or five. For Michael, it was a magical sight.

He waited for a moment, steeling himself.

When *was* the last time? Murphey's Skating Rink . . . Orlando, 1963.

He murmured a short, conventional Baptist prayer. Werner was never there when he needed him.

He wasn't half bad, actually.

A little wobbly on the turns, but nothing to snicker at.

After five minutes, he had gained enough confidence to concentrate on serious cruising.

So far, his favorite was a blond guy in chinos and a blue Gant shirt. He looked like the vice president of every high school class in northern Florida. He probably *still* drove a Mustang.

And he was skating alone.

Michael moved in the direction of his quarry, overtaking two small black kids in Dyn-O-Mite T-shirts. The only hindrance now was a couple of sherbet straights, doing a very showy Arthur Murray routine less than ten feet away.

The couple heeled like a yacht in a gale, drifting off to the left, clearing the way for Michael. . . .

He felt like a roller derby star, moving in for the kill.

Fixing his sights on the target, he accelerated at the turn . . . and realized, too late, what was about to happen. The blond man wasn't turning.

He was stopping.

And Michael had forgotten how to stop.

Clutching desperately at the air, his hands sought anchorage on the sacred oxford-cloth shirttail. His right leg buckled under him, as he skidded unceremoniously into the iron railing, dragging his Galahad behind him.

The two black kids backtracked momentarily, studied the carnage with undisguised glee, and skated off again.

* * *

Michael's face was covered with blood. The blond man helped him to his feet.

"Jesus. Are you all right?"

Michael poked his face cautiously with his fingertips. "It's my nose. It's O.K. It bleeds if you don't talk nice to it."

"Are you sure? Can I get you a Kleenex?"

"Thanks. I think I'll hobble off to the head."

When he returned, the blond man was waiting for him. "They just announced 'couples only,' " he grinned. "You man enough for that?"

Michael grinned back. "Sure. Just tell me when you're gonna stop."

So this time they moved as a unit, hand gripped in hand, under the twirling mirror ball.

"My name is Jon," said the blond man.

"I'm Michael," said Michael, just as his nose started to bleed again.

Coed Steam

VALENCIA STREET, WITH ITS UNION HALLS AND MEXI-
can restaurants and motorcycle repair shops, was
an oddly squalid setting for the gates of heaven.
For Brian, though, that was part of the turn-
on.

He *basked* in the squalor, the teenager-in-Tijuana feeling
that came over him whenever he caught sight of that seedy
neon sign:

FOR BETTER HEALTH—STEAM BATHS.

Behind the façade, in a tiny entrance alcove, he flashed his
laminated photo ID card and forked out five dollars to the guy
in the admission booth.

Four dollars for admission.

One dollar for The Party.

The Party made Mondays special at the Sutro Bath House.

Women were admitted free, and tonight there were at least
a dozen.

There were twice as many men, mingling with the women

in a space that seemed strangely reminiscent of a rumpus room in Walnut Creek: rosy-shaded lamps, mismatched furniture, and a miniature electric train that chugged noisily along a shelf around the perimeter of the room.

A television set mounted on the wall offered *Phyllis* to the partygoers.

On the opposite wall a movie screen flickered with vintage pornography.

The partygoers were naked, though some of them chose the shelter of a bath towel.

And most of them were watching *Phyllis.*

Brian stripped in the locker room. Overhead, in a plastic arbor, a mechanical canary twittered incessantly. He smiled at it, then wrapped a towel around his waist and headed back to the television lounge.

In the hallway, he met one of the hostesses.

"Hi, Frieda."

"How's it goin', Brian?"

"Just got here. Any hassles tonight?" Frieda's job was to ensure that women at the baths weren't harassed by the men . . . unless they wanted to be.

She shook her head. "Mellow as ever."

"That's too bad."

Frieda grinned, pinching him on the butt. "Go play with yourself, pig."

Then she was off again, walking her rounds in a T-shirt that said: WE DARE YOU.

Brian decided it was still too early to head for the orgy room. The Party was going full tilt. Most people would chow down on cheese and cold cuts before heading upstairs. And *Phyllis* wasn't over.

Adjusting his towel, he sauntered up to a blond woman with an all-over tan.

"Can I buy you some salami?"

"Now *that's* a new one."

He grinned. "I swear I didn't mean it that way."

"I'm a vegetarian." She smiled back.

"Me too." He extended his hand. "Put it there."

She studied him for several seconds, then asked flatly: "What kind?"

"Uh . . . you know, strict."

"With occasional lapses into lacto and ovo, huh?"

"Yes. Except on weekends and nights when I'm stoned. Then I'm a steako-lacto-ovo . . . or maybe a porkchopo-lacto-ovo . . ."

She smirked at his fraud. "You're a turko . . . that's what you are!"

"I knew we'd hit on it."

"Actually, I almost *never* make it with vegetarians."

"The woman has taste."

"We've met before, haven't we?"

"I like my line better."

"No . . . I'm serious. Didn't we play Earth Ball together at the New Games this year?"

"No, but I . . ."

"You into whales?"

"What?"

"Whales. Saving whales."

Brian shook his head apologetically, wishing to hell he'd saved a whale or two.

"Baby seals?"

"Nope. I used to be into lots of things. Now I'm into this."

"That's up front, anyway."

"Thank God for small favors."

"Hey . . . are you making fun of me?"

"Hell, no. I just feel like I'm . . . applying for a position, that's all."

She smiled again. "You are."

They both laughed. Brian decided it was time to take the initiative. "Look . . . I don't have a room, but maybe we could . . . you know . . . go upstairs. . . ."

"I can't handle the exhibitionism trip."

"Then maybe we could . . ."

"It's cool," she smiled. "I've got a room."

Hillary's Room

BRIAN WAS WRECKED. SHE WAS A *GODDESS*. A YOUNGER sister of Liv Ullmann, maybe . . . and Christ almighty, she had a room!

The girl meant business!

"I'm Hillary," she said, closing the door. The room was no bigger than a walk-in closet.

"You would be."

"Huh?"

"It fits you. You fit it."

"You don't have to compliment me. I've processed through all that."

"I meant it."

"What's your name?"

"Brian."

She patted a spot next to her on the bed. "Sit down, Brian." She sounded oddly clinical, despite her nakedness. "Have you done this often?"

"Come to the baths?" She *couldn't* mean fuck.

"No. I mean got it on with girls . . . women?"

He flashed his best Steve McQueen grin. "A fair amount."

"How long have you been gay?"

"*What?*"

"It's cool if you don't wanna talk about it."

"Uh . . . I think you've made a mistake."

"Fine . . . whatever." Her look was professionally compassionate. It irritated the piss out of him.

"No, Hillary . . . not fine. I'm not gay, understand?"

"You're not?"

"No."

"Then what are you doing here?"

"I'm losing my mind! What am I doing here, she asks? What the fuck do you *think* I'm doing here?"

"A lot of guys who come here are gay . . . or at least bi."

"Well, I'm not, got it? I have a well-rehearsed but limited repertoire." Gently, he placed his hand on her leg.

Gently, she removed it.

"All of us are a little homosexual, Brian. You must not be in touch with your body."

"It's not *my* body that I want to be in touch with!"

"You don't have to be macho all the time, you know."

"Who's trying to be macho? I'm trying to get laid."

"Right. A heartless, mechanical exploitation of . . ."

"Look . . ." He adopted a softer tone. "I don't think you're being entirely fair when you imply that I'm a male chauvinist or something. I mean, we're equals, aren't we? Look at us. You invited me to your room . . . and I accepted. Right?"

She stared at the wall. "I thought you needed help."

"I *do!* Oh, God, do I need help!"

"It's not the same."

"Can I help it if I'm weird? I've had this perverse craving for women as long as I can remember."

"Don't be so goddamn flip! You're not any better than a gay person, you know."

"Did I say that, Hillary? Did I, huh? I like gay people. I *accept* gay people. Christ almighty, don't make me say that some of my best friends are gay!"

"I wouldn't believe you if you did."

"Hillary, look . . ."

"I think you'd better leave, Brian."

"Would you please just . . ."

"Don't make me call Frieda."

He stood up, retrieving his towel from the floor. He wrapped it around himself. She was at the door now, holding it open for him.

"Once," he blurted, "when I was twelve, this guy who was in my scout troop and I took off our . . ."

"That doesn't count," she said.

He stood in the doorway and watched wistfully as she pulled the door closed again.

Venus reentering the clam shell.

Breakfast in Bed

MICHAEL WOKE WITH COTTONMOUTH.
He slipped out of bed as quietly as possible
and went to the bathroom, squeezing Aim onto
his toothbrush and his sterling Tiffany toothpaste roller. He brushed with the door closed.
When he tiptoed back to the bedroom, the shape under the
sheets spoke to him. "You cheated."

Michael crawled back into bed. "I thought you were
asleep."

"Now I'll have to brush *my* teeth."

"No you won't. I'm paranoid about *my* breath, not yours."

Jon threw back the covers and headed for the bathroom.
"Well, there's something *else* we have in common."

Mona knocked at the wrong time.

"Uh . . . yeah . . . wait a minute, Mona."

Mona shouted through the door. "Room service, gentlemen. Just pull the covers up."

Michael grinned at Jon. "My roommate. Brace yourself."

Seconds later, Mona burst through the doorway with a tray of coffee and croissants.

"Hi! I'm Nancy Drew! You must be the Hardy Boys!"

"I like her," said Jon, after Mona swept out. "Does she do that every morning?"

"No. I think she's curious."

"About what?"

"You."

"Oh . . . Are you two . . . ?"

"No. Just friends."

"You've never . . . ?"

Michael shook his head. "Never."

"Why not?"

"Why not? Well . . . let's see now. How about . . . I'm queer as a three-dollar bill."

"So?"

"So I'm a virgin with women. A perfect Kinsey six."

"Oh."

"That freaks you?"

"No, I just . . . How old are you?"

"I hope you're not a chicken queen. I'm twenty-six."

"I'm twenty-eight . . . and I'm not a chicken queen."

"That's a relief."

"What about high school?"

"B-minus average."

Jon smiled. "I mean *girls* in high school. Didn't you ever get it on with them?"

"All I ever did in high school was tool around with the guys and a six-pack of Bud, looking for heterosexuals to beat up."

"Is that right?"

Michael nodded. "You can't miss 'em. They walk funny and carry their books against their hips. That's what you did, wasn't it . . . when you were a heterosexual?"

Jon studied his face for a moment. "Don't be so defensive. I wasn't criticizing you."

"If it helps any, I didn't come out until three years ago. I was a eunuch in high school."

"I wish I'd known you then."

"As opposed to now?"

"In *addition* to now." Jon tousled his hair. "I *like* you, turkey!"

Michael was abuzz after Jon left. "He's *incredible,* Mona. He's well-adjusted and self-assured . . . and he's a goddamn *doctor!* Can you imagine me with my very own live-in doctor?"

"He's proposed?"

"Don't get technical."

"What kind of doctor?"

"A gynecologist."

"That oughta come in handy."

Michael slapped her on the fanny. "Just let me fantasize, will you?"

"You're gonna wanna move out, aren't you?"

"Mona!"

"Well?"

"You're my *friend,* Mona. We'll always be together in one way or another."

"Oh, yeah? What are you gonna do? Adopt me?" She walked to the door and opened it, addressing an invisible guest. "Oh, hi, Mrs. Plushbottom! May I present my father, Michael Tolliver, the famous raconteur and bon vivant, and my mother, the gynecologist!"

Michael shook his head, laughing. "I'd marry you in a second, Mona Ramsey."

"If you were the only boy in the world, and I were the only girl. What else is new?"

He kissed her on the forehead. "Don't worry. I'll screw this up."

"It sounds like you want to."

"Spare me the Jungian analysis."

"Take out the garbage, then. If it happens, it happens."

The Maestro Vanishes

THE PR WOMAN WAS ALMOST AS SHAKEN AS FRANNIE was.

"Mrs. Halcyon . . . believe me . . . we've tried our best to . . ."

"The party *starts* in two hours. I've notified *Women's Wear Daily,* the *Chronicle* and the *Examiner,* Carson Callas. . . . How on God's green earth can you *lose* a conductor?"

The opera publicist's voice turned starchy. "The Maestro is not . . . lost, Mrs. Halcyon. We've simply been unable to locate him. We've left word for him at the Mark, and there's a good chance he'll . . ."

"What about Cunningham? She'll come without him, won't she?"

"We're trying to find an alternate escort, in the event that . . . We're doing our best, Mrs. Halcyon. Miss Cunningham is not generally compatible with tenors."

"Are you telling me she won't . . . ? Oh, God . . . Really, this is the shoddiest excuse for . . . What am I supposed to tell my guests?"

* * *

Beauchamp and DeDe arrived at Halcyon Hill later than
planned. DeDe had popped the zipper on her Galanos. Beauchamp, to survive the ordeal, had downed four jiggers of J&B.

"Mother must be *dying*," said DeDe.

"Stop trying to cheer me up."

"God . . . Carson Callas is here already. He *loves* to write
no-show stories. He absolutely humiliated the Stonecyphers
with that article about . . . Beauchamp, would you please try
not to look so bored?"

"There's Splinter."

"I want a drink, Beauchamp."

"Help yourself. I'll be talking to Splinter."

"Beauchamp, if you expect me to go to the bar
alone . . ."

"Prue Giroux makes her own drinks."

"Goddammit, Beauchamp! I don't want to . . . talk to
Oona."

It was too late. The Rileys were next to them now, radiating
marital bliss. DeDe forced a smile. Her gown felt like a sausage casing.

"So where's the diva?" Splinter asked cheerfully. "That's
the right word, isn't it?"

Oona smiled and squeezed her husband's arm. "He's such
an oaf! How did you manage to marry an intellectual, DeDe?"

The message came through loud and clear. An *impotent*
intellectual.

Splinter had told Oona about the phone call. DeDe was
sure of it.

Beauchamp broke the silence. "Well, this intellectual
needs to kill a few brain cells. Join me at the bar, Splinter?"

The men walked off together.

Oona remained, smiling at DeDe, but only around the
mouth.

* * *

"I'm sorry, DeDe."

"About what?"

"Your ordeal."

"What ordeal?"

"Oh . . . I see. I'm sorry. I guess we should talk opera or something."

"I haven't the slightest idea what you're talking about."

"Forget it. You must think me *terribly* insensitive."

"Oona, will you please . . ."

"The grocery boy, darling. The *Chinese* grocery boy."

Silence.

"Shugie told me about The Forum, and we *all* feel for you dreadfully. It must have been awful." Oona smiled diabolically. "It *was* awful, wasn't it?"

"I have to go, Oona."

"I won't say a *thing,* darling. We Sacred Heart girls have to stick together, don't we?"

"Besides," she added, tucking DeDe's bra strap back under her dress, "a girl has to make do *somehow.*"

Frannie Freaks

FRANNIE HAD BEGUN WOBBLING SLIGHTLY. "EDGAR, what am I gonna *do*?"

"I'd say it was in the lap of the gods."

"Don't be ridiculous! We can't just stand here and let things . . . go to hell."

"They look like they're having a good time."

"Of course they're having a good time! They're *crucifying* me, Edgar. Look at Viola! She hasn't stopped giggling with Carson all evening!"

"Frannie . . . look . . . if you need entertainment or something, I could call the accordionist who plays at the club. It's late notice, but maybe he'd . . ."

Frannie groaned. "You don't just *swap* an accordionist for the greatest soprano in the world, Edgar!"

"I didn't know she was going to sing."

"She doesn't have to *sing*, Edgar! God! Do you do that on purpose?"

"What?"

"Act like such a philistine."

"I *am* a philistine."

"You are not a . . ."

"My father ran a department store, Frannie."

"He bought a box at the opera!"

"He ran a department store."

Beauchamp chatted with Peter Cipriani on a quiet corner of the terrace.

"So what's *your* theory on La Grande Nora?"

Peter shrugged. "Who cares? I didn't come for that. My new passion is Troyanos."

"Your pupils are dilated."

"They'd better be. Psilocybin."

"Jesus."

"I'm dating Shugie Sussman, for Christ's sake."

"Is that your excuse for an altered consciousness?"

"Got a better one?"

"I pass."

"I hope the little darling can drive. I had two drinks at The Mill before I picked her up."

"I'm *so* bored," said Margaret van Wyck Montoya-Corona.

DeDe fish-eyed her. "Mother will be so glad to hear that."

"Oh, no, DeDe . . . not *here* . . . I mean, in general. Jorge's been in Madrid for three weeks. It's *no* fun being married to a contraceptive czar, lemme tell you."

"I can imagine."

"It's the company I miss mostly."

"Get a dog, then."

Muffy smirked. "I've thought about getting a Samoan."

"You mean a Samoyed."

"No. I mean a *Samoan*. Penny and Trinka have *both* got Samoans. Matching Samoans. They're mechanics in the Mission . . . and, my dear, they are *big.*"

DeDe grimaced. "I don't like fat men."

"Not fat." She held her hands up. "Big."

"Oh. I see."

"Well, it's a helluva lot better than sending away for one of those plastic doohickies."

Edgar pulled his daughter aside. "I need your help," he whispered.

"What?"

"Your mother's locked herself in the john."

"Again?"

"Would you mind, DeDe. She's upset over . . . that singer."

Upstairs, DeDe bellowed at her mother through the bathroom door. "Mother!"

Silence.

"Mother, goddammit! You are *not* Zelda Fitzgerald. This act gets *real* old."

"Go away."

"If you're freaked over Nora Cunningham . . . I talked to Carson Callas. He says she does this all the time."

"It doesn't matter."

"He's giving you nine inches, Mother. Nine inches."

"What?"

"In *Western Gentry.* He's devoting most of his column to . . ."

The bathroom door swung open. Frannie stood there, red-eyed, holding a Mai Tai. "Did you ask him to stay for breakfast?" she said.

The Case of the Six Batons

THE CATERERS MADE SCRAMBLED EGGS FOR THE REM-
nants of the party at Halcyon Hill. While Frannie
was cornering Carson Callas, Edgar slipped away to
his den and placed a phone call to Barbary Lane.
"Madrigal."

"It's me, Anna."

"Hello, Edgar."

"I'm sorry about Mona, Anna."

"You don't need to apologize."

"Yes I do. I shouldn't have snapped at you this morning."

"I . . . you have a job to do, Edgar."

"If I had known how much Mona means to you . . ."

"I shouldn't have called. I meddle too much."

"I have a free day next week. We could beach it again."

"Fine."

"Thank God!"

"Go on, now. Get back to your guests."

*　　*　　*

142

Back at Barbary Lane, Mona was prone on the sofa with *New West* when Michael dragged in.

"Well," she said. "How's the wonderful world of gynecology?"

"I wasn't with Jon."

"My! How soon the flame of love can die!"

"He had a meeting tonight."

"So you went to the tubs?" She frowned at him, only half-jokingly.

"It isn't good to put all your eggs in one basket."

"So to speak."

He grinned. "Yeah."

"My lips are sealed."

He wriggled onto the sofa next to her. "Guess who was there?"

"The Mormon Tabernacle Choir."

"O.K., if you don't wanna dish, we won't dish."

"No. Go ahead. I want to."

"No. First I have to tell you about Hamburger Mary's."

"I hate it when you punish me."

"I'm setting the stage, Mona. Relax. Pretend I'm your guru. Maharishi Mahesh Mouse. I bring you the Keys to the Kingdom of Folsom Street. The Holy Red Bandanna That Sitteth on the Left Hand of the Levi's. The . . ."

"Michael, you fucker!"

"All right, all right. There I was at Hamburger Mary's, eating a bean sprout salad and wondering if my new Sears work boots looked *too* new, when this couple waltzed in and took a seat in the middle of a heavy biker contingent."

"A couple of guys?"

"Hell, no. A guy and his wife, slumming. Radical chic, vintage 1976. She was wearing a David Bowie T-shirt to show where her sympathies lay, and he was looking *grossly* uncomfortable in a Grodins sports ensemble. I mean, five years ago you could have caught these turkeys down in the Fillmore, chowing down on chitlins and black-eyed peas with the Brothers and Sisters. Now they're into faggots. They want *desperately* to relate to perverts."

"It's nothing but heartbreak, I can tell 'em!"

"O.K., so the scene gets more rough-trade by the minute. And then this dude sits down next to them and he's wearing a ring in his nose and a Future Farmers of America jacket and Mr. Grodins Ensemble is freaking out so badly that he may have to split for El Cerrito *any* minute."

"What about his wife?"

"Oh, God . . . *extremely* PO'ed that hubby's not getting off on the decadent ambience. Finally, she looks at him intently and says, in a voice *fraught* with meaning: 'Which do you think you'd prefer, Rich? S or M?' "

"And?"

"He thought it was something to put on the hamburger."

"So who did you meet at the tubs, Mouse?"

"Well . . . I met him after I'd been there a couple of hours. I was walking down the hall, looking into rooms, and this gray-haired guy motioned me to come into his room. He seemed pretty old, but he had a nice body. So I went in and sat down on the edge of his bed, and he said, 'Had a busy night?' and I immediately knew who it was by his accent. I also recognized him from his album covers."

"Who?"

"Nigel Huxtable."

"The conductor?"

"Yep. Nora Cunningham's husband, no less."

"Did you two . . . ?"

"Are you kidding?"

"Well, I didn't . . ."

"I got out of there as soon as I saw what he had in his bag."

"Go on, go on. . . ."

"A cassette recorder . . . a tape of his lovely wife singing the 'Casta Diva' . . . a piece of gold brocade cord which he *said* came from the curtain at La Scala . . . and six rubber batons!"

"Jesus Christ!"

"I didn't do anything, Mona. With anybody."

"Tell that to your gynecologist!"

Back to Cleveland?

DAYS DRAGGED LIKE WEEKS AT HALCYON COMMUNICA-
tions.

Beauchamp would smile as he passed Mary
Ann's desk, and sometimes even wink at her in
the elevator, but there were no more invitations,
no more anguished pleas for friendship.

It was as if Mendocino had never happened.

Fine, thought Mary Ann, if that's the way he wants it. There
were lots of other outlets for her energies . . . and miles to
go before she slept.

She cleaned out Edgar Halcyon's coffee machine.

She bought a glass-cutter and made a wine-jug terrarium
for her desk.

She created a "personal corner" of her bulletin board,
filling it with *Peanuts* cartoons, fortune cookie messages and
postcards from friends on vacation.

Once a morning, she sat perfectly still at her desk, closed
her eyes, and uttered the brave new litany of the seventies:

"Today is the first day of the rest of my life."

*　*　*

One night, Michael showed up at her door, bearing a clay pot shaped like a chicken.

"It's half of my *poulet Tolliver,*" he grinned, pronouncing his name *toe-lee-vay.* "Mona's out either raising her consciousness or lowering her expectations, and I thought . . . well, here."

"Michael, that's very sweet."

"Don't get gushy until you've seen it. It looks like a seagull that tangled with a 747."

"It smells delicious."

"Shall I put it on the parsons table?"

"Fine. Thanks."

He set the crock down, then smiled, shaking his head.

"What?" asked Mary Ann.

"They do this in the South when somebody dies. Bring food, I mean."

"Well, you're close."

"What do you mean?"

"Are you . . . have you eaten the other half of that chicken yet?"

He shook his head.

"Would you like company?"

Michael rolled his eyes. "Sometimes to the point of obsession."

Mary Ann made a salad, while Michael was retrieving his half of the chicken.

They dined by candlelight.

"This is my first formal dinner . . . for a guest."

"I'm honored."

"I hope you like Green Goddess."

"Mmm. Next time we'll have asparagus and you can show me your hollandaise recipe."

"How did you know I . . . oh . . ."

Michael nodded. "Robert. I lost the recipe in the divorce settlement."

146

Mary Ann reddened. "It's easy."

"I shouldn't have brought up ancient history. I'm sorry."

"It's O.K. I've always felt a little dumb about that."

"Why? Robert's a hot number. I would have done it. Hell, I *did* do it. Where do you think *I* met him?"

"The Safeway?"

"Not *that* one, actually. The one on Upper Market. From *my* standpoint, it's a lot cruisier." He slapped his own cheek. "Stop that. You're embarrassing the girl."

She laughed. "Do I look that out of it?"

"No, I . . . yeah, sometimes."

"Well, I am."

"It's very becoming, actually."

"I've heard *that* one before."

"Oh . . . who?"

"It doesn't matter."

Michael smiled wryly, studying her expression. "Is that why you're close to death?"

"Michael, I . . ."

"Look . . . let's plan a big night next week. We can go out to someplace impossibly straight . . . like the Starlight Roof or something. You haven't lived until you've done business with the Tolliver Gigolo Service."

She managed a grin. "That might be nice."

"Try to control your ecstasy, will you?"

"I might not be here, Michael."

"Huh?"

"I think I'm going home to Cleveland."

Michael whistled. "That's not close to death. That *is* death."

"It's the only thing that makes sense right now."

"You mean"—he threw his napkin down—"I just wasted a whole chicken making friends with a transient?" He stood up from the table, walked to the sofa, sat down and folded his arms. "Come over here. It's time for a little girl talk!"

Michael's Pep Talk

M ARY ANN STOOD UP UNCERTAINLY, ILL AT EASE with Michael's new role as mentor. She was sorry she had ever mentioned going home to Cleveland.

"Can I get you some crème de menthe?"

"Why are you leaving, Mary Ann?"

She sat down next to him. "Lots of reasons . . . I don't know . . . San Francisco in general."

"Just because some turkey dumped on you . . ."

"It isn't that. . . . Michael, there's no stability here. Everything's too easy. Nobody sticks with anybody or anything, because there's always something just a little bit better waiting around the corner."

"What did he *do* anyway?"

"I can't handle all this, Michael. I want to live somewhere where you don't have to apologize for serving instant coffee. Do you know what I like about Cleveland? People in Cleveland aren't 'into' anything!"

"Boring, in other words."

"I don't care what you call it. I need it. I need it badly."

"Why go home? We have boring people here. Haven't you

ever been to Paoli's at lunchtime?"

"There's no point . . ."

The phone rang. Michael jumped up and grabbed it. "The boring residence of Mary Ann Singleton."

"Michael!" Mary Ann jerked the phone away from him. "Hello."

"Mary Ann?"

"Mom?"

"We've been worried sick."

"What else is new?"

"Don't talk to me like that. We haven't heard from you in *weeks.*"

"I'm sorry. It's been hectic, Mom."

"Who was that man?"

"What man? Oh . . . Michael. Just a friend."

"Michael what?"

Mary Ann covered the receiver. "What's your last name, Michael?"

"De Sade."

"Michael!"

"Tolliver."

"Michael Tolliver, Mom. He's a real nice guy. He lives downstairs."

"Your daddy and I have been talking, Mary Ann . . . so hear me out on this. We both agree that you deserved a chance to . . . try your wings in San Francisco . . . but the time has come now . . . well, we can't just sit by and watch you throw your life away."

"It's *my* life to throw away, Mom."

"Not when you apparently don't have the maturity to . . ."

"How would you know?"

"Mary Ann . . . a strange man answered your phone."

"He's not a strange man, Mom."

"Who says?" grinned Michael.

"You don't even know his last name."

"We're more informal out here."

"Apparently . . . if you have no more judgment than to invite some perfectly . . ."

"Mom, Michael is a homosexual."

149

Silence.

"He likes *boys,* got it? I know you've heard of it. They've got it on TV now."

"I think you've completely lost your . . ."

"Not completely. Gimme another week or two."

"I can't believe I'm . . ."

"Mom, I'll call you in a few days, O.K.? Everything is fine. Night-night."

She hung up.

Michael beamed at her from the sofa.

Mona was the second assault wave.

"Christ, Mary Ann! No wonder you're miserable. You sit around on your butt all day expecting life to be one great big Hallmark card. Well, I've got news for you. There's not a single goddamn soul out there who cares enough to send the very best."

"So what point is there in . . . ?"

"You've got to *make* things work for you, Mary Ann. When you're down to the seeds and stems, get out there and grab life by the . . . Get a pencil. Take down this address. . . ."

War and Peace

A PLATOON OF SANDPIPERS PATROLLED THE BEACH at Point Bonita, pecking at the poptops in the shiny black sand. The water was sometimes blue, sometimes gray.

Edgar slipped his arm around Anna's waist. "I'll take her back, you know."

"Who?"

"Mona . . . If you tell me to, Anna, I will."

Anna shook her head. "I wouldn't do that. Furthermore, she wouldn't come back, even if you *did* change your mind."

"I'm a horse's ass, then?"

"No. Your son-in-law."

"She told you that?"

Anna nodded. "Is she right?"

"Absolutely."

"I thought she might be."

"Have you told her, Anna?"

"About you?"

"Yes."

Anna shook her head. "This is us, Edgar. Just us."

"I know, but . . ."

"What?"

"She's like a daughter to you, isn't she?"

"Yes."

"Isn't it hard *not* to tell her?"

"Yes."

"I want to tell the whole goddamn world."

Anna smiled. "Not so much as a memo to your secretary."

"She'll figure it out before Mona does."

"I hope not."

"Why? I have more to lose than you do."

Anna gazed at him for a moment. "C'mon. Let's get the blanket out of the car. It's colder than a witch's titty out here."

Edgar chuckled. "I didn't know nice girls knew that expression."

"They don't."

"We used to say that in France. During the war."

"That's when I learned it."

"What are you talking about?"

"I was in the Fort Ord campaign."

"You were a WAC?"

"I typed munitions requests for a colonel who was drunk most of the time. Hey, are we gonna get that blanket or not?"

They huddled together behind a sand dune, out of the wind. "What was it like growing up in a whorehouse?" Edgar asked.

Anna pursed her lips. "What was it like growing up in Hillsborough?"

"I didn't grow up in Hillsborough. I grew up in Pacific Heights."

"Oh, my! You *have* been a gypsy, haven't you?"

"C'mon. I asked you first."

"Well . . ." She scooped up a handful of sand and let it trickle through her fingers. "For one thing, I was fourteen years old before I realized that American currency does *not* bear the inscription 'Good for all night.' "

Edgar laughed.

"Also, I developed a number of quaint superstitions that hound me to this very day."

"For instance?"

"For instance . . . I can't abide cut flowers, so don't send me a dozen long-stems, if you want to maintain our strange and wonderful relationship."

"What's wrong with cut flowers?"

"Ladies of the evening consider them to be a sign of impending death. Beauty cut down in its prime and all that."

"Oh."

"Not pleasant."

"No."

Anna looked down at the sand, tracing a line there with her finger.

And it seemed to Edgar that she not only sensed, but shared, his pain.

Once More into the Breach

THE BAY AREA CRISIS SWITCHBOARD WAS LOCATED IN A renovated Victorian house in Noe Valley. Its exterior was painted persimmon, mole, avocado, fuchsia and chocolate. A sign in the window informed visitors that the building's occupants did not drink Gallo wine.

Mary Ann felt weird already.

She rang the buzzer. A man in a Renaissance shirt came to the door. Mary Ann's gaze climbed from the shirt past a scraggly red beard to the place where his left ear should have been.

"I . . . called earlier."

"Far out. The new volunteer. I'm Vincent."

He led her into a sparsely furnished room dominated by a gargantuan macramé hanging that incorporated bits of shell and feather and driftwood. She had no choice but to comment on it.

"That's . . . really wonderful."

"Yeah," he beamed. "My Old Lady made it."

She assumed he didn't mean his mother.

To her great relief, he turned out to be a very nice guy. He worked the Tuesday to Thursday shift at the switchboard. He was an artist. He fixed her a cup of Maxim, without apologizing.

"We'll probably . . . like . . . work together," he explained. "We get enough calls between eight and eleven to keep us both pretty busy."

"Are they all . . . trying to kill themselves?"

"No. You'll learn to psyche out the regulars."

"The regulars?"

"Loonies. Lonelies. The ones who call just to talk. That's cool too. That's what we're here for. And some of 'em just need referral to the proper social agency."

"For instance?"

"Battered wives, gay teen-agers, senior citizens with questions about social security, child abusers, rape victims, minorities with housing problems . . ." He rattled off the list like a Howard Johnson's employee reciting the twenty-eight flavors.

"Then what about the suicides?"

"Oh . . . we get maybe two or three a night."

"You know, I haven't had any special training in . . ."

"It's cool. I'll handle the hairy ones. Most of the time they're just trying to get your attention."

Mary Ann sipped her coffee, drawing strength from Vincent's casual confidence. "It's pretty rewarding, isn't it?"

Vincent shrugged. "Sometimes. And sometimes it's a real drag. It depends."

"Has it been . . . hairy lately?"

"I don't know. I've been off for a couple of weeks."

"Vacation?"

He shook his head, holding up his right hand. Mary Ann had already noticed that his little finger was bandaged . . . but not the fact that it appeared to have been severed at midpoint.

"You poor thing! How did that happen?"

"Aww . . ."

The ear . . . the finger . . . She was suddenly embarrassed. Vincent saw her redden. "I get on downers."

"Pills?"

He smiled. "No . . . just downers. Depressed. Bummed out."

"I'm afraid I don't . . ."

"No big deal. I'm gettin' it together. Hey, hey! Almost eight o'clock. All set?"

"Yeah. I guess so." She sank into the chair in front of the telephone. "I guess I'll just . . . play it by ear."

She could have bitten her tongue off.

Fantasia for Two

AFTER WATCHING *YOUNG FRANKENSTEIN* AT THE Ghirardelli Cinema, Michael and Jon walked onto the pier at Aquatic Park.

The pier was dark. Clusters of Chinese fishermen broke the silence with laughter and the tinny blare of transistor radios. A helicopter made a *whup-whup* noise in the sky over Fort Mason.

The couple sat at the end of the pier on a mammoth concrete bench.

"It's a question mark," said Michael.

"What?"

"The pier. It's a giant question mark."

Jon looked across the black lagoon defined by the curve of the pier. "No it's not. It bends the other way. It's a backwards question mark."

"Doctors are so literal."

"Sorry."

"I never told you about my chimp, did I?"

"As in monkey?"

"Uh huh. Do you wanna hear it?"

"By all means."

"Well . . . ever since I was a kid I've always wanted a chimp. I used to fantasize about training a chimp to burst into my fifth-grade classroom and throw water balloons at my teacher, Miss Watson." He laughed. "She was probably a dyke, come to think of it. I should've been nicer to her. . . . Anyway, I *never* outgrew it . . . the desire to own one . . . and last year I happened to mention this to my ex-lover. . . . I mean, he's my ex-lover now. . . . He was my lover at the time."

"Stick to the chimp."

"O.K. . . . The *big* coincidence was that Christopher had had this *exact same* fantasy ever since *he* was a kid. Sooo . . . we talked about it for a while and decided we were two responsible adults and there was no reason in the world why we shouldn't have one. Anyway, Christopher contacted this friend of his at Marine World who knew how to handle all the red tape and everything and eventually . . . we ended up the proud parents of a teenaged chimp named Andrew."

Jon smiled. "Andrew, Michael and Christopher. Very nice."

"We thought so. And it worked out *beautifully,* after we got past the toilet-training part and all. We took him *everywhere* . . . Golden Gate Park, the Renaissance Faire . . . and the *zoo.* Christ, he *adored* the zoo! Then one day our friend at Marine World asked if we would . . . like . . . mate him with a lady chimp that belonged to a friend of his. Naturally, we were pretty excited about this, since it would make us grandparents, in effect."

"In effect."

"So the big day came . . . but Andrew didn't."

"Oh, no!"

"Hell, he wouldn't even go in the same *room* with her."

"O.K., let me guess."

Michael nodded soberly. "Queer as a goddamn three-dollar bill!"

"Now wait a minute!"

"I could handle it O.K., because I really *loved* Andrew, but Christopher took it personally. He was *convinced* that if he had played more ball with Andrew . . ."

Jon began to laugh. "You're too much!"

"It was *awful*, I tell you! Christopher accused me of molly-coddling Andrew and taking him to too many Busby Berkeley movies and . . . letting him see the men's underwear section of the Sears catalogue!"

"Stop it!"

Michael grinned finally, forsaking the game altogether. "You like that one, do you?"

"Do you always make things up?"

"Always."

"Why?"

Michael shrugged. " 'I want to deceive him just enough to make him want me.' "

"What's that from?"

"Blanche DuBois. In *Streetcar.*"

Jon threw an arm around Michael's neck. "Come over here, Blanche." They kissed for a long time, pressed against the cold concrete.

When they separated, Michael said, "Would it sound better if the lover was named Andrew and the chimp Christopher?"

"You made up the lover too?"

"Oh . . . *especially* the lover."

The Mysterious Caller

THE WIND WAS RISING ON THE BEACH, SO ANNA READ-
justed the blanket that sheltered them. "Here,
Edgar . . . cover up. Somebody might see your
Brooks Brothers ensemble."

"Watch it."

"Say . . . those socks are adorable . . . pardon the expression. I understand *everybody* in St. Moritz is wearing charcoal
over-the-calves these days!"

"That tickles, Anna. Cut it out."

"Ticklish? Edgar Halcyon? Is *nothing* sacred?"

"Anna, I'm warning you . . ."

"Tough talk for a city boy!" She jumped up suddenly,
giving his loosened tie a yank, and pranced down the beach.
Edgar chased her back into the dunes, then tackled her with
a Samurai yelp.

They lay there together, laughing and gasping.

"C'mon," said Anna, taking his hands. "Let's go find some
flotsam and/or jetsam."

"Wait a minute, Anna."

"Are you all right?"

"Yes. I . . ."

"Are you sure?"

"Yes, I'm fine."

"I keep forgetting you're an old buzzard."

"I'm two years older than you."

"Right. An old buzzard."

The sky cleared at four o'clock. They walked barefoot up the beach.

"This reminds me of something," Edgar said.

"A bourbon commercial?"

He smiled and squeezed her hand. "When I was nineteen, my parents sent me to England for the summer. I stayed with some cousins in a village called Cley-next-the-Sea. I used to walk on the beach looking for carnelians."

"Stones?"

"Beautiful red ones. Orangish-red. One day I met an old lady on the beach. At least, I *thought* she was old at the time. Her daughter was with her. She was eighteen and beautiful. They asked me to walk with them. They were looking for carnelians too."

"Did you do it?"

"What do you think?"

"I think Edgar was too busy . . . or too embarrassed."

Edgar stopped and turned to face her. He looked like a lion with a thorn in his paw. "It's too late, isn't it, Anna?"

She dropped her shoes in the sand and wrapped her arms around his neck. "It's too late for the girl, Edgar. The old lady's a pushover."

They were under the blanket again.

"We should get back, Anna."

"I know."

"I told Frannie I would . . ."

"Fine."

"Are we making a big mistake?"

"Oh, I hope so!"

161

"You don't know much about me."

"No."

"I'm dying, Anna."

"Oh . . . I thought you might be."

"You've known about . . . ?"

Anna shrugged. "Why else would Edgar Halcyon do this?"

"Jesus."

She toyed with the white curls on the back of his neck. "How much time have we got?"

Back at Barbary Lane, Anna soaked in a hot tub. She was humming a very old tune when her buzzer rang.

She dried off, slipped into her kimono, and buzzed in her visitor.

"Who is it?" she shouted down the hallway.

"A friend of Mary Ann Singleton's," came the reply. It was a young woman's voice.

"She's out, dear. At the Crisis Switchboard."

"Would it be all right if I waited here? In the foyer, I mean? It's kind of important."

Anna walked into the hallway. The young woman was blond and plump, with the face of a lost child. She was carrying a Gucci tote bag.

"Have a seat, dear," said the landlady. "Mary Ann should be home soon."

Back in the tub, Anna puzzled over the visitor. She looked familiar somehow. Something about the eyes and the line of the jaw.

Then it hit her.

She looked like Edgar.

So Where Was Beauchamp?

THE WOMAN'S FACE WAS IN THE SHADOWS. SHE HAD gained so much weight that Mary Ann didn't recognize her immediately.

"Mary Ann?"

"Oh . . ."

"Beauchamp's wife. DeDe. Your landlady let me in."

"Yes. Mrs. Madrigal."

"She was very nice. I hope you don't mind. I was afraid I'd miss you."

"No . . . that's fine. Can you come up for a drink?"

"You're not expecting . . . company?"

"No," said Mary Ann, already denying the accusation.

DeDe sat in a yellow vinyl director's chair, folding her hands across the surface of her tote bag.

"Would you like some crème de menthe?" asked Mary Ann.

"Thank you. Do you have white?"

"White what?"

"Crème de menthe."

"Oh . . . no . . . just the other."

"Oh . . . I think I'll pass."

"A Tab or a Fresca?"

"Really. I'm fine."

Mary Ann sank to the edge of the sofa. "But not *that* fine." She smiled feebly.

DeDe looked down at her hands. "No. I guess not. Mary Ann . . . I'm not here to make a scene."

Mary Ann swallowed, feeling her face turn hot.

"I wanted to bring you this." DeDe fumbled in the tote bag and produced Mary Ann's brown-and-white polka-dot scarf. "I found it in Beauchamp's car."

Mary Ann stared at the scarf, dumfounded. "When?"

"The Monday after you went to Mendocino with him."

"Oh."

"He told me about that."

"I see."

"It's yours, isn't it?"

"Yes."

"I don't care. I mean . . . I *care,* but I've stopped . . . exhausting myself over it. I've dealt with it. I think I even understand how he . . . got you involved."

"DeDe, I . . . Why are you here, then?"

"Because . . . I'm hoping you'll tell me the truth."

Mary Ann made an impotent gesture with her hands. "I thought I just had."

"Were you with him last weekend, Mary Ann?"

"No! I was . . ."

"What about Tuesday before last?"

Mary Ann's jaw dropped. "DeDe . . . I swear to God . . . I was with Beauchamp one time and one time only. He asked me to go to Mendocino with him because . . ." She cut herself off.

"Because what?"

"It sounds dumb. He . . . said he wanted someone to talk to. I felt sorry for him. I've barely talked to him since."

"You're with him every day."

"In the same building. That's about it."

"You *did* sleep together in Mendocino?"

"I . . . yes."

DeDe stood up. "Well . . . I'm sorry to bother you. I think that's enough of this soap opera for both of us." She turned and headed for the door.

"DeDe?"

"Yes?"

"Did Beauchamp *tell* you I was with him last weekend and . . . whatever that other time was?"

"Not in so many words."

"He implied it?"

"Yes."

"I wasn't, DeDe. I want you to believe me."

DeDe smiled bitterly. "I do. Isn't *that* the pits?"

Back on Montgomery Street, DeDe tore ruthlessly into the mail she had ignored all day.

There were new bills from Wilkes and Abercrombie's, the latest issue of *Architectural Digest,* a plea for money from the Bennington Alumni Association, and a letter from Binky Gruen.

She took Binky's letter into the kitchen, where she fixed a bowl of Familia and milk. She opened the envelope with a butter knife.

The letter was written on Golden Door stationery.

DeDe Dear,
    Well, here's old Bink, wallowing in luxurious misery at America's most elegant fat farm. We get up at some godawful hour of the morning to jog through the boonies in very unflattering pink terry-cloth jumpsuits called "pinkies." (Please, darling, no jokes about Binky in her Pinky.) I've lost six pounds already. Trumpet fanfare. Movie stars everywhere you turn. I feel déclassé if I don't wear my Foster Grants in the steam room. Try it, you'll hate it.

Love and kisses.
Binky

*   *   *

Beauchamp walked into the kitchen. "Where did you go to-night?"

"Junior League."

He looked at the cereal bowl. "They didn't feed you?"

"I had a *small* bowl, Beauchamp!"

"Suit yourself. It's too late to get in shape for the opening of the opera, anyway." He smiled maddeningly and walked out of the room.

DeDe glowered at him until he was out of sight. Then she picked up Binky's letter and read it again.

What the Simple Folk Do

THE BEAST IN THE DOORWAY MADE MARY ANN'S FLESH crawl.

Its face was chalk white with lurid spots of rouge on the cheekbones. It was bare-chested and furry-thighed, and two gnarled goat horns rose hideously from its brow.

It spoke to her.

"How horny can ya get, huh?"

"Michael!"

"*Wrong,* O boring one. I am the Great God Pan."

"You scared me to death!"

"But I am a gentle, playful creature . . . the spirit of forests and shepherds. . . . Screw it! How can anybody stay in character with you?"

Mary Ann smiled. "A costume party?"

"No. Actually, I'm meeting my Aunt Agnes at the Greyhound station."

"You're going to the bus . . . ? Why do I even *talk* to you?"

"Aren't you gonna invite me in?"

She giggled. "My mother would love you."

"This may come as a rude shock to you, but I don't particularly *want* your mother to love me. Look . . . if you don't let me out of the hallway, that man on the roof is gonna have a heart attack."

"Come on in. *What* man on the roof?"

Michael bounced into the room and sat down, adjusting the brown Afro wig that held his horns. "The new tenant. Somebody Williams. I saw him on the steps to the roof a little while ago. He nearly *freaked.*"

"There's an apartment on the roof?"

"Sorta. I call it a pentshack. It doesn't rent very often, but it has a *gorgeous* view. He moved in a couple of days ago. Hey, can I have something to drink?"

"Sure . . . there's some . . ."

"Say crème de menthe and I'll gore you!"

She wiggled one of his horns. "White wine, Your Holiness."

"Sure . . . no, I take it back. I've gotta leave soon. I kinda hoped you'd go with me."

"As what? A nanny goat?"

"A shepherdess. I've got a neat-looking peasant dress with a ribboned bodice and . . . Don't look at me like that, woman. It's Mona's!"

Mary Ann laughed. "I'd love to, Michael . . . but tonight's my night at the Crisis Switchboard."

"This *is* a crisis! Lonely, horned homophile with hairy legs seeks attractive but boring lady for freewheeling evening of . . ."

"What about that guy I saw you with?"

"Jon?"

"Blond hair?"

Michael nodded. "Tonight's the opening night of the opera."

"Oh . . . you don't like opera, huh?"

"No . . . well, that's true, as a matter of fact . . . but that isn't it. Jon bought season tickets with a friend. But you're right . . . I can't really handle opera. I don't think I would've . . . you know."

She kissed him cautiously on his rouged cheek. "How about a rain check?"

He stood up, sighed and readjusted his horns. "That's what they *all* say."

"Where's the party?"

"Not far. The Hyde and Green Plant Store. I'm gonna walk it."

"Dressed like that?"

"Don't be so . . . Cleveland. Half the people on Russian Hill look like this."

"Well, be careful."

"Of what?"

"I don't know. . . . Other people who look like that, I guess."

"Have fun with the suicides."

"Thanks." She pushed him playfully out the door. "Go find yourself a nice billy goat."

Intermezzo

EANWHILE, AT THE OPERA HOUSE, THE GENTLE-
men came and went in the shadows, preening
their plumage amid the red leather and dark
wood and gleaming fixtures of the men's room
at The Boxes. For the next two hours, it would
be the most elegant toilet in town.

"Guard the door," ordered Peter Cipriani.

"What?" said Beauchamp.

"The *last* thing we need is one of those tight-assed old
dinosaurs stumbling in here ripped to the tits!"

From his pocket Peter took a Gump's envelope embossed
with the Cipriani crest. He dug into it with a tiny gold spoon
and lifted the spoon to his left nostril.

"Ah! Uncut! The way I like my coke *and* my men!"

Beauchamp was nervous. "C'mon! Hurry up!"

"Ladies first!"

The spoon went down and up again, catering to Peter's
other nostril. Beauchamp followed suit, then inspected his
tails for lint in front of the mirror.

"God, this is dreary!"

Peter grinned at him. "Are you going to L'Orangerie with the Halcyons afterwards?"

"Check with DeDe. She and her mother are calling the shots tonight."

Peter extracted a Bill Blass bronzer from his breast pocket and began to touch up his cheekbones. "Why don't you split with me at intermission and go to The Club?"

"The club has something planned?"

Peter groaned. "You poor naïve heiress! I'm talking about the one at Eighth and Howard."

"I think you're on your own tonight, Peter."

"Chacun à son goût. Personally, I'm sick of these pseudo-patricians. I'm ready for a few pseudo-lumberjacks."

Ryan Hammond swept into the room. Ryan was an Englishman, or at least *talked* like one. He was renowned in the social columns as an escort of widows and a star of musical comedies on the Peninsula.

"Well," purred Peter, "haven't the walkers crawled out of the woodwork tonight?"

Beauchamp glared at his friend.

Ryan ignored him, heading for the urinals.

"Your date's real cute, Ryan. How old is she? A hundred and eight?"

"Peter!" snapped Beauchamp.

Going about his business, Ryan fixed Peter with his best George Sanders evil eye. "Good evening, Mr. Cipriani. I didn't know Massenet was your cup of tea."

"Well, not ordinarily . . . but opening night is *such* a spectacle, isn't it? Hell, it's the only night of the year that *you* wear less jewelry than your girlfriends."

The bathroom was empty again when Edgar entered with Booter Manigault.

Booter was adorned with his European Campaign ribbons

and the earplug of a transistor radio. He was listening to the Giants-Cincinnati game.

The two men faced the wall. "Almost time for ducks again," Edgar said expressionlessly.

"What? . . . Sorry, Edgar." He pulled out the earplug.

"I said it's almost time for ducks again. Seems like the Grove was just yesterday, and now it's almost time for ducks again."

"Yeah . . . the old tempus really fugits, doesn't it?" Booter chuckled to himself. "Who says we haven't got seasons in California? Just about now the hookers are leaving their nests in Rio Nido and migrating to Marysville. I'd say that was a sure sign of fall, wouldn't you?"

Silence.

"Edgar . . . are you all right?"

"Yeah . . . I'm fine."

"You look a little white."

"Opera." He forced a grin.

Booter reinstated the earplug. "Goddamn right!"

Vincent's Old Lady

MICHAEL UNCAPPED A TUBE OF DANCE ARTS CLOWN white and repaired his Pan face in the foyer of 28 Barbary Lane. He loved that old foyer, with its tarnished Deco ladies and gilt mirrors and pressed-tin ceiling full of thirties hieroglyphics.

Somehow it made him feel debonair—gay in the archaic sense of the word—like Fred Astaire in *Top Hat* or Noel Coward off to meet Gertie Lawrence at the Savoy Grill.

Thank heavens, he thought, for Mrs. Madrigal, a landlady of almost cosmic sensitivity who had never felt called upon to defile the building with polyethylene palm trees or Florentine stick-on mirror tiles from Goodman Lumber.

He gave himself a thorough inspection and smiled in approval. He looked damned good.

His horns were outrageously realistic. His mock-chinchilla Home Yardage goat haunches jutted out from his waist with comic eroticism. His belly was flat, and his pecs . . . well, his pecs were the pecs of a man who hardly ever cheated on a bench press at the Y.

You're hot, he told himself. Remember that.

Remember that and hold your head up later when your parents call from Orlando and wonder if you've met any "nice girls" . . . when that cute trick from The Midnight Sun turns out to have a lover on the diving team at Berkeley . . . when someone at the tubs says, "I'm just resting right now" . . . when the beautiful and aloof Dr. Jon Fielding furrows his Byronesque brow and declines to step out of his white porcelain closet.

Well, eat your heart out, Dr. Beautiful! Pan is on the rampage tonight!

When Mary Ann arrived at the Bay Area Crisis Switchboard, Vincent seemed to be on a bummer.

She checked his extremities for recent ravages.

He was still wearing a bandage on his truncated little finger, but nothing else—other than his left ear—was missing. Mary Ann heaved a secret sigh of relief and sat down in front of her phone.

"Bad day, huh?"

Vincent smiled wistfully and held up a string of Greek worry beads. "I haven't let go since breakfast."

"What's the matter?"

"I don't think . . ." He turned away from her, nervously twisting a Rolodex with his good hand. "I don't like to lay heavy trips on people." His sad eyes and scraggly red whiskers reminded Mary Ann of some pitiful zoo animal on the verge of extinction.

"Go ahead," she smiled. "It's good practice for this." She patted the telephone.

Vincent stared at her. "You are really . . . a very far-out person."

"C'mon."

"No. I really mean it. When I first met you, I thought you were just another Hostess cupcake. I thought you were probably . . . like . . . slumming here, doing your bit for the Junior League or something . . . but you're not like that at all. You're really together."

Mary Ann reddened. "Thank you, Vincent."

Vincent smiled at her warmly, scratching his stub.

His problem, it turned out, was his Old Lady.

He had met his Old Lady when he was a house painter and she was a waitress in an organic pizzeria called The Karmic Anchovy. Together, they had fought for peace, forging their love in the fires of zealotry. They had named their first child Ho and joined a commune in Olema.

A union made in Nirvana.

"What happened?" asked Mary Ann softly.

Vincent shook his head. "I don't know. The war, I guess."

"The war?"

"Vietnam. She couldn't take it when it was over. She fell all to pieces."

Mary Ann nodded sympathetically.

"It was the biggest thing in her life, Mary Ann, and nothing after that quite fulfilled her. She tried Indians for a while, then oil spills and PG&E, but it wasn't the same. It just wasn't the same."

He looked down at the worry beads twined around his fingers. Mary Ann hoped he wouldn't start crying.

"We tried everything," Vincent continued. "I even sold our food stamps to send her to an awareness retreat on the Russian River."

"A what?"

"You know. A place to go to get centered. Feminist therapy, bioenergetics, herbology, transcendental volleyball . . . It didn't work. Nothing has worked."

"I'm really sorry, Vincent."

"It isn't fair, is it?" said Vincent, blinking back the tears. "There ought to be an American Legion for pacifists."

Now Mary Ann was certain that *she* was going to cry.

"Vincent . . . it'll work out."

Vincent just shook his head in desolation.

175

"It *will,* Vincent. You love her, and she loves you. That's all that matters."

"She left me."

"Oh . . . well, then run to her side. Tell her how much she means to you. Tell her . . ."

"I can't afford to go to Israel."

"She's in Israel?"

Vincent nodded. "She joined the Israeli Army."

Abruptly, he pushed back his chair and fled from the room, locking himself in the bathroom.

Mary Ann listened at the door, white with fear.

"Vincent?"

Silence.

"Vincent! Everything is going to work out. Do you hear me, Vincent?"

She heard him rummaging in the bathroom cabinet.

"Vincent, for God's sake! Don't cut anything off!"

Then her phone rang.

The Anniversary Tango

So where's our wandering boy tonight?" asked Mrs. Madrigal, pouring Mona a glass of sherry.

"Michael?"

"Do you know any other wandering boys?"

"I wish I did."

"Mona! Have you two quarreled or something?"

"No. I didn't mean it like that." She ran her palm along the worn red velvet on the arm of the chair. "Michael's gone to a costume party."

The landlady pulled her chair closer to Mona's. She smiled. "I think Brian's at home tonight."

"Christ! You sound just like my mother!"

"Stop avoiding the issue. Don't you *like* Brian?"

"He's a womanizer."

"So?"

"So I don't need that right now, thank you."

"You could have fooled me."

Mona gulped her sherry, avoiding Mrs. Madrigal's eyes. "Is that your answer for everything?"

The landlady chuckled. "It isn't *my* answer for everything.

It's *the* answer for everything. . . . C'mon, Calamity Jane, get your coat. I've got two tickets to *Beach Blanket Babylon.*"

Warmed by a pitcher of sangria, the two women unwound amid the rococo funk of Club Fugazi. When the revue was over, Mrs. Madrigal stayed seated, chatting easily with the wine-flushed strangers around her.

"Oh, Mona . . . I feel . . . immortal right now. I'm very happy to be here with you."

Sentiment shot from the hip embarrassed Mona. "It's a wonderful show," she said, burying her face in a wineglass.

Mrs. Madrigal let a smile bloom slowly on her angular face. "You'd be so much happier if you could see yourself the way I see you."

"Nobody's happy. What's happy? Happiness is over when the lights come on."

The older woman poured herself some more sangria. "Screw that," she said quietly.

"What?"

"Screw that. Wash your mouth out. Who taught you that half-assed existential drivel?"

"I don't see why it should matter to you."

"No. I suppose you don't."

Mona was puzzled by the hurt look in her companion's eyes. "I'm sorry. I'm a bitch tonight. Look . . . let's go somewhere for coffee, O.K.?"

The sight of the Caffè Sport gave Mona an instant shiver of nostalgia.

Mrs. Madrigal had planned it that way.

"God," said Mona, grinning at the restaurant's Neapolitan bric-a-brac. "I'd almost forgotten what a trip this place is!"

They took a small table in the back, next to a dusty "Roman ruin" basrelief which a loving, but practical, artist had protected with chicken wire. A tango was playing on the jukebox.

Mrs. Madrigal ordered a bottle of Verdicchio.

When the wine came, she lifted her glass to Mona. "To three more," she said merrily.

"Three more whats?"

"Years. It's our anniversary."

"What?"

"You've been my tenant for three years. Tonight."

"How in God's name would you ever remember a thing like that?"

"I'm an elephant, Mona. Old and very battered . . . but happy."

Mona smiled affectionately, raising her glass. "Well, here's to elephants. I'm glad I chose Barbary Lane."

Anna shook her head. "Wrong, dear."

"What?"

"You didn't choose Barbary Lane. It chose you."

"What does that mean?"

Mrs. Madrigal winked. "Finish your wine first."

Bells Are Ringing

ETTING THE CRISIS PHONE RING, MARY ANN POUNDED on the bathroom door.

"Vincent, listen to me. Nothing's as bad as you think it is! Do you hear me, Vincent?"

She made a hasty mental inventory of the items in the cabinet over the sink. Were there scissors? Or knives? Or razors?

RRRRINNNGGGG!

"Vincent! I have to answer the phone, Vincent! Will you just say something? Vincent, for God's sake!"

RRRINNNNGGGG!

"Vincent, you are a child of the universe! No less than the trees and the stars! You have a right to be here, Vincent! And whether or . . . whether or not . . . Today is the first day of the rest of your life. . . ."

Nausea swept over her in waves. She ran from the bathroom door and lunged at the telephone. "Bay Area Crisis Switchboard," she panted.

The voice on the other end was high-pitched and wheezy, like some Disney forest creature receding into senility.

"Who are you?"

"Uh . . . Mary Ann Singleton."

"You're new."

"Sir, could you hold . . . ?"

"Where's Rebecca? I always talk to Rebecca."

She held her hand over the mouthpiece. *"VINCENT!"*

Silence.

"VINCENT!"

The reply was strangely subdued. "What?"

"Are you all right, Vincent?"

"Yes."

"This guy wants somebody named Rebecca."

"Tell him you're Rebecca's replacement."

Mary Ann spoke into the phone. "Sir . . . I'm Rebecca's replacement."

"Liar."

"Sir?"

"Stop calling me sir! How old are you, anyway?"

"Twenty-five."

"What have you done to Rebecca?"

"Look, I don't even *know* Rebecca!"

"You *don't,* huh?"

"No."

"You wanna suck my weenie?"

Vincent stood in the middle of the room like a frightened rodent, his sad eyes blinking rhythmically above the brush pile of his beard.

"Mary Ann?"

She didn't look up. She was still on her knees over the wastebasket.

"Can I get you something, Mary Ann? A Wash'n Dri, maybe? I think there's a Wash'n Dri in the desk drawer."

She nodded.

Vincent handed her the moist towelette, placing his hand lamely on her shoulder.

"I'm sorry . . . I really am. I didn't mean to freak you out. God, I'm really . . ."

She shook her head, pointing to the dangling telephone

receiver. It was beeping angrily. Vincent returned it to its hook.

"Who was that?"

She straightened up warily, assessing Vincent. Everything seemed to be there. "He . . . a crank, I think."

"Oh . . . Randy."

"Randy?"

Vincent nodded. "Rebecca called him that. I should have mentioned him."

"He calls a lot?"

"Yeah. Rebecca figured if he called *anybody* it might as well be us."

"Oh . . ."

"It's like . . . you know . . . we're here for everybody, and . . ."

"What happened to Rebecca?"

"Oh . . . she OD'd."

Once again they sat by the phones.

Vincent offered her a kindly smile. "You a junkie or something?"

"What?"

He picked up her box of Dynamints. "You've eaten half a box in five minutes."

"I guess I'm edgy."

"Have some of mine." He handed her a bag of trail mix. "I got it at Tassajara."

"In Ghirardelli Square?"

He smiled indulgently. "Near Big Sur. A Zen retreat."

"Oh."

"Lay off the sugar, O.K.? It'll kill ya."

The Landlady Bares Her Soul

O.K.," SAID MONA, DOWNING HER VERDICCHIO. "What was that cryptic comment all about?"

Mrs. Madrigal smiled. "What did I say?"

"You said Barbary Lane *chose* me. You meant that literally, didn't you?"

The landlady nodded. "Don't you remember how we met?"

"At the Savoy-Tivoli."

"Three years ago this week."

Mona shrugged. "I still don't get it."

"It wasn't an accident, Mona."

"What?"

"I engineered it. Rather magnificently, I think." She smiled, swirling the wine in her glass.

Mona thought back to that distant summer evening. Mrs. Madrigal had come to her table with a basket of Alice B. Toklas brownies. "I made too many," she had said. "Take two, but save one for later. They'll knock you on your ass."

A spirited conversation had followed, a long winy chat about Proust and Tennyson and the Astral Plane. By the end of the evening, the two women were solid friends.

The next day Mrs. Madrigal had called about the apartment.

"This is the madwoman you met at the Tivoli. There's a house on Russian Hill that claims it's your home."

Mona had moved in two days later.

"But why?" asked Mona.

"You intrigued me . . . and you were also a celebrity."

Mona rolled her eyes. "Right."

"Well, you were. *Everybody* knew about your swimwear campaign for J. Walter Thompson."

"In New York?"

Mrs. Madrigal nodded. "I read the trade journals from time to time."

"You blow me away sometimes."

"Good."

"What if I had said no?"

"About the apartment, you mean?"

"Yeah."

"I don't know. I would have tried something else, I guess."

"I guess I should be flattered."

"Yes. I guess you should."

Mona felt herself reddening. "Anyway, I'm glad."

"Well . . . here's to it!"

"Uh uh," said Mona, watching the landlady's upraised glass. "Not until I find out what 'it' is."

Mrs. Madrigal shrugged. "What else, dear? Home."

Mary Ann was already there, recuperating from her night at the switchboard.

She had installed her new walnut-grained shelf paper, scrubbed the ick off the back of the stove, and replaced the blue-water thingahoochie in the toilet tank.

When Mona stopped by, she was hunched over the kitchen table.

"What the fuck are you doing?"

"Alphabetizing my spice rack."

"Jesus."

"It's therapeutic."

"The switchboard was supposed to be your therapy."

"Don't even bring it up."

"Why? What happened?"

"I don't wanna talk about it."

"That's right. Repress it. Keep all that prom queen neurosis locked up inside, so . . ."

"I was *never* a prom queen, Mona."

"It doesn't matter. You were the type."

"How do *you* know? How the hell do you know *what* type . . . ?"

"Ladies, ladies . . ." It was Michael, standing in the doorway. His furry Pan legs were matted and wine-stained.

"Mouse . . . you're back."

"You think it's *easy* getting picked up dressed like this?"

Suppressing a smile, Mona moved next to him and touched the mock chinchilla. "Yuck!"

"O.K., O.K. So Nair doesn't work for everybody."

At the Fat Farm

SAGEBRUSH, AND AVOCADO TREES SHIMMERED IN THE afternoon heat as the huge gold limousine sped north through the hills of Escondido.

DeDe settled back in the seat and closed her eyes. She was bound for The Golden Door!

The Golden Door! America's most sumptuous and blue-blooded fat farm! A jeweled oasis of sauna baths and facials, pedicures and manicures, dancing lessons, herbal wraps and gourmet cuisine!

And not a moment too soon.

DeDe was *sick* of the city, sick of Beauchamp and his deception, sick of the guilt she had suffered over Lionel. Furthermore, she had had it with the puffy-cheeked wretch who stared at her morosely from mirrors and shopwindows.

She wanted the old DeDe back, the DeDe of Aspen and Tahoe, the golden-maned temptress who had teased the Phi Delts, tantalized The Bachelors and devastated Splinter Riley not *that* many years ago.

She had done it before.

She could do it again.

*　*　*

The driver peered over his shoulder at her. "Your first time, madam?"

DeDe laughed nervously. "I look that far gone, do I?"

"Oh, no, madam. It's just that your face is a new one."

"I guess you see some pretty famous faces."

He nodded, apparently pleased she had brought up the subject. "Just last week, Miss Esther Williams."

"Really?"

"The Gabors were here last month. Three of them, in fact. I've also driven Rhonda Fleming, Jeanne Crain, Dyan Cannon, Barbara Howar . . ." He paused, though presumably only for effect; DeDe was sure he had memorized the list. "Also, Mrs. Mellon and Mrs. Gimbel, Roberta Flack, Liz Carpenter . . . I could go on and on, Mrs. Day."

The sound of her own name jolted her, but she tried not to show it.

The Gabors would *never* have shown it.

A stately row of Monterey pines lined the highway on either side of the security gates. The driver mumbled something into an intercom and the gates swung open.

The driveway beyond was a sinuous downhill sweep, flanked on one side by the spa's private orange grove and on the other by thickets of pine and oak.

Then The Door appeared, gleaming in the sunshine like the gates of Xanadu.

DeDe felt like Sally Kellerman on the brink of Shangri-la!

Her Calvin Klein T-shirt was already two shades darker under the arms.

The driver parked at a gatehouse next to The Door, collected her luggage, and led the way through the mythical gates. On the other side, DeDe crossed a pussy-willowed stream by means of a delicate Japanese bridge, then passed through shoji screens and finally a massive wooden door.

The reception area was an elegantly sparse chamber of bamboo furniture and Japanese silk paintings. After a short but pleasant interchange with a fortyish directress, DeDe Halcyon Day signed her name to one of the world's most rarefied registers.

Her $2,500 transformation had begun!

Her room, as arranged, opened onto the Camellia Court. ("Don't let them stick you in the Bell Court or the Azalea Court," Binky had warned. "They're O.K., but very Piedmont, if you know what I mean.")

DeDe wandered amid her private Oriental splendor, checking out her tokonoma (a niche housing a bronze Buddha) and her "moon-watching deck" overlooking the garden. On her night table lay a copy of Erich Fromm's *The Art of Loving,* which she perused idly, totally transported from the agonies of San Francisco.

Then the phone rang.

Would she kindly report to the weigh-in room at her convenience?

The weigh-in room!

She grabbed a handful of fanny flab, said a small prayer, and braced herself for the cold, steel reality of the Toledo.

Michael's Shocker

LUNCH FOR MONA AND MICHAEL CONSISTED OF TWO cheesedogs and an order of fries at The Noble Frankfurter on Polk Street.

"I should have changed my nail polish," said Mona.

"Beg pardon, ma'am?"

"Green nail polish at a weenie stand is not Divine Decadence. It's just plain tacky."

Michael laughed. "It's very *Grey Gardens,* actually. It makes you look shabby genteel."

"Well, you're half right. We are bordering on financial embarrassment, Mouse. My unemployment check will not keep us living in the style to which we have become accustomed."

She was only half kidding, and Michael knew it.

"Mona . . . I signed up with an agency this week. They might be coming up with a waiter's job for me really soon. I don't want you to think I'm just sitting around on my ass mooching off . . ."

"I know, Michael. Really. I was just thinking out loud. It's just that we're already a month behind on the rent, and I feel funny about Mrs. Madrigal. She'll overlook it . . . but she's gotta pay taxes and all, and I . . ."

"Aha!" said Michael, raising a french fry as an exclamation point. "I haven't told you about my instant cash plan yet!"

"God. Am I ready for this?"

"A hundred bucks, Babycakes! In one night!" He popped the french fry into his mouth. "Think you can handle that?"

"Won't it get a little chilly, working the corner of Powell and Geary?"

"Very funny, Wonder Woman. Do you wanna hear my plan or not?"

"Shoot."

"I, Michael Mouse Tolliver, am going to enter the jockey shorts dance contest at The Endup."

"Oh, please!"

"I'm serious, Mona."

And he was.

Across town, at Halcyon Communications, Edgar Halcyon called Beauchamp Day into his office.

"Sit down."

Beauchamp smirked. "Thank you." He was already seated.

"I think we should talk."

"Fine."

"I know you think I'm a horse's ass, but we're stuck with each other, aren't we?"

Beauchamp smiled uncomfortably. "I wouldn't exactly put . . ."

"Are you serious about this business, Beauchamp?"

"Sir?"

"Do you give a good goddamn about advertising? Is this what you want to do with your life?"

"Well, I think I've amply demonstrated . . ."

"Never mind what you've *demonstrated*, goddammit! What do you *feel*? Can you honestly stomach a lifetime of pushing pantyhose?"

The thought made Beauchamp cringe, but he knew what the answer should be. "This is my career," he said forcefully.

Edgar looked weary. "It is, is it?"

"Yes sir."

"You want my job, don't you?"

"I . . ."

"I don't *hire* men who don't want my job, Beauchamp."

Beauchamp uncrossed his legs, now totally unsettled. "Yes sir, I can understand that."

"I want to talk to you while DeDe's out of town. Are you free for drinks tonight at the club?"

"Fine. Yes sir."

"What I'm going to tell you is in strictest confidence. Do you understand that?"

"Yes sir."

The Family Myth

ANNA WAS WAITING FOR HIM AT THE SEAL ROCK INN.
"Did the desk clerk give you a funny look?"
she asked.

"No, goddammit. I've never been so insulted."

She grinned at him. "My ego's a little bruised too. I thought maybe you'd had second thoughts and run off with a nude encounter girl from Big Al's."

"I'm sorry," he said, kissing her forehead. "Beauchamp and I had a couple of drinks at the Bohemian Club. It took longer than I planned."

"What?"

"Nothing. Nothing important. Business . . . God, you look good!"

"A trick of the light." She took his arm and led him to the window. "There's the best example I know anywhere."

Beyond the dark trees, Seal Rock gleamed eerily against the ocean, white as an iceberg under the moon.

"Magic," she said, squeezing his arm.

Edgar nodded.

"That's what I mean," she winked. "In the right light, even seal shit looks good."

"Anna?"
  "Mmm?"
  "Thanks."
  "Anytime."
  "I feel . . ."
  "I know."
  "Let me finish."
  "I thought you had."
  "Will you let me be serious?"
  "Not for a second."
  "I love you, Anna."
  "Then we're even, O.K.?"
  "O.K."

She leaned on her elbow and studied his face. "I'll bet you don't even know where your name came from?"
  "Something to do with birds, right?"
  "You know the legend?"
  "I heard it once, but I've forgotten it. Tell it to me, why don't you?"
  "All right. Once upon a time there was a just and peaceful ruler named Ceyx, who reigned over the kingdom of Thessaly. Ceyx was married to Halcyone, daughter of Aeolus, keeper of the winds. . . ."
  "Where in God's name did you learn all this?"
  "Margaret used to read to me from *Bulfinch's Mythology.*"
  "Margaret?"
  "At the Blue Moon Lodge. The lady who got first crack at you. Stop interrupting now."
  "Sorry."
  "Anyway, Ceyx went off on a sea voyage to consult an oracle because his brother had died and he was convinced

that the gods had it in for him. Halcyone, on the other hand, had a terrible premonition that Ceyx would die during the voyage and begged him not to go."

"But he went anyway, of course."

"Of course. He was a busy executive, and she was an hysterical female. Naturally, there was a godawful storm and Ceyx was killed. Halcyone found his body several days later, floating offshore at the very spot where he had set sail."

"Delightful."

Anna pressed her fingers to his mouth. "Here comes the sweet part. Suddenly, Halcyone was transformed into a beautiful bird. She flew to her lover's body and lighted on his chest, and instantly he became a bird, and Aeolus decreed that for one week each winter the seas would be calm, so that the halcyon birds could build their nest on a raft of twigs and hatch their young and live happily ever after."

"That's nice," said Edgar, looking up at her. "My father had more imagination than I gave him credit for."

"You just lost me."

"He made up the name. The real one was Halstein."

"Why on earth?"

Edgar smiled and kissed her. "He wanted to be a Bohemian, I guess."

DeDe Triumphs

SUBMERGED IN FOUR FEET OF WARM WATER, DEDE HAL-cyon Day gripped a volleyball uneasily between her knees.

"Stay there," she muttered, gritting her teeth. Twice in ten minutes she had torpedoed the movie star exercising next to her.

The movie star smiled gamely, indicating no hard feelings. "It's a bitch, isn't it? I feel like I've got the *Hindenburg* between my legs."

Somehow still clutching the volleyball, DeDe went through her gyrations again, swinging her arms frenetically above her head. Every muscle in her body was screaming in pain.

"Stretch it!" shouted the instructress at the edge of the pool. "Strrrreeetch that gorgeous body."

"Gorgeous?" groaned the movie star. "My ass is so water-logged it looks like a Sunsweet prune."

DeDe grinned at her companion, delighting in the earthiness of a woman who had always seemed larger than life on the screen. Up close, the tracheotomy scar at the base of her neck testified to her mortality.

But her eyes *were* violet.

This was her second week at The Golden Door. For six rigorous days she had driven her body to its limits, rising at six forty-five to flop about the countryside in a pale-pink sweatsuit, her face stripped of makeup, her hair drab and icky in a thick coat of Vaseline. It was murder, but she was getting there.

Wasn't she?

Well, at least she *felt* better. Breakfast in bed was enhanced by the fact that she actually looked forward to her nine o'clock Leonardo da Vinci exercises. Then there was the Jump for Joy session and the morning facial and yoga and a Kneipp Herbal Wrap and . . . goddammit, something *must* have been happening!

At twilight, she would soak in the fan-shaped whirlpool bath, giggling happily with the movie star and half a dozen other members of the elite sisterhood. She felt like a girl again, placid and simple and whole. Her pride had returned, and somehow, miraculously, so had her self-control. Not once, but twice, she had talked the movie star out of leading a raid on the orange grove.

She was over the hump now.

The old DeDe—the pre-Beauchamp DeDe—was running her life again, and it felt damn good!

"God, I can't believe it!"

"If it's good," the movie star scowled, "I *don't* wanna hear it."

DeDe stepped off the scales, then on again, fiddling with the weights. "Look at that, would you? Would you just look at that? Eighteen pounds! I've lost eighteen pounds in two weeks!"

"That's abnormal. You should see a doctor."

"It's a miracle!"

"What the hell do you expect for three grand?" The movie star gave up the tough façade and burst into a radiant smile, enveloping DeDe in her still flabby arms. "Oh, I hope it makes you happy, DeDe!"

For a moment, DeDe thought she would cry. Here was this idol—this goddess—and *she* was envious of DeDe! Nobody at home would ever believe it!

They would simply have to believe their eyes.

She felt like a different woman on the flight from San Diego to San Francisco.

Her skin was tanned and glowing, her eyes danced with self-esteem. Her peach-colored T-shirt clung to her waist— her waist!—as if she had nothing to hide.

In the seat next to her, an aggressive sailor made inane conversation about "Frisco," boring her with endless details about his tour of duty on Treasure Island.

It didn't matter. She was enjoying the warm friction of his leg against hers. She felt deliciously single, free from Beauchamp's petty intrigues and the dreary quagmire of her marriage.

Well, why shouldn't she? Beauchamp hadn't missed her. She was sure of that. And she sure as hell hadn't missed *him*. Period.

Period?

Dear God. She had missed her period.

Boris Steps In

O N A WARM AUTUMN SATURDAY AT BARBARY LANE, Mary Ann stretched lazily in bed, savoring the musk from the eucalyptus tree outside her window.

A fat, tiger-striped cat lumbered into view along the window ledge, scratching its back against the open sash. Bored with that exercise, it took several half-hearted swats at the stained-glass butterfly hanging from the curtain rod.

Mary Ann grinned and tossed a pillow at the cat. "Boris . . . don't!"

Boris accepted the gesture as an invitation to play. He landed with a muffled plop on Mary Ann's mock flokati and sauntered in the direction of the bed.

"Lucky ol' Boris," said Mary Ann, scratching the cat behind his ears. Boris, she couldn't help thinking, was beautiful, independent and loved. He belonged to no one in particular (at least, no one at 28 Barbary Lane), but he moved freely through a wide circle of benefactors and friends.

Why couldn't *she* do that?

She was sick and tired of being dumped on—romantically, emotionally and every other way. Wasn't it time to take control of her life again? To deal with her problems directly and experience each moment to the fullest?

Yes! She bounded out of bed, startling Boris, and twirled around the room on her toes. God, what a day! Here in this magical city, here on this storybook lane! Where little cable cars climb halfway to the stars and cats crawl in your window and the butcher speaks French and . . .

Boris darted past her, intent on avoiding this lunatic altogether.

He raced through the living room, only to find the front door closed.

"You want out, Boris? Is that what you want, baby?" Mary Ann opened the door for him, instantly recognizing the folly of that decision. Boris sped down the hallway and sought the protection of elevation by heading up the stairway to the roof.

The house on the roof.

Downstairs on the second floor, Michael was serving Mona breakfast in bed: poached eggs, nine-grain toast, Italian roast coffee and French sausages from Marcel & Henri. When he set the tray on the bed, he was whistling "What I Did for Love."

"Well," said Mona, grinning at him, "a little nookie does you a world of good."

"You said it, Babycakes!"

"Where's Jon? Ask him in. We can all have breakfast together."

"He's at home. I stayed there last night."

"You little dip! Did you come all the way back here to fix me breakfast?"

"I have to drop off my laundry too."

"Drop off your laundry, my ass!"

"Sorry. Mr. Lee only does shirts and sheets." He leaned over and kissed her on the forehead. "O.K. . . . So I missed you a little."

Michael's evening had begun at a cocktail party given by *After Dark* magazine at the Stanford Court. "What can I tell you, Mona? It was sheer piss-elegance!"

Next to "affairette," "piss-elegance" was Michael's favorite word.

"Jon got the invitation, actually. I didn't know a soul . . . unless you count Tab Hunter, of course."

"Of course."

"He looked damn good for forty-five, and I kinda wanted to talk to him, but he was *surrounded* by GQ types, and what the hell do you say to Tab Hunter, anyway? 'Hi, I'm Michael Tolliver, and I always liked you better than Sandra Dee'?"

"It doesn't read. You're right."

"Sooo . . . I gorged myself on pizza canapés and did my best to avoid the guy from Brebner's who once told me I was too average-looking to make it as a model."

"Poor Mouse!"

"Well, he was right! Christ, Mona, you should have *seen* the beauties in that room! There was so much hair spray they probably had to make an Environmental Impact Report before they could hold the party!"

"Is the plan still on?" Mona asked after breakfast.

"What plan?"

"The jockey shorts dance contest."

"I've been practicing all *week,* woman. You're coming, aren't you? It's tomorrow at five-thirty."

"What the hell for?"

"I don't know . . . moral support, I guess."

"Jon'll go with you."

"No. I'd rather Jon didn't know about this, Mona."

"O.K.," she said quietly. "I'll go."

Renewing Vows

BEAUCHAMP WAS WAITING FOR HER AT THE PSA TERMI-nal, surrounded by stewardesses in pink-and-orange mini-skirts. When DeDe caught his eye, he smiled phosphorescently and pushed his way through the crowd to her side.

He was deeply tanned, and his eyes danced with genuine surprise.

"You look great!" he beamed. "God, you're a new person!"

It's possible, she thought, that I am *two* new people. But even that prospect couldn't dim the triumph she felt at Beauchamp's reaction.

She had planned on being cool with him, but one look at his face melted her Catherine Deneuve icicle.

"It wasn't easy," she said finally.

Then he crushed her in his arms and kissed her passionately on the mouth. "I swear to God I've missed you!" he said, burying his face in her hair.

It was almost more than she could take. Was *this* what he had needed all along? Two weeks alone in the city. Enough time to put things in perspective, to discover what she had meant to him.

Or was he simply intrigued by her new body?

On the way back to Telegraph Hill he briefed her on the fortnight she had missed.

The family was fine. Mother had spent several days at the house in St. Helena, catching up on correspondence while Faust received treatment from the family vet. Daddy seemed in good spirits. He and Beauchamp had chatted amiably over drinks. Several times.

DeDe smiled at that. "He really likes you, Beauchamp."

"I know."

"I'm glad you got a chance to talk . . . man to man, I mean."

"So am I. DeDe?"

"Uh huh?"

"Is there anything I can do to let you know I still love you?"

She turned to study his profile, as if uncertain that the words had come from him at all. His hair was swept back in the wind; his eyes were fixed firmly on the freeway. Only his mouth, boyishly vulnerable, betrayed the turmoil within.

DeDe reached over and placed her hand gently on his thigh.

Beauchamp continued. "Do you know when I missed you the most?"

"Beauchamp, you don't need . . . When?"

"In the morning. Those few terrible moments between sleeping and waking when you're not sure where you are or even *why* you are. I missed you then. I *needed* you then, DeDe."

She squeezed his thigh. "I'm glad."

"I want to make things better between us."

"We'll see."

"I *do*, DeDe. I'm going to try. I promise you."

"I know."

"You don't believe me, do you?"

"I *want* to, Beauchamp."

"I don't blame you. I'm an asshole."

"Beauchamp . . ."

"I am. I'm an asshole. But I'll make it up to you, I promise."

"A day at a time, O.K.?"

"Right. A day at a time."

At Halcyon Hill a dying sun slipped behind the trees as Frannie strolled in the garden with her only confidante.

"I don't know what's happened to Edgar," she said, sipping disconsolately at her Mai Tai. "He used to care about things . . . about us. . . . You know, it's funny, but when Eddie was in France during the war, I used to miss him terribly. He wasn't *with* me, but he was, you know. . . . Now he's with me, but he's not . . . and goddammit, I like missing him the other way more!"

Her eyes were brimming with tears now, but she didn't brush them away. She was lost in another time, when loneliness wasn't barren but beautiful, when snapshots and love letters and the honeyed voice of Bing Crosby had eased her gently through the most difficult winter of her life.

But now it was summer, and Bing lived just over the next hill. Why hadn't things worked out?

"'I'm . . . dreammminnngg . . . of a . . . whiiite . . . Chrissssmusss . . . juss like the ones I usssse to know . . . '"

Her tears kept her from finishing. "I'm sorry," she whimpered to her companion. "I shouldn't burden you with this, baby. You're *so* patient . . . so good. . . . If it weren't for you, baby, I'd be like Helen . . . yes, I would . . . lunching with her *decorator,* for God's sake! C'mon. There's a teensy-weensy little bit of Mai Tai left in the pitcher."

She poured some Mai Tai into a large plastic bowl on the terrace.

Faust, her Great Dane, lapped it up with relish.

The Man on the Roof

BORIS' TAIL MARKED TIME LIKE A METRONOME AS HE sped down the hallway and up the stairs to the roof. Mary Ann slipped into her bathrobe and set off in pursuit of the unofficial tenant, fearful that he might get trapped in the building.

The steps to the roof were uncarpeted, painted with dark-green deck enamel. At the top, next to an ivy-choked window, a bright-orange door blocked the cat's escape. Boris was indignant.

"Here, kitty . . . come on, Boris . . . nice Boris. . . ."

Boris was having none of it. He stood fast, answering her with a terse saber rattle of his tail.

Mary Ann climbed higher, now less than a yard away from the door. "You really are a *pain,* Boris! You know that, don't you?"

The door banged open, grazing Boris's side, sending the startled cat bounding down the steps with a howl. Mary Ann stiffened.

Before her stood a large, middle-aged man.

"Sorry," he said uncomfortably. "I didn't hear you out here. I hope I didn't hurt your cat."

She struggled to regain her composure. "No . . . I don't think so. . . ."

"He's a nice-looking cat."

"Oh . . . he's not my cat. He sort of belongs to everybody. I think he lives down at the end of the lane. I'm sorry . . . I didn't mean to intrude."

The man looked concerned. "I scared you, didn't I?"

"It's O.K."

He smiled, extending his hand. "I'm Norman Neal Williams."

"Hi." She returned his shake, noticing how huge his hand was. Somehow, though, his size made him seem especially vulnerable.

He was wearing baggy gray suit pants and a short-sleeved drip-dry shirt. A little tuft of dark-brown hair spilled over the top of his clip-on four-in-hand tie.

"You live just below, don't you?"

"Yeah . . . oh, sorry . . . I'm Mary Ann Singleton."

"Three names."

"Excuse me?"

"Mary Ann Singleton. Three names. Like Norman Neal Williams."

"Oh . . . do you go by Norman Neal?"

"No. Just Norman."

"I see."

"I like to say Norman Neal Williams first off, because it flows nice, you know."

"Yes, it does."

"Would you like some coffee?"

"Oh, thanks, but I've got lots of things . . ."

"The view's real nice."

That got her. She *did* want to see his view, as well as the layout of the Lilliputian rooftop house.

"O.K.," she smiled. "I'd love to."

The view was dazzling. White sails on a delft-blue bay. Angel Island, wreathed in fog, faraway and mystical as Bali Ha'i.

Wheeling gulls over red tile rooftops.

"That's what you pay for," he said, obviously apologizing for the size of the place. There was nowhere to sit but the bed and a kitchen chair next to the window facing the bay. The coat to his suit was folded over the back of the chair.

Mary Ann sighed at the panorama. "You must *love* getting up in the morning."

"Yeah. Except I'm not here that much."

"Oh."

"I'm a salesman."

"I see."

"Vitamins." He indicated a carrying case in the corner of the room. Mary Ann recognized the company logo.

"Oh . . . Nutri-Vim. I've heard of those."

"Completely organic."

She was sure his enthusiasm was strictly professional. There was nothing about Norman Neal Williams that struck her as organic.

The Ol'-Time Religion

O N SUNDAY MORNING, MONA WENT TO CHURCH.
In the old days—post-Woodstock and pre-
Watergate—she had gone to church a lot. Not
just *any* church, she was quick to point out, but
a *People's* church, a church that was Relevant.
That was a long time ago. She'd had it with the People, and
Relevance was as obsolete as puka shells. Still, there was
something nostalgically *comfortable* about returning to Glibb
Memorial.

Maybe it was the light show or the rock ensemble . . . or the
Afro-aphrodisia of the Reverend Willy Sessums, bojangling
the bejeezus out of Third World Socialism.

Or maybe it was the Quaalude she took at breakfast.

Whatever.

Today she felt mellow. Together. A karmic cog in the great,
swaying mechanism of Glibb Memorial. She sang out with the
fervor of a Southern Baptist, flanked by a Noe Valley wood
butcher and a Tenderloin drag queen in a coral prom gown.

He's got the Yoo-nited Farm Workers
In His hands!
He's got the Yoo-nited Farm Workers
In His hands!

"That's right!" shouted Reverend Sessums, darting through his flock with a leather pouch full of black juju dust. "Chairman Jesus loves you, brother! And he loves you too, sister!"

He was talking to Mona. *Directly* to her. He smiled radiantly and embraced her, sprinkling her with juju dust.

Even with the Quaalude, Mona stiffened. She hated herself for it, for the cynicism that cloaked her embarrassment over anything personal. She wanted him to go away.

He would not.

"Do you hear me, sister?"

She nodded, smiling feebly.

"Chairman Jesus loves you! He loves all of us! The black and the brown and the yellow and the white . . . and the lavender!" The last color was directed to the man in the prom gown.

Mona looked at the drag queen, praying that Sessums had shifted his focus.

He had not.

"If you believe Willy . . . if you believe that Chairman Jesus loves you more than oil companies, more than Big Business and Male Chauvinists and the House Armed Services Committee . . . if you believe that, sister, then let ol' Willy hear a 'Right on!' "

Mona swallowed. "Right on," she said.

"What's that, sister?"

"Right on."

"Make it *loud,* sister, so Chairman Jesus can hear you!"

"Right on!"

"Awwwwwwwriiiight! You're *beautiful,* sister!" He began to sway and clap to the music again, winking privately at Mona like a nightclub comedian who had just had harmless fun at her expense.

The band broke into "Love Will Keep Us Together" as Sessums moved on.

"This is to die over," said the drag queen, recognizing the song. "Don't you absolutely *adore* the Captain and Tennille?"

Mona nodded, collecting herself.

Her fellow churchgoer fumbled in his purse and produced a bullet-shaped inhaler. He handed it to her.

"Have a popper, honey."

After church, she drove back to Barbary Lane and fell into a black, contemplative mood.

She was thirty-one years old. She needed a job. She was living with a man who might leave her at any moment for another man. Her mother in Minneapolis had somehow lost the power to communicate with her.

Her only *real* guardian was Anna Madrigal, and the landlady's interest had recently assumed an intensity that made her nervous.

Seeds and stems, seeds and stems.

The phone rang.

"Yeah?"

"Mona?"

"Right."

"This is D'orothea."

"Jesus. Where are you?"

"Here. In town. Are you glad?"

"Of course, I'm . . . Are you on vacation?"

"Nope. This is it. I did it. I'm here for good. Can I see you?"

"I . . . sure."

"Try not to sound so ecstatic."

"I'm just a little surprised, D'or. What about lunch tomorrow?"

"I was hoping for dinner tonight."

"I can't, D'or. I'm going to . . . a dance contest."

"Good reason."

"I'll tell you about it tomorrow."

"What time?"

"Noon? Here?"

"Twenty-eight Barbary Lane?"

"Yeah . . . O.K.?"

"I've missed the hell out of you, Mona."

"I've missed you too, D'or."

Child's Play

ARY ANN STOPPED BY MONA'S JUST BEFORE NOON. She was wearing what Michael referred to as her "Lauren Hutton drag."

Levi's and a pink button-down shirt from the boys' department at Brooks Brothers . . . with a pale-blue crew-neck sweater knotted cavalierly around her neck.

"Hi," she chirped. "Do you guys feel like brunch at Mama's?"

Mona shook her head. "Michael's not eating. The big contest is tonight, and he thinks he's fat."

"Where is he?"

"Down in the courtyard . . . bronzing his fat."

Mary Ann laughed. "What about you, then?"

"Thanks. I think I'll pass."

"Are you . . . O.K., Mona?"

"Don't I look it?"

"Sure . . . I didn't mean . . . You look . . . distracted, that's all."

Mona shrugged and looked out the window. "I just hope it's not terminal."

*　*　*

The line at Mama's snaked out of the building and up Stockton Street. Mary Ann was considering alternative brunch spots when a familiar figure in the crowd signaled her sheepishly.

"Oh . . . hi, Norman."

"Hello. I've been saving your spot." He winked at her rather obviously, fooling no one around him. Mary Ann slipped into the line behind him.

A little girl tugged on Norman's leg. "Who's she?" she asked.

Norman smiled. "She's a friend, Lexy."

"Well," said Mary Ann, looking down at the child. "Where did *you* come from?"

"My mommy."

Mary Ann giggled. "She's *precious,* Norman. Does she belong to you?"

Before he could answer, the child reached up and tugged at Mary Ann's sweater. "Are you breaking in line?"

"Well, I . . ."

Norman laughed. "Alexandra . . . this is Mary Ann Singleton. We live in the same building . . . right up there on that big hill." He winked at Mary Ann. "She belongs to some friends of mine in San Leandro. Sometimes I give them a breather on Sundays."

"That's sweet."

Norman shrugged. "I don't mind. I get the best of both worlds." He tugged playfully on one of the child's braids. "Isn't that right, Lexy?"

"What?"

"Never mind. Tell ya later."

"Can I feed the pigeons, Norman?"

"After breakfast, O.K.?"

Mary Ann knelt down in front of the child. "That's a *beautiful* dress, Alexandra!"

The child stared at her, then giggled.

"Do you know what it's called, Alexandra?"

"What?"

"Your dress. It's called a Heidi dress. Can you say that?"

Alexandra looked slightly put out. "This is a *dirndl,*" she said flatly.

"Oh, well . . ." Mary Ann stood up, grinning at Norman. "I asked for that, didn't I?"

The trio dined on omelets at Mama's. Alexandra ate in silence, studying Mary Ann.

Afterwards, in Washington Square, the grownups talked, while Alexandra chased pigeons in the sunshine.

"She's very bright, isn't she?"

Norman nodded. "She gives me a complex sometimes."

"Have you known her parents long?"

"About . . . oh, five years. Her father and I were in Vietnam together."

"Oh . . . I'm sorry."

"Why?"

"Well . . . Vietnam . . . It must have been awful."

He smiled, holding up his arms. "No wounds, see? I was a chief yeoman in Saigon. Office job. Navy intelligence."

"How did you get interested in vitamins?"

He shrugged. "I got interested in making a living."

"I see."

"I'm afraid there's nothing very interesting about me, Mary Ann."

"Oh, no . . . I think you're very . . . ."

"There's a movie I'd like you to see tonight, if you haven't already. . . ."

"What is it?"

"An oldie. *Detective Story.* Kirk Douglas and Eleanor Parker."

"I'd love to," she said.

What Are Friends For?

BEAUCHAMP AND DEDE SPENT A LEISURELY SUNDAY morning in Sausalito, brunching at the Altamira.

They were a pair again, a matched set—bronzed and blooded and beautiful. People looked at them with hungry eyes, whispering speculations over Ramos fizzes in the brilliant sunlight of the hotel terrace.

And DeDe loved every minute of it.

"Beauchamp?"

"Mmm?" His eyes were *exactly* the color of the bay.

"Last night was . . . better than our wedding night."

"I know."

"Was it . . . ? Is it me that's changed, or you?"

"Does it matter?"

"It does to me. A little."

Beauchamp shrugged. "I guess I've . . . sorted out my priorities."

"It confuses me a little, Beauchamp."

"Why?"

"I don't know. Things are . . . working now and . . . well, I just wanna know what I'm doing right, so I can keep on doing it."

He rubbed his knee against hers. "Just keep being yourself, O.K.?"

"O.K.," she smiled.

Back at Montgomery Street, Beauchamp clipped a leash on the corgi. "I think I'll take Caesar up to the Tower. Feel like a walk?"

"Thanks. I should catch up on my letters."

As soon as he had gone she called Binky Gruen.

"Bink?"

"DeDe?"

"I'm back."

"Well?"

"Well, what?"

"How much, dummy? How much did you lose?"

"Oh . . . eighteen pounds."

Binky whistled. "That sounds like anorexia to me!"

"Binky, I need . . ."

"I am *convinced,* by the way, that Shugie Sussman has anorexia. I mean, there's no doubt in my mind. She's wasting away to *nothing,* and nobody can persuade her that she isn't *obese.* It's too tragic, DeDe. We may have to ship the poor thing off to the Menninger Clinic in a Manila envelope!"

"Binky, as much as I'd like to hear about Shugie Sussman . . ."

"Sorry, darling. Did you have a marvelous time? I mean, aside from those godawful Leonardo da Vinci exer . . . ?"

"I need your help, Binky."

"Sure."

"I . . . need a doctor."

"Oh, God! You *are* sick! Jesus, I am such a . . ."

"No, not sick. I just need a doctor."

"Oh."

"I was thinking about the one you saw last spring."

"Uh oh."

"It isn't an item yet. I'm not sure. I'd just feel better if . . ."

"It may have been the exercise, DeDe. Sometimes a physi-

215

cal change like that can screw up your cycle."

"I've considered that."

"Hell, it could even be anorexia."

"Will you *stop?* It could be almost anything. I just want . . ."

"Almost anything but Beauchamp, huh?"

Silence.

"You want a gynecologist who doesn't know the family, right?"

"Yes."

"O.K. This guy's a prince. Gentle, discreet and a *treat* to look at. Got a pencil?"

"Yeah."

"Jon Fielding. The Jon doesn't have an *h.* He's at 450 Sutter. You can tell him I sent you."

The Beach Boys

MRS. MADRIGAL'S TENANTS HAD DUBBED THAT COR-
ner of the courtyard "Barbary Beach."

Well, thought Michael, spreading his towel
on the bricks, it ain't Sunday at Lake Temescal,
but it'll have to do.

In less than seven hours he would be on the platform at
The Endup.

He needed all the rays he could get.

"Hi," said a voice somewhere between him and the sun.

He looked up, shielding his eyes. It was the guy from the
third floor. Brian something. He was carrying a towel im-
printed with a Coors label.

"Hi. Come on in. The water's fine."

Brian nodded and tossed his towel on the ground. Five feet
away, Michael noted. Close, but not *too* close. A perfect HBU.
Hunky But Uptight.

"Think it's worth it?" asked Brian.

"Probably not, but what the hell? Who are we to disappoint

all those *other* pink bodies in the bars?"

Brian laughed, obviously catching the irony of the remark. O.K., thought Michael, he knows we're not heading for the same bars. Much less the same bodies. Still . . . he knows, and he knows that I know he knows. It's O.K.

"You're Brian, and I'm Michael. Right?"

"Right."

They shook hands, still on their bellies, reaching out over the void in order to touch.

Michael laughed. "We look like something off the ceiling of the Sistine Chapel!"

Fifteen minutes later, Michael felt like talking again.

"You're single, right?"

"Yeah."

"This must be a great town to be single in. I mean . . . for a straight guy."

"Oh?"

"Well, I mean . . . there are so many gay guys that a straight guy must be a hot property with the women. At least . . . you know what I mean."

Brian grunted. He was on his back now, his hands folded behind his head. "I spent four fucking hours at Slater Hawkins last night, trying to plug a chick I wouldn't have sneezed at in college."

"Yeah," said Michael, somewhat jarred by the remark. "It kinda gets to be a game, doesn't it? Unwrapping the package is more fun than the package itself. At least, sometimes . . ." He looked over at Brian, wondering if they were communicating at all. "Do you know Mary Ann Singleton?"

"Yeah."

"Well, Mary Ann and I had this really heavy session where she told me she wanted to go back to Cleveland, and I gave her the whole est trip about taking control of her life and all . . . but the creepy thing is that sometimes I think she's right. Maybe we should all go back to Cleveland."

"Yeah. Or go live in a farm town in Utah or something. Get back to basics."

"Uh huh. I have that one too. A mountain village in Colorado, maybe, with just the bare essentials. One nice French restaurant and a branch of Design Research."

They both laughed. Michael felt instantly more comfortable with him.

"The thing that bugs me," said Brian, "is that you never really know what women are like . . . not for a long time, anyway. They only show you what they want you to see."

Michael nodded. "So you fantasize over all the wrong things."

"Yeah." Brian began to tear blades of grass from between the bricks.

"Christ! That happens to me all the time," said Michael. "I meet some person . . . male-type . . . at a bar or the baths, and he seems really . . . what I want. A nice mustache, Levi's, a starched khaki army shirt . . . strong . . . Somebody you could take back to Orlando and they'd never know the difference.

"Then you go home with him to his house on Upper Market, and you try like hell not to go to the bathroom, because the bathroom is the giveaway, the fantasy-killer. . . ."

Brian looked confused.

"It's the bathroom cabinet," Michael explained. "Face creams and shampoos for *days*. And on the top of the toilet tank they've all always got one of those goddamn little gold pedestals full of colored soap balls!"

Ebony Idol

THE BLACK WOMAN ATE SUNDAY DINNER ALONE IN THE back room at Perry's.

She was an image of grace and sophistication, dark and sleek as a patent-leather dancing slipper. She was avoiding her french fries, Brian noticed, and her eyes seldom wandered from her plate.

"More coffee?"

She looked up and smiled. Wistfully, he thought. She shook her head and said, "Thanks." She was devastating.

"What about dessert?"

Another no.

O.K., he thought, so much for the standard conversation ploys. It's time for the heavy-duty back-up patter.

"Didn't like the french fries, huh?"

She patted her tiny waist. "I'm allergic to them. They look wonderful, though."

"One or two won't hurt you."

"I've never seen round ones like that. They look like potato chips with a thyroid condition."

He chuckled manfully. *Now* we're getting somewhere, kiddo. But keep it loose as a goose. Nothing heavy. And move slow, for God's sake, move slow. . . .

She folded her napkin across her plate. Shit! She was going to ask for her check!

She smiled again. "May I . . . ?"

"Do you know you look exactly like Lola Falana?"

Subtle as shit. If *that* didn't scare her off, nothing would.

Her face didn't change, though. She was still smiling. "You want to buy me a drink, don't you?"

"Uh . . . yeah, as a matter of fact."

"What time do you get off work?"

"Ten o'clock."

"It's a date, then?"

"You bet. My name is Brian."

"I'm D'orothea," she said.

Across town at The Endup, Michael Tolliver threaded his way through a forest of Lacoste shirts. Mona was with him.

"Well, this clinches it, Mouse."

"What?"

"I am *definitely* a fag hag."

"Oh, for Christ's sake!"

"Look around the goddamn room, would you? I'm the only woman here!"

Michael grabbed her shoulder, spinning her around to face the bar. A robust-looking woman in Levi's and a work shirt was tending bar. "Feel better now?"

"Terrific. Look . . . are you gonna change or what?"

"I think I'm supposed to register. Will you be all right if I leave you here?"

"Probably. Goddammit." She winked and slapped him on the behind. "Give my regards to Bert Parks."

The bartender directed Michael to a man in charge of registration. The man took Michael's name and vital statistics and issued him a numbered paper plate on a string.

He was Number 7.

"Where do I . . . uh . . . change?"

"In the ladies' room."

"Figures."

There were already three guys in the ladies' room. Two of them had stripped down to their jockey shorts and were placing their clothes in plastic bags provided by the management. The third was smoking a joint, still decked out in recycled Vietnam fatigues.

"Hi," said Michael, nodding to his fellow gladiators.

They smiled back at him, some with more calculation than others. They reminded him of his competition in the 1966 Orlando High School Science Fair. Artifically flippant. And hungry for victory.

Well, he thought, a hundred bucks is a hundred bucks.

"Can we . . . are we supposed to stay in here until our turn comes up?"

A blond in Mark Spitz briefs smiled at Michael's naïveté. "I don't know about you, honey, but I'm gonna mingle. They might be giving out a Miss Congeniality award."

So Michael slipped into the crowd, wearing only his paper plate and the jockey shorts he had bought at Macy's the day before.

Mona rolled her eyes when she saw him.

"It'll pay the rent," said Michael.

"Don't get too cocky. I think I just saw Arnold Schwarzenegger come out of the ladies' room."

"You're such a comfort, Mona."

She snapped the elastic in his shorts. "You'll do all right, kid."

D'orothea's Lament

A S ARRANGED, BRIAN MET HER AT THE WASHINGTON Square Bar & Grill.

She was draped decoratively against the bar, brown eyes ablaze with interest as she chatted with Charles McCabe. The columnist seemed equally fascinated.

"You know him?" asked Brian, when she broke away to join him.

"I just met him."

"You work fast, don't you?"

She gave him a playful shove. "Haven't you figured *that* out yet?"

D'orothea was a model, he learned. She had worked in New York for five years, peddling her polished onyx features to *Vogue* and *Harper's,* Clovis Ruffin and Stephen Burrows and "everybody else who was hopping on the Afro bandwagon."

She had made money, she admitted, and lots of it. "Which ain't half bad for a girl who grew up in Oakland B.A."

"B.A.?" asked Brian.

She smiled. "Before Apostrophe. I used to be Dorothy Wilson until Eileen Ford turned it into Dorothea and stuck an apostrophe between the *D* and the *o.*" She arched an eyebrow dramatically. "Verrry chic, don't you think?"

"I think Dorothy was good enough."

"Well, so did I, honey! But it was either the apostrophe or one of those godawful African names like Simbu or Tamara or Bonzo, and I'd be goddamned if I'd go around town sounding like Ronald Reagan's chimpanzee!"

Brian laughed, noticing that her face was even more beautiful when animated. He was silent for several seconds, then asked soberly: "Was it tough growing up in Oakland?"

She did a slow take, staring at him through heavy-lidded eyes. "Oh . . . I get it! A lib-ber-rull!"

He reddened. "No, not exact . . ."

"Gimme a hint, then. A Vista Volunteer, maybe? A civil rights lawyer?"

Her accuracy annoyed the hell out of him. "I did some work for the Urban League in Chicago, but I don't see what that . . ."

"And all that guilt exhausted you so much that you decided to hell with it and chucked it all for a waiter's job. I hear you, baby. I hear you."

He downed his drink. "I don't think you're hearing a goddamn thing but your own voice."

She set down her glass of Dubonnet and stared at him expressionlessly. "I'm sorry," she said softly. "I guess I'm nervous about being back here."

"Forget it."

"You have a nice face, Brian. I need somebody to talk to."

"A therapist."

"If you like. Does that bother you?"

"I'd hoped for something more basic."

She ignored the implication. "Sometimes it helps to tell things to strangers."

He signaled the bartender for another drink. "Go ahead, then. The doctor is in."

She told her story without embellishment, seldom meeting his eyes.

"Four years ago, when I was just beginning to catch on in New York, I met this person who was working on a swimsuit campaign at J. Walter Thompson. We were together almost all the time, shooting at locations all over the East Coast. It took us about three weeks to fall in love."

Brian nodded, abandoning his hopes.

"Anyway, we moved in together, fixing up this wonderful loft in SoHo, and I experienced the happiest six months of my life. Then something happened . . . I don't know what . . . and my lover accepted a job in San Francisco. We corresponded some after that, never completely losing touch, and I just kept on . . . making money."

She sipped her Dubonnet and looked at him for the first time. "Now I'm back home, Brian, and all I want is to have this person back in my life again. But that's completely up to . . ."

"Her."

She smiled warmly. "You're quick," she said.

"Thanks."

"This drink's on me, O.K.?"

The Winner's Circle

THE MASTER OF CEREMONIES FOR THE JOCKEY SHORTS dance contest was someone called Luscious Lorelei. His platinum wig hovered over his rotund frame like a mushroom cloud over an atoll.

Michael groaned and readjusted his shorts. "What the fuck am I doing here, Mona? I used to be a Future Farmer of America!"

"You're paying the rent, remember?"

"Right. I'm paying the rent, I'm paying the rent. *This* is a recording. . . ."

"Just take it easy."

"What if I lose? What if they laugh? Jesus! What if they don't even *notice* me?"

"You're not gonna lose, Mouse. Those assholes can't dance, and you look better than any of 'em. You've gotta believe in yourself!"

"Thank you, Norman Vincent Peale."

"Cool it, Mouse."

"I think I'm gonna throw up."

"Save it for the finale."

*   *   *

Five contestants had already vied for the hundred-dollar prize. Another was competing now, thrashing across the plastic dance floor in nylon leopard-skin briefs.

The crowd howled its approval.

"Listen to that, Mona. It's all over." Michael chided himself silently for selecting the standard white jockey briefs. This mob obviously went in for flash.

"C'mon," said Mona, pulling him through the crowd to the edge of the dance floor. "You're next, Mouse." She stayed by his side as they waited in the glow of an electrified American flag.

Luscious Lorelei moved to the microphone when the applause for Contestant Number 6 had subsided. "How about that, guys? Could you *BUHLIEVE* the pecs on that humpy number? I mean, *PULLEASE*, Mary!" He gripped the contours of his sequined bosom. "Rice bags never looked so good."

Michael felt the color leave his face.

"Call Mary Ann," he whispered to Mona. "I'm going back to Cleveland with her." Mona reassured him with a pat on the rump.

"O.K.," bellowed Lorelei, "our next contestant is . . . Contestant Number 7! He hails from Orlando, Florida, where the sun shines bright and they grow all those *BEEYOOTIFUL* fruits, and his name is Michael . . . Michael Something . . . Honey, I can't read your handwriting. If you're out there, how 'bout telling Lorelei your name?"

Michael raised his hand half-heartedly and said, "Tolliver."

"What, honey?"

"Michael Tolliver."

"OKAAY! Let's hear it for Michael Oliver!"

Now bright red, Michael climbed onto the dance platform as Lorelei slipped back into the darkness. The revelers at the bar turned in unison to assess the newcomer. The music began. It was Dr. Buzzard's Original Savannah Band doing "Cherchez la Femme."

Michael slipped his body into gear and his mind into neutral. He moved with the music, riding its rhythm like a madman. He was merely having that dream again, that ancient high school nightmare about appearing in the senior play in his . . . jockey shorts!

His eyes unglazed long enough to see the crowd. The shining, tanned faces. The muscled necks. A hundred tiny alligators leering from a hundred chests . . .

Then his blood froze.

For there in the crowd, somber above a silk shirt and Brioni blazer, was the one face he didn't want to see. It linked with his, but only for a moment, then wrinkled with disdain and turned away.

Jon.

The music stopped. Michael leaped off the stage into the crowd, oblivious of the congratulatory hands that grazed his body. He pushed his way through a fog of amyl nitrite to the swinging doors in the corner of the room.

Jon was leaving.

Michael stood in the doorway and watched the lean figure retreat down Sixth Street. There were three other men with him, also in suits. A brief burst of laughter rose from the foursome as they climbed into a beige BMW and drove away.

An hour later, he got the news.

He had won. A hundred dollars and a gold pendant shaped like a pair of jockey shorts. Victory.

Mona kissed him on the cheek when he climbed off the platform. "Who *cares* if there's a doctor in the house?" Michael smiled wanly and held on to her arm, losing himself in the music.

Then he began to cry.

Fiasco in Chinatown

LEAVING THE GATEWAY CINEMA, MARY ANN AND NORMAN headed west up Jackson toward Chinatown.

When they reached the pagoda-shaped Chevron station at Columbus, a thick pocket of fog had begun to soften the edges of the neon.

"On nights like this," said Norman, "I feel like somebody in a Hammett story."

"Hammond?"

"Hammett. Dashiell Hammett. You know . . . *The Maltese Falcon?*"

She knew the name, but not much else. It didn't matter, however.

The only Falcon in Norman's life was parked at the corner of Jackson and Kearny.

"Do you have to get home right away?" He asked it cautiously, like a child seeking permission to stay up late.

"Well, I should . . . no. Not right away."

"Do you like Chinese food?"

"Sure," she smiled, suddenly realizing how much she liked this bumbling, kindly, Smokey the bear man with a clip-on tie. She wasn't particularly *attracted* to him, but she liked him a lot.

He took her to Sam Woh's on Washington Street, where they wriggled through the tiny kitchen, up the stairway and into a booth on the second floor.

"Brace yourself," said Norman.

"For what?"

"You'll see."

Three minutes later she made a discreet exit to the rest room. There was no sink in the cramped cabinet, and she was halfway back to the table before she discovered where it was.

"Hey, lady! Go wash yo' hands!"

Thunderstruck, she turned to see where the voice had come from. An indignant Chinese waiter was unloading plates of noodles from the dumbwaiter. She stopped in her tracks, stared at her accuser, then looked back toward the rest room.

The sink was outside the door. *In the dining room.*

A dozen diners were watching her, smirking at her discomfort. The waiter stood his ground. "Wash, lady. You don't wash, you don' eat!"

She washed, returning red-faced to the table. Norman grinned sheepishly. "I should have warned you."

"You *knew* he would do that?"

"He specializes in being rude. It's a joke. War lord-turned-waiter. People come here for it."

"Well, *I* didn't."

"I'm really sorry."

"Can we go, Norman?"

"The food's really . . ."

"Please?"

So they left.

Back in the dark canyon of Barbary Lane, he took her arm protectively.

"I'm sorry about Edsel."

"Who?"

230

"That's his name. The waiter. Edsel Ford Fung."

She giggled in spite of herself. "Really?"

"I meant it to be fun, Mary Ann."

"I know."

"I really blew it. I'm sorry."

She stopped in the courtyard and turned to face him. "You're very old-fashioned. I like that."

He looked down at his black wing tips. "I'm very old."

"No you're not. You shouldn't say that. How old are you?"

"Forty-four."

"That's not old. Paul Newman is older than that."

He chuckled. "I'm not exactly Paul Newman."

"You're . . . just fine, Norman."

He stood there awkwardly, as her palm slid gently along the contour of his jaw. She pressed her cheek against his. "Just fine," she repeated.

They kissed.

Her fingers moved down across his chest and clutched at the ends of his tie for support.

It came off in her hand.

Starry, Starry Night

THERE WERE MORNINGS WHEN VINCENT FELT LIKE THE last hippie in the world.

The Last Hippie. The phrase assumed a kind of tragic grandeur as he stood in the bathroom of his Oak Street flat, fluffing his amber mane to conceal his missing ear.

If you couldn't be the first, there was something bittersweet and noble about being the last. The Last of the Mohicans. The Last Supper. The Last Hippie!

He had mentioned the concept once to his Old Lady, just hours before she had run off to join the Israeli Army, but Laurel had only sneered. "It's too late," she said, lifting the hair on the left side of his head. "You're only seven eighths of The Last Hippie."

She hadn't always been that way.

During the war, she had been coming from a different place. Her Virgoan anal retentiveness had been channeled into positive trips.

Astral travel. Sand candles. Macramé.

But postbellum, things had got heavy. She had enrolled in a women's self-defense course and would practice holds on him while he was saying his mantra. Later, despite the efforts of her instructors at an Arica forty-day intensive, she developed an overnight obsession for Rolfing.

But not as a patient. As a practitioner.

That budding career came to an abrupt end when a dentist from Marin threatened to have her arrested for assault and battery.

"He was paranoid," Laurel claimed afterward.

"He said you were getting into it," Vincent replied quietly.

"Of course I was getting into it! It's my *job* to get into it!"

"He said you said things while you Rolfed him."

"Like what?"

"Let's drop it, Laurel."

"Like what?!"

"Like . . . 'Bourgeois pig' and 'Up against the wall.' "

"That's a lie!"

"Well, he said . . ."

"Look, Vincent! Who are you gonna believe, anyway? Me or a goddamn paranoid bourgeois pig?"

Well, she had gone now. She had left Amerika for good.

That's the way she had spelled it. With a *k*.

The very thought of that quirk made him tearful now, clinging desperately to the last vestiges of their life together.

He shuffled into the kitchen and stared balefully at his Day-Glo "Keep on Truckin' " poster.

Laurel had put it there. A hundred years ago. It was yellow and cracked with age now, and its message seemed a cruel anachronism.

He had stopped truckin' a long time ago.

Lunging at the poster with his five-fingered hand, he crumpled it into a ball and hurled it across the room with a cry of primal anguish. Then he stormed into the bedroom and did the same to Che Guevara and Tania Hearst.

It was time to split.

The switchboard, he decided, was the best place to do it. It was neutral ground somehow. Public domain. It had nothing to do with him and Laurel.

He arrived there at seven-thirty and made himself a cup of Maxim from the tap in the bathroom. He tidied the desk, emptied the wastebaskets and cleaned his scalpel with a Wash'n Dri.

Mary Ann would arrive at eight o'clock.

There was time to do it properly.

He made his last entry in the log book, feeling a twinge of remorse for the tortured souls who would call tonight seeking his solace.

What would Mary Ann tell them?

And what would she do when she found him?

The scalpel wasn't fair, he decided, fingering his worry beads for the last time. There had to be a cleaner way, a method that would lessen the horror for Mary Ann.

Then he thought of it.

The News from Home

BEFORE LEAVING FOR THE CRISIS SWITCHBOARD, MARY Ann stopped by Mona and Michael's.

A red-eyed Michael opened the door.

"Hi," he said quietly. "Welcome to Heartbreak Hotel."

"Company?" A stereo was playing in the bedroom.

"I wish."

"Michael . . . is something the matter?"

He shook his head, forcing a smile. "Come on in. I want you to hear something."

He led her into his bedroom and pointed to a chair. "Sit down and have a good cry. This woman is God's gift to romantics." He held up an album cover. Jane Olivor's *First Night.*

Mary Ann propped her head on her hand and listened. The chanteuse was singing "Some Enchanted Evening," wrenching still more tears from Michael.

"Every faggot in town adores her," explained Michael. "It's real washing-up music."

"Washing-up music?"

"You know. Post-whoopie. You play it afterwards, while

he's lighting a cigarette and . . . washing up."

Mary Ann reddened. "Why not before?"

"Uh . . . good question. I guess it's . . . a threat before. Afterwards, there's no danger."

"Oh." She laughed nervously.

Michael flopped on the bed and stared at the ceiling. "I hope I don't become cynical."

"You won't."

"Do you believe in marriage, Mary Ann?"

She nodded. "Most of the time."

"Me too. I think about it every time I see a new face. I got married four times today on the 41 Union bus."

There was embarrassment in Mary Ann's laugh.

"I know," said Michael unaccusingly. "A bunch of fairies in caftans, tripping through Golden Gate Park with drag bridesmaids and quotations from 'Song of the Loon' . . . That's not what I mean."

"I know."

"It would be like . . . friends. Somebody to buy a Christmas tree with."

"Sure." She tried in vain to picture herself choosing a Scotch pine with Norman.

Mona had been gone all day. Her absence began to gnaw at Michael again as soon as Mary Ann had left. Mona wasn't much fun these days, but she was at least a distraction.

She kept him away from Lands End.

Big deal, he thought, turning off the stereo and skulking into the kitchen. *Your whole goddamn life is at Lands End.* You belong to nobody, and nobody belongs to you. Your sacred chastity doesn't mean *shit.*

He foraged in the refrigerator for munchies, emerging with a grapefruit half and a flat Tab. Next to the ice tray, a bottle of Locker Room sat in stoic isolation, waiting for the next time.

He glared murderously at the squat brown bottle and slammed the freezer door. "Freeze your ass off, you little mother!"

That was when the phone rang.

"Mikey?"

"Mama?"

"How are you, Mikey?"

"Fine, Mama. There hasn't been . . . ? Everything's all right, isn't it?"

"Oh . . . fair to middlin', I guess. Papa and I've got a surprise for you, Mikey."

His fingertips traced the furrows in his brow. Please God, don't do this to me. "What, Mama?"

"Well, you know Papa's been trying for _years_ to wangle one of those trips with Florida Citrus Mutual. . . ."

Come _on,_ God! I'll join the church of my choice! I'll never lust in my heart again!

"So guess what happened just this afternoon?"

"You got the trip."

"Uh huh. And guess where?"

"Fire Island."

"What?"

"Nothing, Mama. I was being silly. You're coming to San Francisco, right?"

"Isn't it wonderful? We've got four whole days to visit, Mikey! And we've already got the hotel reservations and everything!"

The reservations, it turned out, were at the Holiday Inn on Van Ness. October 29 through November 1.

The horrible significance of those dates didn't hit Michael until he checked a calendar.

Mr. and Mrs. Herbert L. Tolliver were forsaking their orange groves, their Sizzlers and their Shakey's and their _Saturday Evening Posts,_ to spend four fun-filled days in Everybody's Favorite City.

On Halloween weekend.

Jesus H. Christ.

237

A Place for Strays

ANNA'S BEDROOM HAD BEEN CAREFULLY GROOMED for Edgar's arrival.

The linens were fresh, the ferns were misted, and the photograph that usually stayed on the dresser was tucked away in the bottom of the lingerie drawer.

"No waterbed?" Edgar grinned slyly, surveying the room for the first time.

"Sorry." Anna shrugged. "It's in the shop for repairs. I had a gentleman caller last night and we nearly drowned the cat."

"What cat?"

She threw a pillow at him. "You're supposed to say, 'What gentleman caller?' goddammit!"

"O.K. What gentleman caller?"

"I've forgotten. There've been so many!"

He wrapped his arms around her and held her for half a minute, then leaned down and kissed her lightly on the eyelids. When he was done, Anna looked up and said, "Fitzgerald."

"Ma'am?"

"That's from *The Great Gatsby* . . . 'She was the kind of

woman who was meant to be kissed upon the eyes.' Something like that, anyway . . . Do you want something to drink, or are you already drunk?"

"Anna!"

She nudged him in the ribs. "You smell like expensive scotch."

"I've been to a cocktail party at The Summit."

"With Frannie?"

Edgar nodded.

"How did you . . . ?"

"DeDe took her home."

"Edgar . . . surely she *notices* when you . . ."

"She was barely conscious, Anna."

Anna rested her hand on his chest and pointed a long, delicate forefinger toward the window.

"There," she said, adjusting the pillow under his head. "You want proof?"

He rolled over to face the window and saw a plump tiger-striped cat inching along the ledge. The animal stopped for a moment, mewed at Anna, then moved on.

"His name is Boris," said Anna.

"You don't let him in?"

"He doesn't belong to me."

"Ah . . . then it doesn't count."

"I love him," she said flatly. "That counts, doesn't it?"

"There's a theory," said Anna, handing him a cup of tea as she climbed back into bed, "that we are all Atlanteans."

"Who?"

"Us. San Franciscans."

Edgar grinned indulgently, bracing himself for another yarn.

Anna caught it. "Do you want to hear it . . . or are you getting stuffy on me?"

"Go ahead. Tell me a story."

239

"Well . . . in one of our last incarnations, we were all citizens of Atlantis. All of us. You, me, Frannie, DeDe, Mary Ann . . ."

"Are you *sure* she's out of the building?"

"She's gone to her switchboard. Will you relax?"

"O.K. I'm relaxed."

"All right, then. We all lived in this lovely, enlightened kingdom that sank beneath the sea a long time ago. Now we've come back to this special peninsula on the edge of the continent . . . because we *know,* in a secret corner of our minds, that we must return together to the sea."

"The earthquake."

Anna nodded. "Don't you see? You said *the* earthquake, not *an* earthquake. You're expecting it. We're all expecting it."

"So what does that have to do with Atlantis?"

"The Transamerica Pyramid, for one thing."

"Huh?"

"Don't you know what dominated the skyline of Atlantis, Edgar . . . the thing that loomed over everything?"

He shook his head.

"A pyramid! An enormous pyramid with a beacon burning at the top!"

When Edgar slipped into the lane an hour later, Anna was watching him from the window. She rapped once, but he didn't hear her.

Someone else was watching too, concealed in the shrubbery at the edge of the courtyard.

Norman Neal Williams.

Hanging Loose

MARY ANN WAS RUNNING LATE, BUT THE MERCEDES parked at the foot of the Barbary Lane stairway caught her eye. Its personalized plates said FRANNI. She recognized it instantly as Edgar Halcyon's.

A small town, she thought. Smaller, in a lot of ways, than Cleveland. She wondered which celebrated Russian Hill hostess was serving cocktails to the Halcyons tonight.

"Off to the body shops?"

It was Brian Hawkins, striding down Leavenworth with a *definite* smirk on his face.

"I'm late for the switchboard," she said crisply.

"Oh . . . the suicide place."

She frowned. "That's only part of it."

"What time are you off?"

"Pretty late."

"I see. O.K. . . . Well, if you feel like it, come on up for a joint afterwards."

"I'm usually pretty tired, Brian."

He brushed past her, heading up the stairway. "Right. Can't get much plainer than that, can you?"

As usual, the J Church streetcar was a zoo.

Once past the scowl of the conductor, Mary Ann inched through a cloud of Woolworth's cologne to an empty seat in the back. She sat next to an old woman in a pink cloth coat and a battered brown wig.

"Warming up."

"Ma'am?"

"Seems to be getting warmer." A talker, thought Mary Ann. It never fails.

"Yes, ma'am. It does."

"Where you from?"

"Cleveland."

"My sister went to Akron once."

"Oh . . . Akron's very nice."

"I was born and raised here. Castro Street. Before all the you-know-whats moved in."

"Yes, ma'am."

"Have you found Jesus yet?"

"Ma'am?"

"Have you accepted Jesus as your personal Saviour?"

"Well . . . I'm . . . I was raised a Presbyterian."

"The Bible says until ye be born again, ye shall not enter into the Kingdom of Heaven."

If there's a God, thought Mary Ann, He must get his jollies by bringing these people into my life. Fundamentalist crones. Hare Krishna flower peddlers. Scientologists offering "personality tests" on the corner of Powell and Geary.

When the streetcar stopped at Twenty-fourth Street, Mary Ann wasted no time in heading for the door.

The old woman reached into the aisle and said "Praise Jesus," handing her convert a dog-eared pamphlet. Mary Ann accepted it with a blush and a nod of thanks.

As the streetcar departed, she stood on the corner and read the pamphlet's boldly emblazoned headline: JIMMY CARTER FOR PRESIDENT.

* * *

The world was changing, she decided. Even to her untrained Midwestern eye, Twenty-fourth Street seemed almost quaintly anachronistic. Men still wore their hair in ponytails here, and women slumped around in vintage granny dresses.

"Far out" had the sound of "Oh, you kid."

So what's next? she wondered. What will come along to take the place of free clinics and crisis switchboards and alternative newspapers and macrobiotic everything?

The entrance hall of the Switchboard was dark. A sliver of light from the back room guided her feet to the sound of a ringing phone.

"I'm here, Vincent. I'm really sorry! I just lost track of the time. I know you must be . . . *No!* . . . *Oh, God, Vincent, no!* . . . *You didn't . . . ?*"

His tongue was the worst part, protruding from his mouth like a fat black sausage.

He was swinging very slowly from the ceiling, his neck a hideous mass of twine and shells and feathers. Laurel's macramé had finally served a purpose.

He had died as organically as possible.

Nightcap

T HE POLICEMAN WHO DROPPED HER OFF AT BARBARY Lane was so young that he had zits. But he was gentle and he seemed to be genuinely worried about her.

"You sure you're gonna be O.K.?"

"Yes. Thank you." She had come very close to inviting him up for a crème de menthe. . . . Anything to keep from being alone tonight.

Bounding up the stairway into the dark lane, she found herself praying that Mona or Michael would be at home. But no one answered their buzzer.

Upstairs, she fumbled in her purse for her key, then noticed the light spilling under Brian's door. She reversed her course without a moment's hesitation.

He was wearing boxer shorts and a sweatshirt when he opened the door. His face was shiny with sweat.

"Sit-ups," he grinned, jerking his head toward his incline board.

"I'm sorry if I . . ."

"It's O.K."

"I . . . Does that offer for a joint still hold?"

He listened to her account of the horror with a face almost devoid of expression. When she had finished, he whistled softly. "He was a good friend?"

She shook her head. "Not at all."

"That's the part that hurts, doesn't it?"

"God, Brian, if I had only *talked* to him a little more . . ."

"No. It wouldn't have done any good." He shook his head, smiling ruefully. "So we've *both* had a good day."

"What happened to *you?*"

"Not much. A house party at Stinson Beach."

"You didn't like it?"

He took a toke off the joint. "Picture this, O.K.? Five young married couples and me. Well . . . semi-young. Thirty to thirty-five. Still in Topsiders, mind you, but driving an Audi now and sending a couple of rug rats to the French-American School and swapping notes on their Cuisinarts . . ."

"Their what?"

He handed her the joint. "Next image: a beach full of pink people, the women on one side, chattering about hot tubs and cellulite and the best place for runny Brie . . . and the guys out by the volleyball net, huffing and puffing in twelve-year-old Madras bermudas their wives have let out at least twice . . . and all these yellow-haired kids fighting over who gets to play with Big Bird and G.I. Joe . . ."

Mary Ann smiled for the first time. "I got it."

"So here's our hero, in the middle of all this . . . wondering if he can get food stamps if he quits at Perry's . . . hoping to hell the Clap Clinic doesn't call this week. . . ." He stopped, seeing the look on her face. "A joke, Mary Ann . . . And then this guy runs out of the house with his guitar slung around his neck like some refugee from *Hootenanny,* only he's a *lawyer,* right? . . . and he drops down in the sand and starts singing 'I don't give a damn about a greenback dollar' . . . and everybody claps along and sings and jiggles kids in their laps. . . ."

She nodded, confused by his cynical tone. The whole thing sounded rather *sweet* to her.

"Christ! I went back to the house when the singalong started and sat in an empty bedroom and smoked a joint and thanked my fucking lucky stars I wasn't trapped in that *pathetic*, middle-class prison!"

"I see."

"This kid . . . about six years old . . . walks into the room, right? She asks me why I'm not singing and I say I'm a lousy singer and she says that's O.K. because she is too."

"How cute."

"She was all right."

"Did she stay there with you?"

"She asked me to read her a story."

"Did you?"

"For a little while. Hell, I was stoned."

"Well, that doesn't sound so bad."

"Her old man and I went to George Washington together."

"Where?"

"Law school. He was the one who didn't give a damn about the greenback dollar."

"You were a lawyer?"

The roach was so short that it burned his fingers. He threw it on the floor and stepped on it. "Oh, yes . . . only I *really* didn't give a damn about the greenback dollar. I was everybody's favorite freebie."

"You didn't charge?"

"Not if you were black in Chicago . . . or a draft resister in Toronto or an Indian in Arizona . . . or a Chicano in L.A."

"But you could've . . ."

"I *hated* law. It was the causes I loved . . . and . . . well, I ran out of them." He looked down at his hands dangling between his knees. "Ol' Vincent and I would have gotten on like a house on fire."

"Brian . . ."

"Go on."

"Thanks for listening."

"Out. Gotta finish my sit-ups."

Words of Comfort

MR. HALCYON WAS NICER THAN SHE EXPECTED when she asked for the day off.

"I'm sorry about your friend, Mary Ann."

"He wasn't really a *friend* exactly. . . ."

"Just the same."

"I really appreciate it."

"It's not easy living in Atlantis, is it?"

"Sir?"

"Nothing. Take your time. I can call Kelly Girl."

She was more out of it than ever. She sat on her wicker sofa, munching a Pop-Tart and watching the bay. The water was so *blue* . . . but was the price too high?

How many times now had she threatened to go home to Cleveland?

How many times had the lure of family china and split-level security beckoned her from the slopes of this beautiful volcano?

Would she *ever* stop feeling like a colonist on the moon?

Or would she wake up one morning to find herself a cloth-coated old lady, tottering about Russian Hill in slightly soiled gloves, prolonging her choice of a single lamb chop at Marcel & Henri, telling the butcher or the doorman or the nice young gripman who helped her onto the cable car that any day now, when her social security check came in, when the weather turned, when she found a home for her cat . . . she was going home to Cleveland?

Her buzzer rang.

When she opened the door, the face of her visitor was obscured by a huge pot of yellow mums.

"Hello, Mary Ann."

"Norman?"

"I didn't wake you up, did I?"

"No. Come in."

He set the flowers on one of her teak nesting tables from Cost Plus. "Are those for me?" she asked.

He nodded. "I heard about last night."

"How sweet . . . Who told you?"

"That guy across the hall. I ran into him in the courtyard this morning."

"Brian."

"Yeah. Look, are you sure I'm not . . ."

"I'm delighted to see you, Norman. Really." She pecked him on the cheek. "Really."

Norman flushed. "I thought you might like the yellows better than the whites."

"Yes." She touched the flowers appreciatively. "Yellow's my favorite. Hey, can I fix you some coffee?"

"If it's not too much trouble."

"Of course not. I'll be right back." She dashed into the kitchen and began fussing with her French stainless-steel-and-glass Melior pot from Thomas Cara Ltd. She had paid thirty-five dollars for it a month ago . . . and used it exactly twice.

She was almost positive that Norman was a Maxim-type person, but there was no point in risking it.

Norman seemed to like the coffee. "Boy!" he grinned, looking up from his cup. "Brian showed me what the landlady grows in the garden."

"Oh . . . the grass, you mean?" She marveled at the matter-of-fact tone of her voice. Her growing sophistication sometimes astounded her.

"Yeah. I guess that's pretty common around here, huh?"

She shrugged. "She only grows it for us . . . and herself. Well, you know . . . you got one when you moved in, didn't you?"

"One what?"

"A joint . . . taped on your door?"

Norman looked puzzled. "No."

"Oh . . . well . . ."

"She taped a joint on your door when you moved in?"

Mary Ann nodded. "It's a house custom, sort of. I guess she must've . . . forgotten or something."

Norman smiled. "My feelings aren't hurt."

"You don't smoke, huh?"

"No."

"Well, maybe she could tell. She's awfully intuitive."

"Yeah . . . maybe. Brian says she used to work in a bookshop in North Beach."

Mary Ann failed to see the connection. "Yeah. He told me that too. I've never asked her."

"She's not from around here, is she?"

"Are you kidding?" said Mary Ann, grateful for the chance to use the line herself. "*Nobody's* from around here."

"She sounds Midwestern to me."

"Yeah . . . she and Mona talk a lot alike, I think."

"Mona?"

"The red-headed woman on the second floor."

"Oh."

He looked a little lost, Mary Ann felt. Poor thing. *Someday,* she hoped, he would learn to feel part of the family.

The Clue in the Bookshop

NORMAN LEFT MARY ANN'S APARTMENT JUST BEFORE noon.

He spent the next three hours exploring bookshops, with no success. Finally, on Upper Grant, he discovered a dusty hole-in-the-wall sandwiched between a leather shop and an organic ice cream parlor.

He sniffed around for several minutes before approaching the old man in the back.

"Anything on sky-diving?"

"Huh?"

"Sky-diving. Parachuting."

"Sports?"

"Yeah. A sport."

The old man lifted his cardigan to scratch his side, then pointed to a shelf just above eye level. "That's all we got on sports." He conveyed an air of mild disgust, as if Norman had asked him for the pornography section.

"Well, it doesn't matter, anyway. I just wanted to get a look at the old place. I used to come here a long time ago. You've fixed it up real nice."

"Think so?"

"Yeah. Real tasteful. You don't see many places like this anymore. It's nice to know some people still have respect for the past."

The old man chuckled. "I got plenty of past . . . I guess I oughta have plenty of respect."

"Yeah . . . but you're young at heart, aren't you? That's what counts. You're a lot easier to deal with than that woman who used to run the place."

The old man eyed him. "You knew her?"

"Not well. She struck me as a real disagreeable lady."

"Never heard *that* about her. A little peculiar, maybe."

"Peculiar as hell. You bought the place from her?"

The old man nodded. "About ten years ago. Been here ever since."

"That's nice to hear. A place like this needs some . . . stability. I guess Mrs. Whatshername went back East . . . or wherever she came from?"

"Nope. Still here. I see her off and on."

"I wouldn't have figured that. She didn't seem too happy here. She was always gabbing about . . . hell, *someplace* back East. Where was she from, anyway?"

"I guess you could call it back East. She was from Norway."

"Norway?"

"Maybe Denmark. Yeah . . . Denmark."

"I guess I've got her mixed up with somebody else."

"Name Madrigal?"

"Yep. That was it."

"She was from Denmark, I'm sure. Born here . . . I mean the States . . . but she lived in Denmark before she bought the shop. I guess that's where she picked up her funny customs."

"She had some funny ones, all right."

The old man smiled. "See that cash register?"

"Yeah?"

"Well, when I took the place over . . . the day I moved in . . . I found a note pasted there that said, 'Good luck and God bless you' . . . and you know what else?"

Norman shook his head.

"A cigarette. A hand-rolled cigarette. Stuck up there with a piece of tape."

"Peculiar."

"Mighty peculiar," said the old man.

As Mona and D'orothea entered Malvina's, Norman was striding down Union Street toward Washington Square.

Mona nodded to him, but the gesture went unnoticed.

"He's in our building," she explained. "He's afraid of his own shadow."

"I can tell."

"He watches me, though. He doesn't talk much, but he watches me."

Upstairs at Malvina's, they sipped cappucinos and reconstructed the missing years.

"I've lost track," said Mona. "What happened to Curt?"

"Lots . . . *Sleuth* for a year or so. A couple of new soaps, then one of the big roles in *Absurd Person Singular*. He's done all right."

"And so have you?"

"So have I."

"I lost my job."

"I know."

"How the . . . ?"

"I'm doing some modeling for Halcyon. Beauchamp Day told me."

"Small fucking world."

"I'm finished with New York, Mona. I want this to be my home again."

"Comin' home to go roamin' no more, huh?"

"You sound so cynical."

"Sorry."

"I need you, Mona."

"D'or . . ."

"I want you back."

Mona Moves On

THE MORNING WAS BRIGHT AND BLUSTERY. MICHAEL tossed a pebble into the bay and flung an arm across Mona's shoulders. "I love the Marina Green," he said.

Mona grimaced and stopped in her tracks, scraping an ancient Earth Shoe against the curb. "Not to mention the Marina Brown."

"You're such a romantic!"

"Fuck romanticism. Look where it gets *you.*"

"Thanks, I needed that."

"Sorry. I didn't mean it to sound that way."

"Well, you're right."

"No, I'm not. I'm a coward. I'm scared shitless. One of these days, Mouse, something really nice is going to happen to you. And you'll deserve it when it comes, because you never stop trying. I gave up a long time ago."

Michael sat down on a bench and dusted off the space next to him. "What's bugging you, Mona?"

"Nothing in particular."

"Bullshit."

"You don't need another downer, Mouse."

253

"Says who? I *thrive* on downers."

She sat down next to him, fixing her eyes glassily on the bay. "I think I may move out, Mouse."

His face was blank. "Oh?"

"A friend of mine wants me to move in with her."

"I see."

"It's got nothing to do with you, Mouse. It really doesn't. I just feel like *something's* gotta change soon or I'll freak. . . . I hope you . . ."

"Who is it?"

"You don't know her. She's a model I used to know in New York."

"Just like that, huh?"

"She's really nice, Mouse. She's just bought this beautiful remodeled Victorian in Pacific Heights."

"Rich, huh?"

"Yeah. I suppose."

He stared at her without a word.

"I need . . . some sort of security, Mouse. I'm thirty-one years old, for Christ's sake!"

"So?"

"So I'm sick of buying clothes at Goodwill and pretending they're funky. I want a bathroom you can clean and a microwave oven and a place to plant roses and a goddamn dog who'll recognize me when I come home!"

Michael bit the tip of his forefinger and blinked at her. "Arf," he said feebly.

They walked for a while along the quay.

"Was she your lover, Mona?"

"Uh huh."

"How come you never told me?"

"It never really seemed important, I guess. I wasn't exactly . . . into that scene. I was a lousy dyke."

"But you aren't now, huh?"

"It doesn't matter."

"The hell it doesn't."

"She's a sweet person, and . . ."

"She'll take good care of you, and you can stay at home and eat bonbons and read movie magazines to your heart's . . ."

"That's enough, Mouse."

"Christ! Maybe you *did* give up a long time ago, but I'm not going to stand by and watch you throw your life away. You're not even being fair to *her,* Mona! What the hell does she need with some half-assed lover who's got the hots for tile bathrooms?"

"Look, you're not . . ."

"Nothing's free, Mona! Nothing!"

"Oh, yeah? What about your rent?"

The words stung harder than she expected, silencing Michael completely.

"I didn't mean that, Mouse."

"Why not? It's the truth."

"Mouse . . . I don't care about that." He was crying now. She stopped walking and reached for his hand. "Look, Mouse, you'll have the whole place to yourself, and Mrs. Madrigal is bound to give you some slack on the rent until you can find a job."

He rubbed his eyes with the back of his hand. "Why does this sound like the end of a B-movie affair?"

She kissed him on the cheek. "It does, doesn't it?"

"Some affair. You didn't even stick around long enough to meet my parents."

At the Gynecologist's

THE WAITING ROOM WAS THE SAME SHADE OF GREEN that once oppressed DeDe at the Convent of the Sacred Heart. There were clowns on the walls— weeping clowns—and nothing to read but a July 1974 issue of *Ladies' Home Journal.*

She might as well have been waiting to get a tooth pulled.

The receptionist ignored her. She was ravaging a bag of barbecue potato chips while she read the *Chronicle.*

"Will it be much longer?" DeDe asked, hating herself for sounding apologetic.

"What?" This chinless Bryman School graduate was plainly irked that her reading had been interrupted. "Uh . . . the doctor will be with you in a moment." She brightened a little, holding up the paper and pointing to a serial on the back page. "Have you read this today?"

DeDe stiffened. "I don't read that."

"Ah . . . c'mon!"

"I don't. It's nothing but trash. A friend of mine almost sued him once."

"Far out. Have you ever . . ." She cut off the sentence and

covered the newspaper with an IUD catalogue, just as a door swung open next to her booth.

DeDe looked up to see a lean, blond man in a blue oxford-cloth shirt, chino pants and a white cotton jacket. He reminded her instantly of Ashley Wilkes.

"Ms. Day?"

That was one point in his favor. She hadn't explained her marital status on the telephone. She had said simply that she was "a friend of Binky's," sounding as quaintly furtive as a flapper approaching a speakeasy.

"Yes," she said colorlessly, extending her hand.

Obviously sensing her discomfort, he led her out of the waiting room and into the room with the stirrups.

"Any nausea recently?" he asked softly, going about his work.

"A little. Not much. Sometimes when I smell cigarette smoke."

"Any foods bother you?"

"Some."

"Like?"

"Sweet and sour pork."

He chuckled. "But half an hour later you feel fine again."

That was *not* funny. She froze him out . . . or as much as she could in that position.

"Have you felt tired lately?"

She shook her head.

"How's Binky?"

"What?"

"Binky. I haven't seen her since the film festival."

"She . . . I guess she's fine." It enraged her that anyone could talk about Binky Gruen at a time like this.

When he was done, he came away from the sink with a smile on his smooth, Arrow collar face. "It's yours, if you want it."

"What?"

"The baby. There's no point in waiting for the urinalysis. You're going to be a mother, Mrs. Day."

She wondered later if some automatic defense mechanism

had dulled her response to the announcement. Most women, surely, would not have chosen that particular moment to dwell on the luminous blue pools of their doctor's eyes.

She warmed to him after that, freed from embarrassment by his loose-limbed easiness, his toothy, prep-school smile. She could trust him, she felt. Baby or no baby. She was certain that he sensed the delicacy of the situation.

"When you make up your mind," he said, "give me a call. In the meantime, take these." He winked at her. "They're pink and blue. It's a subtle propaganda campaign."

He said good-bye to her in the waiting room, turning to the receptionist as DeDe headed for the door.

"Through with the paper?"

She nodded, handing him the *Chronicle.*

He opened the newspaper to the same page that had occupied the receptionist. A slow smile crept over his face, and he began to shake his head.

"Sick," said the doctor. "Really sick."

The Diagnosis

STUPEFIED, FRANNIE STARED AT HER DAUGHTER.

"God, DeDe! Are you sure?"

DeDe nodded, fighting back the tears. "I talked to him this morning."

"And . . . he's sure?"

"Yes."

"Dear God." She clutched at the trellis in the morning room, as if to support herself. "Why didn't . . . we know before? Why didn't he *tell* us?"

"He wasn't sure, Mother."

Frannie's voice grew strident. "Wasn't *sure?* Who gave him the right to play God? Don't we have a right to know?"

"Mother . . ."

Frannie turned away from her daughter, hiding her face. She fidgeted with a pot of yellow spider mums. "Did the doctor . . . did he say how long he has?"

"Six months," said DeDe softly.

"Will he . . . be uncomfortable?"

"No. Not until the end, anyway." Her voice cracked. Her mother had begun to cry. "Please don't, Mother. He's awfully old. The vet says it was time."

259

"Where is he now?"

"On the terrace."

Frannie left the morning room, brushing the tears from her eyes.

Out on the terrace, she knelt by the chaise lounge where Faust lay sleeping.

"Poor baby," she said, stroking the dog's graying muzzle. "Poor, sweet baby."

Later that day, Frannie poked morosely at her cheese soufflé and raised her voice over the noontime din at the Cow Hollow Inn.

"I said . . . I hope I can prepare myself for it."

"Of course you do." Helen Stonecypher was busying herself with a wet napkin, removing a chunk of Geminesse lipstick from her front tooth.

"Am I being maudlin?"

"Not at all."

"I thought I might have his dish bronzed . . . as a kind of . . . memorial."

"Sweet."

"You *know* how I abhor women who get hysterical about their dogs . . . but Faust was . . . is . . ." Her voice trailed off.

Helen patted her hand, jangling their bangle bracelets in unison. "Darling, do whatever makes *you* feel best. You remember Choy, don't you? My grandmother's cook in the big house on Pacific?"

Frannie nodded, blinking back the tears.

"Well, ol' Choy was Nana's dearest friend in the world . . . and when he died . . ."

"I remember that. Wasn't he wheeling her around the fair at Treasure Island?"

Helen nodded. "When he died, Nana had his queue cut off and made into a choker."

"A . . . ?"

"A necklace, darling . . . with three or four *very* understated little ivory beads worked into the strands. It was quite lovely, actually, and Nana *adored* it. As a matter of fact, she was wearing it when she died in our box in 1947."

"I remember," said Frannie, smiling bravely. *"Götterdäm-merung."*

Helen dropped her compact back in her purse. "C'mon, darling. Let's go pour a stiff one at Jean's."

"Helen . . . not just yet."

"Darling, you *are* down!"

"I'll be all right in a . . ."

"He was an old, old pooch, Frannie."

"Is."

"Is . . . Frannie, look at it this way. He's had a full, rich life. *No* dog's had it as good as he has."

"That's true," said Frannie, brightening somewhat. "That's very, very true."

The Tollivers Invade

ALL THINGS CONSIDERED, HALLOWEEN WEEKEND
had gone quite well.

So far.

Michael's parents had rented a Dodge Aspen
upon their arrival in the city, so it was easy
enough to fill up their time with Muir Woods and Sausalito,
The Crooked Street and Fisherman's Wharf.

But now it was Sunday. The Witches' Sabbath was upon
them.

If he was careful, very careful, he could ease them through
it, protect their fragile, *Reader's Digest* sensibilities from the
horror of The Love That Dares Not Speak Its Name.

Maybe.

In *this* town, he thought, The Love That Dares Not Speak
Its Name almost never shuts up.

His father chuckled when he saw the apartment for the first
time. "Took you all weekend to clean it up, huh?"

"I'm neater than I used to be," Michael grinned.

"Looks like a lady's neatness, if you ask me." He winked at his son.

Michael's mother frowned. "Herb, I told you not . . ."

"Aw, it's O.K., Alice. Christ, we're not a couple of old fuddy-duddies. I remember what *I* was like at Mike's age. Hell, son . . . I hope you didn't move her out on our account."

"Herb!"

"Your mother's too old-fashioned, Mike. Go snoop around the kitchen, Alice. I'm surprised you could hold off this long."

Michael's mother pushed out her lower lip and trudged out of the room.

"Now," said his father. "What the hell's going on? Your mother and I thought you'd like to introduce us to . . . what's her name?"

"Mona . . . Papa, she's only . . ."

"I don't give a damn *what* she is, Mike. Frankly, I'm a little disappointed you felt you had to hide the poor little thing. I've seen *Hustler,* son. I know a thing or two about 1976."

"Papa . . . she moved out. She wanted to."

"Because of us?"

"No. She just wanted to. She found another roommate. There's no hard feelings."

"You're a damned idiot, then! She just up and left you and there's no hard feelings? Jesus, Mike . . ."

He stopped talking when he heard his wife return. She was standing in the kitchen doorway with a small brown bottle in her hand.

"What's this stuff, Mikey?"

Michael went white. "Uh . . . Mama, that's something . . . my roommate left behind."

"In the freezer?"

"She used it to clean her paintbrushes."

"Oh." She looked at the bottle again and returned it to the refrigerator. "You need to scrub your vegetable bin, Mikey."

"I know, Mama."

"Where do you keep your Ajax?"

"Mama, can't we just . . . ?"

263

"It's disgusting, Mikey. It won't take me a second."

"Alice, for God's sake! Leave the boy alone! We didn't come three thousand miles to scrub his goddamn vegetable bin! Look, son, your mama and I want to take you out to dinner tonight. Why don't you show us one of your favorite places?"

Peachy, thought Michael. We'll just boogie on down to The Palms, sip Blue Moons in a window seat, and watch the Cycle Sluts wave leather dildos at the traffic cops.

The Aspen was parked up on Leavenworth, near Green. Michael's mother was out of breath by the time they reached Union. "I've never seen a street like that in my life, Mikey!"

He squeezed her arm, taking sudden pleasure in her innocence. "It's an amazing city, Mama."

Almost on cue, the nuns appeared.

"Herb, look!"

"Goddammit, Alice! Don't point!"

"Herb . . . they're on roller skates!"

"Goddamn if they aren't! Mike, what the hell . . . ?"

Before their son could answer, the six white-coifed figures had rounded the corner as a unit, rocketing in the direction of the revelry on Polk Street.

One of them bellowed at Michael.

"Hey, Tolliver!"

Michael waved half-heartedly.

The nun gave a high sign, blew a kiss, then shouted: *"Loved your jockey shorts!"*

Trick or Treat in Suburbia

MARY ANN TUGGED ON HER DRIVER'S ARM. "OH, Norman . . . beep, will you?"

"Who is it?"

"Michael and his parents. Mona's room-mate."

Norman tapped on the horn. Michael looked towards them as Mary Ann blew a kiss from the window of the Falcon. He smiled feebly and pretended to yank out a handful of hair. His parents were charging ahead, oblivious.

"Poor baby!" said Mary Ann.

"What's the matter?"

"Oh . . . it's complicated."

"He's queer, isn't he?"

"Gay, Norman."

Lexy poked her head over the seat. "What's queer?"

"Sit down," said Norman.

Mary Ann turned around and fussed with Lexy's Wonder Woman cape. "You look so *nice,* Lexy."

The child bounced on the back seat. "Why don't *you* have a costume?"

"Well . . . I'm a grownup, Lexy."

The child shook her head vehemently and pointed out the window to three men dressed as high school majorettes. *"Those* grownups have costumes."

Norman chuckled, shaking his head.

Mary Ann sighed. *"How* old did you say she was?"

It was almost dark by the time they reached San Leandro. Norman parked the car in a pseudo-Spanish subdivision and opened the door for Lexy.

The little girl bounced down the sidewalk with a mammoth plastic trick-or-treat bag.

"Are you sure she'll be all right?" asked Mary Ann.

Norman nodded. "Her folks live over in the next block. I told them I'd . . . you know . . . let her get this out of her system."

"I hope they appreciate all this."

"I wouldn't do it if I didn't like it." He grinned sheepishly. "Rent-a-kid, you know."

"Yeah. It's kinda nice, isn't it?"

"It isn't boring for you?"

"Not at all."

He looked at her solemnly for a moment, then squeezed her hand.

"Norman?"

"Yeah?"

"Have you ever been married?"

Silence.

"I'm sorry. It's just that you're so good with kids that . . ."

"Roxanne and me were gonna have kids. That was the plan, anyway."

"Oh . . . she died?"

Norman shook his head. "She ran off with a ceramic-tile salesman from Daly City. When I was in Nam."

"I'm sorry."

He shrugged. "That was a long time ago. About the time Lexy was born, in fact. I got over it."

She looked out the window, embarrassed by this new insight into his personality. Was Lexy his only link with a vanished dream? Had he given up all hope of building a home again?

"Norman . . . I don't see how *anyone* could leave you."

"It doesn't matter."

"Of course it matters, Norman! You're a gentle, kind, loving man, and no one should . . . Norman, you've got *so* much love to give someone."

His hands were fidgeting in his lap. He looked down at them. "Someone," he repeated vacantly.

He needed a sign from her. He was *pleading* for a sign.

She was reaching up to touch his sad bear's face when a hand on her shoulder made her yelp.

Lexy was back.

"Oh, Lexy . . ." Mary Ann laughed, somewhat relieved. "How did you do?"

"A crummy apple."

"Well, apples are good. I'll eat it if you don't want it."

The child looked at her for a moment, then produced the apple and sunk her teeth into it defiantly.

Norman shouted in horror. "Lexy . . . no!"

Lexy grinned at him as the juice dribbled down her face. "It's O.K.," she said. "I already checked it for razor blades."

Chip off the Old Block

MICHAEL ENDED UP TAKING HIS PARENTS TO THE Cliff House. It was the straightest place he could think of.

It was also far enough away from the Halloween madness of Polk Street that roller-skating nuns were not likely to invade the family circle again.

The nuns, he explained as cavalierly as possible, were "some crazy friends of Mona's." And, yes, they were men.

"Fruits?"

"Herb!" Michael's mother dropped her fork and glared at her husband.

"Well, what the hell do you want me to call them?"

"That's not a very nice word, Herb."

"Why not? I'm a citrus grower, Alice. We *raise* fruits!" He laughed raucously.

"You just shouldn't talk that way about people who can't help themselves."

"Can't help themselves! Who the hell can't help skatin' down the middle of the street dressed up like a goddamn nun?"

"Herb . . . don't raise your voice. There might be Catholics in the room."

Michael looked up from his plate, speaking as offhandedly as possible. "It's kinda like Mardi Gras, Papa. There's lots of crazy stuff going on. A lot of people do it."

"A lot of fruits."

"Not just . . . them, Papa. Everybody."

His father snorted and reattacked his steak. "I don't notice *you* out there making a goddamn fool of yourself."

"He's with *us,* Herb. Maybe he'd *like* to be out there . . . going to a party or something. It sounds like a lot of fun to me."

"Well, you two go right ahead. I'll just sit here and finish my steak with the normal people."

A waiter refilling Herbert Tolliver's water glass caught the remark and rolled his eyes in pained forbearance.

Then he winked at Michael.

Back at 28 Barbary Lane, Alice Tolliver recapped the social history of Orlando for the past six months.

A new shopping mall had been built. The Henleys' daughter, Iris, was addicted to pot and living with a professor in Atlanta. A colored family had bought the McKinneys' split-level down the road. Aunt Miriam was doing fine, despite her overlong recovery from a female operation, and everybody in central Florida agreed that Earl Butz would never have been fired if he had made that remark about an Irishman.

They weren't expecting an early frost.

Herbert Tolliver sat quietly through the telling of this saga, embellishing only occasionally with a chuckle or a nod of his head. He was mellower now, softened by the wine at dinner, and he beamed at his son in open affection.

"Is . . . everything goin' O.K. for you, Mike?"

"Pretty good, Papa."

"Don't you worry about your ladyfriend, you hear?"

"I won't, Papa."

"Your mama and I are gonna miss you at Christmas."

"Now, Herb, he's grown up now, and he's got friends of his . . ."

"I know that, goddammit! I just said we'd miss him, didn't I?"

His wife nodded. "We will, Mikey."

"I'll miss y'all too. It's just so expensive to fly back there for . . ."

"I know, Mikey. Don't you worry about that."

"Mike . . . if we can help out a little bit until you can find a job . . ."

"Thanks, Papa. I think I can manage. I've picked up a little on odd jobs."

"Well, you let us know, O.K.?"

"O.K., Papa."

"We're mighty proud of you, son."

Michael shrugged. "Not much to be proud of, is there?"

"Don't be a damn fool! You're as good as the best of 'em! Some things take a little time, son. You'll work it out before you know it. Hell, I kind of envy you, son. You're young and you're single and you're livin' in a beautiful town full of beautiful women. You got no sweat at all, son!"

"I guess you're right."

"Course I'm right. Smooth sailin' all the way." He chuckled and grazed his son's cheek with a playful fist. "Long as you can keep those fruits away."

Michael made a manly grin. "I'm not their type, anyway."

"Attaboy!" said Herbert Tolliver, tousling the hair of his pride and joy.

DeDe's Growing Dilemma

WHEN DEDE CALLED BEAUCHAMP AT WORK, HE was briefing Halcyon's hottest new model on the Adorable Christmas campaign.

"Look, I'm right in the middle of . . ."

"Sorry, darling. I just . . . I was afraid you'd forget about Pinkie and Herbert's opening tonight."

"Shit."

"You forgot."

"What time do we have to be there?"

"I can meet you after work. We just need to make an appearance."

"Six o'clock?"

"Fine . . . I love you, Beauchamp."

"Me too. Six o'clock, then?"

"Yeah. Be good."

"Always."

He hung up and winked at D'orothea. "My wife. Sometimes I think God put women on this earth to remind men of cocktail parties."

D'orothea merely grunted.

"Ah," Beauchamp grinned. "That makes me sound like a chauvinist pig, I guess."

"No," she said coldly. "Do you want it to?"

The Hoover Gallery was jammed with patrons, a canvas of kelly green and pink. The women were decked out in understated Lilly Pulitzers, while their blue-blazered husbands expressed their individuality in madras patchwork trousers.

Beauchamp and DeDe headed directly to the bar, wearing identical smiles and flaunting their new-found bliss like Tahitian tans.

DeDe was still clinging to Beauchamp's arm when Binky Gruen intercepted them.

"Oh, thank God you two showed up! Beauchamp, quick, gimme a kiss! I have to look occupied!"

Beauchamp pecked her on the cheek. "I've heard better excuses, Ms. Gruen."

"Keep talking, goddammit! He's looking this way!"

"Who?"

"Carson Callas. He's been blowing pipe breath at me for the past fifteen minutes, telling me how sexy he is! Yecchh!"

Beauchamp recoiled in mock surprise. "You don't think Carson Callas is sexy?"

"Sure. If you get off on midgets in puka shells."

"Naughty, naughty. He won't put you in his column, Binky."

"Or vice versa, if *I* can help it. Look, be an angel and fill this up with scotch. I feel an attack of ennui coming on. Your skinny wife looks thirsty too."

Beauchamp took Binky's glass, then turned to DeDe. "Champagne, Skinny Wife?"

"Please." Her tone was deliberately chilly. She *hated* it when Binky and Beauchamp did their Lombard and Gable routine.

By the time Beauchamp had disappeared into the crowd, Binky was ready to pounce.

"Well?"

"Well, what?"

"Did you see Dr. Fielding?"

"Binky . . . this is hardly the place."

"Yes or no?"

"Yes."

Binky whistled. "I've got a good abortion man, if you need one."

"Binky . . . will you just shut up, please!"

"Well, *pardonnez-moi!* I thought you could use a friend about now. I guess I was mistaken."

"Binky, I . . . Look, I'm sorry . . . it's just that you make it sound so . . . A good abortion man, for heaven's sake! Does he cater parties too?"

Binky giggled. "No, but he's *marvelous* with windows and floors!"

"That's not funny."

"Well, I think you're getting *much* too heavy about this whole business." She patted DeDe's stomach. "No pun intended, darling. Look . . . if all that nasty Catholic guilt is gonna be too much for you, why don't you just go ahead and have the little bastard?"

"I thought you had that one figured out already."

"What the hell? Beauchamp can play along. He needs an heir, doesn't he? Who's gonna know the difference?"

"Binky . . . you don't know what you're talking about. . . ."

"Don't tell me it would *show?*"

DeDe glared at her for several seconds, then nodded.

"Hair?" asked Binky, her eyes fairly dancing with excitement. "A different color hair?"

"No."

"Not *skin?*"

Another nod.

"Oh, you poor baby! Oh, DeDe, I didn't mean to be so . . . What color?"

DeDe pointed to her daffodil Diane von Furstenberg and burst into tears.

*   *   *

273

After repairing her mascara in the bathroom, she merged with the mob again. Beauchamp was waiting with lukewarm champagne.

"I'm with Peter and Shugie," he said. "Wanna join us?"

She shook her head with a watery smile. "Not right now, Beauchamp. Binky and I are catching up."

Alone again, she plastered a smile on her face and headed toward the corner where Binky was holding court. A hand stopped her, clamping onto her forearm.

"Well, doesn't Mrs. Day look good enough to eat?"

If her arm had been free, she might have crossed herself. It was the society editor of *Western Gentry* magazine.

Carson Callas.

Mrs. Madrigal and the Mouse

MICHAEL WAS SHIFTING HALF OF HIS CLOTHES INTO Mona's closet when Mrs. Madrigal phoned.

"Michael, dear. Could you come down for a moment?"

"Sure. Three minutes, O.K.?"

"Take your time, dear."

Well, he thought, hanging up the phone, here it comes. Eviction time. She's been more than lenient about the rent so far, but enough is enough.

He slipped into corduroy trousers and a white shirt, brushed his teeth, Pro-Maxed his hair into place, and ran a wet towel across his Weejuns.

There was no point in *looking* like a deadbeat.

The landlady's angular face, usually so mobile, was locked into the smile of a corporate receptionist.

She seemed artificially restrained, moving with such deliberate dignity that her kimono looked as dowdy as a housecoat.

"Mona's left, hasn't she?"

He nodded. "Yesterday."

"For good?"

"So she says. But you know Mona."

"Yes." Her smile was off-kilter.

"I'm gonna stay, Mrs. Madrigal. I mean . . . I'd *like* to. Mona's gonna pay off the rest of this month's rent, and I've registered with an employment agency, so if you're worried . . ."

"Where did she go, Michael?"

"Oh . . . uh . . . a friend's house. In Pacific Heights."

Mrs. Madrigal walked to the window, where she stood motionless, keeping her back to Michael. "Pacific Heights," she echoed.

"Didn't she . . . talk to you, Mrs. Madrigal?"

"No."

"I'm sure she planned to. Things have been kinda hectic for her lately. Anyway, *I'm* still here. It's not like she's breaking a lease or anything."

"Do you know this person, Michael?"

"Who? . . . Oh . . . no, I've never met her."

"A woman?"

He nodded. "Somebody she knew in New York."

"Oh."

"Mona says she's really nice."

"I'm sure . . . Michael, you don't have to answer this if you don't want to. . . ."

"Uh huh?"

"Is this woman . . . are she and Mona special friends?"

"Uh . . ."

"Do you understand me, dear?"

"Sure. I don't know, Mrs. Madrigal. They *used* to be . . . in New York. I think they're just . . . regular friends now."

"Well . . . then why on earth . . . ? Michael, has Mona ever said anything to you about me? Anything that . . . might make you think she was unhappy here?"

"No, ma'am," he said earnestly, reverting to Central Floridian custom. "She was *crazy* about Barbary Lane . . . and she liked you a lot."

Mrs. Madrigal turned to face him. "Liked?" she asked.

"No. Likes. She's *very* fond of you, I'm sure she'll call. Really."

The landlady turned crisply businesslike again. "Well, *you're* staying. That's something."

"I'll try to be better about the rent."

"I know. Look, dear, I've got a brand-new lid, and the night is young. Will you join me?"

Her fingers trembled noticeably as she worked the roller. She set it down, drew a breath, and massaged her forehead with both hands. "I'm sorry, Mouse. I'm being awfully silly."

"Please don't . . . Where did you hear that name?"

She chewed her lower lip for a moment, observing him. "I'm not the only one that Mona was fond of."

"Oh . . . yeah."

"My stupid fingers won't behave! Would you do the . . .?"

He took the roller from her, avoiding her eyes as they began to fill with tears. "Mrs. Madrigal, I wish I could say . . ."

She moved no closer, but her long, slender hand came to rest on his knee as she pressed a handkerchief to her face. "I *hate* weepy women," she said.

The Shadow Knows

THE RAT-FACED MAN IN THE SAFARI SUIT MOVED SO close to DeDe that she could smell the Cherry Blend on his breath. "You've lost weight," he smirked, flashing an uneven row of Vuitton-colored teeth.

DeDe nodded. "How have you been, Carson?"

"Hangin' in there. A fat farm, huh?"

"The Golden Door." She smiled when she said it, without elaborating. He was pumping her, she knew, and she didn't relish the thought of reading about her weight problem in *Western Gentry* magazine.

"Well, it looks damn good."

"Thanks, Carson."

"What do you think of the artist?"

That threw her for a moment. Paintings were the *last* thing she noticed at an opening. "Oh . . . a very individual style. Quite sensitive, I think . . ."

"You and Beauchamp in the market?"

"Oh . . . no, I don't think so, Carson. Beauchamp and I are into Western art."

He sucked on his pipe, never taking his tiny eyes off her

face. "This man's Western," he said finally.

"I mean . . . you know . . . the old stuff."

"Yeah, the old stuff. Sometimes the old stuff's better." He winked at her, chewing methodically on his pipestem until she acknowledged the joke with a thin smile.

"Excuse me, will you, Carson? I think Beauchamp . . ."

"I was hoping you'd tell me about the Fol de Rol."

"Oh . . . sure." Her spirits brightened instantly. This could be a *coup* that would drive Shugie Sussman up the wall!

Callas pulled a pad and pencil from the pocket of his safari suit. "You're on the committee, right?"

"Yeah. Me and a few others."

"Who's performing this year?"

"Oh, it's *fabulous,* Carson! The theme is 'Wine, Women and Song' and we've got Domingo, Troyanos and Wixell. . . ."

"First names?"

"Placido Domingo . . ."

"Oh, sure . . ."

"Tatiana Troyanos and Ingvar Wixell." She stopped herself from spelling the names, remembering Callas' vanity. He could look them up when he got back to his office.

The columnist returned the pad and pencil to his pocket. "Fun evening, huh?"

"Should be."

"But not as fun as most of yours?"

"Uh . . . what, Carson?"

The leer was back again. "I think you heard me, sweetheart."

The crowd in the gallery had grown thicker and noisier, but now the din seemed oddly remote. DeDe swallowed and forced herself to look blasé.

"Carson, really! Sometimes you can be *too* much!"

"I think we've got a lot in common."

"Carson, I don't know what . . ."

"Look . . . we're both grownups. Nobody ever accused me of not knowing my way around an orgy . . . and I think I can recognize a kindred spirit when I see one."

279

God, she thought, how many times had he used *that* one?

It was a standing joke in town that Callas had once unsuc-
cessfully propositioned the entire cast of a local musical
revue, starting with the women and working down to the less
attractive men.

"Carson . . . I love chatting with you, but I think I need a
drink."

"One more question about the Fol de Rol?"

"Sure."

"Are you gonna have the abortion before or after?"

The glass slipped from her hand almost instantly, shatter-
ing as a punctuation to the horrid question. Callas dropped
to his knees and helped her gather the pieces in a cocktail
napkin.

"Ah, c'mon! It's not that bad, DeDe. I'm sure we can work
it out . . . if you'd like to talk about it some night." He stuffed
his business card into the belt of her dress and stood up
again.

"Your friends are *concerned,*" he added. "Surely there's
nothing wrong with that?"

She didn't look up, but continued picking up the pieces in
silence.

Discretion was too much to expect of Binky Gruen.

How to Cure the Munchies

BRIAN CRASHED AT MIDNIGHT AFTER A GRUELING SHIFT at Perry's, only to wake up five hours later with a bitch of an appetite.

Stumbling into the kitchen in his boxer shorts, he rummaged through the refrigerator for something to placate his growl.

Ketchup. Mayonnaise. Two bluish Ball Park franks. And a jar of cocktail onions.

Had he been stoned, he might have hacked it. (Once, after smoking half a joint of Maui Wowie, he'd been reduced to using Crisco as a dip for Ritz crackers.)

But not tonight.

Tonight—hell, five o'clock in the morning!—he lusted for a Zim-burger. And a fat, greasy side order of fries, and maybe a chocolate malt or a . . .

He excavated in his laundry bag until he found a rugby shirt that would pass the sniff test, climbed into Levi's and Adidas, and almost sprinted out of the house into Barbary Lane.

Hyde Street was freakishly quiet. Asleep in its iron cocoon, the ancient cable seemed more intrusive than ever. From the crest of Russian Hill, the wharf was a colorless landscape, a black-and-white postcard from the forties.

Even the Porsches parked on Francisco suggested abandonment.

It felt like the last scene of *On the Beach.*

Zim's, by contrast, was jarringly cheery. The all-night eatery was humming with efficient waitresses, frazzled insomniacs and the remnants of parties that couldn't stop.

Brian's waitress was dressed in commercial country-western. Orange blouse and jumper. Orange-checked kerchief. Her name tag said "Candi Colma."

" 'The City of the Dead.' " Brian grinned as she slapped a napkin and fork in front of him.

"What?"

"You're from Colma. Cemeteryland."

"South San Francisco, really. Just over the border. South San Francisco was too long to put on the name tag."

"Candi Colma sounds nicer, anyway."

"Really." Her smile was nice, implying an intimacy that didn't exist. She was in her late thirties, Brian guessed, but it showed only around the eyes. Her waist was small and firm, her legs wickedly long.

Never mind the teased blond hair, he thought. You can't get picky at five o'clock in the morning.

After she had taken his order, he watched her move across the room. She walked like a woman who knew she had an audience.

"Zimburger O.K.?"

"Fine. Perfect."

"Anything else? Dessert, maybe?"

"Whatcha got to offer?"

"It's on the menu there, sugar."

He flapped the menu shut and gave her his best Huck Finn grin. "I bet it's not . . . sugar."

Moving closer to him, she tapped her pencil against her lower lip, cast her eyes left and right, and whispered, "I don't get off till seven o'clock."

Brian shrugged. "It's not *when* you get off, is it? It's *how.*"

Candi's Camaro was parked around the corner next to the Maritime Museum. It was plum-colored and its bumper sticker said: I BRAKE FOR ANIMALS.

When the seat-belt buzzers had stopped, she looked at him apologetically. "I'd feel better if we went to my place."

"Colma?"

She nodded. "If you don't mind."

"Christ, that's a half hour's drive!"

"The traffic's not bad when you're going this direction."

"How the hell am I gonna get home?"

"I'll drive you. Look . . . I've got a roommate."

Brian slammed his palm against his forehead. "Oh, shit."

"No. It's a girl. It's cool, really. It's just that she'll worry if I'm not home."

"Call her, then."

She shook her head. "I'm sorry, Brian. If you'd like to forget it, I'll understand."

"No. Let's go."

"You don't have to, if . . ."

"I said let's go, didn't I?"

She stuck the key in the ignition. "I live in a trailer. I hope you don't mind."

He shook his head and stared out at the pewter surface of the early-morning bay.

He was sure of it now.

This had all happened before.

The Hungry Eye

NORMAN WAS WOLFING DOWN A BREAKFAST OF COLD egg rolls when the telephone rang.

The noise startled him. He wasn't used to receiving calls in the little house on the roof.

"Hello."

"Mr. Williams?"

He recognized the grating Midwestern twang immediately. "I hope this is important."

"Well, I . . . I was just wondering how it was going."

"Look, I gave you the number of my answering service, right?"

"Mr. Williams . . . I've left three messages with your service in the last two . . ."

"Do you think you're my only client?"

"Of course not . . . but I don't see why you can't . . ."

"You're perfectly free to find another man, if you want." He knew it was safe to say that. He was too valuable to her now.

"I have the utmost confidence in you . . ."

"I'm working on *three* missing husbands right now . . . plus a runaway kid from Denver and more guys messing around on their wives than I can . . . You're paying me by the job, remember? Not by the hour."

"I know." Her tone was placating.

"You could've blown the whole thing by calling me here. I've got no privacy at all in this cracker box. There could've been somebody sitting two feet away from me who would've figured out the . . ."

"I know, Mr. Williams. I'm sorry I . . . Could you just tell me if you've found out anything?"

He waited for a moment, then said, "It's going O.K."

"Do you think . . .?"

"I think she's the one."

That rocked her. "God," she said incredulously.

"I have to go slow, though. It's ticklish."

"I understand."

"People are sticky out here about privacy, you know."

"Of course."

"It should be a matter of weeks. I can tell you that."

"I hope you can understand why I'm so . . ."

"Look . . . look at it this way, O.K.? You've waited thirty years already. Another month or so won't kill you."

"I thought you said two weeks."

"Mrs. Ramsey!"

"All right. O.K. Did you find out if the name is . . ."

"Yeah. Phony. It's an anagram."

"Anna Madrigal? You mean it spells . . .?"

"Look, lady! Will you wait for my goddamn report!"

"I won't bother you again, Mr. Williams."

She hung up.

The call unsettled him for the rest of the morning. Who the hell was he kidding?

The kid from Denver had shown up *weeks* ago, canceling the most potentially lucrative job of his career. Most of his missing-persons clients had switched to slicker agencies, and he hadn't been offered a philandering-husband case since 1972.

He prolonged the Ramsey case because it was his *only* case

285

. . . and he couldn't confront the reality of failure.

If things kept up like this for long, he might be selling Nutri-Vim for real.

"Paul?"

"Yeah?"

"It's Norman."

"Hey, man . . . the proofs aren't ready yet. I'll call you when they're ready, O.K.?"

"I didn't call about that. I thought . . . well, I thought you might wanna schedule the next session."

"Nah. Too soon. Besides . . . I think we're gonna film this week."

"How's it pay?"

"Not bad. You wanna . . .?"

"Yeah. I can arrange it."

"How much notice do you need?"

"Couple days."

"Can do."

"I want the money in advance, Paul."

"You got it."

Trauma in a Travel-Eze

THE TREASURE ISLAND TRAILER COURT WAS A DREARY little encampment just off El Camino Real at the Colma-South San Francisco border.

Its nearest neighbor was Cypress Lawn Cemetery.

As Candi's Camaro swung off the highway into the court, Brian winced at the ugly row of Monopoly board houses snaking along a distant hillside.

Rows.

Peninsula people often condemned themselves to rows, thought Brian. Rows of houses, rows of apartments, rows of tombstones . . .

Ah, but not so at the Treasure Island Trailer Court. The Treasure Island Trailer Court had *rues.*

French. Much classier.

Rue 1, Rue 2, Rue 3 . . . Candi's home was a faded pink Travel-Eze mired in a bed of succulents on Rue 8. An engraved redwood sign out front said: CANDI AND CHERYL.

And that was all he needed to know.

"Uh . . . Candi. There's something I should tell you."

"Uh huh?"

"You're not gonna believe this, but . . . I think I know your roommate."

"Cheryl?"

"Does she work at Zim's too?"

Candi grinned. "The morning shift. That's O.K., Brian. We hardly ever see each other."

"I've been here before, Candi."

She squeezed his thigh. "I said it was O.K., didn't I?"

Apparently it was O.K. with Cheryl too.

Wolfing down a breakfast of Froot Loops, she looked only mildly surprised when Brian slumped in with Candi. "Well, look what the cat drug in."

She was younger than Candi. Considerably. Brian did a heavy déjà vu number on her pouty Bernadette Peters mouth. He would have swapped on the spot, given the chance. "Small world, huh?"

She grinned lewdly. "Not particularly. I'd say you've just run out of material."

Candi slammed her way into the bedroom, shouting over her shoulder at her roommate. "You're late again, Cheryl. I'm not gonna keep makin' excuses for you. It's gettin' embarrassing."

"I was waiting for my fuckin' *wig*, if you don't mind!"

Silence.

"Did you hear me?"

The voice from the bedroom was low and menacing. "Cheryl, come in here a minute."

"I'm finishing my Froot . . ."

"Goddammit, Cheryl!"

Cheryl pushed her chair back noisily, rolled her eyes at Brian and left the room. A muffled catfight followed. When Cheryl reemerged several minutes later, she was wearing a Zim's uniform and Candi's head of hair.

"Don't break the bed," she purred to Brian, goosing him as she walked out the door.

288

"Brian?"

"Huh?"

"Would you like something to drink? A Pepsi or something?"

"Hey. You're off duty, remember?"

"I just thought . . . well, you know. Sometimes people get thirsty afterwards."

"I'm fine."

"Was I . . . ? Do you think I'm as pretty as Cheryl? I mean . . . I know I'm older and all, but, you know, like for my age . . . do you think I look O.K.?"

He wiggled her earlobe and kissed the tip of her nose. "Better than O.K. Even without that damn wig."

She beamed. "You know what? I've got the whole day off, and the Camaro's full of gas. . . ."

"I've gotta get home, Candi. I'm expecting a phone call."

"It wouldn't take long. I could show you a pumpkin patch. They're beautiful right now."

He shook his head, smiling.

"Do you want me to drive you home?"

"There's a bus, isn't there?"

"Yeah. If you want. It's no trouble for me, Brian."

He climbed out of bed. "I don't mind the bus."

"I'd like it if you'd call me."

"Sure. You in the book?"

She nodded.

"I'll call you, then."

"It's Moretti."

"O.K."

"Two *t's.*"

"Good. I'll give you a buzz in a week or so."

He got out without giving her his last name, but not without noticing a photograph framed on the bathroom wall.

Cheryl in a high school cap and gown.

Candi in street clothes, giving her a hug.

And this inscription: "To the best Mom in the whole wide world."

And Baby Makes Three?

A WAGNERIAN FOG WAS SETTLING OVER THE AVE-nues when DeDe drove away from Carson Callas' house in her husband's silver Porsche.

Done.

She shivered a little, thinking of it. That icky little body. The yellowed fingernails digging into her flesh. The . . . thing . . . he kept in the bedside table.

Her secret, however, was still intact, and she doubted very seriously that the columnist would demand a repeat performance. By the time she reached Upper Montgomery Street the horrid indignity of it all seemed as dim and distant as Cotillion days.

Riding the elevator to the penthouse, she felt almost noble about it. She had sacrificed something, bitten the bullet . . . for the sake of her marriage, for the sake of the Halcyon family name.

* * *

"How were the whales?" asked Beauchamp.

"Same as before," she lied. "We're still trying to set a date for the benefit."

"I think you'd be better off in Leukemia."

"Muffy does Leukemia. It's not very original."

"Crippled children, then."

"God, no. We went to at *least* three crippled children tea dances last month. Anyway, you don't have to have your picture taken with whales." She sat in his lap and planted a kiss on his mouth. "You don't look like you missed me that much."

"I've been reading."

"What?"

"You're sitting on it."

"Oh." She shifted onto the arm of the wing chair as Beauchamp held up a copy of *Some Kind of Hero*.

"James Kirkwood," he said.

DeDe studied the book jacket. "It's about Vietnam?"

"Yeah. Sort of."

"Beauchamp?"

"Huh?"

"Take me to bed, will you?"

"It's been a long day, DeDe."

"Just to cuddle, O.K.?"

He dropped the book on the floor and smiled at her. "O.K."

"Beauchamp?"

"Mmm?"

"We're doing better, don't you think?"

"At what?"

"You know . . . living together."

"What do you want? A Good Housekeeping Seal of Approval?"

"Really, though, I think . . ."

"Marriage is a bitch, DeDe . . . for *everybody*. Other people don't do much better than we do. I've told you that all along."

"Still . . . I think we're learning more . . . growing."

"O.K. If that makes you feel any better."

"Doesn't it make *you* feel better?"

"I suppose."

"Before . . . I really didn't think we were *mature* enough to raise children."

"Jesus Christ!"

"Well, you have to admit we've weathered . . ."

"How many times do I have to tell you, DeDe? I have no intention of . . ."

"You! *You!* It's *my* body! What if I *want* a baby? What about *that,* huh?"

He sat up in bed and smirked at her. "Fine. Go get somebody else to knock you up."

"You're disgusting!"

"Don't expect me to pay for it, though. *Or* to live with it."

"It? It's not a thing, Beauchamp. It's a *human being!*"

His eyes burned into her. "Christ! Are you pregnant?"

"No."

"Well, shut up, then . . . and go to sleep. I've got a long day tomorrow."

Ties That Bind

MARY ANN SPENT HER LUNCH HOUR AT HASTINGS, picking out just the right tie for Norman. The hint might not be terribly subtle, she decided, but *somebody* had to do something about that gross, gravy-stained clip-on number.

Walking back to Jackson Square, she watched as a big yellow Hertz truck parked on Montgomery Street in a commercial zone.

The burly driver sauntered to the back of the truck and opened the double doors.

Inside were at least two dozen young women, packed as tightly as cattle in a disinfectant chamber. They were giggling nervously, and most of them appeared to be dressed for office work.

"O.K.," said the driver. "Stand on the lift. Six at a time." He returned to the front of the truck, as the young women waited obediently to be lowered to the street. When the last of them had stepped off the hydraulic lift, the driver came back to issue them each a cardboard box with a neck strap attached.

The boxes contained complimentary mini-packs of Newport Lights.

Mary Ann shuddered. So *that's* where they came from! Those pathetic creatures who stood on street corners, pushing free cigarettes and lucky wooden nickels and garish fliers for yet another soup-and-sandwich spot.

There were worse jobs than hers. Plenty of them.

She quickened her pace. She was already fifteen minutes late.

Back at the agency, she breathed a sigh of relief. Mr. Halcyon was still in conference with Adorable.

She opened the tie box and looked at her purchase again. It was silk, with maroon and navy stripes. Conservative but . . . sharp. Just the thing Norman needed.

She doodled on a note pad with a Flair, ending up with this:

> *don't listen when they scoff*
> *that you are old and i am young,*
> *for i am old enough to know better*
> *and you are young enough not to care.*

Not bad, she concluded. And poetry was fabulous therapy, taking her back to simpler days at Central High when she cranked out anguished, e.e. cummings-style verses for the *Plume and Palette.*

But *this* poem made her uncomfortable somehow, touching a little too close to the defensiveness she felt about her relationship with Norman.

What relationship? So far, they had only kissed. A perfectly tame good-night kiss, at that. Norman was like . . . a big brother? No . . . and not exactly an uncle, either.

She felt toward Norman what she felt toward Gregory Peck when she was twelve and saw *To Kill a Mockingbird* five times . . . just to experience that goose-bumpy, dry-throated, shivery feeling that came over her whenever Atticus Finch appeared on the screen.

294

But Norman Neal Williams was no Gregory Peck.

She tore up the poem.

Mr. Halcyon was still in conference when Beauchamp sidled up to her cubicle.

"Rough day?"

"Not particularly," she answered with deliberate blandness.

"You look a little . . . bummed out."

"I guess it's my biorhythms." She wasn't exactly sure what that meant, but it kept things impersonal.

"Can I buy you a drink tonight?"

She stared at him icily. "I don't believe you. I really don't."

"Just trying to be nice."

"Thank you very much. I have a date tonight."

"Aha! Where's the lucky man taking you?"

She slipped a sheet of paper into her typewriter. "I don't see why you should care about . . ."

"Oh, c'mon! I'd like to know."

She began to type. "Some place called the Beach Chalet."

"Ah."

"You know it?"

"Sure. You'll love it. The VFW meets there."

She looked up to see a smirk curl across his face. He headed into the hallway again, where he saluted her crisply. "Don't OD on Beer Nuts, toots!"

New York, New York

RIVETED TO THE RECEIVER OF HER ANTIQUE FRENCH telephone, D'orothea wielded a gold-tipped Sherman like a conductor's baton.

She was talking to New York again.

The fourth time in two days.

Mona watched in cynical silence, curled up comfortably on their new buff suede Billy Gaylord banquette. She was sick of competing with New York.

"Oh, Bobby," shrieked D'orothea, "that's the third time this month you've taken Lina to The Toilet. . . . Well, I know, honey, but . . . Well, look, Bobby. Once is slumming, three times is just plain *sick*. . . . It isn't at *all* like The Anvil. The Anvil was fun in the old days. I mean, Rudi went there, for God's sake! . . . I never saw that. . . . They weren't, Bobby. I never saw any of that business with the fists. . . . Anyway, The Toilet is just plain flat-out *scuzzy*. I totaled a perfectly good pair of Bergdorf Goodman shoes. . . ."

It went on like that for ten minutes. When D'orothea hung up, she smiled apologetically at Mona. "Shit, I got out just in time. The Big Apple's getting too wormy for words."

"Is that why you need a progress report every night?"

"It *isn't* every night."

"We have depravity here too, you know . . . and what the hell's The Toilet?"

"It's a bar."

"Of course."

"It's in *Vogue* this month."

"How gauche of me not to . . ."

"Hey . . . what is it with you, Mona?"

"I'm just sick of dealing with New York, that's all. I mean, you've moved back here now, and it seems to me that you could . . ."

"That isn't it, Mona. You've been brooding about something."

"I'm not brooding. I'm always like this."

"I think you miss Michael."

"Don't overanalyze things."

"Hon, if we don't talk about it . . ."

"It's nothing. I'm in a bitchy mood. Forget it."

"I'm a little claustrophobic myself. C'mon . . . let's take a walk."

Back at Barbary Lane, Brian Hawkins was boiling a bag of frozen chow mein. When it was ready, he gulped it down at the kitchen table while he leafed through his mail.

Not much. An Occupant notice about a new pizzeria. A circular from the Chicago Urban League. A garish pink envelope listing the Treasure Island Trailer Court as the return address.

The envelope contained a note card bearing the face of a Keane child, a sugary nymphet staring mawkishly from a tenement window.

Dear Brian,
    They gave me your address at Perry's. I hope you don't mind. I just wanted to tell you what a fabulous time I had with you. You are a real sweet guy, and I hope you will call

me some time. I can't call you cuz I'm not aggressive. Ha ha.
Seriously, you are really a neat person. Don't feel like you
have to write back.

Luff ya,
CANDI

She had dotted the *i* in "Candi" with a Happy Face.

He dumped the mail into his garbage bag, left the dishes in
the sink, and went into the bedroom to roll a joint. There was
a little Maui Wowie left. Enough for a good buzz, anyway.

He lay on his back on the Busvan sofa, sorting out the
half-assed little escapades of the last six months. Mary Ann
Singleton, who *still* tormented him . . . Connie Bradshaw, a
veritable museum of kitsch . . . that chick at the Sutro Baths
. . . and now a goddamn mother-and-daughter team!

He laughed out loud at himself.

Either he was a masochist or God was a sadist.

Minutes later, he was up again, changing into Levi's and a
khaki army shirt. He headed for the door, stopped, and returned to roll another joint.

Then he bounded downstairs to the second floor and rang
Michael's buzzer.

Full Moon in Sea Cliff

JON FIELDING COULDN'T HELP BUT FEEL A TWINGE OF ENVY when the Hampton-Giddes' houseboy offered him a stuffed mushroom.

Harold was an absolute *find.*

Efficient, courteous and intelligent. With just enough café au lait skin and gray at the temples to make him seem like an old family retainer . . . a spare servant that Mother had shipped from Bar Harbor.

"He's a gem," Jon said to Collier Lane as soon as Harold had moved on.

Collier nodded. "Perfect. Sort of a gay Uncle Ben."

"He's gay?"

"Better be. He's the one who shows the movies."

"Here?"

"Over there. In front of that Claes Oldenburg that looks like a couple of Hefty bags. A screen comes down. They're showing *Boys in the Sand* after cigars and brandy."

The Hampton-Giddes, John observed, hadn't skimped on anything. Brown suede walls. A chrome bin for the fireplace logs. Travertine marble for *days* and a lighting system that would have functioned nicely for a smallish production of *Aïda.*

The doctor grinned at his lawyer friend. "Somebody told me they've even got the television on a dimmer switch."

Collier smiled back. "They've got their whole *life* on a dimmer switch."

There were eight people at the dinner party. Rick Hampton and Arch Gidde (the Hampton-Giddes), Ed Stoker and Chuck Lord (the Stoker-Lords), Bill Hill and Tony Hughes (the Hill-Hugheses), and Jon Fielding and Collier Lane.

Jon and Collier sought refuge in the Hampton-Giddes' black onyx bathroom.

"Christ, Jon, aren't you sick of hearing about remodeled kitchens?"

"Have a line," said the doctor. "Things go better with coke."

The Hampton-Giddes had provided the cocaine for their guests. In the bathroom only. Out of sight from the servants. Collier snorted a line.

"Let's go to the tubs," he said, straightening up.

"We can't just walk out, Collier."

"Who can't? I'm bored shitless."

"Have another line, then."

"Where are the twinks, anyway? They usually have the decency to provide one or two decorative twinks. . . . Jesus, who needs to waste a night staring at these tired old Gucci queens."

"I can't leave now. Maybe after the movie . . ."

"Fuck the movie! Whatever happened to the real thing? My God, there's a full moon tonight! Can't you imagine the tubs . . . ?"

Jon tweaked Collier's cheek. "There's such a thing as social obligation, turkey."

"You're a jellyfish, Fielding."

Jon smiled. "Take a cold shower. It'll keep."

* * *

"So," said William Devereux Hill III, passing the braised endive to Edward Paxton Stoker, Jr., "Tony and I checked the St. Louis Social Register, and they are *not* in it. Neither one of them."

"Jesus."

"And let's face it, honey. In St. Louis, it's *not* that difficult!"

"How about the eighth?" asked Archibald Anson Gidde.

Charles Hillary Lord checked his black leather Hermès appointment book. "Sorry. Edward's taking Mrs. Langhurst to hear Edo that night. Once again, I'm a symphony widow."

"What about the following Wednesday?"

"That's our ACT night."

"I give up."

"It's mad, isn't it?" sighed Charles Hillary Lord.

"How's the twink?" asked Richard Evan Hampton, smirking across the travertine table at Jon Philip Fielding.

"Who?"

"The twink in the jockey shorts. At The Endup."

"Oh . . . I haven't seen him for a while."

"Well, he was hardly your type, was he?"

"Oh?"

"Well, I mean, how many people do you know who enter jockey shorts dance contests?"

"I knew *him*. And I liked him, Rick."

"Well, pardon me, Mary."

"No, pardon me."

"What?"

"It's a full moon, Mr. Hampton, and I've had just about as much of this DAR meeting as I can take. Will you excuse me, gentlemen?" He pushed back his chair, stood up and nodded to his friend. "I'll get a cab," he said.

"The hell you will," said Collier Lane.

They wore their Brioni blazers to the tubs.

Norman Confesses

AFTER THREE WHITE WINES AT THE BEACH CHALET, Mary Ann felt much better about the bar's Archie Bunker ambience.

"I like this place," she told Norman honestly. "It's very . . . down-to-earth." Beauchamp could just go to hell with his snotty crack about the VFW.

"I thought you might get a kick out of the muriels," said Norman.

"The . . . ?"

"The paintings on the walls."

"Oh . . . yes, they're beautiful. Art Nouveau, right?"

Norman nodded. "Good ol' Mr. Roosevelt and the WPA. Hey, how about a little walk on the beach?"

The idea didn't particularly appeal to her. It was cold outside, and there was something really cozy about the glowing beer signs and the bowling-jacketed patrons bellied up to the bar.

She smiled at him. "*You'd* like to, wouldn't you?"

"Yes."

"Is something the matter, Norman?"

"No. I'd just like to take a walk, O.K.?"

"Sure."

He smiled and touched the tip of her nose.

She took Norman's arm when they reached the sand, fortifying herself with his warmth. Beneath a full moon, the Cliff House gleamed like a mansion out of Daphne du Maurier.

She was the first to speak.

"Do you want to talk?"

"I wish . . . never mind."

"What, Norman?"

"I wish I was better-looking."

"Norman!"

"The *old* part wouldn't be so bad, if . . . forget it."

She stopped walking and made him turn to face her. "In the first place . . . you are *not* old, Norman. There's no reason for you to go around apologizing for that all the time. And in the second place, you are a *very* strong, masculine and . . . appealing man."

He acted as if he hadn't heard any of it. "Why do you go out with me, Mary Ann?"

She threw her hands up and groaned. "You're not even *listening.*"

"Lots of guys are after you. I've seen the way Brian Hawkins looks at you."

"Oh, please!"

"Don't you think Brian's handsome?"

"Brian Hawkins thinks any woman who goes to bed with him is . . ." She cut herself short.

"Is what?"

"Norman . . ."

"Is *what?*"

"A whore."

"Oh."

"Norman . . . I wish I could show you the things you've got going for you."

"Don't strain yourself."

"Norman, you are *gentle* . . . and considerate . . . and you believe in a lot of . . . traditional values . . . and you don't make

303

me feel like I'm out of it all the time."

He laughed bleakly. "Because I'm more out of it than you are."

"I didn't say that. And thanks a lot!"

"Do you think I could make you happy, Mary Ann?"

She had been afraid of that one. "Norman . . . I always have a good time with you."

"That's not what I asked."

"We haven't known each other very long."

The line was so weak she was instantly sorry she had used it. She studied his face for damage. He seemed to be struggling with something. His features were strangely distorted.

"I don't push pills, Mary Ann."

"What?"

"I don't sell Nutri-Vim. I just told you that to . . . I just told you that."

"But what about the . . . ?"

"I'm coming into a lot of money really soon. I can buy you anything you want. I know I must look like a failure now, but I'm . . ."

"Norman," she said as gently as possible, "I don't want you to *buy* me anything."

His face had eroded completely. He stared at her in desolation.

"Norman . . ." She reached up and readjusted his new tie. "It looks . . . real nice on you."

"I'll take you home."

"Please don't feel like . . ."

"It's O.K. I just . . . want too much sometimes."

He said almost nothing on the way back to Barbary Lane.

What D'or Won't Tell Her

A FLUORESCENT PHONE BOOTH GLOWED LIKE ECTO-plasm against the black slope of Alta Plaza as Mona and D'orothea strolled west up Jackson Street.

Mona shuddered. "What a creepy place to make a phone call!"

"You're afraid of the dark?"

"Terrified."

"I never would've guessed."

"I thought everybody was afraid of the dark. It's the only thing that distinguishes us from animals."

D'or grinned. "Not me. Black is Beautiful, remember?"

"It looks good on *you,* anyway."

D'or stopped walking and took Mona's hands in hers. "Hon . . . would you still . . . ?"

"What?"

"Nothing." She dismissed the thought with a wave of her hand and began walking again. "No big deal."

Mona frowned. "I hate that."

"What, hon?"

"The way you weed out things you think I can't handle."

"I don't mean to seem . . ."

"I'm not all that fucking fragile, D'or. Don't you think you could *communicate* a little more?"

"Fine." D'or looked hurt.

"And I don't need to hear that you love me. I *know* you love me, D'or. The thing is . . . you don't really share your . . . your thoughts with me. Sometimes I feel like I'm living with a stranger."

Silence.

"I'm sorry. You asked what was bothering me."

"You want to move out. Is that it?"

"No! I never expected miracles, D'or . . . ever. I just . . ."

"Is it the sex part? I've told you that isn't important to me if . . ."

"D'or . . . I *like* you a lot."

"Ouch."

"Well, goddammit . . . that's a lot, isn't it? I mean, I'm not sure I even need a lover, male *or* female. Sometimes I think I'd settle for five good friends."

They walked in silence for several minutes. Then D'orothea said: "So what do we do?"

"I want to stay, D'or."

"But I have to shape up. Is that it?"

"I didn't say that."

"Look, Mona . . . you're bitching about *something.*"

Mona glared at her. "Do you really think it's my function in life to sit here on my ass all day while you're out there making another hundred thou off the same son-of-a-bitch who fired me?"

"Mona . . . I could talk to Edgar Halcyon about . . ."

"You do and I'll pack tomorrow."

"Well, *what* then? What do you want me to do?"

"I don't know . . . I feel cut off, somehow. I can't hack all these blue-haired old ladies with Mace in their pocketbooks, marching their poodles endlessly up and down the . . ."

"There's nothing I can do about . . ."

"You could let me share your life, D'or. Introduce me to

306

your friends . . . and your family. Christ, your parents are in Oakland and I've never even *seen* them!''

D'orothea's tone grew chilly. "Let's not drag my parents into this."

"Ah!"

"What's *that* supposed to mean?"

"It means you're *petrified* that Mommy and Daddy will find out you're a dyke!"

"It does not."

"Well, what, then?"

"I don't . . . talk to my parents. I haven't exchanged a word with them since I got back from New York. Not a word."

"C'mon!"

"Have you seen me do it? When have I talked to them?"

"But why?"

"When did you last talk to *your* mother?"

"That's different. She's in Minneapolis. It wouldn't take that much for you to . . ."

"You haven't the slightest *idea* what it would take, Mona."

Mona stopped walking and turned to confront her. "Look, I know you must be a lot more . . ." She cut herself off.

"A lot more what?"

"I don't know . . . sophisticated?"

D'orothea laughed ruefully. "That ain't the half of it, honey!"

"Well, so what? Do I look like a snob to you? I've done a thing or two for Third World people, you know!"

"My father is a baker in the Twinkie factory, Mona!"

Mona stifled a grin. "You made that up."

"Drop it, will you?"

"No. You think I can't relate to older black people, don't you? Racist *and* agist, in spite of myself!"

Silence.

"That's it, isn't it?"

"I think you're very good with people. Now let's drop it, O.K.?"

So Mona shut up.

307

Her liberal consciousness, however, wouldn't permit her to discard the issue.

She would pursue the matter on her own.

There couldn't be *that* many Wilsons working at the Twinkie factory.

Michael's Visitor

ICHAEL WAS MAKING HIS BED WHEN THE DOOR
buzzer rang. He sped up the procedure, laughing at himself. He never made his bed for *himself.* He did it for others . . . or the hope of
others.

The same reason, really, that he kept the toilet clean and
a fresh guest toothbrush in the bathroom cabinet. You never
knew for sure when you were auditioning for the role of
housewife.

He opened the door on the second ring, prepared once
more to be a sympathetic ear for Mary Ann.

"Brian!"

"I'm not . . . interrupting anything?"

"As a matter of fact, Casey Donovan is languishing in my
boudoir."

"Oh, I'm . . ."

"A joke, Brian. Esoteric. What can I do for you?"

"Nothing . . . I . . . I've got some Maui Wowie. I thought
you might like to smoke a little and . . . rap for a while."

Such a quaint word, thought Michael. Rap. Straight people
still *longed* for the Summer of Love.

*　　*　　*

The grass took hold quickly.

"Jesus," said Michael. "How much *is* this stuff, anyway?"

"Two hundred a lid."

"Please!"

"Swear to God."

"My teeth are numb."

"Who needs 'em?"

Michael laughed. "Damn right! Is this stuff *local*, Brian?"

"Uh uh. L.A."

"Good ol' Lah!"

"Huh?"

"Lah. L.A. . . . get it?"

"Oh . . . yeah."

"L.A. is Lah. S.F. is Sif."

"Is it ever!"

They laughed. "Jesus, Brian. One more toke and I'll see God."

"Too late. He moved to Lah."

"God's in Lah?"

"Who you think sold it to me?"

"Sometimes," said Brian, "I get the feeling that the New Morality is over. Know what I mean?"

"Sorta."

"I mean . . . like . . . what's left? You know?"

"Yeah."

"Guys and chicks, chicks and chicks, guys and guys."

"Right on."

"But now . . . you know . . . the pendulum."

"Yeah . . . the fucking pendulum."

"I mean, Michael . . . I think . . . I think it's gonna be all over, man."

"What?"

"Everything."

"Sodom and Gomorrah, huh?"

"Maybe not that . . . dramatic, but something like that. We're gonna be . . . I mean people like you and me . . . we're gonna be fifty-year-old libertines in a world full of twenty-year-old Calvinists."

Michael winced. "Lusting in their hearts like Jimmy . . . but nowhere else."

"Yeah . . . Are you horny?"

Michael's heart stopped. "Uh . . ."

"Grass always makes me horny."

"Yeah . . . I know what you mean."

"Why don't we . . . do something about it?"

The room was so still that Michael could hear the hair growing on Brian's chest.

"Brian . . . that's kind of . . . complicated, isn't it?"

"Why?"

"Why?" repeated Michael. "Well, I . . . you and I aren't exactly coming from the same place, are we?"

"So? There must be *some* place in this fucking city where they've got straight chicks *and* gay guys."

"You want us to . . . go cruising together?"

"Kind of a kick, huh?"

Michael looked at him for several seconds, then broke into a slow grin. "You're really serious, aren't you?"

"Fuckin' A."

"It's truly twisted."

"I knew you'd get into it."

"Maybe," said Michael, turning into Pan again, "we could break up a couple."

Three Men at the Tubs

LEAVING THE HAMPTON-GIDDES', JON FILLED HIS LUNGS with the cleansing fog that had spilled into Seacliff from the bay.

Collier grinned at him. "I knew you'd OD, sooner or later."

"Shut up."

"You're stuck on that Tolliver kid, aren't you?"

"I'm not *stuck* on anybody, Collier. I just get sick of that bitchy talk about twinks. That's just a queen's way of being a male chauvinist pig!"

"Can I send that to Bartlett's *Quotations?*"

"Just drive, will you?"

"The tubs, right?"

"That's what you want, isn't it?"

"I could drop you off at the twink's house."

"Collier, if you mention that one more . . ."

"The tubs it is, milord."

* * *

Jon kept silent on the long ride to Eighth and Howard. He hated these unsettled moments when the stuffiness of the Hampton-Giddes and the aimlessness of the Michael Tollivers seemed equally inapplicable to his own life.

At times like this, the tubs was an easy way out.

Discreet, dispassionate, noncommittal. He could diddle away a frenzied hour or two, then return unblemished to the business of being a doctor.

It was really his only choice.

Decorators, hairdressers and selected sheriff's deputies were *expected* to be gay in San Francisco.

But who wanted a gay gynecologist?

Most women, he observed, expected their gynecologist to be detached in dealing with their most intimate specifics. They did *not*, however, expect detachment to come easy. In their heart of hearts lurked the tiniest hope that they were driving the poor devil mad.

Gay was not Good in OB/GYN.

The television lounge of the Club Baths was jammed with terry-cloth Tarzans.

For once, they were genuinely engrossed in the television.

"Forget about the orgy room," said Collier. "It empties during *Mary Hartman.*"

Jon grinned, already feeling better. "I'm hungry, anyway. We never got past the braised endive, remember?"

They microwaved a couple of hot dogs, laughing over the oven's obligatory warning about pacemakers. A pacemaker at the Club Baths was about as common as an Accu-Jac at the Bohemian Club.

Then they parted, each seeking his own private adventure in Wonderland.

Jon prowled the corridors for fifteen minutes, finally settling on a dark-haired number in a room near the showers. He was resting on his elbows in bed.

His towel was still on, his rheostat turned up.

A good sign, thought Jon. The desperates invariably kept their lights down and their towels off.

When they had finished, Jon said, "Let me know when you want me to leave."

"No problem," said the dark-haired man.

"It's nice to rest."

"Yeah. It's a mob scene out there."

"Full moon."

"I like it better on slow nights. I mean . . . sometimes I come here just to . . . get away."

"Me too."

The dark-haired man folded his hands behind his head and stared at the ceiling. "I wasn't even particularly horny tonight."

"Neither was I. I usually tell myself I'm here for the steam, but it never seems to work out that way."

The man laughed. *"Quelle coincidence!"*

Jon sat up. "Well, I guess I'd better . . ."

"Can I buy you a cup of coffee?"

"Thanks. I'm here with a friend."

"A lover?"

Jon laughed. "God, no!"

"Are you . . . one of the reachables?"

"Sure."

"Can I give you my phone number?"

Jon nodded, extending his hand. "My name's Jon," he said.

"Hi. I'm Beauchamp."

Cruising at The Stud

FOR HIS NIGHT ON THE TOWN WITH BRIAN, MICHAEL settled on The Stud. The Folsom Street bar was suitably megasexual, and its pseudo-ecological décor would probably be the least intimidating to Brian.

It might even remind him of Sausalito.

"It reminds me of The Trident," he said, as they walked in the door.

Michael grinned. "That's the Code of the Seventies, isn't it? It doesn't matter what you do, as long as you do it in something that looks like a barn."

"Christ! Look at those tits by the bar!"

"Yeah. He's gotta been pumping iron since junior high school, at least!"

"The chick, Michael!"

"Hey," said Michael. "You look at your tits and I'll look at mine!"

* * *

The other patrons were grouped undramatically around the central bar, some in knots of three or four. They laughed in short, stony spasms, while a scruffy-looking band imitated Kenny Loggins singing "Back to Georgia."

"Here's the plan," said Michael in a stage whisper. "If I run into anything that might interest you, I'll send it your way."

"Not *it,* Michael. *Her.*"

"Right. And you do the same for me."

"Don't worry."

"See anything you like?"

"Yeah. Ol' Angel Tits over there."

"You'll have to pry her away from that guy she's with."

"Maybe he's gay."

"Forget it. He's straight."

"Now, how can you tell?"

"Look at the size of his ass, Brian!"

"Gay guys don't have fat asses?"

"If they do, they don't go to bars. That's the *other* Code of the Seventies."

The woman who sat down next to Brian was wearing a beige French T-shirt that said "bitch" in discreet lower-case letters.

"You guys here together?"

"Yeah. Well . . . not exactly. He's gay and I'm straight."

"How nice for you."

"I didn't mean it like that. Michael's a friend."

"What do you do?"

"Me and Michael?"

"No. You. For a living, like."

"I'm a waiter. At Perry's."

"Oh. Heavy."

That irked him. "Is it?"

"Well, I mean . . . that's kind of . . . plastic, isn't it?"

"I like it," he lied. No radical-chic cunt in a bitch T-shirt was calling *his* job plastic.

"I work for Francis."

"The Talking Mule?"

She rolled her eyes impatiently. "Ford Coppola," she said.

Michael was standing alone by the bar when Brian rejoined him.

"Any luck?"

Brian took a swig of his beer. "I didn't stick around long enough to find out. She was weird."

"How so?"

"Aw, forget it."

"C'mon. Gimme the dirt. Bondage and Discipline? Water sports? Satin sheets?"

"She wanted to know if I was into . . . cockrings."

Michael almost shrieked. "You're kidding!"

"What the hell do they do, anyway?"

"A cockring? Well, Jesus . . . lemme see. It's this steel ring about . . . yea big . . . although sometimes it's brass or leather . . . and you put it around your . . . equipment."

"Why the fuck would you do that?"

"It helps you to keep it up longer."

"Oh."

"Isn't life interesting?"

"Do you have one?"

Michael laughed. "Hell, no."

"Why not?"

"Well . . . it's just one more thing to remember. Christ, I can't hang on to a pair of *sunglasses* for longer than a week." He laughed suddenly, thinking of something. "I used to know this guy . . . a very proper stockbroker, in fact . . . who wore one *all* the time. But he soon got cured of *that.*"

"What happened?"

"He had to fly to Denver for a conference, and they caught him when he passed through the metal detector at the airport."

"God! What did they do?"

"They opened his suitcase and found his black leather chaps!"

Brian whistled, shaking his head.

"It's not too late for a cup of coffee at Pam-Pam's."

"You got a date, man!"

She Is Woman, Hear Her Roar

SHORTLY AFTER SEVEN, BEAUCHAMP STUMBLED OUT OF bed and into the bathroom.

DeDe rolled over and continued to breathe heavily, pretending to be asleep.

This time she didn't want to hear his excuse. She was numb from excuses, drained by the effort it took to believe in him.

He had come in at 4 A.M. Period.

There might not be Another Woman, but there were definitely other women.

Her response to that fact must be forceful, reasoned and intrinsically feminine. She tried to imagine how Helen Reddy might have handled it.

The phone woke her at nine-fifteen.

"Hello."

"You asleep, darling?"

"Not exactly."

"You sound down."

"Do I?"

"Look . . . if it's about the you-know-what . . . well, it's a simple little procedure and you . . ."

"Binky, I . . ."

"It's not like the old rusty coat hanger days."

"All *right,* Binky!"

Silence.

"Binky . . . I'm sorry, O.K.?"

"Sure."

"I . . . had a bad night."

"Of course. Look . . . I called with a juicy one. Wanna hear it?"

"All ears."

"Jimmy Carter is a Kennedy!"

"Uh . . . once more."

"Isn't that the absolute *ripest* gossip you've heard in *months?*"

"Rank is more like it."

"Look . . . I'm only telling you what *everybody* was talking about at the Stonecyphers' last night. Apparently there's been some hush money paid to make sure that . . ."

"What *are* you talking about?"

"Miss Lillian used to be Joe Kennedy's secretary."

"When?"

"Oh, don't be such a spoilsport, darling. I think it's a divine story."

"Divine."

"Well, it explains all those *teeth,* doesn't it?"

When she finally got off the phone, she headed for the bathroom with a shudder.

A half-hour conversation with Binky was like eating a Whitman Sampler in one sitting.

Avoiding the kitchen, she dressed hastily in a cashmere turtleneck and Levi's, throwing on her Anne Klein suede jacket as an afterthought.

She wanted to walk. And think.

As usual, she went to the Filbert Steps, where the gingerbread houses and alpine cul-de-sacs provided a Walt Disney setting for her woes.

She sat down on the boardwalk at Napier Lane and watched the neighborhood cats promenading in the sun.

Once there was a cat who fell asleep in the sun and dreamed she was a woman sleeping in the sun. When she woke, she couldn't remember if she was a cat or a woman.

Where had she heard that?

It didn't matter. She didn't feel like a cat *or* a woman.

All her life, she had done as she was told. She had moved, without so much as a skipped heartbeat, from the benevolent autocracy of Edgar Halcyon to the spineless tyranny of Beauchamp Day.

Her husband ruled her as certainly as her father had, manipulating her with guilt and promised love and the fear of rejection. She had never done *anything* for herself.

"Dr. Fielding?"

"Yes?"

"I'm sorry to bother you at home."

"That's all right. Uh . . . who is this, please?"

"DeDe Day."

"Oh. How are you?"

"I . . . I've made up my mind."

"Good."

"I want the baby, Dr. Fielding."

The Doctor Is In

BEAUCHAMP DECIDED TO DRINK HIS LUNCH AT WILKES
Bashford.

There, amidst the wicker and lucite and cool
plaster walls, he downed three Negronis while he
tried on a pair of $225 Walter Newberger boots.
He was fitted by Walter Newberger himself.

"How does it feel?" asked the designer.

"Heaven," said Beauchamp. "*Exactly* the right amount of
Campari."

"The *boots*, Beauchamp. You *can* stand up, can't you?"

Beauchamp grinned roguishly. "Only when absolutely necessary . . . Look, where's your phone?"

"There's one in the mirror room."

Beauchamp lurched into the mirror room and dialed Jon's
office at 450 Sutter.

"Hi, Blondie."

"Good afternoon."

"I'm in the neighborhood, Hot Stuff. Why don't we rent a

321

room at the Mark Twain and have a nooner?"

"I'm quite busy right now. If you'll check with my receptionist later, I'm sure . . ."

"Oh, I get it!"

"Good."

"You've got a customer in the office with you?"

"That's correct."

"Is she cute?"

"I'm sorry . . . I can't discuss . . ."

"Awww . . . c'mon! Just tell me if she's cute."

"I have to go now."

"She *can't* be cuter than me, can she?"

The doctor hung up.

Beauchamp laughed out loud, leaning against the stuffed cotton cactus in the mirror room. Then he sauntered back to the bar, where the shoe designer was standing.

"Charge 'em," said Beauchamp.

The Old Man was apparently still having lunch at the Villa Taverna.

Beauchamp ambled into the executive suite and made a few mental notes to himself.

The space wasn't bad, actually. Clean lines and fairly decent track lighting. Once you got rid of those *godawful* hunt prints and tired Barcelona chairs, Tony Hail could probably do something really stunning with baskets and a few ficus trees and maybe some ostrich eggs on the shelf behind the . . .

"Is there something you're looking for?"

It was Mary Ann, being *very* territorial about the Old Man's lair.

"No," he said flatly.

"Mr. Halcyon won't be back until two."

Beauchamp shrugged. "Fine."

She stood stonily in the doorway until he had walked past her and back to his own office down the hall.

That night Mary Ann submitted to an urge that had plagued her all week.

She told Michael about Norman . . . and the weird night at the Beach Chalet.

Michael shrugged it off. "What's the big deal? You're a foxy lady. You break hearts. That's not *your* fault."

"That's not the *point*, Mouse. I just can't shake the feeling that he's . . . up to something."

"Sounds to me like he's blowing smoke."

"What?"

"Trying to impress you. Have you talked to him since then?"

"Once or twice. Just superficial stuff. He bought me an ice cream cone at Swensen's. There's something terribly . . . I don't know . . . desperate . . . about him. It's like he's biding his time . . . waiting to prove something to me."

"Look . . . if you were forty-four years old and selling vitamins door to door . . ."

"But he *isn't*. I'm sure of that. He *told* me he isn't . . . and I believe him."

"He sure carries that stupid Nutri-Vim case around with him enough."

"He's *fooling* people, Michael. I don't know why, but he is."

Michael grinned devilishly. "There's one way to find out."

"What?"

"I know where Mrs. Madrigal keeps the extra keys."

"Oh, Mouse . . . no, forget it. I couldn't."

"He's gone tonight. I saw him leave."

"Mouse, no!"

"O.K., O.K. How 'bout a movie, then?"

"Mouse . . .?"

"Huh?"

"Do you really think I'm a foxy lady?"

Not Even a Mouse

THE CITY ITSELF, NOT THE WEATHER, LET MARY ANN know that winter had finally come.

Ferris wheels spun merrily on the roof of The Emporium. Aluminum cedars sprouted in the windows of Chinese laundries. And one bright morning in mid-December a note appeared on her door.

Mary Ann,
   If you haven't made plans, please join me and the rest of your Barbary Lane family for a spot of eggnog on Christmas Eve.

Love,
A.M.

P.S. I could use some help in organizing it.

That news—and the joint attached to the note—boosted her spirits considerably. It was good to feel part of a unit again, though she rarely regarded her fellow tenants as members of a "family."

But why shouldn't Mrs. Madrigal be permitted that fantasy?

The Christmas party became Mary Ann's new obsession.

* * *

"... and after we light the tree, maybe we could have some
sort of caroling thing ... or a *skit!* A skit would be *fabulous,*
Mouse!"

Michael deadpanned it. "Great. You can be Judy Garland
and I'll be Mickey Rooney."

"Mouse!"

"O.K., then. *You* be Mickey Rooney and *I'll* be Judy Garland."

"You're not into this at all, are you?"

"Well, *you* certainly are. You've been running around for
three days acting like Gale Storm organizing a shuffleboard
tournament."

"Don't you *like* Christmas?"

He shrugged. "That isn't the point. Christmas doesn't like
me."

"Well ... I know it's gotten commercial and all, but that's
not . . ."

"Oh, *that* part's O.K. I *like* all the tacky lights and the mob
scenes and the plastic reindeer. It's the ... gooey part that
drives me up the wall."

"The gooey part?"

"It's a conspiracy. Christmas is a conspiracy to make single
people feel lonely."

"Mouse ... *I'm* single and . . ."

"And *look* at you ... scrambling like mad to make sure
you've got someplace to go." He swept his hands around the
room. "Where's your tree, if you're so crazy about Christmas? And your wreath ... and your mistletoe?"

"I might get a tree," she said defensively.

"It wouldn't make sense. It wouldn't make a damn bit of
sense to trek down to Polk Street to pick out some pathetic
little tabletop tree and spend two days' pay decorating it with
things you used to like back in Cleveland, just so you could
sit there alone in the dark and watch it blink at you."

"I have friends, Mouse. *You* have friends."

"Friends go home. And Christmas Eve is the most horrible
night of the year to go to bed alone ... because when you

325

wake up it's not going to be one of those Kodak commercials with kids in bunny slippers . . . It's going to be just like any other goddamned day of the year!"

She slid closer to him on the sofa. "Couldn't you ask Jon to the party?"

"Hey . . . drop that, will you?"

"I think he liked you a lot, Mouse."

"I haven't seen him since . . ."

"What if *I* called him?"

"Goddammit!"

"All right . . . all *right!*"

He took her hand. "I'm sorry. I just . . . I get so sick of the We People."

"The what?"

"The We People. They never say I. They say, 'We're going to Hawaii after Christmas' or 'We're taking the dog to get his shots.' They wallow in the first person plural, because they remember how shitty it was to be a first person singular."

Mary Ann stood up, tugging on his hand. "C'mon, Ebenezer."

"What for?"

"*We're* buying Christmas trees. Two of 'em."

"Mary Ann . . ."

"C'mon. Don your gay apparel." She giggled at the inadvertent pun. "That's funny, isn't it?"

He smiled in spite of himself. "We are *not* amused!"

Enigma at the Twinkie Factory

FTER WEEKS OF WORRYING ABOUT IT, MONA FI-
nally embarked on her secret plan to reunite
D'orothea with her parents.

There wasn't that much to go on.

She learned that Twinkies were made by the
Continental Baking Company and that there were two loca-
tions in the Bay Area. One was the Wonder Bread bakery in
Oakland. The other was on Bryant Street.

"Thank you for calling Hostess Cakes."

"I . . . do you make Twinkies?"

"Yes, we do. Also Ho Hos, Ding Dongs, Crumb
Cakes . . ."

"Thank you. Do you have a Mr. Wilson there?"

"Which one?"

"Uh . . . I'm not sure." She almost said "the black one," but
somehow it sounded racist to her.

"Donald K. Wilson is a wrapper here . . . and we have a
Leroy N. Wilson, who's a baker."

"I think that's the one."

"Leroy?"

"Yes . . . May I speak to him, please?"

"I'm sorry. The bakers work the night shift. Eleven to seven."

"Can you give me his home number?"

"I'm sorry. We're not allowed to divulge that information."

Christ, she thought. What is this? A nuclear power plant or a fucking Twinkie factory? "If I came down there . . . tonight, I mean . . . would it be possible to talk to him?"

"I don't see why not. On his break or something?"

"Around midnight, say?"

"I guess so."

"You're on Bryant?"

"Uh-huh. At Fifteenth. A big brown brick building."

"Thanks a lot."

"May I leave a message for him or anything?"

"No . . . Thanks, anyway."

D'orothea got home at eight o'clock, devastated by a ten-hour session before the cameras.

"If I *never* see another plate of Rice-a-Roni, it'll be too soon!"

Mona laughed and handed her a glass of Dubonnet. "Guess what's for supper?"

"I'll kill you!"

"Hang on . . . pork chops and okra!"

"What!"

Mona nodded, smiling. "Just like your mother probably used to make."

"What a shitty thing to say about somebody's mother!"

"Well . . . your foremothers, then."

"Have you been reading *Roots* again?"

"I *like* soul food, D'or!"

D'or scowled at her. "Would you like *me* if I weren't black?"

"D'or! What a thing to say!"

After studying Mona's face for a moment, D'or ended the

328

discussion with a smile and a wink. "I'm just tard, honey. Les go eat dem poke chops."

After dinner, they lay by the fire and looked at color transparencies of D'orothea modeling Adorable Pantyhose.

It seemed like a good time to tell her.

"D'or . . . Michael's asked me to go with him to a late show at the Lumiere tonight."

"Good."

"You won't mind if . . . ?"

"You don't have to ask my permission to go to the movies."

"Well, normally I'd want you to come along . . ."

D'orothea patted her hand. "I'm gonna crash in ten minutes, hon. You go have a good time, O.K.?"

Shortly after midnight, Mona's heart was pounding so fast that the Twinkie factory might as well have been the House of Usher.

The waiting room reminded her of the lobby of an ancient Tenderloin hotel.

She rang a buzzer at the information desk. Several minutes later, a man who appeared to be a baker asked if he could help her.

"Do you know Leroy Wilson?" she asked.

"Sure . . . wanna talk to him?"

"Please."

The man disappeared into the back, and another ten minutes passed before Leroy Wilson presented himself to a mystified Mona Ramsey.

The baker was dusted with a fine coating of powdered sugar.

And his skin was as white as the sugar.

Anna Crumbles

THE COUPLE TRUDGED UP THE DARK MOUNTAINSIDE along a narrow mud path that was slick from similar pilgrimages.

"What time is it?" he asked.

She checked her watch. A man's Timex. "A little before midnight."

Something other than the fog caused him to shiver as they moved through the eucalyptus forest. His companion seemed unperturbed.

"You're a stout-hearted woman, Anna."

"What's the matter? Can't keep up? This little jaunt was your idea, remember?"

"I don't know what the hell got into me."

She didn't say anything. He looked down at her and brushed a strand of hair away from her face.

"Yes I do, Anna. Yes I do."

At the crest of Mount Davidson, they caught their breath beneath the giant concrete cross.

Edgar swept his arm over the city beneath them.

"All my life . . . all my goddamn life and I never came up here."

"Pretend you were saving it."

He took her hand and pulled her next to him. "I swear it was worth it."

Silence.

"Anna?"

"We didn't come here to neck, did we, Edgar?"

He sat down on the ledge under the cross. "I . . . no."

She joined him. "What is it?"

"I don't know exactly. I got a call today."

"About what?"

"A man who wants to talk to me about madrigals."

"What?"

"That's what he said. That's *all* he said, actually. 'I'm a friend and I want to talk to you about madrigals.' He was maddeningly coy about it."

"Do you think he . . . ?"

"What else? He wants money, I guess."

"Blackmail?"

Edgar chuckled. "Quaint, isn't it? Six months ago that might have shaken me up real bad."

"But how would he know?"

"Who knows? Who *cares?*"

"*You* do, apparently. You just marched me up Calvary to tell me about it."

"That wasn't the reason."

"Will you see him?"

"Long enough to memorize his face and kick his ass down the steps."

"Are you sure that's wise?"

"Hell, what can he do? I'm a goner. Christ, I never thought that would come in handy someday!"

Anna picked up a twig and traced a circle in the damp earth. "We're not the only ones to consider, Edgar."

"Frannie?"

Anna nodded.

"He won't go to her. Not when he sees how little it matters to me."

"You don't know that for certain."

"No . . . but I'm not losing sleep over it, either."

"Are you sure it's . . . blackmail?"

"Positive."

Anna stood up and walked away from the cross, closer to the lights of the city. "Did he tell you his name?"

"Just Williams. Mr. Williams."

"When does he want to see you?"

"Christmas Eve afternoon." He grinned. "Gothic, eh?"

Anna didn't smile. "I don't want to hurt your family, Edgar. Or you."

"Me? Anna, you've *never* caused me a single moment of . . ."

"I *could,* though, Edgar. I could hurt you very badly."

"Bullshit!"

"Your family needs you now, Edgar. It isn't right or fair for me . . ."

"What the hell is the matter with you? Christ, *I'm* supposed to be the nervous one in this relationship! I brought you up here to ask you to go away with me!"

She spun around to face him. "What?"

"I want you to go away with me."

"But we . . . Where?"

"Any place you want. We could take a cruise to Mexico. I could make it look like a business trip. Look at me, Anna! You can see how much time I've got left!"

There were tears in her eyes. "I can see . . . a beautiful man."

"It's yes, then?"

"You can't do that to Frannie."

"Would you let me worry about that!"

"I don't . . ." Her voice choked up. "I don't want you caught up in this, Edgar."

"I'm *already* caught up in it, goddammit!"

"It's not too late. You can tell Mr. Williams . . . you can tell him . . . Hell, I don't know . . . deny it. He can't have positive proof about us. If we never see each other again . . ."

He grasped her shoulders and looked into her eyes. "You're way out of line, lady."

"God help me . . . I know!" She was sobbing now.

"Anna, please don't . . ."

"I'm a liar, Edgar. I love you with all my heart, but I'm a liar!"

"What the hell are you talking about?"

She composed herself somewhat and turned away from him. "It's worse than you think," she said.

The Baker's Wife

FOR A MOMENT, MONA WAS SPEECHLESS, CONFRONTING this stranger at the Twinkie factory at midnight.

This *white* stranger.

"Yes, ma'am," he said pleasantly. "What can I do for you?"

"I . . . excuse me . . . I think I must want the other Mr. Wilson."

"Don? The wrapper? I'll get him, if you'd . . ."

"No. Wait, please . . . Do you have a daughter named Dorothy?"

Leroy Wilson's face went whiter still. "Oh, my God!"

"Mr. Wilson, I . . ."

"You're from the Red Cross or something? Something's happened to her?"

"Oh, no! She's fine. Really! I saw her tonight."

"She's in San Francisco?"

"Yes."

The relief in his expression gave way to bitterness. "I wouldn't expect we'd hear from her."

"She lives here now, Mr. Wilson."

"Who are you?"

334

"I'm sorry . . . Mona Ramsey. I room with your daughter."

"What do you want from me?"

"I want to . . . Wouldn't you like to see Dorothy, Mr. Wilson?"

He snorted. "What *we* want doesn't have much to do with it, does it?"

"I think . . . I think Dorothy would really like . . ."

"Dorothy doesn't even *approve* of me and her mother."

So *that* was it, thought Mona. The sophisticated Miss D'orothea Wilson was the product of a lower-class interracial marriage. And it bugged the hell out of her.

Which explained, among other things, D'orothea's semi-Caucasian features and her fierce reluctance to deal with her African heritage.

She was, in short, an Oreo.

Leroy Wilson bought Mona a cup of coffee in the bakery's second-floor snack bar. Obviously wounded by his daughter's behavior, he allowed his visitor to do most of the talking.

"Mr. Wilson, I don't know why Dorothy decided to . . . cut off communications with you and Mrs. Wilson . . . but I think she's changed now. She wants to live in San Francisco, and I'm sure that means . . ."

"I don't even remember the last time Dorothy wrote us."

"It's easy to lose touch in New York, especially if you're a model and . . ."

"C'mon. Get to the point."

Mona set her cup down and looked him in the eye. "I want you and your wife to come to dinner this week."

He blinked at her, slack-jawed.

"It would just be the four of us."

"Dorothy knows about this?"

"Well, uh . . . no."

"I think you'd better run along home."

"Mr. Wilson, please . . ."

"What do *you* get out of this, anyway?"

"Dorothy's my *friend.*"

"That's not all of it."

"It's such a *waste,* dammit!"

He stared at her soberly, and Mona sensed a sort of primitive intuition at work. "Do you talk to your daddy?"

"Mr. Wilson . . ."

"Do you?"

"I . . . never knew him."

"He passed away?"

"I don't know. He left my mother when I was a baby."

"Oh."

"Go ahead. Psyche out my motives, if you want. All I . . ."

"O.K. When?"

"What?"

"When do you want us to come?"

"Oh, I'm so . . ." She flung her arms around his neck and hugged him, then backed off, embarrassed. "Is Christmas Eve O.K.?"

"Yeah," said Leroy Wilson. "I guess so."

Old Flames

CHRISTMAS. SOME YEARS IT HAPPENS. OTHERS IT doesn't.

This year, thought Brian, finishing off a bottle of Gatorade, it isn't going to happen.

Not if it snows on Barbary Lane. Not if you OD on eggnog. Not if Donny and Marie and Sonny and Cher and the whole fucking Mormon Tabernacle Choir show up on your doorstep with a partridge in a pear tree . . . it isn't going to happen.

As far as he was concerned, Mrs. Madrigal's party would be just like any other.

"Cheryl?"

"Yeah."

"Brian."

"Uh . . . Brian who?"

"Hawkins. From Perry's." The one who nailed your mother, dingbat!

"Oh . . . Hi!"

"What's up?"

"Oh . . . not much."

"Still living in the trailer park?"

"Yeah . . . *I* am."

"Swell."

"Candi's left. She's working in Redwood City now. At Waterbed Wonderland."

"Terrific."

"She's got an old man now. A hot-shit celebrity. Larry Larson."

"Don't know him."

"You know . . . Channel 36?"

"No."

"The Wizard of Waterbeds."

"Oh."

" 'We'll help you make a splash in bed'?"

"Got it."

"Larry might let her do a commercial soon."

"Well . . . star time. Look, Cheryl . . . you wanna go to a Christmas party?"

"When?"

"Christmas Eve."

"Oh . . . I'd *love* to, but Larry's taking us to Rickey's Hyatt House for turkey with all the trimmings."

"Oh."

"I could check with Larry. He might not mind if you came along."

"That's all right."

"I hate for you to be alone on . . ."

"I won't be alone, Cheryl."

"I'd try to get out of it, but Larry's called ahead for Mateus and everything."

"Ol' Larry thinks of everything."

"Yeah. He's real nice."

"Well, I hope you find one for yourself . . . some rich asshole in a leisure suit who can buy you all the Mateus and . . . Mediterranean furniture and . . . steel-belted radials . . ."

"You're just as fucked up as ever, aren't you?"

"And you're about as liberated as a goddamn hamster."

338

"I *never* said I was liberated!"

"Right you are!"

"I am really, really sorry for you!"

"I can tell."

"You really hate women, don't you?"

"What makes you think you're a woman?"

She slammed the phone down.

"Connie?"

"Just a sec. Lemme turn down the stereo." The Ray Conniff Singers were murdering "The Little Drummer Boy" in the background.

"Hi," she said, returning. "Who's this?"

"Your birthday boy."

"Byron?"

"Brian."

"Oh . . . sorry. Long time no see, huh?"

"Yeah, look . . . It might turn out to be a big bore, but I'm invited to this Christmas party my landlady's giving and . . . well, that's it."

Silence.

"Whatdya say?"

"Was that an invitation, Brian?"

"Yeah."

"I see. When?"

"Uh . . . the twenty-fourth."

"Just a sec, O.K.?" She left the phone for a matter of seconds. "Sure," she said finally. "The twenty-fourth is fine."

A Lovers' Farewell

T HE NOONTIME PERRY'S CROWD WAS THICKER THAN usual. Beauchamp pushed his way to the far end of the bar and nodded to the blue-blazered maître d'.

"I'm meeting a friend," he said.

Jon was waiting for him at a table in the tiny back courtyard.

"Sorry," said Beauchamp. "I got tied up in pantyhose again."

The gynecologist smiled. "Still trying to wreck my business, huh?"

"That's funny. I hadn't thought of that."

"I ordered you a Bullshot."

"Perfect."

"I can't stay long, Beauchamp."

"Fine. Neither can I."

"I don't think this is such a good idea, anyway."

Beauchamp frowned. "Look, there's no goddamn reason in the world why two men can't have a perfectly . . ."

"You don't consider a wife a *reason?*"

"Don't start on that again!"

"I hadn't planned to."

"Anyway . . . why should *you* care, if I don't. DeDe doesn't know you from Adam. You could be *anybody.* You could be a friend from the club, for all she knows!"

"That isn't the point."

"Well, what the hell *is* the goddamn . . . ?"

"Can I take your order now?" The Bullshots had arrived, along with a waiter whose green eyes and chestnut hair temporarily diverted both men from the crisis at hand.

Beauchamp flushed and chose the first thing he saw on the menu. "Yeah. The shepherd's pie."

"Same here," said Jon.

The waiter left without a word.

"Surly bastard," said Beauchamp.

Jon shrugged. "But pretty."

"You *would* notice that, wouldn't you?"

"Didn't you?"

"Not when I'm with somebody I care about!"

Jon looked down at his drink. "I think you're expecting too much of me, Beauchamp."

Silence.

"I think this should be . . . it."

"Just like that, huh?"

"It isn't 'just like that' and you know it. It's been coming on for a long time."

"It's DeDe, isn't it?"

"No. Not entirely."

"Well, *what,* then?"

"I'm not sure exactly."

"Yes you are."

"Beauchamp . . . I don't think I *trust* you."

"Jesus!"

"I *know* DeDe can't trust you. Why should *I* trust you?"

"That's different."

"It's *not* different. She hurts the same way you and I do."

"Look, what is this shit with DeDe? What the hell has DeDe got to do with . . . ?"

"She's pregnant, Beauchamp."

Silence.

"She's a patient of mine."

"Fuck."

341

"Well, *somebody* did."

"Jesus Christ."

"He's as good a possibility as any, I suppose."

"How can you *joke* about this, Jon?"

"It isn't *my* joke, Beauchamp. It's yours. I'm not gonna be part of this."

The food arrived. Neither of them spoke until the waiter had gone.

"I still wanna see you, Jon."

"It figures."

"There's a party at the club on Christmas Eve."

"I have plans on Christmas Eve." He pushed his chair back and stood up, dropping a ten-dollar bill on the table. "I'm not hungry. It's on me."

Beauchamp grabbed his wrist. "Wait a minute, goddammit! Did you tell DeDe about us?"

"Let go."

"I wanna know!"

Jon jerked his arm free and straightened his tie. "She's a nice woman," he said. "She could have done better than you."

342

Edgar on the Brink

THE CRAMPS HAD BEGUN AGAIN.

Edgar stood up from his desk and stretched his arms out slowly, arcing them from his body like a tired semaphorist.

He repeated the exercise four or five times, long enough to realize that it wasn't working, then confronted the mirror in his office washroom. His face was waxy white.

Chronic pyelonephritis. Renal disease. Toxic products that would back up just so long until one day . . . acute pericarditis would cause his heart to stop.

A lot of fancy words for bum kidneys.

Mary Ann buzzed him from the outer office. "Mildred called from Production. She wants to talk to you about the mail-boy."

"For Christ's sake! Can't you keep that old bat off my neck long enough . . ."

"I'm sorry, Mr. Halcyon. She was really upset, and I didn't know what . . ."

"Did he flip her the bird again?"

Mary Ann giggled. "You're not gonna believe it."

"The suspense is killing me."

"She caught him Xeroxing his . . . privates."

"What!"

"She came in early this morning and found him on top of the Xerox machine . . . with his pants down."

Edgar began to laugh. So hard, in fact, that he broke into a coughing jag.

"Are you all right, Mr. Halcyon?"

"That's the funniest . . . goddamn thing I've . . . What was he going to do with it?"

Now Mary Ann broke up. "He's . . . he's been doing it for *weeks*, Mr. Halcyon." She paused for a moment to collect herself. "Everybody in Production called him the Xerox Flasher, but nobody knew who it was. Mildred . . ." She began to giggle again, losing control.

"Mildred what?" Christ, he thought. Am I gossiping with my secretary?

"Mildred thought it was somebody from Creative. . . ."

"Mmm. Perverts all."

"Anyway . . . he always made a lot of copies and left them in the secretaries' desks every morning . . . until Mildred found out about it."

"Hell, he's the only person in the building who isn't guilty of false advertising!"

"Well, not exactly."

Edgar began to laugh again. "Oh, God! Don't tell me . . ."

"Yes, sir. He was using the enlarger."

Frannie called after lunch, obviously distraught.

"Edgar, I want you to do something about those people at Macy's."

"What is it this time?"

"I have *never*, Edgar . . . in all my life . . . been so *humiliated*. . . ."

"Frannie . . ."

"I went to Loehmann's this morning, out at West-lake. . . ."

"I thought you said Macy's?"

"Let me finish. I went to Loehmann's, because I wanted to get something nice for Helen for Christmas, and Loehmann's has perfectly *darling* designer-line clothes like Anne Klein, Beene Bag, Blassport . . ."

"Frannie."

"I have to *explain* this, Edgar! Loehmann's has these marvelous clothes, see, only they cut the labels out because they're overruns, so you can get them for practically *nothing* . . . and since I'm crazy about Helen, but not *that* crazy, I though I'd buy her this precious Calvin Klein cashmere cowlneck sweater that I could *tell* was a Calvin Klein, even though they'd cut the label out, because it had GJG in it."

Edgar gave up and let it wash over him. "GJG?" he asked blandly.

"That's the *code.* Anyway, it's just plain tacky to give your best friend a sweater without a label in it, so I asked them at Loehmann's if they had any extra labels, and they said that they were all cut out by the manufacturers, so . . ."

"Macy's, Frannie."

"I'm getting to that. I went to Macy's . . . well, not exactly Macy's, but that new place called the Shop on Union Square, and I picked out a couple of Calvin Klein sweaters . . . and when I was in the dressing room I noticed one of the labels was so loose it was practically *falling off,* so I took out a pair of nail scissors and . . ."

"Jesus Christ!"

"Oh, don't be so sanctimonious, Edgar! They've got *hundreds* of labels, and I wasn't . . . Well, when that horrid little Chicano clerk barged in, you would have thought I was *stealing* or something!"

He was back on the phone two minutes after Frannie had hung up.

"Anna?"

"Hello."

"I have to see you, Anna."

"Edgar . . . I don't think that's . . ."

"No arguments. I want to show you something."

"What?"

"You'll see. I'll pick you up tomorrow after breakfast."

"What about Mr. Williams?"

"He's not coming until six. We'll be back by then."

Breaking and Entering

ON THE NIGHT BEFORE CHRISTMAS EVE, MICHAEL phoned Mona in Pacific Heights.

"Hi, Babycakes!"

"Mouse!"

"Don't Mouse me! I thought you were becoming a dyke, not a nun! Where the hell have you been?"

"Mouse . . . I'm sorry . . . It's just that I've had so much adjusting . . ."

"*Tell* me. It's a strain being pissy. I tried it once for three days in Laguna Beach . . . and I nearly OD'd on kaftans."

Mona managed a laugh. "I've missed you, Mouse. I really have."

"Prove it, then, and come to Mrs. Madrigal's wingding."

"When?"

"Tomorrow night."

"I can't. Jesus . . . I don't even want to *think* about it."

"What?"

"I'm having D'or's parents over for dinner."

"Christ . . . in-laws and everything! D'or must be a *lot* of fun!"

"She doesn't even know about it."

"She . . . ? What are you up to, Babycakes?"

"It's a long story. Suffice it to say I'm freaked."

"Mrs. Madrigal will be disappointed."

"I know. I'm sorry."

"Maybe you should give her a call or something. I think she thinks you're . . . bummed out with her."

"Why should she . . . ?"

"You haven't talked to her in weeks, Mona."

"Thanks for the guilt trip."

"It isn't a guilt trip. She asked me to call you. She really misses you."

Silence.

"I'll explain about your dinner party. She'll understand. But give her a call, O.K.?"

"O.K." Her voice seemed unusually weak.

"You doin' all right, Babycakes?"

"Mouse . . . I think D'or has a drug problem."

Michael couldn't help but laugh.

"I'm *serious*, Mouse!"

"What's the matter? She pinching your Quaaludes or something?"

"For your information, smartass, I found some totally *unidentifiable* pills in her dresser last night, and she started acting really spooky when I asked her about them."

"Has she been acting spooky otherwise?"

"No. Not particularly."

"Well, relax, then."

"I can't. I'm saving my last Quaalude for tomorrow."

Mary Ann, meanwhile, was trying to decide what to do about Norman.

He had made himself unreachable for days, avoiding Barbary Lane during daylight hours, often returning to his house on the roof as late as 3 or 4 A.M., when Mary Ann could hear his labored footsteps on the stairs.

He was drinking heavily, she guessed, and it made her uncomfortable to think that *she* might be the reason.

Mrs. Madrigal had left him two notes about the party, nei-

348

ther of which he had answered. He seemed to be a man of single purpose now, moody and slightly manic, lunging uncontrollably toward a Holy Grail that no one but himself could see.

Something *had* to be done.

It was dark in the foyer of the house when Mary Ann opened the door under the stairwell leading to the basement. Fumbling in the blackness for the light switch, she listened carefully for sounds on the stairs above her. She would *die* if anyone caught her doing this.

The key board was just beyond the fuse box, shrouded in cobwebs. She searched for half a minute until she found the key marked "Roof House." Then she closed the door as quietly as possible and crept up three flights of stairs to the door that was painted orange.

Although she was *certain* that Norman was gone, she rapped twice on the door. The sound reverberated in the stairwell. She froze. Had anyone heard it?

The house was completely still.

She slipped the key into the lock. A tight fit. She jiggled it until the door swung open and the darkness of the little house engulfed her.

It took her less than a minute to find the Nutri-Vim suitcase.

At the Grove

THE FORESTER WHO ADMITTED THEM NEVER ONCE looked at Anna, curled up placidly on the front seat of Edgar's Mercedes.

She winked at the stony sentinel as they drove in.

"I hope he thinks I'm a hooker."

"It wouldn't be the first time."

Anna squeezed his knee. "For him or you, sir?"

He wouldn't joke about it. "You're the only woman I've ever brought here, Anna."

They parked the car in a lot adjacent to the entrance and began their odyssey on foot.

"Well, well," said Anna, as they moved through the towering redwoods. "Anna Madrigal at the Bohemian Grove."

"I think that's as it should be."

"Just the same . . . thank you."

"I wish I'd thought of it twenty years ago."

"Twelve."

Edgar grinned. "Twelve," he repeated.

Slipping her arm through his, Anna simply smiled and shook her head in amazement.

Edgar switched easily into the role of White Rabbit. His Alice blinked her wide blue eyes at him when he showed her the Grove Stage.

"You *performed* here?"

"I stopped the show once as a Valkyrie."

"In *drag*, Edgar?"

"Hell . . . the Greeks did it."

"The Greeks did a lot of things."

He smiled. "Get off my back, will you?"

"That's what the Greeks used to say."

Edgar slapped her on the behind and chased her up the River Road, ignoring the tightness that had begun to grow in his chest.

The camps they passed had names like honeymoon suites at the Madonna Inn: Pink Onion, Toyland, Isle of Aves, Monastery, Last Chance. . . .

Edgar's camp was Hillbillies.

A two-story chalet dominated the enclave, opening onto a courtyard with a barbecue pit. Admitting himself with a key, Edgar led Anna to the second floor, where a couch and a stone fireplace awaited them.

Anna grinned slyly. "Oh, I get it!"

He smiled like a satyr.

"Don't look so smug, Edgar Halcyon. I can match your decadence any day!"

She reached into the pocket of her peacoat and produced a thin tortoise-shell cigarette case. She extracted a joint.

"Anna . . ."

"It's good for what ails you."

He arched an eyebrow. "Wanna bet?"

"I'm sorry. I . . . Damn, I'm usually so *good* with words."

His smile forgave her. She kept the joint held out for him.

"Anna . . . can't you just make do with the last of a breed?"

She tapped the joint against her lower lip, then returned it to the case. "Damn right," she said softly.

Wrapped in an Indian blanket, they sat in front of the fire.

"If this were the old days, we could run away together to the wilds."

She rearranged his white mane with her fingers. "We're already in the wilds, aren't we?"

"Then . . . wilder wilds."

"That would be lovely."

"We don't have to go back, Anna."

"Yes we do."

He turned and stared into the fire. "Would you have told me, if Mr. Williams hadn't come along?"

"No."

"Why not?"

"It wasn't . . . necessary."

"You're still beautiful, Anna."

"Thank you."

"What shall I tell him tonight?"

Anna shrugged. "Tell him . . . his rent's due."

Edgar laughed, hugging her. "One more question."

"What?"

"Why haven't you invited me to your party?"

"Now, how on earth . . . ?"

"I heard Mary Ann talking about it."

She smiled at him in wonderment. "You dear man."

"That doesn't answer my question."

"Is eight o'clock O.K.?"

He nodded. "Right after I finish with Mr. Williams."

Art for Art's Sake

MARY ANN'S MORNING WAS A HELLISH BLUR OF RE-
membered images. Petrified of meeting Norman in the hallway, she crept out of the house
and ran down the lane to Leavenworth Street.
She caught the first cab she saw.

"Where to?"

"Uh . . . what's a nice museum?"

"The Legion of Honor?"

"Out beyond the bridge?"

"Yep. Lotsa nice Rodin stuff."

"Fine." It was perfect, really. She *needed* Art now . . . and
Beauty . . . and anything else with a capital letter that would
pull her through the worst Christmas Eve of her life.

She wandered through the museum for almost an hour, then
returned to the therapeutic sunlight of the colonnade courtyard. She sat at the base of *The Thinker* until the comic irony
of the scene drove her back indoors to the Café Chanticleer.

After three cups of coffee, she made up her mind.

353

She found a phone booth near the entranceway on the ground floor, dug Norman's Nutri-Vim business card from her purse, and dialed the number scribbled in pencil on the back.

"Yeah?"

"Norman?"

"Yeah?"

"It's Mary Ann."

"Hello." He sounded drunk, *very* drunk.

"I have . . . sort of a problem. I was hoping you could come meet me."

There was a pause, and then he said, "Sure." Even now, knowing what she did, she hated herself for the way she could govern his feelings.

"I'm out at the Palace of the Legion of Honor."

"No problem. Half an hour, O.K.?"

"O.K. Norman?"

"Huh?"

"Drive carefully, will you?"

She was waiting for him in the parking lot, under the statue of *The Shades*. Norman crawled out of the Falcon with exaggerated dignity. He was blitzed.

"How ya doin'?"

"Pretty good, pretty good." Why did she *say* that? Why was she being nice to him?

"You wanna go in the museum?"

"No, thanks. I've been there all morning."

"Oh."

"Could we take a walk?"

Norman shrugged. "Where?"

"Over there?" She pointed across the road to what appeared to be a golf course with a network of footpaths. She wanted to get away from people.

Norman extended his arm with drunken gallantry. Everything he did, in fact, seemed a hideous parody of the things she had once admired about him. She took his arm, suppressing a shudder. If nothing else, it would keep him from falling flat on his face.

They crossed the road and descended a path along the edge of the golf course. The fog had begun to roll in, blurring the Monterey cypresses on a distant rise. Somewhere beyond those trees lay the ocean.

Mary Ann let go of Norman's arm. "I wanted to talk to you in private, Norman."

"Yeah?" He smiled at her, apparently allowing his hopes to rise again.

"I know about the pictures."

He stopped in his tracks and stared at her, slack-jawed. "Huh?"

"I've seen the pictures, Norman."

"What pictures?" Of *course* he wasn't going to make it easy for her.

"You know what I'm talking about."

He stuck out his lower lip like a petulant child and began to walk again. Faster now. "I *don't* know what you're talking about!"

" 'Tender Tots'? 'Buxom Babies'?"

"You must be . . ."

"I know about you and Lexy, Norman!"

Guess Who's Coming to Dinner?

HOVERING OVER A TABLE SET FOR FOUR, MONA hummed her mantra in a last-minute effort to calm her nerves.

D'orothea's parents were arriving in ten minutes.

And D'orothea still didn't know.

"I'm not kidding, Mona. I hate surprises. If you've invited those dreary backpacking dykes from Petaluma, you can count me out. I know all I need to know about skinning squirrels, thank you."

Mona didn't look up. "You'll like them. I promise, D'or."

Shit, she thought. What if she *doesn't*? What if she feels more alienated than ever? What if the Wilson's oddly bourgeois interracial marriage had left unimaginable scars on the psyche of their daughter?

"And another thing, Mona . . . the *minute* one of those garage-sale gurus of yours starts spouting off about The Third Eye or whose moon is in . . ."

"I'll split a Quaalude with you, O.K.?"

"You can't *drug* me into submission, Mona."

Mona turned away and readjusted a fork. "Forget it, then."

"I'm sorry. That wasn't fair."

"Will you *try* to act human, D'or?"

"Sure. What the hell."

"I want this to be . . . well, I want it to be nice."

"I know. And I'll try."

The next fifteen minutes were the worst in Mona's memory.

She scurried around the house, pretending to busy herself with housekeeping, *certain* her terror would show if she stayed in one place.

The Wilsons were late.

D'orothea was upstairs, fixing her face in the bedroom.

Mona forsook her mantra and recited a childhood prayer. She was halfway through it when the doorbell rang. There was no way out now. No excuses. No postponements.

She opened the door just as D'or reached the landing on the stairs.

"I'm sorry we're late," said Leroy Wilson quietly. "This is Mrs. . . ."

His eyes, climbing to the stairs, grew large and glassy. "Dorothy? My God! Dorothy, what in God's . . .?"

D'orothea stood frozen on the landing. "Mona . . . Jesus, Mona, what have you . . .?" She spun around and dashed back up the stairs, weeping like a madwoman.

Mona was wrecked, speechless before Leroy Wilson and the short, dumpy woman who had come in too late to witness the bizarre scenario.

The short, dumpy *white* woman.

With the Wilsons in limbo downstairs, D'or wept like a baby in Mona's arms.

"I swear, Mona . . . I swear to God . . . I never meant to lie to you. I wanted to work . . . I just wanted to work. When I moved to New York five years ago, nobody would hire me. Nobody! Then I did a couple of jobs in dark makeup . . . one of those Arab harem girl things . . . and all of a sudden people started asking for the foxy black chick . . . I didn't *plan* it. It just sort of . . ."

"D'or, I don't see what . . ."

"I'm a fraud, Mona!" Her sobs grew louder. "I'm nothing but . . . a white girl from Oakland!"

"D'or . . . your skin . . .?"

"Those pills. The ones you found in my drawer. They're for vitiligo."

"I don't . . ."

"It's a disease that causes white spots to break out on your body. People with vitiligo take the pill to make their pigment darker. If you're white, and take enough of them over a two-month period . . . Didn't you ever read *Black Like Me?*"

"A long time ago."

"Well, that's what I did. I found a dermatologist in New Orleans who would give me the pills, along with ultraviolet treatments, and I disappeared for three months and came back to New York as a black model. I made *money,* Mona . . . more money than I had ever seen in my life. Naturally, I dropped all contact with my parents, but I never intended . . ."

"But doesn't it wear off?"

"Of course. It's a constant strain. I had to sneak off every few months or so to get more ultraviolet treatments . . . and, of course, I kept taking the pills . . . and finally one day I just couldn't take the sham anymore, so I decided . . ."

". . . to move to San Francisco and go white."

D'or nodded, wiping her eyes. "Naturally, I felt that you would be my refuge until . . . I had changed back . . . and I always planned to see my parents again, but not until . . ."

"Why didn't you *tell* me, D'or?"

"I *tried.* I tried lots of times. But every time I got close you would whip up a mess of chitlins or start talking about my beloved African heritage . . . and I felt like such a phony. I didn't want you to be . . . ashamed of me."

Mona smiled. "Do I look ashamed?"

"This really is my hair, Mona. I *do* have naturally curly hair."

"Do you have any idea what I thought, D'or?"

D'or shook her head.

358

"I thought you were dying. I freaked. I thought you were taking those pills because you were dying."

"Of what?"

"What else? Sickle cell anemia."

The Confrontation

NORMAN WAS ALMOST RUNNING NOW, LURCHING recklessly toward the cypresses on the edge of the rise.

"Jus' shuddup, O.K.? Jus' shuddup!"

"I'm not shutting up, Norman! I'm not standing by while you exploit that child in such a horrible, *disgusting* . . ."

"It's none o' your business!"

"I saw those magazines in your suitcase, Norman!"

"What were you doin' in my suitcase?"

"You're sick, Norman. You're . . ." She was breathing almost as heavily as he was. She pulled at his arm. "Will you *stop?*"

He obeyed, jerking to a halt at the top of the rise. Swaying for a moment, he clutched at her to regain his balance. She gasped, not at him, but at the stomach-churning scene that confronted them in the fog.

"Norman . . . *get back!*"

"Wha . . . ?"

"It's a cliff! Get back! Please!"

He stared at her dumbly, then staggered several steps in

her direction. She latched on to his arm, hooking her other arm around a tree.

Norman was indignant. "Thass not what I do, ya know."

"Norman, if you don't . . ."

"Those stupid pictures are nothin'! I got bigger things'n *that* going for me!"

"Norman . . ." She softened her tone somewhat, leading him away from the precipice. "What you are doing is . . . against the law, for one thing."

"Ha! You think I don't know that?"

"How *could* you, Norman? You've always been so sweet to Lexy."

"So?"

"I won't stand for it, Norman. I'm calling that child's parents."

"You think they don't *know?*"

She clenched her teeth. "Dear God!"

"How the hell you think they make a livin', huh? Lexy's a goddamn *star!* She's a goddamn famous little . . . Hell, I'm jus' . . . her agent!"

"But you're in the magazines!"

He nodded almost proudly. "A few movies too."

"Jesus."

"I can't help it. She won't do it with anybody else."

"Norman!"

"You think I'm chickenshit, don't you? You think I'm a chickenshit child pornographer!"

"Norman, stop . . ."

"I've got news for you, Miss Fancypants! I'm a goddamn private investigator and I'm jus' about to break the biggest goddamn case of my goddamn career!"

"Norman, get away from the . . ."

She couldn't look.

When she turned around again, he was lumbering down the path along the edge of the cliff. To her relief, he had moved beyond the precipitous portion to a place where the drop-off seemed less pronounced.

361

"Norman, come back!"

He snarled over his shoulder at her. "Find your own goddamn way home!"

Then, suddenly, he lost his footing, sliding off the path into the loose rock and sand on the slope leading to the sea.

She ran to him, horror-stricken. He was spread-eagled on his back, thrashing like an overturned cockroach. A dozen feet below him another cliff awaited. He whimpered pathetically.

"Please . . . jus' help me, please. . . ."

Mary Ann dropped to the ground and reached as far as she could down the slope. "Don't move, Norman. Just hold still, O.K.?"

He wasn't listening. His limbs flailed wildly until the ground beneath him began to shift and rumble like molten lava. She lunged desperately for his arm and missed.

His progress to the edge of the cliff was slow, steady and horrible.

He left behind his clip-on tie, dangling limply from her hand.

She ran back to the museum in the swirling fog, his screams reverberating in her head.

In the phone booth, she checked her purse. Thirty-seven cents. She had counted on riding home with Norman.

She dialed 673-MUNI.

"Muni," said a man on the other end.

"Please . . . how do I get to Barbary Lane from the Legion of Honor?"

"Barbary Lane? Let's see. O.K. . . . walk down to Clement and Thirty-fourth and take the Number 2 Clement to Post and Powell, then transfer to the Number 60 Hyde cable car."

"The Number 2 Clement?"

"Yes."

"Thank you."

"Sure. And Merry Christmas!"

"Merry Christmas to you," she said.

362

The Party

WHERE'S MARY ANN?" ASKED CONNIE BRADSHAW, standing under Mrs. Madrigal's red-tasseled archway. "I thought you said she'd be here."

Brian selected a joint from a Wedgewood plate. "She's here. At least . . . I saw her upstairs."

"Jeez, it's been a zillion years since I've seen her!"

"You two are good friends, huh?"

"Oh, the best! I mean . . . we haven't been too good about keeping in touch or anything, but . . . well, *you* know how it goes in this town."

"Sure."

"Uh . . . I think someone wants to talk to you, Brian."

"Oh . . . Hi, Michael."

"Hi. You haven't seen Gale Storm, have you?"

"Who?"

"Mary Ann."

Brian took a toke off the joint, then passed it to Connie. "We were just talking about that. What's with her, anyway? I thought she was orchestrating this orgy."

"She was. I guess she's fixing her face or something. Hey,

363

don't go 'way. I've got something for you." He ducked into the kitchen and returned with a small package wrapped in silver foil.

Brian flushed. "Hey, man . . . we said no presents, remember?"

"I know," said Michael, "but this isn't for Christmas, really. I just forgot to give it to you earlier."

"That's nice," Connie beamed.

Brian glanced at her, then back at Michael. There was something more impish than usual about Michael's grin. "Hey, Michael, this isn't . . .?"

"Go on," squealed Connie. "I can't stand the suspense!"

Brian looked directly into Michael's eyes. "Shall I?" He smiled.

"What the hell. The sooner you open it, the sooner you can use it."

"Right!" Connie agreed.

Brian tore into the package. He was fully prepared when the heavy brass ring emerged from the tissue paper. "It's a nice one, Michael. Very handsome."

"Are you sure? I can take it back if . . ."

"No. I'm . . . nuts about it."

Michael stayed poker-faced. "I hope it's your size."

"What is it?" asked Connie.

Brian held it up so she could look at it. "Nice, huh?"

"It's *gorgeous.* What's it for?"

Brian's eyes flashed toward Michael for a split second, then back to Connie. "It's . . . an ornament," he said appreciatively. "You hang it on your tree."

Michael picked up a tray of brownies in the kitchen. "Are these loaded?" he asked.

Mrs. Madrigal merely smiled at him.

"I thought so," said Michael.

"Has Mary Ann come down yet?"

"Not yet."

"What on earth could have . . .?"

"I can check, if you want."

"No. Thank you, dear . . . but I need you down here."

"Are you expecting any others?"

She checked her watch. "One," she said vaguely, "though I'm not sure. . . . It's nothing definite, dear."

"Is everything . . . all right, Mrs. Madrigal?"

She smiled and kissed him on the cheek. "I'm with my family, aren't I?"

When Michael returned to the living room, he almost dropped the brownies.

"Mona!"

"In the firm but pliant flesh."

"Hot damn! What happened to D'orothea?"

"She's having a White Christmas with her parents in Oakland."

"It's *snowing* in Oakland?"

"It's too long a story, Mouse."

He set the tray down and flung his arms around her. "Goddammit, I've missed you!"

"Yeah. Same here."

"Well, you don't look any worse for wear."

"Yeah," she grinned. "Same ol' Mona . . . smiling in the face of perversity."

Saying Good-bye

WHEN MARY ANN FINALLY APPEARED, SHE MADE her apologies to Mrs. Madrigal.

"I hope it hasn't been a hassle. I . . . well, I guess I just lost track of the time with Christmas shopping and all."

"Don't be silly, dear. It's been no problem at all, and Michael's been the perfect . . . You haven't seen Mr. Williams, have you, dear? If he's in the house, we should certainly invite him to . . ."

"No. No, I haven't. Not for a day or so, anyway."

"Well, that's too bad."

"He's been gone a lot recently. He hasn't seemed himself . . . to me, anyway."

"No, he hasn't, has he?"

"It's nice to see my friend Connie again."

"I know. Isn't that a *coincidence?* And Mona was able to make it, after all, and . . . well, God bless us, every one!" She kissed Mary Ann a bit too breezily on the cheek and rushed past her out of the room.

It seemed to Mary Ann that she was crying.

Fifteen minutes later, Mona looked for the landlady and found her on the stairway at the entrance to the lane.

"Waiting for somebody?" she asked, sitting down beside her.

"No, dear. Not anymore."

"Anybody I know?"

"I wish you had."

"Had?"

"I meant . . . It's hard to explain, dear."

"I'm sorry I haven't kept in touch with you more."

Mrs. Madrigal turned and looked at her. There were tears in her eyes. "Oh, thank you for saying that!" she cried. She held on to Mona for a moment, then straightened up again, regaining her composure.

"I'd like to move back in," said Mona, "if you can stand me."

"*Stand* you? You simple child! I've missed you more than you'll ever know!"

Mona smiled. "Thank you . . . and Merry Christmas."

"Merry Christmas, dear."

"Why don't you come back in? It's *cold* out here!"

"I will. In a minute. You run along."

"Couldn't your friend meet you inside?"

"He's not coming, dear. He's already left us."

He left at Halcyon Hill.

Dr. Jack Kincaid administered a sedative to his wife, while his daughter and son-in-law said good-bye to him.

He was flat on his back in bed. His skin was so pale that it seemed translucent.

"Daddy?"

"Is that you, DeDe?"

"It's me and Beauchamp."

"Oh."

"We have a surprise for you, Daddy."

Beauchamp flashed an uneasy glance at his wife. DeDe glared back at him, then turned and knelt at her father's bedside.

"Daddy . . . we're going to make you a grandfather."

Silence.

"Did you hear me, Daddy?"

Edgar smiled. "I heard."

"Aren't you glad?"

He lifted his hand feebly. "Could you . . . show me?"

"She's so small." DeDe stood up, taking his hand, pressing it gently against her belly. "I don't think you can feel . . ."

"No. I can feel her. You think it's a girl, huh?"

"Yes."

"So do I. Have you picked out a name yet?"

"No. Not yet."

"Name her Anna, will you?"

"Anna?"

"I've . . . always liked the name."

Smiling again, he kept his hand pressed against the warm new life. "Hello, Anna," he said. "How the hell are you?"

The Golden Gate

BUNDLED UP AGAINST THE WIND, MARY ANN AND MI-
chael set out across the bridge on New Year's Day.

"I've never done this," she said.

"I can't believe it," he grinned. "There's something *you've* never done?"

"Lay off, Michael!"

He squeezed her arm. "You've had a busy year, Lucrezia."

"Michael, look! You can joke about it with me, but we've
got to be very, very careful about . . ."

"You think I don't know what being an accomplice
means?"

"I'm still so freaked out about it I could die!"

Michael leaned against the rail. "Show me where it happened."

She looked faintly annoyed, then nodded toward the cliffs.
"Over there. See where that buoy is? Right behind it."

He pointed at the buoy. "*That* one?"

"Don't *point,* Michael!"

"Why?"

"Somebody'll see you."

"Oh, please! The body hasn't even turned up yet."

"But it *could*. It could turn up at any time."

"So?"

"Well, it's possible that the police could think it was . . . foul play. And it's possible that some witness somewhere could identify me as the person who was with him at the museum. And . . . there are *lots* of things that could implicate me in . . ."

"I still don't see why the hell you just didn't report the accident. It *was* an accident, wasn't it?"

"Yes!"

He grinned. "Just checking."

"Michael . . . if I tell you something, will you *swear* on a stack of Bibles that you'll never, *ever* tell another living soul?"

"You think I'd cross you, baby? I've *seen* what you do to your enemies!"

"Forget it."

"No, please! I promise! C'mon, tell me."

She studied him sternly, then said, "Norman wasn't *just* a pornographer, Michael."

"Huh?"

"He was a private eye."

"Jesus! How do you know?"

"He told me. Right before he fell. He also told me he was working on a big case that was going to make him a lot of money. It made me start to wonder about why he came to Barbary Lane in the first place and why he would question me about . . . certain things."

"Wow! Go on!"

"Well . . . when I got back to the house after . . . you know . . . I got his spare key out of the basement again and went through his room again. And this time the child porn didn't stop me!"

Michael whistled. "Nancy Drew, eat your heart out!"

"He had a huge file, Michael. And do you know what he was investigating?"

"What?"

"Mrs. Madrigal!"

"What!"

"I couldn't believe it, either."

"Well, what did it *say*?"

"I don't know."

"Now *wait* a minute!"

"I burned it, Michael. I took it back to my room and burned it in a trash can. Why do you think I was late for the party?"

Down the Peninsula at Cypress Lawn Cemetery, a woman in a paisley turban climbed out of a battered automobile and trudged up the hillside to a new grave.

She stood there for a moment, humming to herself, then removed a joint from a tortoise-shell cigarette case and laid it gently on the grave.

"Have fun," she smiled. "It's Colombian."

About the author

About the book

Insights,
Interviews
& More . . .

Read on

Meet
Armistead Maupin

BORN IN Washington, D.C., in 1944,
Armistead Maupin grew up in Raleigh,
North Carolina and graduated from the
University of North Carolina at Chapel
Hill. After serving as a naval officer with
the River Patrol Force in Vietnam, he
moved to San Francisco, where, in 1976, he
launched his groundbreaking Tales of the
City series in the *San Francisco Chronicle*.

The now-iconic residents of
Mrs. Madrigal's apartment house at
28 Barbary Lane have blazed a singular trail
through popular culture—from a sequence
of globally bestselling
novels, to a Peabody
Award–winning television
miniseries, to a stage
musical at San Francisco's
American Conservatory
Theater. The nine novels in
the Tales series are *Tales
of the City, More Tales of
the City, Further Tales
of the City, Babycakes,
Significant Others, Sure
of You, Michael Tolliver
Lives, Mary Ann in
Autumn,* and *The Days
of Anna Madrigal.*

Maupin is also the
author of the bestselling
novels *Maybe the Moon*
and *The Night Listener.*
In 1997 he received the
Publishing Triangle's Bill

Christopher Turner

2

Whitehead Award for Lifetime Achievement. In 2002 he was honored with the Trevor Project's Life Award "for his efforts in saving young lives." Maupin was the first recipient of Litquake's Barbary Coast Award for his literary contribution to San Francisco. In 2012 he received the Lambda Literary Foundation's Pioneer Award. He lives in Santa Fe, New Mexico, with his husband, the photographer Christopher Turner. ❧

"A Pleasing Shock of Recognition"
On Writing *Tales*

I REMEMBER this guy. He usually dressed like a clone in flannel shirts and Levi's 501s, so he must have thought that a loosened knit tie would make him look more journalistic. He had just moved into a cottage in the Castro, having bounced between Russian and Telegraph Hills for most of the seventies.

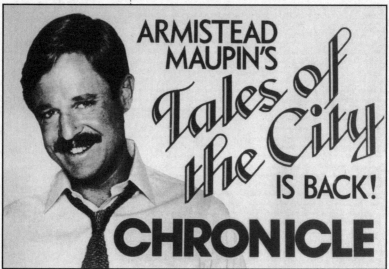

Newspaper rack card, 1981

For five years, off and on, he'd been writing a column for the morning newspaper that was, in effect, a story without an ending. He wrote his columns on carbon paper, keeping one copy and delivering the other to the newspaper office, often in a frantic last-minute dash in his Volkswagen convertible.

There were times when he was barely two days ahead of his readers. Like them, he was waiting breathlessly for what would happen next—but counting on his life to provide it.

In that regard San Francisco never failed him. His tales were often fueled by the people around him: a closeted movie star who lured him (rather easily) to his suite at the Fairmont Hotel; a socialite who threw a fancy luncheon "to rap about rape"; a homeless man who offered him coffee in a hidden lean-to on Telegraph Hill; a hulking construction worker who slow-danced with him at a gay rodeo. When a "co-ed bathhouse" opened on Valencia Street, this young man was there, taking notes. When the newspaper offered him cruises to Mexico and Alaska, he went on them—in part to see where they would lead his imagination. His never-ending story was a snuffling, ravenous beast that had to be fed on a daily basis, so anything meaty and available was tossed into its waiting maw.

When, for instance, he went home one night with someone aroused by his shoes (the Weejuns he wore with his rugby shirt), he folded that incident straight into the mix. He even wrote about the things that hurt, the "affairettes" that broke his still-adolescent heart—the gorgeous but uptight doctor named Jon who performed mastectomies, the harmonica-playing Marine recruiter who read German poetry to him in bed and gave him a keychain that said: "The Marines are looking for a few good men." It helped him make something useful—or at least entertaining— out his romantic misadventures.

Which is not to say that his tales were especially autographical. The guy in this photo was all of his characters and none ▶

> " His never-ending story was a snuffling, ravenous beast that had to be fed on a daily basis, so anything meaty and available was tossed into its waiting maw. "

"A Pleasing Shock of Recognition"
(continued)

of them; reality was just his jumping-off point. He used to say that he was far more like DeDe Halcyon Day, the "recovering debutante" in *Tales of the City*, than Michael Tolliver, the romantic gay Floridian. After all, he had never entered a Jockey shorts dance contest nor swum naked into the Bohemian Grove with his clothes in a garbage bag; he would not have had the nerve. His nerve was largely confined to the written word and his insistence that gay folks were part of the human landscape and therefore deserved a place—and equal billing—in his chronicle of modern life. He was often at odds with his editors about this. One of them even kept an elaborate chart in his office to insure that the homo characters in "Tales" didn't suddenly outnumber the hetero ones and thereby undermine the natural order of civilization.

And this guy loved that. He loved frightening the horses with that goofy grin on his face. He had kept his heart (and his libido) under wraps for most of his life, only to discover that the thing he feared the most had actually become a source of great comfort and inspiration. It thrilled him to testify for his own kind, to offer a pleasing shock of recognition to people whose stories were rarely told anywhere, much less in a "family newspaper." He used his column, in fact, as a means of finally telling the truth about himself, coming out to his parents in North Carolina in the very letter that Michael Tolliver wrote to his folks in Florida. He would not have been able to do any of this had he not felt so embraced by a city where

> **❝** He was often at odds with his editors.... One of them even kept an elaborate chart in his office to insure that the homo characters in *Tales* didn't suddenly outnumber the hetero ones. **❞**

everyone—gay, straight, and traveling—had learned to recognize, if not yet fully celebrate, the infinite possibilities of humanity.

That was over thirty years ago, but I've been musing on this young man a lot as I await the publication of my ninth novel, *Michael Tolliver Lives*, the tale of a fifty-five-year-old gardener still living in San Francisco. Could that guy in the loosened tie possibly have guessed how long his story would last or imagine the doors it would eventually open for him? It's better, perhaps, that he remained in the dark, living in the moment and sailing on his dreams. Come to think of it, it's always been better that way.

Armistead Maupin
January 16, 2007
San Francisco

Have You Read?
More by Armistead Maupin

The Tales of the City Series

"These novels are as difficult to put down as a dish of pistachios."

—Charles Solomon,
Los Angeles Times Book Review

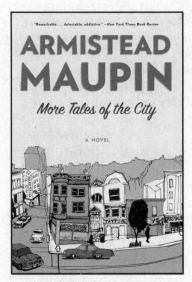

MORE TALES OF THE CITY

The tenants of 28 Barbary Lane have fled their cozy nest for adventures far afield. Mary Ann Singleton finds love at sea with a forgetful stranger, Mona Ramsey discovers her doppelgänger in a desert whorehouse, and Michael Tolliver bumps into a certain gynecologist in a seedy Mexican bar. Meanwhile, their venerable landlady takes the biggest journey of all—without ever leaving home.

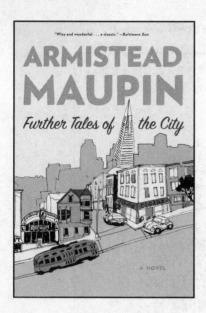

FURTHER TALES OF THE CITY

The calamity-prone residents of 28 Barbary Lane are at it again in this deliciously dark novel of romance and betrayal. While Anna Madrigal imprisons an anchorwoman in her basement, Michael Tolliver looks for love at the National Gay Rodeo, DeDe Halcyon Day and Mary Ann Singleton track a charismatic psychopath across Alaska, and society columnist Prue Giroux loses her heart to a derelict living in a San Francisco park.

BABYCAKES

When an ordinary househusband and his ambitious wife decide to start a family, they discover there's more to making a baby than meets the eye. Help arrives in the form of a grieving gay neighbor, a visiting monarch, and the dashing young lieutenant who defects from her yacht. Bittersweet and profoundly affecting, *Babycakes* was the first work of fiction to acknowledge the arrival of AIDS.

SIGNIFICANT OTHERS

Tranquillity reigns in the ancient redwood forest until a women-only music festival sets up camp downriver from an all-male retreat for the ruling class. Among those entangled in the ensuing mayhem are a lovesick nurseryman, a panic-stricken philanderer, and the world's most beautiful fat woman. *Significant Others* is Armistead Maupin's cunningly observed meditation on marriage, friendship, and sexual nostalgia.

Have You Read? *(continued)*

SURE OF YOU

A fiercely ambitious TV talk show host finds she must choose between national stardom in New York and a husband and child in San Francisco. Caught in the middle is their longtime friend, a gay man whose own future is even more uncertain. Wistful and compassionate yet subversively funny, *Sure of You* could only come from Armistead Maupin.

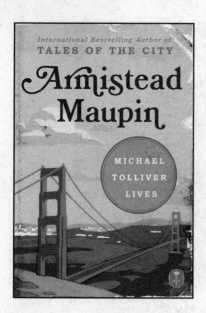

MICHAEL TOLLIVER LIVES

After a hiatus of nearly two decades, Armistead Maupin resumes his classic *Tales of the City* saga with this tender portrait of his all-too-human hero, Michael Tolliver, now a fifty-five-year-old gardener who has survived the plague that took so many of his friends. When a family crisis arises in Michael's boyhood home in Florida, he journeys there with his brand-new, much-younger husband, and finds his loyalties tested as never before.

Have You Read? *(continued)*

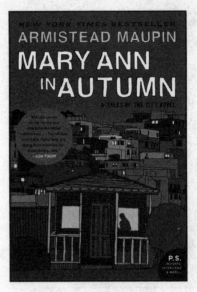

MARY ANN IN AUTUMN

Tales of the City heroine Mary Ann Singleton,
having abandoned San Francisco twenty
years earlier for a career in New York,
returns to the city of her youth in flight
from a pair of unforeseen calamities. When
she seeks a fresh start with her oldest friend
Michael "Mouse" Tolliver (now living
in domestic bliss with his husband), she
discovers that her speckled past has crept
up on her in a most unexpected way.

THE DAYS OF ANNA MADRIGAL

Now in Hardcover

Suspenseful, comic, and touching, the ninth and final novel in Armistead Maupin's bestselling Tales of the City series follows one of modern literature's most unforgettable and enduring characters—Anna Madrigal, the legendary transgender landlady of 28 Barbary Lane—on a road trip that will take her deep into her past.

Also from
Armistead Maupin

MAYBE THE MOON

"Though Cadence Roth, the heroine of Maupin's captivating novel, is only thirty-one inches tall, her impact on the reader's emotions is enormous. . . . A suspenseful story whose subtly foreshadowed ending delivers a dramatic clout."

—*Publishers Weekly*

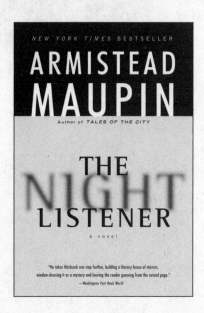

THE NIGHT LISTENER

"With rare authority, humor, and stunning grace, Maupin explores the risks and consolations of intimacy while illuminating the mysteries of the storytelling impulse."
— *Chicago Tribune*

Don't miss the next book by your favorite author. Sign up now for AuthorTracker by visiting www.AuthorTracker.com.